# DEAD-RINGER

JIM YACKEL

Printed in the United States of America.



www.walkthetowpath.com

Cover designed by LLPix Photography

LLPix.com

*For all those who would*
*choose to take the walk...*

# Contents

*And it shall come to pass afterward*
*That I will pour out My Spirit on all flesh;*
*Your sons and your daughters shall prophesy,*
*Your old men shall dream dreams,*
*Your young men shall see visions.*

*Joel 2:28*

# 1

# The Streetwalker

Jesse Same didn't choose to be up at 12:57 a.m. on this clear and chilly Tuesday morning in late October, 2009, but you could say that he was the insomniac's insomniac. Still, Jesse would be quick to point out that it wasn't insomnia but something else that had him walking in his black Cross Trekkers along the peaceful streets of Chittenango, New York. And like an artistic mime scribbling on air, Jesse would feel compelled to draw an image of the town that would be even quieter if that stupid mongrel belonging to that convicted child molester Kenny Harsch wasn't barking its flea-infested head off at oh-dark-thirty!

L. Frank Baum, the writer of that timeless tale *The Wizard of Oz* was born in the rustic burgh of Chittenango, and Jesse counted the film adaptation of Baum's story as one of his favorite movies. Indeed, this man who was sleepless in the "'Nango" was proud of the town's only claim to fame. As Jesse perambulated in a southwesterly direction on Genesee Street past the Redwood Bar and Grill, the streetlamps illuminated the imbedded bricks of the faux "Yellow Brick Road" that was created by the village fathers in honor of Baum to adorn the sidewalks on either side of what was the main thoroughfare through town.

The remnants of the dream that woke Jesse out of his fragile sleep were being dissolved in the sound of *South Central Rain* by R.E.M., from their 1984 album "Reckoning". But just as the voice of Michael Stipe began to sing "I'm sorry, I'm sorry" over the jangling D minor guitar chord and tinkling piano, the mental radio in Jesse's head was unceremoniously unplugged from its cerebral wall socket.

It wasn't so much the blast of beer breath assaulting Jesse's olfactory glands and the slurred proclamation of "Eaguhs winnnnn… Redskinnnnsssssssuck… efff-yeah!" as an inebriated football fan staggered out of the Redwood after earlier watching the Philadelphia Eagles defeat the Washington Redskins 27-17 on Monday Night Football. What was more annoying to Jesse was the drunken, eerily familiar Chittenango resident's insistence on placing his dirty, tattered, green Philadelphia Eagles cap on Jesse's head while he leaned into him to keep from falling onto the yellow brick center of the sidewalk.

Though only 5'5" tall and 135 pounds, the tottering drunk man's weight pushed Jesse into a black vintage-style street lamp post. With the post offering support, Jesse stripped the Eagles hat from his head with his right arm, while pushing the drunk off of him with his left. As the intoxicated reveler wobbled backward, he screeched with a garbled voice "heyyyyyyyy, you look like Elvish Preshley" before collapsing onto his buttocks. As Jesse re-gathered his wits, the drunk who was now sprawled on the "Yellow Brick Road" vomited; spilling some of the chunky yellow and pink liquid onto his faded denim jacket while the remainder steamed on the faux pathway to the fictional merry old Land of Oz.

As an appalled, dazed, and confused Jesse started to quickly stride away from the drunk, he was able to reply to the prone Eagles fan "yeah, a lot of people say I look like Elvis" before affecting a perfect voice impersonation of the King of Rock-n-Roll and adding an "uh-huh."

Jesse was fifteen feet further along on the yellow bricks when a black and white Chittenango Police Department SUV pulled up to the curb on Genesee Street alongside him. Jesse continued to walk, passing a small storefront known as the Oz Museum as he heard the Dodge Durango's driver-side door close. It was then that he heard the command "hey you hold up!"

The man who bore a striking resemblance to Elvis Presley stopped and turned toward the approaching officer named William Brostic. The rotund, terribly out-of-shape, fifty-six-year-old cop waddled up to Jesse and asked him curtly "where you goin' tonight?"

"Just out walking, officer" Jesse answered politely.

"Lemme see some I.D." was the panting cop's brusque follow-up.

As an irritated Jesse retrieved his New York driver's license from his wallet and Brostic's portable radio squawked some indecipherable garble, the intoxicated Eagles fan yelled "heyyyyyyy Billeeee" as he laid on his right side in a puddle of his own steaming reverse peristalsis.

"Hey, Ronny, you celebratin' yer team's win tonight?" the cop replied while snatching the I.D. from Jesse - seemingly embarrassed that he knew the drunk who was hideously prone on the yellow bricks.

"Aah! Elvish pushed me dowwwnnnn... then heeee tried t' take my warrrret, Billeeee! An' I thought heee wassss dead! Whyyy ish shome richeeee rich famoush sing-gher tryna take my warrr... warret? Heyyyy Billeeee - eeeee... duh Eaguhs wonnn!"

"Mr. Same, did you assault that helpless intoxicated man on the sidewalk over there? Did you take his wallet?" the cop inquired of Jesse accusingly.

“Heee gave myyy Eaguhs hat t’ da dog!” the now sobbing drunk screeched as he assumed a fetal position in a fresh pile of puke on the “Yellow Brick Road.”

“What dog… what wallet…what the…?” a confused Jesse asked Officer Brostic as the cop forced him chest first against the side of the police vehicle as he began frisking him.

“Ha-ha-ha! I jus’ messssinnn; my wa… (belch) warret ish right heee-yer” drunk Ronny screeched from his fetal position, no longer crying but laughing, and then stating “Eaguhs wonnnnn, Elvish sucks!”

Brostic halted his frisk of Jesse as two male Redwood patrons emerged from inside and began to help Ronny to his feet. As the men lifted Ronny, the drunk passed out. Both of the men were in their forties, and one sported a green Eagles jersey numbered “1” with a customized player name plate on the back bearing LADY’S MAN. It was this fellow who announced “we got ‘em, Billy. Hey, and next time, don’t buy him so many rounds dude, ya know he can’t hold his liquor - ha ha!”

As the two men dragged the unconscious Ronny back into the bar, the cop glared at Jesse and asked “what are you doing walking around this time of night? I see you out here a lot and I…”

Jesse interrupted the obese cop and asked “what are you doing drinking before work?”

“What? You got no proof of that…”

Jesse angrily interrupted the nervous cop with “the proof is in the form of that macho idiot with LADY’S MAN on his jersey. He just indicted you with his words. And, I’m no lawyer, but I think that waste-case Ronny might be some compelling evidence against you.”

"I oughta arrest you right now for Battery. You…"

"Arrest me for Battery? You must be under the influence, officer! It was that drunk that staggered into *me* as I was walking by this bar, minding my own business" Jesse interrupted the cop, and then continued:

"There is no law against me walking at night. I am committing no crimes. In reality, I could press charges against that Ronny for knocking me into this lamp post here, but I won't. I can see that Ronny has enough problems already. But, you officer, you're the one that might be looking at charges. I can smell the booze on your br…"

Before Jesse could finish the word "breath", Brostic pushed him back against the passenger's side of the Durango; Jesse's spread-legged frame obscuring the the gold-lettered POLICE adornment on the back door. Jesse's left foot was caught between the curb and the vehicle, causing a bolt of pain to shoot like lightning through his ankle, making him wonder for the longest millisecond if it was broken.

The long millisecond stretched into many full seconds, and Brostic froze for a moment before lifting his left hand off of the taller Jesse's shoulder, leaving a puff of stretched fabric in his green Russell Athletic knit hoodie. As the seconds lumbered along, Brostic slowly slid his right hand off of the handcuffs attached to his gun belt and then lifted both hands to their corresponding shoulders with palms facing forward - seemingly affecting a gesture of surrender.

There were no cars passing along Genesee Street and no other witnesses, other than those in the supernatural. No one peered through the windows of the Redwood Bar & Grill. The New York Pizzeria, the Oz Museum, the Just Dance Studio, Delphia's Restaurant, and the other small shops along the "Yellow Brick Road" were closed and uninhabited. The tenants of the apartments above the shops were either asleep or had no interest in looking through their windows. Yes, for this miniscule period of time, it seemed that the world was populated only by Jesse and the fat Chittenango cop whose backup from the Madison County Sheriff's Department never arrived.

"I'm willing to let this go, Mr. Same. I don't think Ronny is gonna wanna press charges against you. He won't even remember this in the mornin'. But, you better watch yer step and don't cause any more trouble around here, got it?"

Jesse was able to stand on the grey concrete section of sidewalk despite his twisted left ankle throbbing with pain. As Brostic announced into his Motorola portable radio that he was "clear", Jesse rebutted sonorously "and you officer had better get some breath mints, the whiskey is strong on your breath."

"Please repeat that unit three zero two, regarding whiskey, over" a response crackled through Brostic's radio as the cop glared at Jesse as he started to limp away from the scene.

Five minutes had passed and Jesse's ankle was hurting less but the thoughts in his head were swirling like cyclone-driven roofing nails. He had passed the La Cocina restaurant - the town's purveyor of "authentic" Mexican food - turned right, and was now setting foot on the "Creek Walk", a gravel pathway that was much like the Erie Canal Towpath that also passed through Chittenango. The Creek Walk paralleled Chittenango Creek - known as Madison County's most popular trout stream - and was a pleasant venue for jogging, biking, or taking a leisurely stroll.

The Oak, American elm, and Yellow Birch trees prevalent along the Creek Walk had dropped many of their leaves on the pathway, creating slippery areas and also serving to cover the fallen fruit of the *Juglans nigra* or Eastern Black Walnut trees - the nuts still shrouded in their brownish-green husks. Jesse could not see the nuts in the dark, but could certainly feel the hard round fruit when by happenstance he'd step on one.

Even easier to feel was the walnut that dropped onto his head, having seemingly been pulled from its parent tree by the intermittent breeze that added to the new morning's chill. "Ow! Ah!" Jesse yelped as the nut's surprise contact caused him to stop walking and spin around, putting extra stress on his tender ankle. Jesse looked up toward the walnut tree and then bent down in confusion. He would have appeared strange to the natural eye of another walker would they have come upon him; he rubbing his left ankle with his left hand while messaging the top of his noggin with his right in what would appear to be an out of sync version of the Hokey Pokey.

After a half-minute of rubbing and messaging, Jesse stood upright and resumed walking; albeit with sore ankle and a growing goose egg. His eyes watered with frustration and pain as he muttered to himself "why does this weird stuff always happen to me - why!?"

What was hidden to the aforementioned natural eye was the supernatural translucent image of a demon that bore an uncanny resemblance to one of L. Frank Baum's "flying monkeys" dressed in bellhop's hat and vest. The mischievous sprite seemingly snickered with glee as it stood weightless on a mere twig of the walnut tree, nineteen feet above where Jesse had just passed.

But what of the aforementioned dream? Wasn't it the dream that woke him at 12:05 a.m. and forced him outside to walk the streets, only to find a modicum of peace on this gravelly path along the rushing rivulets of Chittenango Creek? If it wasn't for the dream, he'd still be asleep and would never have had the bizarre encounter with Ronny the barfing drunk and William Brostic the cop equipped with enough adipose tissue to serve as a second line of defense in the event his Kevlar would be penetrated.

Sometimes the dreams were difficult to separate from the visions. Indeed, it had become difficult for Jesse to know any more if he was awake or asleep. But, as Jesse walked, he was reasonably certain he was awake as he felt with his right hand's middle finger the bump that had grown as a result of the walnut bomb dropped on his head with amazing accuracy. The resulting contusion was trickling blood through his hair and then downward along his right side mutton chop, and as Jesse dragged his hand along the side of his head a red smear was painted on the outside of his index finger.

Jesse ascended the short wheelchair ramp that ran left from the path to a wooden handicap-accessible fishing platform that extended over a hedge of boulders that bordered a swirling pool in the creek. The platform had been constructed over the summer by members of Trout Unlimited Chapter 680. Here was a spot loaded with beautiful Brown Trout and the ubiquitous White Sucker, but thus far the platform rarely saw fisherman. More commonly, the fishing platform was utilized by underage drinkers, smokers, and dopers; all seeking a nighttime hideaway to pursue their vices without being caught.

Bolted to the plywood slats at the front of the platform was a newly installed, white 30" x 30" sign reading *CAUTION - SHALLOW WATER AND HIDDEN ROCKS BELOW - NO DIVING OR JUMPING FROM FISHING PLATFORM*. Below the warning text was an illustration of a male outstretched in a dive about to make contact with water. The illustration was circled in red with the obligatory angled slash through it.

Jesse snickered to himself as strode to the front of the platform, wondering who would be stupid or stoned enough to jump, creating the need for the new sign. The platform was scarcely four months old but it had already become a place of refuge for Jesse. He was glad that it was currently devoid of any other human life, so he might have some time to linger and pull out some of the proverbial roofing nails swirling through his mind and piercing his psyche.

The youthful thirty-something that bore such a striking resemblance to the *'68 Comeback Special* Elvis didn't drink, smoke, or do drugs - and yet it seemed that the hordes around him who did had a better quality of life. If there was pain, most around him would drown it in booze or suffocate it in some manner of illegal substance. And, those painkillers were also recreational and formed friendships while killing time. If the addictions became too powerful, the addicted were coddled and pitied and then celebrated as role models if they managed to overcome. In this world, if you didn't drink to excess or use drugs, you were essentially persona non grata.

No, Jesse did it the hard way by walking the narrow path. Unlike the Creek Walk, the narrow path was strewn with roots and rocks and bordered with untrimmed thorn bushes. This path through Jesse's life was littered with spiritual broken glass that would penetrate his supernatural sneakers and cut his feet. Indeed, it was a narrow path and a rough road, but it was the only way home.

The sky was clear but moonless, so the cool limpid water below looked like motor oil in the darkness. Jesse wiped his right hand on his jeans and believed the minor bleeding from his injured crown had stopped. He could see his breath in the cold as he looked down at the gracefully flowing creek while leaning against the slats that served as the front of the platform. He shoved his hands into his hoodie pockets, shivered, and wished that he would have pulled his Pelle Studio Classic black leather jacket on over the knit garment. But, when he left his upstairs one bedroom apartment in the grey multi-family house with burgundy shutters at 316 Genesee Street, he wasn't thinking clearly and was too distressed to realize that 41 degrees Fahrenheit is cold!

It was a dream this time and not a vision. He had been asleep he was sure. Jesse knew the dream was in some way prophetic, but how could he get anyone to believe him? He was confidant now that these dreams and visions were in fact endowments of the Holy

Spirit. But, these dreams and visions over the last two weeks were causing him to torment in ways that he had never known.

The cold was too much to bear without a warm jacket, and Jesse was quickly back on the Creek Walk, passing behind the brick with white trim single-level structure housing the Chittenango Center for Rehabilitation and Healthcare. He cut through the parking lot and walked the short driveway to Russell Street where he crossed, turned right, and was now walking the sidewalk back toward the center of the village.

Jesse passed the inconspicuously middle class duplexes and bungalows along Russell Street, many of which still had lights on at 1:40 a.m. Street lights were lined along the opposite side of the street, but most of them were non-operational.

After walking two blocks in a distracted daze, Jesse crossed Russell near its culmination at Genesee and ambled along the diagonal sidewalk that bisected Dr. West Memorial Park, which served as the town square as well as food and vendor location for the Oz Fest every June. Scattered about the autumn leaf-strewn park lawn were heavy oak benches shaped like church pews; save for their un-churchlike red and white two-tone paint jobs.

Jesse sat down on the bench closest to the Genesee Street side of the park, with his back to the Ten Pin Restaurant & Tavern at the intersection of Genesee and Seneca Streets. To Jesse's right, where Russell ended at Genesee was the Chittenango Volunteer Fire Department. To his left was Arch Street, that particular block being non-descript and residential. Directly in front of Jesse, Arch Street "arched" to the right and on the arch was situated the stone gothic-style architecture of First Presbyterian Church of Chittenango. The church, built in 1828, featured a large concrete stairway that led to a tall, white, arched entryway with double wooden doors. The two-story edifice featured arched, recessed window sets on either side of the entrance; all trimmed in white. The entryway itself was topped with a peaked roof trimmed with white that pointed to another peaked roof over the main structure, which pointed to a square, white, wooden belfry that sat on a smaller peaked roof.

First Presbyterian Church was a significant part of the dream that woke Jesse and had him out walking in the wee hours of Tuesday, October 27, 2009. The church building itself fit well into the Halloween motif that had overtaken the village like it did every year as of late; with an increasing number of plastic skeletons, inflatable ghosts and witches, strings of orange lights, rubber bats, and plastic tombstones gracing so many porches and front lawns while Jack O' Lanterns lit with candles smiled or grimaced on front steps - the facial expressions dependent on the moods and imaginations of the individuals operating the carving knives.

The Jack O' Lantern's candle lights around town had been extinguished for the night. The church still loomed as a stone-faced monolith, surrounded by street lights that actually worked. As Jesse sat and stared at the church, he shuddered as his tired mind still possessed enough energy to recall the dream from a couple hours before…

…In the dream, Christmas wreaths were hung below the globes of the vintage-style black street lamps along Genesee St. There was snow on the wreaths and a thin layer of slush on the faux Yellow Brick Road that made up the center of the sidewalks on either side of the street. Many of the businesses had twinkling Christmas lights and trees decorated with Wizard of Oz ornaments adorning their street-side bay windows. It was late afternoon and the sun was sinking below the western horizon as Jesse walked in a westerly direction, passing the Redwood Bar and Grill. In the dream, no Ronny the drunken "Eaguhs" fan emerged from the Redwood to accost him. Jesse said to no one in particular "it's kind of quiet for a late Friday afternoon" as there was no one to hear him.

The rumble of a low-flying helicopter broke the relative silence, but Jesse couldn't lift his head to see the whirlybird; such is the state of dreams. But, Jesse was able to see a large shadow sweep across the street in the fading light, and he again spoke to no one, asking "why is that helicopter flying so low?"

As Jesse spoke the word "low", the Chittenango Fire Department's Federal STH10 alert siren began its oscillating wail, and simultaneously all of the lights in the shops along Genesee Street went out. As the siren began its first descent of its five cycle cadence, a mature male voice spoke from a point unknown to Jesse, commanding him to *stop, look, and listen.* As Jesse was frozen in confusion, a sober Ronny, resplendent in a white apron with pizza sauce stains, burst forth from the New York Pizzeria and stopped on the "Yellow Brick Road" in front of Jesse and said with angry astonishment "they friggin' took Sean Hannity off the air, dude! The whole friggin' AM band just ain't there! It's like the whole goddam thing is gone! What the hell!? I've been on the wagon since October 27th man, but this bullcrap makes me wanna drink again!"

"No, Ronny, please, please don't drink… you're gonna die, man!" an ostensibly paralyzed Jesse plead with sober Ronny the pizza chef. Ronny was now sobbing and his image began to dissolve. Jesse was overwhelmed by panic as he tried to run toward the disappearing man but could not move. It was then that the voice again commanded *stop, look, and listen*!

"Lord Jesus, don't let him die without you!" Jesse screamed as he too was now crying, while bearing a crushing level of despair. Simultaneously, residents of the houses and apartments along Genesee began to pour out into the street in frantic, angry, desperate confusion.

"It's an effing free-for-all!" a blond, freckle-faced 18 year old sporting a buzz cut and wearing a white tank top, oversized jeans that hung off of his posterior, and sideways flat-brimmed NY Yankees cap proclaimed with sinister delight as he punched his 89 year old downstairs neighbor in the left temple. After the elderly man toppled backward over a yellow fire hydrant and then fell onto the slush-covered shoulder of Genesee Street, the thug snatched the man's wallet from his grey slacks as he lie twitching in death throes.

"Just take his cash, Homes. The credit cards ain't workin' nowhere" the thug's similarly dressed 19 year old roommate advised his friend. "Cool… let's get some forties, even if we gotta bust the frickin' windows on the Byrne Dairy!" was the killer's ecstatic reply.

As the two walked away from the scene, a 40 inch flat-screen TV burst through the glass of a bedroom window of an apartment above the Just Dance Studio. The 19 year old saw the television falling and yelled "look out" as he scurried out of its path. The projectile landed back-first on the unaware 18 year old roommate, fracturing his skull and shattering five of his upper vertebrae, killing him instantly. The 19 year old whose soul was devoid of any compassion exclaimed "sucks to be you, dude!" and then cackled with laughter as he walked away along the "Yellow Brick Road" as twenty already shocked and frightened Chittenango residents looked on in horror.

In his dream, Jesse attempted to pursue the killer but his right arm was grabbed by the curly-haired redhead with too-tight jeans and too much lipstick who worked as a hairdresser at the Alexander of New York Hair Studio. As he tried to pull free, his gaze was drawn to her piercing blue eyes that were wide with fear as she clung tightly to his arm. There were a number of people gathered under the awning of the salon, and they were speaking in frantic tones as they wondered what exactly had happened. Jesse could not decipher what they were saying but was able to hear the hairdresser.

"The guy on Y-94 FM said that we need to stay in our homes. I need to get home to my daughter but somebody smashed the windshield of my car! I gotta get home and the phones aren't working so I can't even call her. Please help me… please!" the 40 year old panic-stricken woman pled with Jesse.

"Okay, let's walk down the street to my apartment and I'll give you a ride. I think I know where you live, but you have to let go of my arm" Jesse replied calmly; albeit in confusion.

It was then that cocky, swaggering 23 year old Chittenango Police officer Ryan McMaster, who sported the obligatory "high and tight" haircut, grabbed Jesse's left arm and said "you aren't driving anywhere. You return to your home 'hero' before I throw your ass in jail, and you get back to the salon, lady. No vehicular travel is allowed."

Jesse heard the hairdresser's desperate plea of the cop as he found himself suddenly floating toward Dr. West Memorial Park. There were 40 or so panicky individuals gathered there on the snow-covered lawn, asking of each other if anyone knew why the electricity and cellphone service was out. As Jesse heard them speaking, some claimed they still had power and it seemed to be a block by block issue.

In the dream, Jesse now sat on the same bench as he did in the wee waking hours of this Tuesday morning. A hoarsened male voice announced from the crowd "before the juice went out, one of those pretty boys on FOX News said there mighta' been some kinda' nuke in New York City er somethin'. If that's true, we kin jus' bend over and kiss our asses g'by!"

Jesse stood up to walk toward the smaller group of people from which the man spoke, in an effort to glean more information. It was then that the same Chittenango Police officer ordered from behind "hold it right there, sir!" Jesse turned toward the young policeman, and as he did a loud gunshot boomed through the park and the cop's head exploded in a gory mess of bone, brain matter, and blood. A navy blue, late model Dodge Ram pickup truck squealed away from the Genesee Street curb, 10 yards behind where the cop had been standing. Jesse could see seated in the truck's bed as it sped away four middle-aged men dressed in green camouflage who looked more like deer hunters than military personnel. Each man carried what looked to Jesse to be military-grade rifles.

A red-headed 43 year old bar tender named Sandy, with a voice harshened by too many Virginia Slims and too much Miller High Life screeched hysterically from the now growing throng in the park:

"Oh my god, the North Madison Militia shot the friggin' cop! They blew his friggin' brains out! Oh...my...GOD!"

As Sandy cried out in revilement, two Chittenango Police cruisers as well as a silver-hued Ford Explorer with green trim and bearing the MILITARY POLICE insignia on the front doors commenced pursuit of the speeding blue pickup. As the first pursuing black and white Crown Victoria passed the Subway restaurant, it exploded in a ball of flame, having been impacted by a HEAT warhead fired from the back of the pickup by an M72 LAW. The car's hood twirled through the air and then smashed through the eatery's bay window, leaving the upper left corner of the *Five Dollar Foot-Long* poster that adorned the window to dangle in the cold breeze. The militia member had but one shot with this type of shoulder-fired weapon that was last produced in 1983 - and he made it count with practiced precision.

The cop driving the second Crown Vic put the brake pedal to the floor, forcing the vehicle into a three-sixty before it was struck by the trailing Military Police SUV. The police cruiser tipped onto its passenger's side in the center of Genesee Street while the out of control Military Police vehicle wheeled onto the south sidewalk and came to a rest in a vacant lot that now resembled a Christmas card image with the freshly-fallen snow. The two MP's in the front seat were seriously injured and would not be able to exit the smoking vehicle.

Despite the weather, the time, and the appearance, there was nothing "Christmassy" about this scene as smoldering shrapnel littered the street and the smell of burning plastic, rubber, and flesh filled the air.

Seemingly undaunted, Jesse turned his head toward First Presbyterian Church where his dreaming eyes fixated on the white wooden belfry. Standing on top of the structure was what could best be described as a seven foot tall translucent grey gargoyle, with its chiropteran wings folded neatly on its back. The being's head and face possessed qualities that appeared human, but from a distance Jesse could not decipher the finer features.

As Jesse "looked and listened", the being used its muscular arms to tear open its abdomen, releasing fifteen "flying monkeys" in a supernatural Caesarean section. The bird-winged apes were in essence identical to those from *The Wonderful Wizard of Oz* books and film and stood between three and four feet tall, dependent on the individual. Like the gargoyle they were grey in color and translucent, making Jesse think that they did not possess a natural body. The faces of these Hominidae revealed human-like expression, some smiling while others grimaced; all appearing "thoughtful". As they burst from the gargoyle's stomach, the winged monkeys flew down to the snow-covered park lawn and then frolicked about while whispering into the unaware ears of many of the gathered crowd members.

"You can't see them but in your spirit you hear them! Don't listen to them! Don't do what they tell you to do!" Jesse yelled, using his strong diaphragm to full effect.

"Don't do what… you alright, man?" a young volunteer firefighter asked as he shook Jesse's left shoulder. The young man couldn't help but stop as he saw Jesse on the bench and heard him murmur "don't do what they tell you to do" as he walked home through the park after running to the station for what turned out to be a false alarm.

"Yeah, man, I'm fine. I must have fallen asleep here on the bench and had a bad dream" a startled and embarrassed Jesse responded as he quickly stood up.

"Okay, good… glad you're alright" the firefighter said, shrugged his shoulders and continued on his way. Before the alert siren blew, the 21 year-old volunteer had been arguing with his live-in girlfriend, whom he was sure was cheating on him. His anger was again boiling, and he suddenly had the notion that the "unfaithful wench" needed a punch in the mouth to straighten her out. "As a matter a fact, maybe I'll just toss that new TV that I bought for her through the window" he thought to himself as his gait became a purposeful stride.

As a haunted Jesse began heading home, shuffling through the leaf-covered grass to Genesee Street, he thought to himself "I wonder if L. Frank Baum actually saw the stuff that he wrote about?"

Jesse had this terrible dream twice, the first time driving him out of bed on Monday night and then a short time later as he dozed on the park bench.

Was the dream prophetic? This wasn't the first time he'd experienced something like this. Now, Jesse needed someone to believe him as much as he needed sleep.

# 2

# All Shook Up

While seemingly a cursed man with his recent dreams and visions, Jesse Same was likewise blessed. When Jesse's grandfather Richard Same passed away after a long illness in June of 2007, an inheritance was left to Richard's only surviving kin, that being his grandson Jesse, born of his only child - a daughter who never married and passed away before him. After taxes and legal fees, Jesse's cut of Richard's last will and testament was 436,242 Dollars and 14 cents.

At 10:33 a.m. on Monday, July 23rd, 2007, Jesse abruptly quit is day job at the P & C food market in Manlius, NY, having become frustrated that so many of his slacking, UFCW lackey co-workers were taking multiple cigarette breaks each hour while he the non-smoker was left to carry the preponderance of the workload. As Jesse exited the store and walked past a group of employees who were gathered on the front walkway huffing their cancer sticks and chatting about the previous weekend's drinking adventures, 43 year old grocery manager and union steward John Swain blew smoke through his lips and inquired of Jesse, "did you stack that pallet of charcoal briquettes up with the barbeque display yet?" As Swain spoke, he smirked while devouring a 17 year old blond cashier with his eyes and mind as she entered the store to begin her part-time shift.

“Mmm…nice” 35 year old meat department manager Bart “Bucky” McClenthen commented snidely as his eyes followed the cashier toward the store entrance while he crushed his smoke out under a steel-toed shoe.

“Yeah, dude, what my wife wouldn’t know wouldn’t hurt her!” Swain cackled with glee, before continuing with Jesse “so, did you get…”

“Yeah, I stacked them up nice and then put a match and lighter fluid to ‘em. You better run inside and check because I’m not joking, you lazy jackass perverts” Jesse retorted with sneering venom which prompted the entire group of seven staffers to return to the store post-haste as his bluff sounded more than convincing. “Oh, by the way, I quit” Jesse shouted as he set foot into the parking lot and walked with a merry gait toward his awaiting black 2001 Jeep Grand Cherokee Laredo. Jesse had already determined that he could stretch out and live on the inherited money if he was careful. After all, Jesse’s yearly gross salary was only $16,850 as a full-time stock clerk, and he figured that the inheritance equaled 25 years of P & C salary. While he would no longer have health insurance, he took the chance that he’d avoid major illness or injury.

Still, Jesse had another form of income; that being an Elvis Presley impersonator. Other than being green-eyed as opposed to Elvis’s blue, Jesse shared the Dionysus-like facial features, body build, and thick brown hair suitable for the Pompadour. But, if Jesse had a say in the matter, he would not have chosen to grow up to be the spitting-image of the *Memphis Flash.*

As a young boy growing up in the upscale yet idyllic village of Manlius, Jesse would occasionally ask his mother, Tammy Jo, why he didn’t have a father. Always patient but not always fully truthful, the mom who waitressed at Dave's Diner would tell her son that his daddy died when he was three years old, but they had to leave him when Jesse was a baby because he was very "sick" and it wasn't "safe to be around him." When Jesse would occasionally inquire as to where they lived before coming to Manlius, Tammy Jo would patiently answer "a little town near Memphis, Tennessee where your Grandpa lives" with the trace of the dialectical twang that remained years after coming north. Once, when a five year old Jesse asked if they could go see that little Tennessee town that they came from and visit the grandfather he'd only had contact with as a newborn, Tammy Jo welled with tears and uncharacteristically snapped "no! We don't ever want to go near that God-forsaken place. Please don't ever ask me again!"

Tammy Jo's heated response resonated powerfully with Jesse, and he never again pursued knowledge of his past, although his curiosity about his grandfather was almost as strong as that of his father. But, as far as anyone was ever concerned, Jesse was born and raised a central New Yorker.

As a five year old, Jesse would sing while he laid in bed, after his 18 year old babysitter named Angie tucked him in and retired to the living room to watch *Laverne & Shirley*, *Happy Days*, *The Dukes of Hazard*, or whatever sitcom aired on the alphabet networks on a particular weeknight. Tammy Jo usually returned home from waiting tables to the downstairs apartment around 9:00, and would step into Jesse's room to give him a kiss goodnight and make sure that he was "snug as a bug in a rug."

It was on this particular Tuesday night that Jesse was still awake when his mom tip-toed into his bedroom at 9:02, dressed in her gray uniform dress, white apron, and white sneakers. The tippers had been particularly generous for a Tuesday, and a fat wad of cash bulged out of the apron's front pocket.

Jesse was lying wide awake on his right side, staring out over a quiet East Pleasant Street that was the stage for twirling autumn leaves that danced in the glow of the street lights on a cool, persistent breeze. Tammy's long, wavy brown hair had been released from its imprisoning bun once her shift had ended, and it was tousled from the stiff breeze that accompanied her on her walk home. Jesse did not hear his mom push open the door and enter the room, as he quietly sang a song he had heard on WOLF-AM a few hours before, as Angie listened to that pop music station while she did her homework. It was a song that Jesse had never heard before, but it grabbed him and he immediately fell in love with it, and as he stared through the window he sang the only words he could remember up to that point:

*Love me tender, love me true, all my dreams fulfilled... for my darlin', I love you, and I always will...*

Tammy was stunned by the beauty of young Jesse's voice, but conversely the lyrics were like an icicle stabbing her heart. As her emerald green eyes became a dam-break for torrents of tears, she quietly backed out of Jesse's room, ran past a confused and suddenly concerned Angie, and through the front door of the downstairs flat. Jesse saw his mom run under a streetlight with her hands over her face and was confused by what he saw, but was too tired to worry about it as he drifted off to sleep, knowing that she'd come right back home.

Jesse's love for singing had been awakened, and as he progressed through elementary school he became involved in chorus and likewise participated in all of the plays and musicals. Jesse could never get his mother to tell him why his singing of *Love Me Tender* upset her that Tuesday night in October of 1979, but it did not stop him from becoming a fan of Elvis Presley's music. Jesse was always crooning, and found himself singing a myriad of Elvis songs, he saving his allowance money to purchase a "greatest hits" cassette which he would listen to as well as The Beatles, Paul McCartney and Wings, The Knack, The Greg Kihn Band, Split Enz, and likewise a myriad of "New Wave" acts that were popular in the early 1980's.

At the age of ten, Jesse conveyed to his mother his desire for an acoustic guitar, as he "needed an axe to back up his singing." The young songster had been learning to play from his school friend Trey Emerson, who shared an interest in "oldies" like the Beatles and Elvis. The two aspiring pop stars would jam in the basement of the East Pleasant Street colonial where Trey lived with his parents, and Trey's father Dustin would often remark proudly "they sound damn good for just being kids!" While Tammy Jo could give Jesse a small weekly allowance for doing chores and keeping his grades up, she sadly could not afford even a modest guitar on her waitress's wage.

On the last day of school in June of 1984, Jesse arrived home at 11:29 a.m., as the final day of the scholastic year was always a short one. Jesse carried his passing report card, verifying the successful completion of the fourth grade and his progression from elementary school to grade 5 at Eagle Hill Middle School.

"Hi mom, I passed" Jesse announced as he entered through the front door and into the living room.

"Of course you did, and I wouldn't expect anything less!" Tammy Jo replied proudly as she sat on the black faux leather recliner with her long legs folded and bare feet tucked below her bottom. Her toenails were painted a bright pink and she sported tight Jordache blue jeans and a white sleeveless t-shirt with horizontal pink stripes. She had the day off from work, so her long, thick, wavy brown hair was not piled into a bun but instead crept freely across her shoulders and down her back.

"Joan Croghan, c'mon down! You are the next contestant on The Price is Right" blared from the Magnavox TV before Tammy Jo turned the volume down with the remote and then crushed out her twelfth Marlboro of the day. "A parcel came for you today" she said with a mischievous grin as she rose from the recliner and walked spritely to a coat closet with a sticky wooden door near the apartment's entryway. Tammy Jo yanked the door open with a loud squeak and urged Jesse excitedly "well, go ahead, take it out!"

It didn't take Jesse long to tear the packing tape off of the large cardboard box, inadvertently ripping the return address. Styrofoam packing peanuts were hurriedly scooped out of the way -many landing on the living room floor - and the treasure inside the box was quickly excavated.

From within the Styrofoam mess was retrieved a black, tattered, hard-shell guitar case with gold-colored hasps and hinges. A thrilled Jesse could tell that the case was not new, but he cared not one iota. He hurriedly yet carefully laid the case on the floor, unbuckled the hasps and then lifted the worn cover that bore frayed trim. Inside of the case, bordered by burgundy protective fabric, was a blond Gibson J-200 acoustic guitar.

The instrument evidenced a noticeable layer of dust around the sound hole, on the red pick guard, and over the *Gibson* pearl inlay on the headstock. The strings were in decent condition but hardly new. The thin, brown leather strap was attached on one end to the headstock and to a peg at the other end, and the strap itself was well-worn. Jesse was struck with the notion that the guitar had been displayed out of the case but not played in a very long time.

A small white greeting card with the word "congratulations" in gold-colored Harlow Solid font printed on the cover was laying on the living room floor amidst the Styrofoam peanuts, Jesse having first missed it in his excitement. Jesse opened the card and inside in neat cursive handwriting done in blue ink was written:

*I heard you needed a git-fiddle. This is something a dear old friend left to me a long time ago but it's just gathering dust here in my 'Heartbreak Hotel.' Do good with it Jesse, and congratulations on passing the fourth grade.*

*Love,*

*Grandpa Richard*

"Aw…yes…finally! My own guitar, and a Gibson too! I gotta call Trey and tell him!" Jesse exclaimed with absolute joy.

"Yeah, that should do the job for you, but you've got to take good care of it. I think we could probably scrape up enough money to get some guitar polish and some picks" Tammy Jo said with a smile, her emerald eyes revealing joy for her son.

Jesse's sunny jubilation became abruptly stormy: "How did grampa know that I needed a guitar and why can't I meet him? It's not fair that we can't go to Tennessee!"

Tammy Jo's expression evidenced heartbreak and sadness as she lit a cigarette, inhaled deeply, and answered "I'm sorry honey, maybe one day" before exhaling. She squatted down next to Jesse as he stared at the beautiful old Gibson in the case. She pulled Jesse to her chest and embraced him as he heard in stereo two distinctly different sounds: in his left ear the high E, B, and G strings as he plucked them with his left pointer finger and his right ear her fast, irregular heartbeat.

Indeed, Jesse had long possessed the ability to sing just like the King of Rock-n-Roll. As a teenager he mastered the King's moves and mannerisms, and could impersonate his speech patterns. In his mid-thirties, whether regaled in white jumpsuit and cape or black leather jacket and pants, Jesse remained a dead-ringer for "Big El". When not performing as Elvis, Jesse's preferred mode of dress circa 2009 was jeans, the aforementioned Cross Trekkers sneakers, and t-shirt or casual button-down.

*Jesse Same - Elvis Impersonator* played plenty of upstate New York gigs with a band that included his best friend from childhood Trey Emerson on lead guitar, but the big-money work in Las Vegas hadn't materialized. Jesse's agent Mike Wickert, owner of MW Talent, was too often told "we've got more than enough Elvis's around here, so we don't need any from New York."

So it was at 7:30 a.m. on Tuesday, October 27th, 2009 that Jesse was setting his bare feet onto the cool hardwood bedroom floor of his Genesee Street apartment after having slept fitfully for approximately five hours. The dream of the hairdresser, militia, gargoyle, and flying monkeys did not replay a third time, but it clung with Jesse like a hangover from his former drinking days. The events in the previous night's dream took place near Christmas, and Jesse felt confident that it was the upcoming December of 2009.

Jesse didn't hear the phone ring a half-hour before, but Mike Wickert left a message on the answering machine stored on a small, oak TV stand in the living room:

"Hey Jesse, I know you're an early riser so I thought you'd be up. I just wanted to remind you guys that you have the engagement at Mohegan Manor in Liverpool at 1:00 today for the RGIS corporate luncheon. It's just the one hour show so it's quick in and out, but please, this time don't do any of the religious stuff - you know, like Peace in the Valley and How Great Thou Art. These people wanna party hardy and not get preached at, ya know, so give 'em Hound Dog, Love Me Tender, Jailhouse Rock, Suspicious Minds, and all that stuff. You know what to do, bro - and don't forget it'll be 300 bucks for each of the five of you. Alright man, have fun, shake those hips, and I've got more stuff in the pipeline like the Turning Stone Casino. I'll catch ya later - bye."

Jesse pushed the delete button on the answering machine as he muttered sarcastically to himself "yeah, yeah, I know, none of the gospel songs… wouldn't want to take the steam out of anyone's drunken debauchery and marital infidelity. Oh wait, that's why there's Hail Mary's and Rosary Beads, I'm almost forgot!"

By 7:55, Jesse was sipping his first mug of Maxwell House Breakfast Blend black with no sugar, and spooning *magically delicious* Lucky Charms cereal into his mouth as he sat at the 39.5 inch round table with chrome legs that occupied the center of the hardwood floor of his modest kitchen. Lucky Charms were not Jesse's cereal of choice, but he had purchased them for his six year old son Jeremy who had stayed overnight the past Friday and Saturday. Seeing anything that reminded Jesse of Jeremy made him miss his son badly. The frugal Elvis impersonator couldn't allow himself to throw away uneaten cereal, so he felt the need to work on finishing off the box so as to be rid of it.

Jesse came to faith in Jesus Christ in 2004 after being intrigued by a book he saw in the Manlius Library titled *Vanished Into Thin Air* written by evangelist Hal Lindsey. Jesse checked the book out, read it cover to cover in two days and was moved to accept Jesus as Savior and Lord. Allison Same did not appreciate her husband "getting into religion" and would lament that she missed the former "cool guy" who liked to have a good time out with their friends. Additionally, Allison never liked the "Elvis charade" as that music was "old and lame." She was frustrated that Jesse never checked the bid board at work to see what better-paying jobs were available within the P & C grocery store chain. Indeed, she had grown to deeply regret marrying Jesse and desired to be free of him.

Allison hired man-hating Syracuse University Law School graduate Summer Silverman to file on her behalf the divorce that Jesse did not want. The frizzy-haired, googly-eyed Silverman, who was conceived in the Woodstock mud while Jimi Hendrix sang "Purple Haze", described Jesse to Manlius Town Justice Althea Schreiber as "an unstable Jesus freak who thinks he's Elvis

Presley." In April of 2006 Allison Same got her wish and the divorce was final. Jesse would move from the family's quaint Manlius home while Jeremy remained with his mother in residential custody.

On this October 2009 morning, as Jesse was fuzzily crunching on red hearts, orange stars, yellow moons, green clovers, blue diamonds, and purple horseshoes, he thought he heard the leprechaun on the front of the box speak chirpily: "more kids believe in leprechauns than Jesus, tee-hee-hee!"

A shocked Jesse stopped chewing, rapidly shook his head, and then spoke as though others were in the room as he proclaimed "I didn't just hear the cereal box speak!"

"Ooo-hoo-hoo, Americans want their lucky charms, because Jesus doesn't come through with the goods!" the illustrated leprechaun offered up in mocking reply - or at least Jesse thought that it did!

Jesse stood up in a flash and then pounded the top of the 24 oz. box with his right fist while still grasping his spoon, crunching the center of the cardboard package flat against the table, ripping the paper inner packaging and scattering the remaining dry cereal over the table and onto the floor. The "all shook up" Elvis-impersonator then grabbed the ravaged box with both hands and furiously ripped it to shreds, leaving cardboard, paper, marshmallows, and frosted oat cereal scattered about the table and floor. Without forethought and with frosted four-leaf clovers, crosses, and bells crunching under and sticking to his bare feet, he frantically ran his bowl of uneaten cereal over to the sink and dumped it down the drain.

As a dazed and confused Jesse turned from the sink, he heard a woman's voice. The voice sounded as though it was originating from the apartment below him or from outside, he wasn't sure. As he tried to dial in on the sound, he began to think that maybe it came from inside the kitchen walls. The nasally, miserable, carping voice sounded like so many adult women that populated upstate New York, Jesse thought as his mind began to clear. While the voice didn't sound like it was in his apartment, it was close enough that Jesse could decipher much of what it groused about:

"You must really hate your son, the way you destroyed that bax (sic) of his favorite cereal. That's the only reason why he stays overnight with you his boring dad who won't get a real jab (sic) so you can take 'em out to do fun stuff. It's because you give him the food he likes while his manipulative, controlling mother makes him eat healthy. Yup, she's a woman after my own heart, ya know! Gad (sic) love 'er!"

"Hey, whoever the hell you are, I love my son, got it?! That box of cereal was possessed or something! Leave me the hell alone" Jesse yelled in a tone of voice consisting of 63 percent anger and 37 percent panic as he stood alone in the kitchen.

After a moment of what was now silence, save for the sound of a Heartland Express eighteen-wheeler rumbling southwestward on Genesee Street, Jesse rubbed his face with both hands and said to himself "I'm not losing my mind, I know I'm not. This is terribly real."

Fast-forward a few minutes, and the hot shower spray was comforting and invigorating as Jesse lathered Irish Spring first on his face and then around his fit and trim body. Jesse did not maintain an exercise regimen, but his high metabolic rate kept him from becoming paunchy like the Elvis he impersonated did in the last years of his life. As well, all of the walking these recent nights would certainly discourage obesity.

"What the..." a suddenly perplexed Jesse asked of no one as it seemed as though he no longer felt the hot, relaxing water on his body. He could see the soap running down his legs as though it was being rinsed, and yet he didn't hear or feel the spray...

Was it a radio he was now hearing in his bathroom? How could that be, as he didn't keep a radio in there? Were his downstairs neighbors Dean and Cassandra blasting the TV volume yet again, so as to cover up the sound of their loud, violent love-making?

Without question, there was a radio or TV newsman speaking. And while it seemed to Jesse like the voice could have been coming from a source inside the bathroom, at the same time it sounded like it emanated from another room or floor as it spoke…

"So it seems Rob that there is no water pressure anywhere from the east side of Syracuse to as far as western Oneida County and as far south as Marathon in Cortland County. I was just a moment ago on the phone with a FEMA representative, and she confirmed scattered water outages in New Jersey, Massachusetts, and also in Washington, D.C. Additionally Rob, there are now confirmed reports of New York City firefighters not getting any water from hydrants to fight the structure fires in Manhattan resulting from yesterday's terror attack. As to why Fire and Emergency personnel are even being allowed near that area, I don't know.

Again Rob, I have to reiterate as per President Omondi, that the continuing state of Martial Law is…"

Sssssss…..

The announcer then faded away like a distant radio station lost on a clear, starry night. As Jesse struggled to hear the announcer's voice it was replaced by static and then by the sound of rushing water, but not from the shower.

Jesse's shower curtain had morphed into a pseudo open doorway. Although perplexed by what a common everyday morning shower had turned into, he knew and could see that the water he heard rushing was the Mississippi River as it surged through the 28 spillway gates of the Coon Rapids Dam in Coon Rapids,

Minnesota. Jesse's perspective was on the the east side of the river, facing west. He was snatched from his perplexity not by the announcer's voice, but by a now familiar, supernatural, and masculine one. But, it was a voice that had no visible point of origination. It was a voice that commanded him to "look and listen."

The air temperature was hot; Jesse sensing that it was 100 degrees with high humidity. He thought to himself "just like my shower should be." The daytime sky was laden with low grey clouds, appearing as though a thunderstorm was coming. He saw that no one was using the walkway that traversed the dam.

Highway 610 crossed the dam, and the only vehicular traffic Jesse saw pass over was a procession of three M35A2 "deuce and a half "military cargo trucks. The vehicles were adorned in the familiar camouflage paint scheme, but on the driver's side doors the letters "NCSF" were sloppily stenciled in white paint with overspray beyond the 4 characters. Jesse was given the immediate knowledge that NCSF was the acronym for "National Civilian Security Force". The trucks appeared poorly maintained; running rough and belching black smoke out of their loud straight-pipe exhausts.

The cargo beds of the first two trucks were each loaded with six stacks of black, welded-seam body bags, with human "carrion" inside of each one. Each stack was five to six high and these loads were secured with frayed knit strapping. For a few seconds, a large magnifying glass measuring six feet in diameter appeared, revealing MADE IN CHINA FOR NORTH AMERICAN UNION printed in white lettering near a corner of one of the bags.

The bed of the third truck carried what appeared to Jesse to be some variety of soldiers; he estimated there were ten. He was struck with the immediate notion that these motley "soldiers" would not make it through a U.S. Army or Marines boot camp. Even at a distance, Jesse could see that each wore a brown t-shirt, brown baseball-style cap, camouflage BDU pants, and non-descript military boots as they were seated along the edge, fidgeting uncomfortably.

The large magnifying glass reappeared, and Jesse could see the NCSF logo screened on the chest of the shirts and on the caps. The glass remained longer this time, and what Jesse saw next was these second-rate soldiers intermittently scratching their faces, backs, and arms. As the magnifier focused in closer, he could see red sores that looked like large pimples scattered on the uncovered skin of each soldier. As the discomfited soldiers scratched them, some of the sores would begin to bleed.

A human ear, approximately six feet tall, now hovered over the driver's side of the third truck's cargo bed. While human, the ear was translucent and certainly not of this world. With the appearance of the ear, Jesse could now hear over the loud exhaust the distressed conversations from the back of the truck:

"Chobani wants all the dead buried before he gets here. Yes, he's coming tomorrow, praise him our Lord."

"You better praise that son of a bitch, or he'll have you beheaded!"

"Hey, I told you to stop elbowing me, you janky-ass!"

"I can't help it, I'm scratchin' these friggin' sores 'cuz they itch like hell!"

"Listen, Mo-fo, I told you to stop violating my personal space with your boney-ass elbows. That's it - I'm blowin' your friggin' brains out!"

"Screw you, not if I can…"

Jesse was mortified as he heard the pop of a Glock. Next he saw two of the soldiers on the driver's side fall forward into the truck bed; he who first took the bullet from a range of 3 inches, and she who had the bullet bounce around her cranial cavity before settling into her Cerebellum Dura after zipping through one side of the offending scratcher's skull and out the other, taking a small chunk of his Cortex with it. As the remaining seven began to wrestle in the bed of the truck, there were two more shots as the ear and magnifying glass disappeared.

A horrified Jesse was then told to "look at the water" and he immediately fixed his gaze back on the spillway gates. Dead, stinking fish began to pour through; at first just a few but the numbers rapidly increased to hundreds and then thousands. The aquatic carrion were bass, carp, catfish, sunfish, gar, sturgeon, buffalo fish, walleye, perch, and so many other species - large and small. Soon there was so much fish carnage flowing by that Jesse could hardly see the water - the water whose flow was decreasing to a trickle through each spillway gate. Jesse thought that maybe there were so many dead fish congested on the upstream side of the dam that it was impeding the river flow.

As Jesse glanced back at the water that had passed over the dam, he immediately thought of Campbell's tomato soup garnished with Goldfish crackers - but the pleasantness of what would be a tasty lunch was quickly erased. The water had in fact turned red as blood, and the stench was foul as the dead fish rapidly rotted.

"Soon, Jesse, for those who don't repent" the supernatural voice spoke curtly and with frightening clarity.

In his revulsion Jesse tried to cry out; his mouth gaped opened but there was no vibration of his vocal cords. It mattered not, as no one was there to hear. Jesse knew what he was seeing and was immediately overcome with sadness for those who would live through the time in this vision prophesied biblically in Revelation 16 - if this was indeed a vision.

As quickly as the grief overcame him, it began to subside like a parched throat being refreshed with cool water. For it was indeed cool water that Jesse saw next - a rocky creek flowing along a tall bank with green trees and flat stones that restrained the earth from tumbling into the clear, life-giving current. From a low narrow bank opposite the tall one, two brothers - one twelve and the other a year or two younger - were fishing a pool below a small waterfall. The older brother casted a Rooster Tail spinner while the younger a Phoebe spoon, under a vivid blue sky that allowed the sunshine to kiss them.

The older of the two brothers was now reeling in a small but scrappy Rainbow Trout; Jesse could see its pink horizontal stripe glint in the sunshine as the young angler lifted it out of the water. The trout's tail flapped madly as the 12 year old unhooked the spinner from the side of its mouth. The fish had a New York DEC tag in its back, and as the fish was about to be released to fight another time - the magnifying glass enlarged the image of the tag so Jesse could see it from a distance. But, while there were other bits of information printed on the orange tube tag, Jesse could only make out the number 1702.

As Jesse began to wonder what the number meant if anything at all, the supernatural voice spoke poetically:

*"He who dwells in the secret place of the Most High shall abide under the shadow of the Almighty. I will say of the Lord, "He is my refuge and my fortress; My God, in Him I will trust."*

"Psalm 91" Jesse sighed and whispered to himself as he experienced a warm peace growing inside as he again felt the hot shower water spraying. Still, Jesse was stunned as he leaned into the ceramic tile wall of the shower - to both prove to himself he was still in his bathroom and to keep himself from falling down on the porcelain bathtub.

Jesse composed himself, shut off the water, and carefully stepped out of the shower. As he dried himself with a fluffy peach-colored towel, his mind swam through the roiling sea of images left from the vision he had moments ago.

He was looking forward to picking up Trey as they would carpool to the Mohegan Manner for the afternoon's gig. But, would Trey think he was nuts if he was to share the details of his dreams and visions?

Jesse dressed in jeans and tan sweatshirt and then packed "Elvis Suit #1" consisting of black leather pants and jacket, white t-shirt and black boots into a vinyl garment bag, where a black comb and White Rain hair gel were stored in a utility pocket. The J-200 was already in its case and ready to rock-n-roll.

Jesse stared out his bedroom window and into the cloudy, chilly, late October morning. "Oh man, he has no idea" was all Jesse could mutter fretfully as he rapidly shook his head, hoping it would wipe out the scene before him like an illustrator would erase a mistake from a drawing.

What Jesse saw this time was not a dream or a vision. He witnessed in the natural an unwitting elderly man hobble with his cane through the intersection of Genesee and Arch Streets while a translucent scarecrow - apparently in the supernatural - walked alongside, whispering into his ear. A podgy woman with long black hair, dressed in a brocade-patterned Baja hoodie and a tie-die dress walked an English Bull Terrier through the intersection in the opposite direction. As the woman and the hyper, disobedient dog crossed the street, they passed through the scarecrow like it wasn't even there.

# 3

# Jailhouse Rock

As Jesse sped along Salt Springs Road through the high hinterlands between Chittenango and Manlius, the sound of *Number Two* by The Pernice Brothers filled the interior of his Grand Cherokee. "Little power monger sleep tonight, the city lights up like a dirty dime, I hope this letter finds you crying, it would feel so good to see you cry" was sung with heartbroken, back-stabbed bitterness by Joe Pernice over the haunting, lamenting G-Dm-Am-C acoustic guitar chord change.

Jesse loved this song that was the 7th track on this home-burned CD "Mix 47", playing after another Pernice Brothers goodie *The Weakest Shade of Blue*. While Jesse enjoyed the music of Elvis Presley and performed it with uncanny accuracy, he was aching to do something different with his musical gifts. He wished that he could form a new act, performing original material that would reek of pop influences like the Beatles, Guided By Voices, the Pernice Brothers, Fastball, and other similar bands that Jesse enjoyed.

The drive to pick up Trey was helping Jesse to relax and to clear his mind; to sort out the two supernatural occurrences from that morning, following the disturbing dream from the previous night.

If degrees of being shell-shocked were measured on a scale of 1 to five - 1 being the most minor and 5 being of the gravest severity, Jesse was at level 2.43.

He knew that last night's dream, the Lucky Charms incident, and the vision of a blood red Mississippi River and soldiers stricken with sores were not an indication of a traumatized mind coming unhinged. He had the confidence that what he was dreaming and seeing was of the near future and biblically-prophetic. Likewise, he was certain that he had been under demonic assault that morning.

Jesse had been set free by the Son of Man, and yet in this world he felt like a prisoner. He sang the song "Jailhouse Rock" to earn a living, and the song was apropos as he was in essence rocking in a jail - a jailhouse of circumstance.

The critical reviews were always positive. Samantha Styles ("yeah right, like that's her real name" Jesse would often grumble skeptically) the entertainment editor for *Table Hopping*, an upstate New York monthly newspaper self-billed as "Central New York's premier source for Dining, Night Life and Entertainment for over twenty years" wrote of a recent performance of *Jesse Same - Elvis Impersonator* at the Fireside Inn located in Baldwinsville, New York:

*This act should modify its name to be "Jesse Same - Elvis Reincarnate." As I watched Mr. Same wiggle his hips in black leather pants and swing his microphone stand, and as I gazed awestruck at his physical attributes, I was transported back in time - to a much better time. When dressed in a white jumpsuit and cape for the last quarter of the show, I saw what Elvis should have looked like in his last years: fit, trim, and sexy and not heavy, out of shape, and dripping with sweat while reading lyrics he could not remember.*

*When Jesse Same sat on a wooden stool and strummed his acoustic guitar under the spotlight while the band played in the shadows, I saw him shed tears as he wistfully sang "Love Me Tender" with flawless perfection. To say that I was likewise moved to tears would be an understatement. While still seated, he next performed a heartbreaking rendition of "Are You Lonesome Tonight", and as he spoke the forlorn lyrical plea at the end of the song: "now the stage is bare and I'm standing there, with emptiness all around, and if you won't come back to me, then make them bring the curtain down" I was again, if only for a few moments, a swooning teenage girl. The curtain could have come down and if I died right then and there, my life would have been complete.*

*Whether you cherish the music and memories of The King or not, you need to catch Jesse Same at one or both of his remaining Fireside Inn engagements this month. You might think that I've lost my mind, but I believe that Jesse Same is not an Elvis impersonator but in fact the King of Rock-n-Roll back from the dead.*

He would have pulled into the driveway of an old farm house and turned around, but the man referred to as "Elvis back from the dead" had a strong sense of obligation, so he continued on to Trey's residence while the Guided By Voices song *The Brides Have Hit Glass* played from Mix 47.

Jesse desired to know who his father was as well as to know more about his mysterious Grandpa Richard, but strangely in this time of advanced technology and information retrieval, there were gaps that could not be filled and walls that stood as immovable blockades. And, equally as much as he wanted these shadowy issues to be brought to light, he longed to be known as *Jesse Same - Something Other Than an Elvis Impersonator*.

A few minutes later, Jesse's black Jeep Grand Cherokee pulled into the driveway of the same East Pleasant Street house that he and Trey spent so much time in the basement of as kids and teenagers. At 35 years of age, Trey Emerson was the oldest of Dustin and Margaret Emerson's five children; being one of two sons. The 2,468 square foot colonial home painted "Pottery Barn Tan" with black trim was being rented "for a song" by Trey from his parents; they having moved to Dallas in 2006.

Trey had never aspired to be anything other than a guitarist and vocalist; and he played with confidant competence rock, blues, and country music. To earn a living, he was a "gun for hire" live musician and studio session player, performing and recording with everyone and anyone who would pay him. In addition to working lead guitar and backing vocals for Jesse Same - Elvis Impersonator, he was the guitarist and lead vocalist of The Nozeloids, a roots rock trio that planned to release its debut CD in January of 2010. Trey hoped that the CD release would break The Nozeloids open, whereby making that his only gig. But, at this time in 2009, Trey had to play Elvis music as well as provide his guitar chops to Sexxxy Sounds, billed as *Upstate New York's Number One Goodtime Groovalicious Party Band.* Indeed, the hopes of Trey's career path ran through The Nozeloids. While he didn't mind mimicking the guitar licks of Elvis' lead guitarists Scotty Moore and James Burton, he was sick to the back teeth of the "we're Sexxxy Sounds, and we say FUNK YOU" shtick.

The eldest of Dustin and Margaret's brood stood at 5' 11" tall, one inch shorter than Jesse. Like his best friend Jesse, Trey weighed 165 lbs. While the singer who bore an uncanny resemblance to the Memphis Flash had a thick and full head of hair, the talented lead guitarist kept his head shaved as his hair began to noticeably thin at the age of 30. While Jesse would of course be clean shaven, Trey maintained a fashionable soul patch below his bottom lip. As the antithesis of many musicians and hipsters, the fashion accessories that Trey refused to sport were earrings and necklaces.

Trey was waiting in the heated garage when Jesse pulled up. For the gig he would change into black slacks, black ankle boots, and black suit jacket over a powder blue t-shirt. For now, he wore faded Lee jeans, tan Rockport Eureka shoes, and a gold-colored t-shirt with INFOWARS.COM silk-screened across the chest in burgundy lettering. On the back of the shirt, was a square-shaped group of the following logos and symbols: Skull and Bones Society, IMF, UN, CIA, Dept. of Homeland Security, KGB, Free Masons, Council of Foreign Relations, M15, DAPRA, Trilateral Commission, and the World Trade Organization. Inside of the arrayed box of symbols was Nazi official and German military leader Hermann Goering's quote from the Nuremburg Trials:

*"Naturally the common people don't want war: Neither in Russia, nor in England, nor for that matter in Germany. That is understood. But, after all, IT IS THE LEADERS of the country who determine the policy and it is always a simple matter to drag the people along, whether it is a democracy, or a fascist dictatorship, or a parliament, or a communist dictatorship. Voice or no voice, the people can always be brought to the bidding of the leaders. That is easy. All you have to do is TELL THEM THEY ARE BEING ATTACKED, and denounce the peacemakers for lack of patriotism and exposing the country to danger. IT WORKS THE SAME IN ANY COUNTRY."*

The garage door lifted and Jesse walked in. "Hey" was all Jesse needed to say to his best friend, Trey responding with "what's up, haircut?"

Trey pulled on a black Navy Pea Coat and began buttoning it. The coat had been resting on a Fender Twin guitar amp, which Jesse began to roll on its wheels out to his Grand Cherokee. Trey picked up his white Fender Standard Telecaster stored in a black hard-shell case; the case baring a yellow bumper sticker with the DON'T TREAD ON ME slogan and coiled rattle snake. He carried that and a grey suitcase containing several effects pedals, cables, extra strings, and other guitar accessories. After all of that and his garment bag were quickly loaded into the Grand Cherokee, Trey and Jesse were on their way to Liverpool, the busy suburb bordering Syracuse's north side and much of Onondaga Lake.

After a brief period of non-conversation while listening intently to WSYR-AM while Glenn Beck warned that American sovereignty and security was being dangerously and intentionally compromised by the administration of President Jomo Omondi, Jesse broke the silence:

"I really like the band your brother is in."

"Oh, Pie Kite?" Trey responded, in reference to his 23 year old brother Chris, the youngest of the five Emerson children who was lovingly and humorously referred to as "the accident" by his parents. "The accident" worked rhythm guitar, keyboards, and backing vocals for the Manlius-based pop/rock band Pie Kite.
"Yeah. The music sounds so much like mid and late period Beatles stuff. It's amazing that in 2009 guys in their late teens and early twenties would create music like that. Man, I'd love to be doing something like what they do! So, when is their CD coming out?" Jesse spoke with a modicum of excitement, taking his eyes off of Route 92 for a split second and looking over at Trey who was scanning through his iPhone.

Trey looked away from his phone and at Jesse while answering "they plan to release it in mid-December, I guess. They think all the recording, mixing, and graphics will be finished by then. Chris is really geeked about it and I'm happy for him and maybe a little jealous, too. Jake and Josh Zimmer are really talented songwriters and fine singers and musicians. Seth Truax drums like Bun E. Carlos. He's only 19 and thinks that Ringo Starr is one of the best drummers in all of Rock history. Ringo is NOT one of the best drummers in history!"

"You know, I thought I saw the Zimmer brothers in a vision this morning… ah, never mind…" Jesse answered; the smile exiting his face stage-left as his countenance became grim.

"Vision - what?" Trey inquired as he squinted at Jesse while snickering.

“Never mind, just let it go!” Jesse answered through a nervous laugh.

“No, what were you gonna say about the Zimmer brothers?” Trey asked probingly.

“Just let it go!” Jesse retorted forcefully.

After a moment of silence, while Jesse pulled onto the entrance to Routes 690 West and 481 North from Route 5 near the Wegmans food store in Fayetteville, he became furious with an elderly driver in front of him, shouting “why are these old blue-hairs allowed to drive all slow, weaving left and right! We’ve got things to do and places to be! Hey lady, your Depends are leaking, pull over!”

“She didn’t hear you, man. Wow, you are edgy today!” Trey replied with a laugh, yet appearing concerned about his friend.

“Yeah… I’m edgy today. I need to dial it down a few notches. I’m over-tired too. I didn’t sleep well last night and had a rough morning” Jesse answered in rat-a-tat-tat fashion.

“Is what’s happening to America bringing you down?” Trey asked of Jesse earnestly.

“Uh…yeah… that’s it. The people of this country have become pacified and stupid and it shows through the election of Omondi as President. Yeah, that’s it” Jesse answered Trey, hoping that would change the air and the subject.

“Well, bro, it’s not just the pacified; it’s the elites who are the pacifiers. You believe in all of that Book of Revelation stuff. You know a one world government is coming. You know the shit is going to hit the fan, and soon - now that they got Omondi into the White House. That’s why you should join, bro” Trey said, staring with concern at Jesse.

“Join - join what?” Jesse asked, sounding just a bit perplexed.

“The North Madison Militia” Trey answered, nodding his head affirmatively.

As Trey began to read a text message on his iPhone, it seemed that time stood still. Jesse felt his head swim and queasiness in his stomach as he remembered the North Madison Militia shooting a police officer and then destroying a police cruiser in his dream last night. He had never heard of that militia until it appeared in his dream; and now Trey was actually mentioning it as if he either had access to Jesse’s dreams or the organization was real.

Jesse felt for a second that he might lose control of his vehicle before answering Trey in a high, constricted voice: “The North Madison Militia?”

“Yeah, I’ve been involved for a couple of weeks now. We’re preparing for the chaos that will come when America goes down. We’ve got firearms, an underground bun…

“No way, man! I’m not gonna live on some compound with a bunch of trigger-happy rednecks who think they’re the northeastern chapter of the Branch Davidians! Are you crazy there, Skippy?” Jesse cut Trey off at mid-sentence, all while regaining control of his wits and the Grand Cherokee.

“It’s not like that” Trey attempted to reason with Jesse: “I mean, you know that I don’t live on a compound, right?”

“Right” Jesse agreed.

“Okay then, I’ll try to lay it out for you” Trey said, and then began to offer details:

“We meet on Lakeport Road in Chittenango…”

“Yeah, I know where Lakeport Road is” Jesse interrupted facetiously.

“I know you do, so if you’d stop interrupting me!” Trey fired back, a bit hot under the collar.

“Sorry man, tell me about where you guys play army” Jesse replied with a cackle.

Trey drew in a deep breath, released a frustrated sigh, and then began again:

“We meet on Lakeport Road at a house owned by a guy named Steve Sandifer and his wife Eileen. Steve and his friend Galen Moss started the militia and Steve is the commander, while Galen is second in command. Steve and Eileen used to go to Four Corners Community Church with my parents, and that’s how I know them. Steve is a former Green Beret who saw combat at the end of the Viet Nam war, just before Nixon got us out. The guy is 65 years old but he’s in better physical condition than most people I know that are half his age…”

“Sounds like you have a crush on Steve. Does Eileen know?” Jesse interrupted again, endeavoring to sound concerned but finding it difficult to conceal his amusement.

Trey’s patience was being tested, but he was determined to fill Jesse in on the North Madison Militia:

“Look, jackass, America is in deep trouble and probably on its way out. We now have a bona fide Marxist in the White House. It has nothing to do with the guy’s skin color. It has everything to do with his roots, what he stands for, and who stands with him. When Omondi got the Democratic nomination last year, Steve and Galen knew it was time to act. After all the monkey business and recounts before the Democratic Convention, they knew it was a done deal and that he would be elected President, no matter what sort of manipulation it took…"

"…For the wealthy elites who believe they would most benefit from a one world economy, getting a lazy, narcissistic, apathetic, dependent, drugged-out, alcoholic nation of people that is obsessed with computer games and entertainment while being willfully-stricken with the cancer of Political Correctness out to vote for Omondi - that was the easy part. The fraud to make sure that a lot of military votes and votes in historically Republican areas weren't counted and the intimidation to make fence-sitters vote for him took a bit more effort, but they got it done."

"Hey, do you guys play paintball too?" Jesse interrupted, attempting to make light of the heavy subject matter Trey was speaking on, but then quickly turning somber, asking:

"No seriously - so, do you and your friends who get together and play army plan on assassinating Omondi? - I mean, it sure sounds like it!"

Trey reacted with no pretense: "Nah, we won't assassinate Omondi - I'd like to but we can't get that close. The North Madison Militia exists to protect freedom-loving citizens in our immediate area from a government gone rogue - a willingly manipulated government set to destroy America."

"Yeah, I know that what you're saying is true and we need to be prepared, but I'll pass on your invite. I'm not into guns like you are. I'll leave it all to God because it's a supernatural battle" Jesse said, as the dream from last night as well as the vision and the demonic attack from that morning weighed heavily upon him.

"Well, dude, when the feces impacts the air-cooling device, I hope God steps in and saves your ass from citizens recruited into a government-sponsored paramilitary force while other hungry citizens live a zombie apocalypse." Trey delivered his answer as a stern warning, and as he did, Jesse immediately recalled what seemed to be a government-sponsored paramilitary force - the "NCSF" - from his vision a few hours earlier.

How ironic that Trey would at first mention the North Madison Militia, Jesse having never heard of it until last night's dream. Now he was talking of a paramilitary force that could be the NCSF from the morning's vision.

A sudden wave of nausea swept over Jesse, as the apparent irony was too much for his stunned and fatigued mind and body to take. He barked the command "take the wheel" to Trey, and as the confused lead guitarist did as he was told, Jesse rolled down the driver's side window and heaved a steaming mass of Lucky Charms cereal. The vomit splattered onto the windshield of an Onondaga County Sheriff's cruiser that was quickly approaching from behind; the deputy about to put his right index finger on the master switch to turn on the car's flashing lights to pull Jesse over for driving 77 MPH in a double-nickels zone.

The cruiser's lights never got lit, as the suddenly blinded deputy named Brad Ducey hit the brakes, forcing the car into a triple three-sixty spin before harmlessly coming to a rest in the center lane of the three westbound lanes of Route 690, facing oncoming traffic. Fortunately, traffic was light enough at that particular moment that no one was tailgating Ducey; approaching drivers either coming to a stop or veering into the outside lanes and proceeding past the police car with the end product of a "Technicolor yawn" smeared on its windshield.

Jesse retook the steering wheel, drawing in a deep breath while being unaware of the scene behind him. The only words a nonplussed Trey could offer were "uh...wow...was it something I said?"

# 4

# Nostradamus

As the act was known as *Jesse Same - Elvis Impersonator*, Jesse had the last word over what songs would be performed in a given set. And against the suggestion of booking agent Mike Wickert, with the ambivalence of the band, and to the displeasure of some of the RGIS staffers partaking of the company's corporate luncheon, Jesse decided to finish the 1 hour set with "How Great Thou Art."

Indeed, Jesse sang the hymn brilliantly with absolute conviction and was the exact replica - for want of a better term - of a gospel-singing Elvis Presley. As he belted out the line "oh my God, how great thou art" before Trey and the band came in full-force to carry the song home, Jesse felt the Holy Spirit move powerfully through him and he thought he might faint. But, faint he did not, and even keyboardist "T.Z." Tony Zonnerville - ever the unconvinced skeptic - was so moved by Jesse's performance that all he could do was stand and clap after the last notes were played and sung.

As to be expected, not everyone at the corporate luncheon was wowed by the spirit-led performance of the hymn. At the completion of the song, "aw, c'mon sexy man, this ain't Sundee!

(sic) We're like here to party for chrissakes! (sic) No religious songssss" was bellowed by a short, chubby, raspy-voiced redhead named Patty, who evidenced the damaging results of too many trips to the tanning booth on her badly wrinkled face and wore far too much blue eyeliner and red lipstick. As she squawked through a dopey drunken grin, the contents of her bottle of Labatt's Blue Light sloshed onto the floor as she wobbled.

Luanne, Patty's co-worker and near-double, chimed in: "Yeah... what's up, Elvis? Hah? Youse gonna come home wit (sic) me and shake yer hips, honey? Jus' don't be singin' any of those Jesus and Mudder Mary songs 'cuz I've been a really really bad girl... ha-ha-ha!" Luanne's mucus-laden vocal chords had been assaulted by too many years of bourbon shots and too many packs of USA Gold full-flavor.

Jesse ignored the women as he walked off the stage of the Mohegan Manor banquet room. As he grabbed his garment bag and began to head toward the restroom to change, he was stopped by a flitting Neil Belcher, the melodramatic General Manager of the Liverpool RGIS office:

"Jesse, I was elated through ALMOST all of your set as I-LOVE-ELVIS, okay? But, when you ended with that corny gospel song, I was like saying to everybody at my table 'what the hell, ya know? Why does he hafta do this?' Look Jesse, a few of my staffers were really offended by that song, okay? It was like EXTREEEEME right-wing Christian, ya know? There are a lot of really good people here who don't believe that stuff but they're still going to a nice place when they die, okay? They don't need to hear about Jesus or whoever in a song when they just wanna have a good time, right? I know Elvis sang some of those songs, but that was when he was a fat old druggy losing his mind, okay? You shouldn't be like that, 'cuz you've really got it goin' on, ya know! We were gonna book you to do our next event in March, but we've got to think about it now 'cuz of what happened, okay?"

Jesse felt like he'd been run over by a butterfly-powered steamroller, and before he could respond, Neil Belcher was quickly flitting away, calling out in a singsong voice "Marrr-gery, dear, wait uh-up!"

A short while later, after the packing-up was done, neither Jesse or Trey noticed the man sitting with the window rolled down in the front passenger's side of a silver Toyota Corolla parked next to the Grand Cherokee. As Jesse placed his right hand on the Grand Cherokee's driver's-side door handle, he felt warm spittle impact his left cheek, just below his eye.

Startled, Jesse snapped around and saw two middle-aged Pakistani men; one in the driver's seat and the other who had spit on him from the passenger's side. Both were RGIS employees and had been present at the luncheon. Before Jesse could react, the man who had spit on him stuttered and screamed hysterically "You…you… you…you…are a c-c-c-Christian innnnn-fidel p-p-pig in erotic t-t-trousers! You…you…you… who refuse to submit to ah-ah-ah-ah-Allah will have a December to remember! Allah ak-ak-Akbar!"

Although being on the opposite side of Jesse's vehicle, Trey had witnessed the entire event. As a confounded Jesse sat down behind the wheel, Trey was running behind the Grand Cherokee and toward the Toyota. The Toyota backed out of its parking spot with a squeal - nearly striking Trey - and then moved quickly forward toward the exit. Trey's initial impulse was to draw the Colt 45 that was concealed inside of his coat. But, considering the safety of others now entering the parking lot, he decided against that move even though his right hand was on the grip.

"I got the tag number of the Corolla, it's BMT-4580 and I know someone who works for the DMV and can look it up" Trey spoke with teeth-clenched anger as he sat down inside the Grand Cherokee.

Jesse wiped the loogie off of his face with a napkin from McDonalds. "Islam, the religion of peace in action" he uttered, shaking his head while maintaining a wan smile. "I hope the Spitting Jihadist doesn't have any communicable diseases. Man, this has been a weird twenty-four hours" Jesse lamented as he grabbed a small bottle of hand sanitizer from a compartment located in front of the shift lever on the Jeep's console.

"I like that moniker 'the Spitting Jihadist' - that's funny" Trey said with a snicker as he watched his friend apply hand sanitizer to his face in hopes that it would kill whatever germs lived in the Pakistani man's spit. "But, I would have loved to have capped that son of a bitch and his buddy" he finished, his countenance and voice having instantly become incensed.

As Jesse dropped the bottle back into the rectangular-shaped compartment and then started the engine, Trey, now less irate, inquired "so, uh, what other kinds of weird things have been happening?"

It took Jesse a split second to decide not to be too revealing to his best friend Trey. As he backed out of the parking spot and began moving forward through the lot, his answer was "just some really strange dreams last night; they would be too hard to describe. It made it hard to fall back asleep. And then, the miniature terror attack here in the parking lot and you almost shooting the guy."

"Look man, you know Al-Qaeda, Hamas, and Hezbollah have operatives in this country. Bush could have been tougher on those vermin, but Omondi kisses their asses. If people weren't walking out into the parking lot then yeah, I would have released some rounds, dude" was Trey's retort; more irritated by Jesse's apparent displeasure with him wanting to shoot than with the actual events a short time prior.

"Trey, this nation is on the fast-track to destruction, but..."

Before Jesse could finish, Trey was beside himself and interrupted "what the hell, Jesse! That bastard spit in your face and proclaimed 'Allah Akbar!' You claim to be one of those Jesus freaks, right? Well then, that should piss you off, bro! Satan just used that moon god-worshipping creep to violate you! He spit on your cheek! Oh wait, I know, you have to turn the other cheek, right?!"

"I know what's coming, Trey, and the Spitting Jihadist isn't going to get 72 virgins. But yeah, I'm moving forward and turning the other…"

Again, Trey interrupted: "Jesse Same! C'mon man, what's wrong with you? This is a battle between good and evil and we are now fighting an enemy within as well as without!"

"Look, Trey, I know! I know this better than you" Jesse snapped back, and then fell into resignation: "man, I wish I could tell you what I've…ah, never mind."

"Know 'what' better than me? What do you wish you could tell me?" Trey asked, his voice conveying equal parts irritation and paranoia.

"Alright…okay… I've been having strange dreams - dreams that I think are prophetic. Some are directly related to biblical scripture, while others don't appear to be related to it but could be the result of it having been fulfilled. I've had some intense visions as well - I know they are not my imagination" Jesse answered Trey with trepidation.

"Oh, so you're now Jesse Same - Elvis Impersonator and Nostradamus wannabe" Trey replied with a chuckle.

"It's got nothing to do with your Nostradamus. It has much to do with where we are today. You're certainly hip to that, eh? And, it's got everything to do with what's *coming soon to a theater near you* (Jesse affected the drama of a voice-over artist's voice) only the presentation will be super high definition and in your front yard at Camp Reality America" Jesse finished somberly.

"Well, Nostradamus was a biblical prophet, so why is what you claim to be dreaming not like the stuff that he saw, bro?" Trey asked, stone-faced.

"Have you read the Bible?" Jesse answered, finding it hard to conceal his impatience.

"Hell yeah... well little bits of it here and there. You know I believe in God, bro - I'm just not one of those Jesus Freaks" Trey answered with little conviction as he turned and looked out of the passenger-side window.

"If you read the Bible, you'd know that Nostradamus isn't anywhere to be found in it" Jesse's answer conveyed his continued impatience.

"Yeah, well, Emily told me that he is a major biblical prophet. I mean, how else would he have been able to see that stuff that happened already and is coming right at us?" Trey squinted at Jesse in confused disbelief.

"Emily also told you that she's never cheated on you. If you would read the Bible, you'd learn that there are prophets named Isaiah, Ezekiel, Daniel, Jeremiah, and a whole host of others - but none are named Nostradamus" Jesse zinged back.

"Alright, so the wench cheated on me once."

"Once?"

"Okay…you got me, my caring, understanding so-called best friend" Trey snapped back sarcastically, but then continued in a calm and thoughtful manner:

"But, Emily has a degree in Education from Syracuse University. She also minored in Religious Studies and Philosophy. She says that Nostradamus's prophecies were removed from the King James Bible by Catholic priests in the Fifteen Hundreds, because they were too frightening for the believing brainwashed masses. They did that after they excommunicated him from the church - him and his little bowl of water."

"Emily has put multiple bullets into your heart and steaming bull-feces into your mind, Trey. Look, Nostradamus was a 'seer' who was of Jewish origins but followed Catholicism, so the Catholic connection is right. In the end, he was a fraud and his visions were never, ever part of the Word of God. But, I'm not surprised she'd be taught something like that by the indoctrinators at S.U." Jesse answered, shaking his head with a look of exasperation on his face.

"Well, I guess a Bible-thumper like you would know better than a graduate student from Syracuse. But yeah, bro, it's a liberal northeastern university training the cat food-brained junior elites how to become major players in the New World Order" Trey conceded.

Both Trey and Jesse were exhausted and didn't have much energy left for spirited debate. Jesse never did describe on this trip his dreams and visions to Trey. As a light rain sprinkled the windshield and the wipers *wup-wupped* back and forth, both became lost in their own thoughts. Jesse wondered what if anything he would see or dream next, and he silently prayed for peace and discernment. Trey thought about and looked forward to the meeting that night at Steve Sandifer's house, where they would discuss some "intel" that had been relayed to Steve from a friend "still on the inside." Trey also thought about the AK-47 he practiced shooting that past Saturday in the field behind Steve's house. It brought a sense of accomplishment to Trey, knowing that he could now handle the weapon with ease.

As Jesse turned left onto East Pleasant Street from Fayette in the rustic yet bustling village of Manlius, New York, it was Trey who finally broke the silence:

"Jesse, if you're so into Jesus, how come you don't go to church?"

# 5

# Powerball

The past few days had been quiet for Jesse. There were no other gigs that week for *Jesse Same - Elvis Impersonator* and he was glad for some time off. Mike Wickert was putting together an East Coast tour of hotels and casinos for January, but until that time whatever work came up would be local.

There was the dream about UFO's last night, but that was nothing - or was it…?

It was Saturday, October 31st, 2009. While it was an insignificant date for Jesse, most of America was celebrating the pagan holiday of Halloween. For no reason, Jesse found himself browsing the Dollar General store in Chittenango early that afternoon; perusing the picked-over selection of Halloween candy marked down 50 percent. Jesse enjoyed Baby Ruth bars, and the fun-sized trick or treat version did not appear to be popular, as there were plenty of bags left available. Jesse grabbed two bags from a depleted shelf in a center aisle of the small general store and began to walk to the checkout.

“Hey Jesse, long time no see” a voice from behind startled him; slamming the door shut to the room of his racing, jumbled thoughts. Jesse turned to see Matt Carrier, Head Pastor of the Four Corners Community Church standing a few feet behind, holding three bags of assorted candy.

“Hi Matt, how are you?” Jesse inquired.

“Doing well, Jesse, praise the Lord” The pastor replied with an ear to ear grin, and then the grin disappeared as he continued on: “I haven’t seen you in church in quite a while. Is everything going okay?”

“Yeah, Matt, everything is okay. Life is keeping me busy but I’m relying on the Lord to keep me strong” Jesse replied straightforwardly.

It was then that Jesse felt moved to tell the pastor about some of his recent dreams and visions:

“You know Matt; I’ve been having some graphic and somewhat frightening dreams and visions lately. In my spirit I believe they are of the prophetic nature. A few mornings ago, while I was in the shower, I had a vision that I was standing next to the Mississippi River in Minnesota, and it turned blood red and there were thousands of stinking, dead fish. And later, I heard…”

Pastor Matt cut Jesse off with a chuckle: “Wow, sounds like maybe you shouldn’t eat those peanut butter and banana sandwiches that you love so much for breakfast! That’s some crazy stuff, man!”

Jesse responded, speaking in a rapid-fire manner, as though he only had seconds of time: “No Matt, it has nothing to do with that - and I had Lucky Charms - and oh yeah, the leprechaun - well, anyway back to the river vision. I heard a voice at the end of the vision - a strange, masculine voice that said ‘soon Jesse, for those who don’t repent.’ I knew that what I saw was during the Great

Tribulation and prophesied in Revelation 16. There's much more to this, Matt. And in my spirit I know that I am supposed to share what I'm seeing. I've dreamed about Chittenango after some sort of terror event. I've dreamed about the Rapture. I know that it is coming soon, but obviously I don't know the day or hour, and..."

Pastor Matt cut Jesse off again, first addressing an elderly woman who was pretending to be searching for candy but was actually eavesdropping: "Hi Ava, good to see you again - see you tomorrow, for the nine o'clock service, right?"

Then Pastor Matt addressed Jesse: "Look Jesse, there are some Christians that think a lot about the End Times. It sounds like that you have the End of Days on your brain, especially considering what is happening to the economy, to America as a whole, and around the world."

Pastor Matt stopped for a few seconds, breathed deeply, exhaled and then continued again, nodding toward Ava, as if to use her as a point of reference:

"Most Christians - and I'll use those in my congregation as an example - are looking forward to their children and grandchildren graduating college and moving on into good careers. Many are excited that they have sons and daughters that are about to be married and are looking forward to seeing this happen. Some are excited about participating in the Christmas presentation that we put on at the high school every year. Others are starting new careers or getting promotions, praise the Lord, and this is a blessing to be excited about. Still others have babies on the way. And, as you know, we are active in sending out young people on mission's trips to Africa, and we have some teenagers that are just so excited to go! What a thrill it is to get your picture in the church bulletin and to share the amazing stories of God using them in places like Uganda to spread the good news!"

“What about spreading the good news to the poor and homeless in Syracuse - not much church bulletin material there, eh?” Jesse butted in, but it was though the pastor never heard him as he continued to speak:

“Jesse, we like to take the approach of preaching the Social Gospel. My congregation is made up of good, middle class people with lots in this life to be happy about. While they all look forward to being with Jesus one day, they don’t think about the End Times and I don’t preach on it, as you know. The last thing that most in my flock would want is to have some Rapture come along and take them away from those graduations, marriages, promotions, vacations, and wonderful blessings that God has given them in this world.”

Pastor Matt smiled in a way that seemed belittling to Jesse as he finished his lecture. Jesse’s only response was “well, thanks for your time Pastor, and I hope that this world continues to treat you and your happy congregation well. Obviously, I’ve wasted your time.”

Jesse was hurt, insulted, and disappointed as he walked away from the pastor, but he browsed a few minutes longer before heading to the checkout. In another aisle the Christmas ornaments and lights were already beginning to appear on the shelves, and Jesse so enjoyed looking at them. Jesse delighted in the Christmas season and as well he liked performing the Christmas music that Elvis recorded.

Jesse paid for his two bags of “fun-sized” Baby Ruth bars as well as a 16.3 ounce jar of creamy Peter Pan peanut butter. As he walked through the exit, he was nearly bowled over by three pre-teenagers dressed in Halloween regalia. Appropriately enough for Chittenango, a girl was impeccably dressed as Dorothy Gale from the Wizard of Oz, and as Jesse momentarily locked eyes with her he immediately recalled seeing the demon that appeared as a scarecrow that whispered into the unwitting old man’s ear. Jesse felt his stomach twist from the memory, and as a boy in a werewolf costume and another made up as a bloody accident victim brushed hard against him as they entered the store, he was seemingly unaffected. Jesse could only mumble to himself "kind of early in the day to be trick or treating" as he began to proceed along the sidewalk to the parking lot where his Grand Cherokee waited.

As he was about to step off of the sidewalk and into the lot, he was drawn out of his thoughts by a voice speaking "Jesse, wait up." He turned toward the corner of the brick structure that housed the Dollar General and saw Pastor Matt standing there.

"Hey, can I talk to you for a minute?" the broad-shouldered, 5 feet 9 inch tall 55 year old with thinning brown hair and piercing blue eyes asked of Jesse as he stood with one foot on the sidewalk and the other on the parking lot.

"Did you want to tell me that you'll pray for me because I'm losing my mind and living in an End Times fantasy world?" Jesse asked; his face and voice evidencing extreme frustration.

"No, Jesse, not at all, man. I know how I might have come off inside of the store, and I'm sorry. But, everything I said in there is true, but I couldn't tell you everything with nosey Ava McMurtry lurking in the aisle. She attends my church and her husband John is an elder - you know; the guy that owns the two McMurtry Auto Mall dealerships."

"So, alright then, I hope you have a happy 'name it and claim it' sermon tomorrow and I'll head home to a PB and 'nanner sandwich with some Baby Ruth bars for desert. Hopefully, I won't have any scary dreams and visions that might frighten somebody" Jesse spit nails of sarcasm as he began to walk away.

"Jesse, look, I know what's going on. Just hear me out, will you?" the pastor spoke conciliatorily.

"Um, sure, uh, okay" was Jesse's reply as he stopped walking.

"The subject matter of my sermons is dictated by the elders of Four Corners Community Church. They are all middle-aged and senior-aged men; Ava's husband John McMurtry at 82 is the oldest. These men were all instrumental in getting the church off the ground in 1996 as a daughter church to Eastside Bible Church in Manlius."

"Yeah, I know this" Jesse replied impatiently as though he was waiting for the punch-line.

"So, anyway, the elders are all good men who have had some manner of success in their lives, right? They've all had good careers or run their own businesses. They've all had solid Christian marriages with wives who understand their role in the marriage as written in the Bible. With their wives, these men have raised stables of good Christian kids and have been blessed with good Christian grandchildren. Basically, other for then a few serious illnesses that by the healing grace of the Holy Spirit they've recovered from, these men have had predictable, blessed lives. They've done everything that they were supposed to do and always have sought God's leading in their decision making. They have nice homes, vacations, mission's trips, and essentially, everything always works out safely and predictably."

"Yeah, so I've seen" was Jesse's reply as he rolled his eyes, still waiting for the punch-line.

"These guys are leaders of men's groups and they in turn help men to be better Christian fathers. That's all good, right?"

"Right" was Jesse's emotionless reply, silencing the gunshot of sadness in his soul as he wondered who his father was.

"These men lead Bible studies and help others to grow in the word. Yup, they are good church people through and through!"

As Pastor Matt spoke *good church people through and through*, Jesse detected a mixture of irritation and sarcasm in his voice.

"It doesn't matter that Garret Wiley the millionaire gets drunk and pisses his pants. No, it doesn't matter that Brian Taber is an arrogant, snobbish, egotistical know-it-all of a treasurer. No, guys like these are the elders and they decide the tenor of my preaching!" Pastor Matt was noticeably irate now as he continued:

"Jesse, I can't preach on anything that's what they refer to as 'bad for business.' I can't preach on the End Times because it would make far too many in the congregation nervous. I mean, these people have no idea what is going on in America and the world and how it relates to Bible prophecy! Not only that, they aren't interested in becoming familiar with the false teachings like Christian Science, Word of Faith, Kingdom Now, the Prosperity Gospel - which by the way they are forcing me to preach - or any of the stuff that can lead them badly off track. They have no idea what those twisted beliefs even are! No, I can't talk about the End Times or warn them about Mormonism, Catholicism, or whatever. Right now, the one world economy and system is being slowly but steadily built, but I can't teach from Revelation because these are potentially frightening topics that might keep asses out of the pews - or as the elders say, be 'bad for business!'"

"Jesse, I am waiting for the trumpet of rescue to blow and for Jesus to yell 'come up hither!' Like you, it seems to me that it won't be far off, but I can't prepare my flock! I can't teach them how to truly wear the full armor of God, or else I might lose my job and right now man I can't afford that! I have to keep what is tantamount to the chairmen of the board happy! It's la-la-la blessing after blessing in this world God has made for them. Man, for them, Heaven would be anti-climactic!"

The pastor's lips were tight and his eyes began welling with tears as he said "Jesse, I have to go for now." With that, he sat behind the wheel of his blue Dodge Ram pickup, drove out of his parking spot and sped away, leaving a cloud of dust. As Jesse watched the truck turn left onto Tuscarora Road, he was suddenly hit with the notion that the vehicle was identical to the one used by the North Madison Militia in his dream.

"Nah, it can't be the same pick-up truck, could it be?" Jesse said to himself, shaking his head. As Jesse opened the driver's side door of the Grand Cherokee and tossed his bag of candy and peanut butter onto the front passenger's seat, he muttered aloud "sheeple being spiritually chopped into veal cutlets for Satan."

As Jesse lived upstairs at 316 Genesee Street, he didn't get any trick or treat traffic and in that he was glad; but conversely, Dean and Cassandra, who cohabitated downstairs, fully embraced the Halloween celebration. Both of the windows of their flat that faced Genesee Street were trimmed from the inside with strings of orange lights and faux cobwebs stuck to the glass. On the edge of each of the four steps that led to the front porch was a small pumpkin - not carved in Jack O' Lantern fashion but each instead painted by Cassandra in the near-perfect likeness of an original member of the rock band Kiss. From top step to bottom were Paul Stanley, Ace Frehley, Gene Simmons, and Peter Criss. Cassandra had a week before asked Jesse if he minded the pumpkins being on the steps, and he didn't as he used the back entry steps from Rouse Street that went directly up to his flat.

So, as the five o'clock hour arrived on the fifty degree evening and the kiddies began to take to the streets dressed in all manner of costumes, Dean and Cassandra were stocked up with candy, in costume, and ready. "Dr. Dean" was attired in a white physician's coat, mint green colored scrubs, and black Nike sneakers. Hanging from his neck was a Littman stethoscope and in his coat pockets were pens, a prescription pad and a thermometer. In real life 32 year old Dean Dudek was the assistant manager of the Sunrise

Market, which was a convenience store located within walking distance at the intersection of Genesee Street and Route 13. Dean burrowed the medical garb - save for the sneakers - from a friend who interned at SUNY Upstate Medical University.

Twenty-four year old Cassandra Bennett in real life was a waitress at the Applebee's in DeWitt. But, in the fantasy-taken-seriously world of Halloween, she was a witch. Cassandra showed-off in the typical black pointed hat on her shoulder-length brown hair that was as usual streaked with red dye. On her eyes was a heavy layer of black liner and her lips were glossed red. Her fingernails were done in black polish. She sported a black trench coat, opened to reveal a tight, low-cut black shirt. To complete the witch's ensemble was a short black Lycra skirt that barely covered her backside, fishnet pantyhose, and black spiked heels on her feet. As Cassandra was just a tad bit chubby, there was a muffin top resting on her too-tight skirt. When Jesse saw her having a smoke on the porch earlier that afternoon, he thought she looked as much like a prostitute as a witch.

By 5:45 p.m., Jesse was bored and tired. As the lights were all off in his apartment in a successful effort to discourage trick or treaters, he nodded-off on his tan Chenille sofa while watching FOX News. Although he was lonely, handsome, and desirable, he hadn't had much of a dating life since his divorce - so there was no female companionship this evening. Jeremy was doing Halloween with ex-wife Allison's parents this year, dressed as Spider-Man while volunteering at a haunted house near grandma and grandpa's home in Fayetteville.

Sleep…wonderful sleep; there had been precious little of that in Jesse's life these last few weeks, but it was upon him now. He had fallen out of his sitting position and was stretched out on the couch in blue sweatpants and a grey Winnipeg Stags t-shirt; they being his favorite NFL team.

Tonic REM sleep came and then a dream of a locale familiar to Jesse. He was in Sullivan Park in Chittenango; a pretty place of nature trails that wound and rolled through piney woods, pavilions and picnic tables, hills and a playground, and a small pond where Jesse enjoyed fishing. Jesse was sitting on a wooden park bench that overlooked the pond, bundled in his leather jacket, black knit hat, green scarf, black leather Isotoner gloves, blue jeans, and black tie-up Texas Steer boots. It was almost dusk, and there was snow on the ground and a thin layer of ice on the water. The day had been sunny, but now there were clouds moving in from the southeast. "Storm coming" Jesse said to no one as he felt an icy yet refreshing breeze blow across his face. "A few days until Christmas" Jesse then said, but this time there was an answer:

Sung in a deep, warm, mellifluous voice was "hark, how the bells, sweet silver bells, all seem to say, throw cares away." Not at all startled, Jesse looked over his right shoulder and where a moment ago he had the bench to himself, now sat a man who bore a striking facial resemblance to actor Morgan Freeman with a salt and pepper goatee - but his black hair was shoulder length and in cornrows, semi-Rasta style Jesse thought. His hair was graced with a small number of snowflakes.

"Hey, you do a good impression of Elvis - you're a 'dead-ringer' so the expression goes" the man spoke and smiled kindly at Jesse.

"And you look like Morgan Freeman - except for the hair" Jesse replied with a chuckle.

"Yeah, I hear that a lot" the man replied with a laugh, and then asked Jesse, "Did you see the paper today?"

"No, I didn't" Jesse replied, a bit confused.

The man pulled a copy of the Los Angeles Times out from inside of the green hooded parka that he wore. He held it up for Jesse to see, and the headline read: POSSIBLE LARGE SCALE ALIEN

ABDUCTION? The sub line read *Millions Vanish as UFOs Appear Around the World.* The only part of the paper's date that Jesse could see was the month, that being December. Jesse had the immediate sense in this dream that it was the current year, 2009.

"Can you believe this bull-hockey? Can you believe how easily they fall for Satan's lies?" the man asked Jesse, no longer laughing as he shook his head in frustration.

"They love the lie it seems" Jesse said, and he realized that his eyes were tearing up.

"You're not here anymore, right?" the man asked Jesse.

"No, I'm not - no way!" Jesse replied emphatically.

"You're in paradise, aren't you?" the man asked with a smile.

"Yes" was all the Jesse could say, the tears having suddenly stopped.

"You didn't get there in a flying saucer, did you?" The man asked with a smile.

"Praise Jesus, praise his Holy name" Jesse replied, smiling ear to ear.

And then his eyes popped open and he was lying on his couch. It was the second time he dreamed this dream, but this time it was though it was in ultra-high definition.

He was awakened by a woman's screams, the screams coming from Cassandra downstairs. "Oh my God, Jesse, Jesse, help! Get off of him you filthy drunken bastard!"

As Jesse shot to his feet he glanced at the cheap Timex on his wrist and noticed it was 1:29 a.m. Jesse had been asleep for almost 7 1/2 hours. As he gathered his wits, he could hear the sounds of scuffling on the floor below and Dean screaming "aah-aah!"

Pulling on his Cross Trekkers and deciding there was no time to tie them, he heard a somehow familiar male voice - one that sounded inebriated - yelling "Yer a liiierrr! Yer a liiierrr! I'm gonna kill you! You said my Powerball numberrrs would winnnn! Aah! Lierrrrrr!"

Jesse ran down the back stairs and to the front of the house. Bolting up the front steps and inadvertently knocking Gene Simmons and Ace Frehley onto the small front lawn, he saw the door to the downstairs flat open and ran inside.

As Jesse entered Dean and Cassandra's living room, the first thought that popped into his mind was seemingly irrational given the circumstances - the thought that he hated Kiss and was glad that some of the pumpkins fell over.

A heavy glass tan-colored lamp with off-white shade acquired from the local Salvation Army thrift store had been knocked off of an end table and onto the brown and gold Oriental area rug on the hardwood floor of the small, frugal yet welcoming living room. As a testament to the better quality of fixtures that were manufactured in the early 1970's, the lamp was not broken. A large green Tupperware bowl that had held the leftover Halloween candy was face-down beside the lamp. The 40 or so Tootsie Roll midgees in assorted colors that remained undispersed to trick or treaters were now spread about the floor; having been knocked askew in drunken rage by the small yet wiry Ronny, the Philadelphia Eagles fanatic that Jesse had encountered the previous Monday night.

Though Dean was seven inches taller at 6' 0" and 40 lbs. heavier at 175, Ronny had him pinned on the area rug, attempting to choke him as he pushed back on the lightweight drunk. While Ronny maintained the position of dominance, Cassandra was furiously kicking him about the lower body with her spiked heels, but the neurological impulses from the pain and injury of those impacts did not seem to be penetrating Ronny's pickled brain.

"Hey, hey, get off of him you freak!" Jesse yelled and then commanded Cassandra to "stop kicking him and I'll pull him off!"

While the two on the floor uttered guttural noises while maintaining a stalemate - each with hands on the other's throat - Jesse grabbed Ronny's right arm with both hands and pulled as hard as he could. "Let go - aggghhhh" was all that Ronny could scream as his right hand released its grip from Dean's throat. Jesse was then able to bend Ronny's right arm backward, producing the sound of a snap from the little man's right shoulder.

Ronny screeched in pain as Jesse continued to pull on the arm, flinging the drunken little man off of Dean and backward onto the floor with a thud - his dirty Philadelphia Eagles cap remaining intact. As Cassandra stood terrified with her chest heaving while she tried to catch her breath, Dean was able to get up partially from the floor, resting on his elbows while he himself caught his breath. Dean's neck evidenced several bruises and abrasions from where Ronny attempted to choke him, but other than the shock of the little man attacking him, he was none the worse for wear.

Cassandra knelt down next to Dean and asked "are you okay, honey? Oh my God, I love you so much! You're okay, right?"

"Yeah, I'm alright, I think" was Dean's dopey reply as he was still attempting to gather his wits.

Ronny lay on the floor, breathing heavily and staring wide-eyed toward the ceiling. The right leg of his jeans exhibited several growing wet spots; those being bleeding lacerations caused by the impact of Cassandra's black spike heels with pointed toes. His right shoulder was dislocated and he too bore bruises on his stubbly throat from where Dean had fought back.

Muffin, Cassandra's grey tabby cat, entered the scene from the short wood-paneled hallway that connected the living room with the kitchen; from the hallway one would enter the bedroom and also find two storage closets. Ronny lay close to the hallway, and as Muffin approached him she abruptly turned and ran frightened back to the bedroom; letting out a quick meow as the little bell on her collar jingled.

It has been said that animals have the ability to see things that most humans cannot; and perhaps Muffin saw what Jesse was now seeing. Though it squatted on Ronny's chest, its back to Jesse, it would be approximately 3 feet tall if it was standing. Though it was not in the natural, Jesse could see that it was black with scaly skin from head to toe; save for the smooth-skinned bat-like wings. The wings were flapping rapidly as though it was attempting to fly but could not get lift-off. It's small, human-like hands clenched the collar of the tan Carhartt jacket that Ronny wore; appearing as though it was attempting to lift him off of the floor. The being had a scaly tail of about two feet in length, and it extended straight out like that of a pointing hunting dog. The legs appeared to Jesse to be anthropomorphic while the feet were akin to those of a lizard; each foot having five toes with long claws.

Cassandra and Dean were now huddled in embrace on the leather couch, comforting each other and seemingly unaware of the supernatural activity around them. Dean must not have been too seriously injured as Jesse heard him say "mmm...witches turn me on" while Cassandra giggled.

Now, in this moment, Jesse could also hear the supernatural activity around him. He heard the little demon cajoling Ronny in a childlike voice: "c'mon, get up! Get up! I need you to stab the one that looks like Elvis! You'll get away with it because Billy will lie for you! Stab him or the Redwood will burn, you pathetic load of animated human dung!"

Jesse was experiencing this certain sensation with increasing frequency in recent weeks. It was though if just for a few moments at a time, he was able to hear at a level far superior to that of a dog.

Right now, he could hear several others similar to the bat-lizard that crouched on Ronny's chest and also a few of the "flying monkeys" all chattering excitedly albeit indecipherably in the living room. He could faintly hear Dean Martin crooning "Everybody Loves Somebody" on the radio inside of the baby blue 2009 Chrysler 300 driven by 84 year old Madge Tilley as she passed by on Genesee Street. Madge had her windows rolled up, the heater on, and the radio on low volume. He could easily hear Kenny Harsch's mongrel barking a block away on Arch Street. Additionally, there was a cacophony of sounds outside that Jesse could not pinpoint - many coming from the Ten Pin Restaurant & Tavern several doors away.

Inside the flat, Jesse could hear four heartbeats but not his own. Most faintly, he could hear the rapid pitter-patter of Muffin's feline heart in the other room. At his feet he could hear the slow, disorganized work of semi-conscious Ronny's heart and in that Jesse could sense that there was something that needed immediate medical attention. From the couch Jesse could hear the rapid breathing and fast but regular heartbeats of the nearly copulating Dean and Cassandra. In this heightened state of audibility, Jesse could even hear the midsystolic click of Cassandra's prolapsed mitral valve.

There was smoke filling the living room, but Jesse knew that it wasn't in the natural. Now, even without super-sensitive hearing, he'd be able to hear the carnal moans of Dean and Cassandra on the couch.

Jesse wanted to run, but instead he remained steadfast and barked in a powerful voice, using the strength of his diaphragm and the power of his faith: "I command all of you to be gone in the name of Jesus!"

The demon that was crouched on Ronny's chest turned and glared at Jesse. Its eyes were bright, glowing orange - looking identical to the lights that adorned the living room windows. Its elfin head was scaled but the face had smooth black skin and its small nose was more of a pig-like snout. The ears were tiny and pointed. The mouth was small with thin grimacing lips as it called "here, kitty, kitty." As the one that crouched on Ronny spoke this, Jesse heard a "flying monkey" that was on the couch with Dean and Cassandra say "Jesus? Jesus don't live up in this humpy bumpy yo, tee-hee-hee!"

In the matter of a second or two, Jesse saw Muffin leap over the prone Ronny's legs and then take a second leap; onto his own right leg. The cat's claws penetrated the fabric of Jesse's sweatpants and pierced his skin. While Jesse shrieked in surprise and pain, he hopped on his left leg while shaking his right in an effort to remove the cat. Eight seconds passed before Muffin fell loose, and before she did she made sure to urinate on Jesse's leg.

Now, all of the demons were gone. Muffin fell from Jesse's leg, leaped over Ronny and ran terrified back to the bedroom. Likewise, Jesse's hearing had returned to normal human levels.

Chittenango Police Officer William "Billy" Brostic came running through the door with his firearm drawn and his belly bouncing. "Hands up and nobody move" the fat cop ordered while huffing and panting. He drew in a deep, labored breath and then spoke into his portable radio "102 requesting backup and an ambulance at 316 Seneca, over."

Brostic started waddling to where Ronny was attempting to get up off the floor. As he passed Jesse, he barked "keep 'em up" and again, the odor of alcohol was conspicuous on his breath.

Over on the couch, Dean and Cassandra didn't have their hands in the air, as those hands were busy pulling their respective clothing items back into their proper positions.

"Billy" Ronny moaned as he attempted to sit up. "My ssshhhoader ish aaawww meshed (sic) up!"

"Ronny - you (belch) okay, Buddy? What did that bastard do to you this time?" Brostic inquired of his friend.

Before the little drunken twerp could formulate a lie in his pickled brain, it was Dean that provided an answer: "Jesse didn't do anything wrong! It was that animal Ronny that came in here and attacked me, and Jesse came and pulled that freak off of me before I killed him!"

"I was questioning the victim, sir! Now both of you on the couch keep your hands in the air until I can get your statements; you too, Elvis!"

"Victim? - I think you've got to much powdered sugar in your system, officer! My boyfriend here on the couch is the victim! That drunken piece of crap there on the floor came in here and attacked him!" Cassandra spoke with attitude as puffs of smoke burst from her mouth with each word - she having lit a cigarette, obviously not following the directive to keep her hands in the air.

Before the incompetent Brostic could answer, Chittenango police Officer Dan Furman walked onto the bizarre scene - he being the first backup available. As he entered the room speaking into his portable, a Rural Metro ambulance pulled up outside.

Furman asked calmly "so what's going on here, folks? Did Ronny come here looking for trouble?" Officer Furman was forty years of age, not fat like his counterpart, sported a buzz cut and wore wire-rimmed glasses. Unlike Brostic who was a full-time cop, Furman served as a policeman part-time while working on his family's dairy farm full-time, having previously served in the U.S. Army.

Before Brostic could offer a biased explanation, two paramedics walked into the room and proceeded over to Ronny, who was gasping for air while telling Brostic "that Deannnn tol' me dat my Powwwwerballll numberssss would win tonight and they dint (sic). Heee lied and sold me a bad ticket! I-I-I-I came here to eeeeevennnn da scorrrre!"

"My buddy has a dislocated shoulder, poor guy. That Elvis looking guy should pick on people his own size. I'm gonna to be takin' him in for attempted murder and for lottery fraud" Brostic said to one of the paramedics, whose answer was "uh, have you been drinking officer?"

It was Jesse, now with his hands at his side who answered "yeah, he has been drinking again! The booze is strong on his breath."

"Hands behind your head, you son of a bitch, you're under arrest" Brostic bellowed as he began charging toward Jesse.

"Halt, Brostic! Give me your sidearm - NOW!" a New York State Trooper ordered who was now entering the room with his Glock drawn.

"Yeah, he's having a heart attack. Let's get him packaged and out of here" one of the paramedics who attended to Ronny said as he grabbed a blue intubation bag.

After a few minutes had passed, Ronny was being loaded into the ambulance and Billy Brostic was being forced to take a breathalyzer by Trooper Stan Massey with Chittenango Police Chief Charles Waterman assisting. This would be the end of Brostic's law enforcement career, and it was about time. He was a liability to the Chittenango Police Department and to the citizens of the village. Unfortunately, he wasn't the police department's only liability…

Meanwhile, Officer Dan Furman - who was an asset to the police force - was getting a statement from Dean:

"That guy Ronny comes into the Sunrise Market almost every day for beer, gas, and lottery tickets. I'm the Assistant Manager there, and the job sucks because people suck… I mean like the staffers and the customers, ya know!?"

"Powerball draws on Saturday night - which is tonight - and he was in on Friday and got a quick-pick. It also draws on Wednesdays - but anyway, as I rang him out I said 'I think those are the winning numbers.' I was just kidding, right? I mean like how the hell would I know what the winning numbers would be? If I knew, I'd like play the friggin' numbers myself, ya know? For chrissakes! I mean, what kinda idiot is he? Well, obviously he's a stupid-ass drunk just like half the morons in this freakin' town!"

"Okay, Dean, try to stay on point and just explain what happened here" Officer Furman interrupted.

"Okay, sorry, you're right officer. We were watching WYNN News 10 at about midnight and saw that nobody in the country won the jackpot tonight. It's like really strange how fast they know! And then, a little while later, that frickin' Ronny comes bursting in here. We had the door unlocked because we were giving candy to the trick or treaters, and there were some that came late at 11:30. Man, they were about 16 years old! They were too old to be trick or treating and I told them to 'get lost' but Cassie said 'don't be a jerk - let's give them some candy' so of course we did because whatever she wants she gets!"

Cassandra interrupted objectionably through tight lips while she lit another cigarette: "That's not true! Don't make me out to be some kind of wench! Why can't you be a nice guy like Jesse?"

Furman regained control: "Okay Dean, I need you to stay on point here. So, Ronny came through the door and then accused you of selling him a bad ticket. He then jumped on you and started choking you. I can see the welts on your neck. Would you like medical treatment?"

"No, I'm alright, thanks" was Dean's reply.

"And here is the Powerball quick-pick ticket that Ronny had with him. Not that it matters, but is this the one you sold him?" Furman asked with a wan smile and raised eyebrows.

"Yeah, that's it" Dean answered.

"4-11-17-20-39, and a Powerball number of 32. Even though I don't play, I might have chosen a series of number like that if I did" Furman said with a chuckle, and then continued "I got Jesse's statement and it's a good thing that he came down when he did. In his drunken rage, Ronny may have truly hurt you because he had a buck knife inside his coat. I got Cassandra's statement as well. I've noted the damage to the room and Ronny will be facing charges of vandalism as well as assault. He's been a chronic problem and he needs to be kept off of the streets. The guy needs professional help, most certainly. Unfortunately, he's a little too friendly with some of my fellow officers."

The room was quiet for a moment as Officer Furman took a final look around before asking "is there anything else I can do for you?"

"No" was the unanimous answer.

"Alright folks, have a good night - or should I say 'good morning?'"

# 6

# The Eye and the Hourglasses

The November 7th gig at the the Turning Stone Casino was the first job in almost two weeks. It was the full show, which included three costume changes and drew from a song roster that spanned the entire length of Elvis Presley's recording career.

All of the musicians in Jesse's band were professionals; i.e. playing music is what they did for a living. On this night, Chris Emerson, Trey's younger brother and member of Pie Kite, filled in on keyboards for Tony Zonnerville. Tony had been previously booked to tickle the ivories for local rock legend Benny Mardones in a sold-out show at downtown Syracuse's Landmark Theater. Mardones had scored a hit with the ballad "Into the Night" - the recording having the honor of ascending to the top 20 of the *Billboard Hot 100* chart twice; first upon its original release in 1980 and then with a re-release of the same version in 1989.

As the Turning Stone show was relatively late in being booked, Jesse's drummer Mickey Starnes was also engaged elsewhere; playing two shows in Nashville with up and coming country artist Laura Boretti, whose debut single "When Men Were Real Men" was number 21 with a bullet that week on the *Billboard Country* chart. Chittenango native Brian Besser filled in admirably for Starnes on this night.

Along with Trey, bass guitarist Ian LeBeouf was the other permanent member of *Jesse Same - Elvis Impersonator* who performed that night. While being a permanent member, Ian's time with the band was almost up. The 30 year old LeBeouf played bass left-handed - albeit a Fender Precision and not yet a Hofner and Rickenbacker. Indeed, while Jesse was a dead-ringer for Elvis, Ian bore a remarkable resemblance to Paul McCartney. And, when one discussed uncanny resemblances, it could have been said that Ian sang just like the "cute" Beatle and like him was a skilled multi-instrumentalist. Was LeBeouf a Beatles fan? The answer to that question was most indubitably "yes." Could LeBeouf mimic McCartney's riffs, vocalisms, and mannerisms? The answer to that question was "to a tee." So, it would be that Ian LeBeouf would be leaving after the December 17th *Christmas Tribute to Elvis Presley* show at the Turning Stone Casino to become a full-time member of the world-touring Beatles tribute band *The Gear Fabs*.

Tony was on one hand sad to know that Ian was soon leaving, but on the other hand, as he had no dating life at the time, he was happy as he was "sick of Ian getting all the women." Jesse jokingly referred to Ian as "William Campbell" - who was the purported Beatle replacement for the "dead" Paul McCartney of backwards tracks, myths, and conspiracy theories.

Despite two quickly added and rehearsed replacements, the band played well and Jesse's impression of Elvis was as usual, flawless. One gospel song was worked into the early set, that being "(There'll Be) Peace in the Valley." Jesse so loved the song and as he sang, he longed for his real home and missed a place that he had yet to see. As usual for this song, Jesse held the microphone and strolled slowly across the stage while he sang. That night, the song was received well by the crowd, and when Jesse finished singing he noticed a few sets of moist eyes in the audience through the blur of his own.

Jesse and Chris were quick to head home after the show, while Trey, Ian, and Brian stayed behind to gamble. Mike Wickert would be paying the group for the show early the following week, but Trey still had $146.00 in his wallet. After winning a small amount on slot machines, he lost all of his cash playing Keno. He later told Brian that "it doesn't matter really what I lost. The Dollar won't be around in a year anyway."

Sleep came quickly for an exhausted Jesse after he hit the sack at a little after midnight. It had been since Halloween that he'd had any dreams or visions, but as the minutes past into the wee hours of the morning, a dream came and was startling in its vividness…

Jesse was in a Wal-Mart; he was sure it was the superstore that he liked to shop in nearby Oneida. Jesse could hear "Have Yourself a Merry Little Christmas" sung by Frank Sinatra as he walked along the main aisle away from the grocery mart and beside the displays of impulse gifts and twenty sum-odd checkout lines; all of which were deep in customers with loaded carts. Shoppers of all sizes, shapes and colors passed Jesse, headed in the opposite direction. Some looked at him and smiled, while others stared quizzically at him with expressions that asked "what's wrong with you, buddy?"

Many of the cashiers wore Santa hats; that fashion accessory contradicting the looks of stress and fatigue that clung to their faces like paranormal parasites. A group of supervisors was huddled at the bagging carousel of register 3, discussing far too loudly the particulars of a cashier who was fired for stealing from his till. A heavyset African-American cashier named Yolanda, who was stationed at register 5, turned toward the group of supers and yelled "Hey! Jaquan! When y'alls get done wit (sic) yer little chit-chat, I need quarters and dimes. Yo! I NEED THEM NOW!" The cashier then apologized to the 60 year old woman who was left waiting for change from her cash purchase: "I'm sorry, ma'am. I axed (sic) them ten minutes ago for more change and I ain't got it yet; please forgive me." After apologizing to the customer who had become exceedingly irritated, Yolanda bellowed "Yo! Jaquan! Don't make me break my foot offin' (sic) yo ass!"

It was then that in his dream state Jesse realized that the scene playing out had actually occurred in reality during December of 2008. "Why am I doing this again?" Jesse asked in his sleep, but of course no one answered him.

Jesse was now waiting in line at register 5, holding four Wal-Mart gift cards to be loaded for $50.00 each - one for each of his band-mates. Registers 1 through 4 were express lines, but in Jesse's experience it was best to avoid them because there always seemed to be a problem or price checks that brought movement to a halt. It would be a while before Jesse would get to Yolanda, and in the dream as it was in reality nearly a year ago he hoped that Jaquan would stop flapping his gums and bring her the rolls of coins that she needed. In the reality of December 2008 Jesse had to pee and was becoming uncomfortable, but here in the dream he had no such sensation.

While the lines were long and the staffers tired and edgy, the customers were for the most part in high spirits. "I'm not worried about maxing out my credit cards this Christmas because President Omondi is gonna fix all the problems with the economy that Bush caused, ya know?" a woman in her early sixties with a shrill, abrasive, nasally voice and too much lipstick said to a nearly identical friend in line, who answered with a voice and expression of equally poor quality: "yeah, I'm so glad I voted Omondi instead of for McCann and that ditz Susan Patterson. They just would have kept doin' what that moron Bush did, ya know?"

"Yeah, like oh my god, ya know?" affirmed woman number one; in the dream just like in the reality passed. And in the dream just like in the reality, Jesse couldn't help but snicker at their ignorance.

"It's about time, Jaquan!" Yolanda the cashier bellowed.

“Shut up, Yo-Yo!” was Jaquan’s reply, as he popped open her till and loaded in rolls of nickels and pennies in addition to the quarters and dimes she needed, before snatching two 20 Dollar bills to exchange for the change.

“You best not be double-dippin’ on my drawer, punk ass!” Yolanda warned Jaquan.

“Why not - you come up short all the time any-hoo!” Jaquan fired back as he started to walk away.

It was then, as the line still wasn’t moving, that Jesse saw the pieces of a small, wooden Nativity scene spilled on the main aisle in front of register 6. Jesse had been looking at the same model of Nativity scene in the Christmas section just a short while before. Fittingly enough, Jesse could now hear the opening notes of Mannheim Steamroller’s “Stille Nacht” playing - but he didn’t know if it was through the store sound system or from some other place.

All around were joyful people - most swiping credit cards and talking excitedly about new phones, X-Boxes, and getting drunk later after shopping - all while saying “Happy Holidays” to one another. But, in the dream as in the past reality, Jesse felt no joy as he watched a well-coiffed blond woman togged in a brown rabbit fur jacket with fox fur collar, tight blue jeans and black calf-length boots step on the Nativity set’s manger with a crunch. Seemingly, she was unaware as she rattled off through her grimacing lips a list of items she was about to purchase to someone on the other end of her Bluetooth. Her seven year old blond son was with her, dressed in a black snowmobile suit. As they passed, he stopped, turned back, and began stomping on the wooden Christ child in its cradle. “Uh-huh-huh” he shrieked as he stomped, with rage in his voice and a sinister smile contorting his face.

"Look, mom, I just smashed the baby Jesus! I OWNED him, ha-ha-ha" the boy shouted with evil glee as he surveyed the little broken bits on the store floor.

"That's nice, Caleb, now c'mon, buddy" the mom responded patronizingly to the boy before speaking in a sing-song voice "he's headed for another time-out" to whoever was on the other end of her phone call.

As others walked past - including two store employees - the undisciplined boy began stomping the donkey from the Nativity set as his mother released an impatient sigh while standing with her hands on her hips. After a few footfalls the little donkey was broken into several pieces. As an appalled middle-aged woman passing by groused "what a brat" - young Caleb looked up at Jesse with eyes dancing mischievously and asked "yo, you know what another word for 'donkey' is? ASS!"

As Jesse shook his head in disgust, wanting to offer some manner of rebuke to Caleb but biting his tongue, the mom bent down behind the boy, placed her hands on his shoulders and said "okay, dude - after you get home from your play date with Dylan and Ethan, you are gonna have a time-out, and that means no Wii and no Street Fight Four!"

As the mother began to lead Caleb away from the scene and resumed speaking into her Bluetooth - Jesse heard the boy say "I want to live with dad because he plays Grand Theft Auto all the time!"

In the dream as it was in the December 2008 reality, the long checkout line at register 5 had only moved forward one customer since Caleb came into the scene. Yolanda the cashier was becoming increasingly agitated as an elderly woman was trying to get an approval code for a pre-paid MasterCard, but the response for the third time was "declined." Yolanda was lamenting to her co-worker on register 6 that she was supposed to get her break "like a half hour ago" and "nobody has come to help this poor old lady with her stupid card!"

Jesse could hear the joyful voices of young children behind him, one saying "I hope Santa brings me the whole series" while another proclaimed "if I get everything I want it's a good Christmas, but if I don't get everything I want then it's a sucky one!"

The dream focused back on the cash register, and as in the past reality Jesse heard Yolanda - with all of the patience of a wasp trapped in a soda can - ask the elderly woman "well, ain't you got no cash? It seems to me your card ain't gonna work and my line's backin' up and I need a break!"

Unlike most of those around her, the 89 year old woman at register 5 was not purchasing Christmas gifts but instead $33.00 worth of groceries with the MasterCard gift card given to her by a kindly neighbor to help supplement her Social Security. The woman strived to be independent since her husband had passed away - even driving herself to the store and doing her own shopping - but the struggles were becoming difficult to bear.

"I know the card should work because there is enough money on it. Please be patient with me" the woman begged Yolanda as she swiped the card again with her bony, quivering right hand. In her feeble state, the poor woman did not remember that the $100.00 balance on the card had already been used up. Nor, did she remember to bring the new $100.00 card that the kindly neighbor had given her the day before.

Yolanda said: "Mam, old people like you should have somebody else do their shoppin' for them, you know? I hope that our new president Omondi makes that a law! Martha, can you get somebody to re-shop this stuff and I need a break!"

As Jesse began to reach into his wallet for cash to pay for the elderly woman's purchase, she was now teary and with a hitch in her voice she begged "no, no, no - I can pay. The card will…"

She did not complete her plea but instead clutched her chest and squatted down, that action forcing her empty shopping cart into the main entry aisle and into a 16 year old boy with black stringy hair hanging into his eyes that was slumping with his similarly-styled friend toward the exit. "Hey, watch it, you old bag" he spoke rudely as his friend laughed gutturally and added "she's prolly messed up on some good shit! Doctors give old people good drugs, dude!"

The woman was on her knees now and Jesse wanted to help but was trapped. The joyful people that had surrounded Jesse were now voicing their impatience and displeasure:

"Uh, I don't have time for this crap!"

"C'mon lady, just get outta the line and come back when you got the money, geesh!"

"Uh, gross, I think she peed her pants!"

"Mommy, why is that old lady on the floor?"

The elderly woman was suffering a massive heart attack. Those who were in front of Jesse were now pushing back, while those behind him refused to move. He was imprisoned and wanted to be free to help. "Okay, I'm calling 9-11" supervisor Martha said as she held her cellphone to her left ear.

"Hey, can you still ring me out?" the woman with the abrasive, nasally voice who ardently supported President Omondi asked of the scowling Yolanda.

Store manager Greg Pooler attempted to gain control of the situation. He stood at the back end of the line and announced "Ladies and gentlemen, we need to make room for EMS to help that lady. We need you to join other lines and we'll get you on your way ASAP. I'm sorry for the hold-up. There will be coupons for all of you"

In a few moments EMS would arrive and their attempts to resuscitate the 89 year old woman would fail.

"Am I gonna get my break or what!?" Yolanda the cashier bellowed over the din.

Again, Jesse heard Frank Sinatra sing, and it was the final line "so have yourself a merry little Christmas - now" followed by the whimsically haunting strings and backing vocals that carried the recording for its final 14 seconds. This interlude was only in the dream and did not occur in the awful reality.

As the dream faded, Jesse heard the now familiar supernatural voice from other dreams and visions, and his warning was clear:

"The Lord God is loving, patient, and kind and he has watched fallen man make a mockery of his Son and of His creation. He who is the Father of the First and the Last, the Word and the Living Water - He who has offered up His only begotten Son as the ultimate sacrifice for the sins of man and then raised Him into glory - GLORY TO THE LORD MOST HIGH! Remember the scene and the times as you live them through dreams and visions, beloved servant Jesse. He the Ancient of Days has said THEY HAVE FORGOTTEN THE REASON FOR THE SEASON AND IN HIS RIGHTEOUS ANGER DECLARES THAT WAS THE LAST!

Jesse bolted upright - awake in a cold sweat. He was gasping for air and as he slowly caught his breath he began to shiver uncontrollably.

He fell forward on his bed and rolled tight into the fetal position. Jesse moaned and prayed that all of this insanity would stop; the dreams, the visions, the Elvis impersonation, and the world. He missed is dearly departed mother and was frustrated that he could not find out who his father was. Even his Grandpa Richard was a mysterious nut that could not be cracked. Jesse had written letters to the P.O. Box in Cordova, Tennessee - that being the address on the check written by the executor of Richard Same's will - but no answer came.

It was 3:37 a.m. on Sunday, November 8th, and an exhausted Jesse had wept himself back to sleep in the aforementioned fetal position. At 7:40 on that cold, rainy November morning, he was in Tonic REM sleep, and again he dreamed:

In the dream he recalled the Wal-Mart incident of last year and knew that whatever "the last" was that the voice warned of; it was all in God's hands. Jesse knew that time was now at a premium and that time was passing more quickly than man's clocks would indicate.

Jesse saw a giant hourglass, the bulbs supported by three lathed wooden legs, floating on what he instantly knew to be the western sky. It was dusk and while purple clouds covered much of the sky, the horizon was ablaze with a brilliant orange and pink sunset. Jesse had the sensation that he was floating as he saw the hourglass. Below him he saw covered in snow what he was sure was a section of the old Erie Canal Towpath; but it was a section that he was not familiar with. He could see the canal itself covered with a thin coat of ice and light layer of snow, trees on either side of it and woods all around. On the distant hills he could see houses - all strangely without lighting.

Jesse was compelled to turn and look toward the eastern skyline and what he saw was terrifying. At a quick glance it could pass for a sunset in the wrong part of the sky, but Jesse had the immediate knowledge that the red and orange he saw was from an expansive area of fire. He then saw black smoke high above on the dark skyline. "Simultaneous with the dream of Chittenango" was the thought that hit Jesse, and he moaned quietly as little sound came from his throat.

He turned back toward the west, and on the nearly empty top bulb of the hourglass were the words *The Church Age* in glowing silver lettering. Indeed, there was scarcely any sand left in the top and Jesse could see it falling into the nearly full bottom bulb.

To the right of the first hourglass hovered a second identical one, but with a full top bulb and an empty bottom. There was a lustrous silver chain knotted around the tube that connected the top and bottom bulbs. From the knot, a long section of the chain extended diagonally in a northeasterly direction, which was to Jesse's right as he floated. Jesse had the immediate knowledge that the chain was to constrict the tube and keep the sand in the top bulb.

Hovering at an angle above the section of chain that extended from the connecting tube was a silver-colored Parker Pen. The ball of the pen pointed toward the the chain's knot and a steady flare of white flame emanated from the tip; not unlike that of an acetylene torch. The flame came close to the chain's knot but didn't touch it.

Behind the pen and just above the sunset, hovered a large sheet of white paper that rippled on the breeze. Jesse had the immediate knowledge that the paper was a document that would profoundly affect the entire world once the pen was used to ratify it.

As Jesse fixated on the document, a huge magnifying glass that was much larger than that in the dream about the Mississippi River and civilian soldiers appeared. As he focused in on the image in the glass he could see in two rows at the top of the document color images of flags: they being Israel, Lebanon, Saudi Arabia, Iran, Syria, Jordan, Egypt, Iraq, and others that he was certain were form the Middle East but were out of the view of the magnifier.

Below the flags were a number of paragraphs that were too blurry to read. But, what he was able to read clearly was the phrase *FALSE PEACE* that was written in running blood across the center of the document, obliterating the printed text underneath it. Jesse now knew that this symbolized a document would be a significant part of biblical prophecy. In that, he knew that signatures on the paper would serve as fuel to draw the flame in to cut the chain around the connecting tube of the second hourglass and the sand would begin to flow downward. As he now understood the symbolism of this dream, he saw the glowing red lettering of the phrase *Jacob's Trouble* on the top bulb and *Seven Years* in the same glowing red lettering on the bottom bulb that was for now empty.

He was not surprised by what he saw on the sky, as he knew from the Bible what would come. And with the bulb bearing the phrase *The Church Age* being nearly empty, he felt a deep peace mixed with a confidant sense of urgency. But, Jesse was a bit confused by the group of six people he saw walking westward along the towpath below him, all dressed for the cold and each wearing a backpack. "I don't know them, but I know they would believe me if I told them what I see" Jesse said to himself.

Immediately after Jesse spoke in his dream, the entire scene-scape was filled by a human eye. While the pupil was the usual black, the iris and cornea were iridescent and multi-colored: red, orange, yellow, green, blue, indigo, and violet. The colors in the eye were reflective and at the same time radiant and Jesse felt himself gasp as he was amazed by the unspeakable magnificence.

As Jesse had but a moment to gaze into the eye it was still enough time to know that it was part of a face that smiled. As he began to smile with it, the eye blinked and then it was gone…

Jesse felt a tremor that reminded him of a small earthquake, and it forced him to look down. He saw that the six were no longer walking on the towpath. Likewise, it was no longer sunset but now early morning. While fires raged on the eastern horizon, he had the sense in this dream that the sun had risen and a new day had dawned. It was then that the familiar supernatural voice spoke and said "in a moment, in the twinkling of an eye."

As the voice spoke, Jesse again looked into the sky and saw the two hourglasses. The top bulb of the first glass that bore the phrase *The Church Age* was now completely empty of all of its sand. Now, what Jesse saw in the bottom bulb of the first hourglass was to say the least unsettling…

It appeared to Jesse that the grains of sand in the bottom bulb had morphed into human beings; in essence actors in something akin to a movie trailer. But, there was no doubt that these fast-moving graphic scenes would be more suitable for a breaking news bulletin than a Hollywood film.

Some were screaming, crying and pounding on the glass of the bottom bulb in horrible desperation. Others were celebrating what they perceived to be the birth of a wonderful new world order. Grocery store windows were being smashed by the desperate and hungry while tenured professors sitting in ivory towers pontificated on what could be the dawning of the Age of Aquarius. President Omondi urged the citizenry to be calm and offered hope of new found freedoms and opportunities from a secret, secure location while American streets were being shut down by the National Guard, United Nations troops, and an unusual new civilian military force.

It was then, while the scenes still played but the volume had been cut, that the now familiar, supernatural voice spoke and said "how much time passes between the hourglasses? Only God Elohim knows the day and the hour that will end the current age, but nearly all of its time has passed."

Jesse's eyes popped opened and he quickly sat up in his bed. He drew in a deep breath and then exhaled though pursed lips in the manner that a smoker would exhale smoke. As he stood up and pulled on his sweatpants, he recalled the reprise of the Wal-Mart shopping trip in the dream from the wee hours of the morning. And then there was the remembrance of the supernatural voice, speaking with ominous directness the warning *they have forgotten the reason for the season and that was the last*.

The mind of the "dead-ringer" Jesse began to race. It was then without forethought that he himself uttered the words:

"How much time passes between the hourglasses? Only God Elohim knows the day and the hour that will end the current age, but nearly all of its time has passed. They have forgotten the reason for the season and that was the last."

Jesse gasped as he strained to speak through an anxiety-constricted throat: "It must mean that last Christmas was the last Christmas. We're running out of time!"

The anxiety was short-lived and as he sat back down on his bed, Jesse became filled with a sense of peace. He only wished that someone would believe him when he would try to share his dreams and visions...

...Sometimes memories served as visions for Jesse, and as he sat on his bed, he remembered fishing in Sullivan Park Pond one day in early August of 2006. Then, for a moment, the memory of the wintertime dream of the man who resembled a Rasta-styled Morgan Freeman showing him the L.A. Times on a bench overlooking the pond popped into his head, but that was re-filed for another time. The memory that persisted was that of a particular fishing trip...

It was a sunny Tuesday at around 6:30 p.m., a thunderstorm having passed through around 5:45 and the skies having since cleared. While there were many people in the park itself, Jesse had the pond to himself, save for the occasional jogger or dog walker that would pass by on the path that bordered the pond before heading into the woods.

Jesse loved catching all manner of fish; from the highly-esteemed Rainbow Trout, to the pugnacious Largemouth Bass and odd yet scrappy Bowfin; and even the poorly-regarded and oft-vilified Common Carp.

While the pond contained all of the aforementioned species in addition to a variety of panfish, it was carp that Jesse enjoyed pulling from the quaint acre-sized body of water. On that particular Tuesday as he often did, Jesse stood on the rocks at the head of the pond's outlet brook, spanned by a small wooden footbridge that connected the sloping, grassy banks. He was using Aunt Berta's Original Recipe Bread Balls for bait; having just flipped the bail on his spinning reel and tossed his line toward the middle of the pond.

The "dead-ringer" became distracted by a large snapping turtle that floated up from the bottom of the pond near the bank to his right. While its algae-covered shell was submerged by a half inch of water, the turtle's head stuck out of the pond like a periscope as it soaked up the early evening sun - having just a few minutes before lured with its vermiform tongue a tiny Pumpkinseed Sunfish into its mouth as a quick meal.

As Jesse's focus was on the snapper; he remembered the two painted turtles - Gus and Russ - that he kept in an aquarium as a 7 year old during June and July of 1981. The turtles were given to him by his first grade teacher Mrs. Taft, as she was retiring that June and would not need them in a classroom any longer.

Feeding the turtles pieces of lettuce, apple, and lunchmeat was fun for young Jesse, and although the pair of turtles was quiet and unexciting, he loved them just the same.

Tammy Jo Same had a boyfriend that summer, a construction crew supervisor named Eddie Ramsden. Eddie and his crew members were frequent lunch patrons of Dave's Diner and he could be quite the charmer in addition to being a generous tipper and a buddy who would often "pick up the check" at lunchtime. It was Eddie's muscular, suntanned body and boyish good looks that combined with that charm to win waitress Tammy Jo over, and before long he was shacking-up in the East Pleasant Street flat with his new "hottie" and her son.

Eddie was a charmer but he was also a drinker; and a mean one at that. At 5:30, after a hard day of excavating, dropping sewer pipe, and flagging traffic, Eddie and the boys would often convene to the popular Manlius beer joint called Buffoons. Around 7:30 Eddie would come staggering in, and if Tammy Jo was still working he liked to torment and tease Jesse; often saying "I'll kidnap yer mother and leave you here to starve to death" or "one day I'm gonna kill yer stinkin' faggot turtles."

One hot, humid evening charming Eddie came stumbling in after a day of road construction and after losing $30.00 playing pool while consuming shots of Jack Daniels with beer chasers. Tammy Jo had the night off and Jesse was feeding Gus and Russ some apple chunks. That harmless activity sent charming drunken Eddie into a then too familiar rage.

This time the rage turned on Jesse instead of his mother, who had been slapped by Eddie several times within recent days. "You don't feed food that I spend good money on to those filthy animals you little pansy ass" Eddie roared as he pushed Jesse away from the aquarium, grabbed Russ and threw the turtle like a Randy Johnson fastball into the yellow living room wall a mere seven feet away. As Jesse screamed "stop" while seeing the streak of blood on the wall that led to the crushed turtle lying on the floor, charming Eddie grabbed Gus and pitched him in like fashion, the little animal impacting the wall and producing a hole in the sheetrock.

As Jesse cowered on the floor and cried in heartbreak and terror, Tammy Jo shrieked "you evil son of a bitch" as she grabbed a 1/2 liter glass beer stein with pewter lid from a kitchen cupboard and pitched a fastball of her own; causing strike three as it impacted Eddie's forehead between the eyes and knocked him out cold with a severe concussion and bloody laceration.

After his release from serving a short time in jail, Eddie was never again to appear in Tammy Jo's life or at Dave's Diner. And even now, if for a moment, a grown up Jesse felt sadness for his childhood turtles and a deep aching pain in his soul for his mother. But, as quickly as it came on, the sadness was whisked away as he realized that a fish was pulling on his line…

Upstate New York's most popular Elvis impersonator set the hook, and knew right away that one of Aunt Berta's Bread Balls had lured another carp. But, while the carp that Jesse caught from the pond generally weighed from ten to fifteen pounds, he knew by the weight at the end of his line that this fish was smaller, despite its dogged efforts to run back toward the middle of the pond as it fought.

A couple of minutes later, Jesse had a hold of the 12 inch long carp that weighed about two pounds. What was peculiar about this individual member of the family *Cyprinus carpio* was the iridescent silver color of the scales; whereas the majority of carp would be colored a golden brown.

Jesse quickly noted that the fish had swallowed the hook into its gullet. Freeing the hook would be difficult, so the fish was laid back into the water at Jesse's feet, so he could work with absolute care to dislodge the hook while giving the fish sufficient opportunity to breath.

The carp splashed with its tail as it tried to swim free while Jesse held it in the water with his left hand as he reached into his tackle box with his right to grab a pair of needle-nose pliers. With the pliers he believed he would be able to reach into the fish's gullet and remove the hook without causing it serious injury.

As Jesse lifted the fish's head out of the water to insert the pliers, two teenaged boys - one aged seventeen and the other sixteen - were walking the path and stopped to observe. Both boys wore buzz-cuts under their over-sized flat-billed hip hop caps; the sixteen year old blond in a white "NY" logo New York Yankees cap and the brown-haired freckle-faced seventeen year old in a black cap with silver pinstripes with the phrase "Time is Money" embroidered above the bill. This black cap also featured the images of a Rolex watch, rolls of cash, and a blunt. The 17 year old wore a black oversized t-shirt with Al Pacino's character "Scarface" holding wads of cash and the phrase GET EVERY DOLLAR screen-printed on the front. His blond friend also wore an oversized t-shirt, it being white with a large Marijuana leaf screen-printed on the chest. Both boys wore baggy black shorts, no socks, and white Nike Cortez sneakers. The 16 year old had a toothpick protruding from his grimacing mouth.

"Why you tryin' to be so careful with that bro? That's a ghetto fish, man. I'd kill that bitch" the 16 year old inquired of Jesse, before spitting his toothpick into the outlet brook.

"I release the fish I catch. I try not to injure them because I hate to see fish die" Jesse answered, quickly turning his head to look up at the two thugs before turning his attention back to the pliers and the carp.

"Yo, I go fishin' with my Uncle Eddie and my Uncle Ronny and when they catch one a' them carps, they just bash the som' bitch with a rock. Sometimes Uncle Eddie brings his piece and blows those friggers up, yo! You oughta' just cut the line or kill that thang, ya know?" the 17 year old offered his two cents.

It was then that a rock splashed in the pond two feet in front of Jesse, getting droplets of water on his face and shirt. "I jus' tried ta' hit that thing and kill it for you, homes. That way ya'lls can git some good fish n' shit" the 16 year old who appeared to be the dominant member of the duo despite being the youngest said with a smirk, and then both boys started laughing.

Jesse was undaunted by the dirty water that had splashed into his face. The small carp was still in the water and the hook was beginning to loosen.

"Hey T-Maz" Jesse said with a smirk, while still keeping his attention on the fish, "you need to stop peeing your bed at night!"

'What? How did you know my tag, dude?" the 17 year old answered nervously.

"What's more important is how I know you're a little pantywaist that pees his bed at night" Jesse answered with a chuckle, still not looking back at the boys while he worked the pliers with surgical precision.

"Aw, that's gross, yo! What a little momma's boy!" the sixteen year old blond boy guffawed.

"Now D.B., you shouldn't accuse Baby Wee Wee Doll of being a momma's boy, especially since you like to dress in your mother's clothes when she's not around; which is most of the time!" Jesse chortled.

"Screw you dude, I don't do that! This guy is weird, c'mon let's get outta here T-Maz" D.B. uttered in a high panicky voice as he started to walk sprightly back in the direction from which they came.

"Hey fellas, before you run off in denial, I just wanted to remind you that the dealer you mule for, I think Teako is his name? He knows that you're short-changing his customers and he's planning to cap you two. He figures that no one would notice that a couple of dirt bags like you two are missing" Jesse answered, raising his voice as he knew the two hoodlums were now sprinting away.

"We ain't rippin' off nobody man - and I don't wear my mom's clothes anymore" D.B. yelled as they rounded a corner of the pond, his once tough voice now high and whiny. Jesse looked in their direction for a second, just long enough to see T-Maz flipping him the bird; all while his too big shorts were slipping down around his thighs, exposing his "tighty whities" while his cap was falling off of his head.

The hook was nearly free from the carp's gullet, but Jesse was in no mood to rejoice. He didn't know how he knew what he knew about the teenagers. Likewise, he feared that their lives would end abruptly and violently. Jesse was moved to pray out loud: "Lord, it's an emergency; please lead those two boys away from the trouble they are pursuing. They have broken families and bad home lives. They don't stand a chance. Please intervene - in the name of Jesus I pray, amen"

As the "dead-ringer" finished praying, the hook popped free of the carp. Secured in both of his hands, Jesse could see a smeared reflection of a rainbow in the fish's scales. He turned his head over his left shoulder as he squatted at the water's edge, and sure enough there was a double rainbow in the sky above the trees behind him - resulting from the storm a little while before.

After gazing for a moment in amazement, Jesse turned back to the silver carp and lifted his hands from it. It flipped upright from its side and swam away slowly at first, before darting away toward the middle of the pond.

As the ripples caused by the carp's release began to abate, Jesse could see the blue sky, the trees, and the double rainbow reflecting on the water's surface. He set his fishing rod down and slowly stood up and stretched his arms. Looking across the pond to where a parking lot, basketball court, wooden pavilion and inlet brook all were, Jesse saw a man and a girl who could have been 9 or 10 years old standing on the grassy bank. They were a dad and his daughter who had come to fish at the mouth of the inlet brook. The dad held two fishing rods, a blue tackle box, and a teal-colored towel in his left hand while he pointed excitedly at the two rainbows with his right. The girl carried a blue plastic container of nightcrawlers in her left hand while snapping pictures of the breathtakingly-vivid rainbows with a small blue camera in her right.

Desiring to get an even better view of the rainbows, Jesse's first thought was to grab his fishing gear and walk to the opposite side of the pond where the dad and his daughter were. As he picked up his pole, tackle box, and packet of bread balls, he stopped as he heard a friendly male voice speak:

"It was a small one for a carp, but quite a fighter, eh?"

And now in the present, as Jesse sat on the edge of is bed, he realized that the man who spoke to him on that day in August 2006 was the same as the one in the dream of the pond and the L.A. Times article of the so-called mass alien abduction. Quickly, his mind rejoined the replay of the August memory:

"Yeah, not real big, but what a beautiful fish - I've never seen a carp colored silver like that. It was cool how the rainbows actually reflected on its scales" Jesse answered with a grin, having never heard the man who looked like a Rasta Morgan Freeman come down the bank and stand next to him. In this appearance, the man wore a royal blue golf shirt, Khaki shorts, and Birkenstock sandals. As the grass was still slightly wet from the rain, Jesse assumed the man may have slid on his feet as he had done when arriving at this spot.

The man went on, staring across the pond at the dad and daughter as he spoke: "That was a special fish, and the way you made the effort to unhook it without injuring it indicates a loving heart, no doubt - even when those lost boys were giving you a tough time. Who cares about carp, right? Well, God does! They are not trash fish in His eyes! And who cares about the lost boys and dirt balls of this world? God loves those two trash fish that you spoke with, Jesse! And while you may have exposed some awful truths they may have wanted to keep hidden, you started them today on a new path, Jesse - you who hates to see fish die! But it's a path that will take them through an even more dangerous matrix where they will encounter physical controllers and spiritual hackers before a mysterious rebel points their ravaged bodies and minds toward the lover of their souls. Despite what you saw today, trust me when I say that those two rainbows are a message to you Jesse that their names will be written in the Lamb's book of life…"

And then the man who could aptly be described as a Rasta Morgan Freeman was gone. Jesse could only wonder where he went and how he knew his name.

The replay of that memory of the late summer afternoon was over, and Jesse stood up and headed for the shower. Though steamy, the hot shower helped to clear his foggy mind and within a few minutes he was dressed in jeans, black mock turtle neck and black leather jacket. The man who looked and sounded so much like Elvis Presley was headed down the back stairs to the gravel parking area on Rouse Street, situated behind his flat at 316 Genesee, where his Jeep Grand Cherokee Laredo was waiting. Indeed, Jesse had decided it was past time to re-appear at Four Corners Community Church, and he hoped that he wouldn't miss much of the 9:00 a.m. service. However, he did hope that he would miss the worship team singing their quickly rehearsed versions of their K-LOVE favorites that sounded like predictable, overly-repetitive commercial jingles.

It was a ten minute drive to the church's location in North Chittenango. On the way, Jesse passed the baby blue ranch home of Mr. and Mrs. Steve Sandifer on Lakeport Road, and he knew that somewhere in the field behind the house were a shooting range and a buried bunker loaded with doomsday supplies for the members of the North Madison Militia.

It was 9:35 by the time Jesse had made it into the church sanctuary. Four Corners Community Church was modest in size and humble in construction, contrary to the opulent mega-church feel that its mother Eastside Bible Church in Manlius portrayed.

The worship team had closed its opening line-up of songs with "We Fall Down." The offering had been collected and the announcements concerning the Thanksgiving food basket program and rehearsals for the upcoming Christmas musical had been made.

As Jesse walked in and stood along the back, Matt Carrier was sermonizing from his current series "Spirit-led Investments" to a congregation of about sixty people; made up mostly of moms, dads, and grandparents, and also young adults:

"So, as we plan for our future and that of our children, as we strive to invest and save what we can for that day 20 years from now, are we letting Holy Spirit-led men lead us? As an aside, when we gather in groups to watch the Giants or the Bills this afternoon, are we ourselves acting with a spirit of richness as generous Christ-like hosts? Certainly, we nervously prepare for our retirements and hope for that day that we can help our children come up with down payments for their new homes - but are we getting our financial advice from secular advisers on the Fox Business Channel?"

"The Bible says in the second chapter of Corinthians, verses eight and nine, *'For you know what our Lord Jesus Christ gives freely, that though He was rich, for your sakes he became poor, so that by his poverty you might become rich.'* So, does this mean that Jesus' lack of material things was somehow 'flipped' through His resurrection so that his followers would become materially wealthy? Does this verse mean that true followers of Christ have a claim on this unlimited material wealth, and that all we have to do is 'name it and claim it' by asking God to deliver the goods? Can we therefore rest assured that we will have all of the wealth we need - for many years to come in this world - by merely being born-again followers of Christ and claiming the wealth that is a birthright of ours?"

"Yes, child of God, if you're feeling a little light in the pocketbook and little concerned about how the kid's tuition will be paid and those vacations to God's wonderful hideaways will be afforded, there is a breakthrough coming, a blessing for you to name and claim. Yes friends, Dave Ramsey is a financial advisor that God has blessed abundantly, amen? That's why I recommend his book *More Than…*"

After Jesse stood and listened to all he could stand, he interrupted the sermon as Pastor Matt mentioned the book's title:

"Excuse me, but I just need to speak up, ladies and gentlemen. There is a cross on the wall behind the pulpit, but I'm sorry to say that there isn't much of the 'true gospel' that the cross stands for in this church. Instead ladies and gentlemen, what you hear inside of these walls is the 'new gospel.'"

"You see folks, the new gospel is a liberation from low self-esteem, a freedom from emptiness and loneliness, a means of fulfillment and excitement, a way to receive our heart's desires, and means of meeting our needs. The true gospel is about God; but the new gospel is about us…"

"The true gospel is about sin; but the new gospel is all about meeting our needs. The true gospel is about our need for righteousness; the new gospel is about our need for our fulfillment. The true gospel is foolishness to those who are perishing; the new gospel is attractive to those in here who are perishing. Many, and that includes a lot of you people, are flocking to the new gospel but it is altogether questionable how many are actually being saved."

“Now, Pastor Matt, week after week you speak motivational doctrine that excites the flesh, and sure, it's all packed with biblical promises, healings, and miracles. You reference single-line passages pulled from different books of the Bible to make your point. You tell this flock every week that breakthroughs, relief and comfort are coming into their lives as you the charismatic dude at the pulpit declares that what you preach is the uncompromised word of God. And the flock says 'Lord, Lord, amen' but too many of them haven't made Christ Jesus their Lord. Matt, if you'd examine your heart you would be preaching about who Jesus Christ is and not the material things God gives. Folks, listen to me! That cross isn't just an idol to worship. No, it's a reminder that the flesh must be crucified if Jesus is to be the Lord of our lives!”

The church was stunned quiet as Jesse paused for two seconds to collect his thoughts before finishing:

“I don’t think there is going to be much more naming and claiming of wealth in this world, - or graduating, marrying, and la-de-da-ing through the happy horse crap of the perceived privileged American life for true followers of Jesus. You know what’s coming, Matt. I think you ought to start shooting your flock with the straight dope!”

There was a second of silence before most of the congregation began to murmur while turning to gawk at the “nut-job” who interrupted the sermon. Jesse could hear their hushed comments:

“I think I’ve seen him here before.”

“How rude!”

“He looks like Elvis Presley!”

“He’s cute!”

"Guys like him who don't go along with the program are bad for business!"

Then, Pastor Matt Carrier rebutted Jesse: "hey, Jesse, you know that we don't know the day or the hour, right? It could be a hundred years before Jesus comes back and the Great Tribulation begins. For now, I don't think we should be scaring people with 'rumors of wars' and 'signs in the sun and moon…'

Jesse cut Matt off, and continued to sound like a preacher himself: "No one knows the day or the hour, but it's not going to be a hundred years and it may not be a hundred days! The sands of the hourglass have nearly run out on the Church Age. We are in the season, people! Because of some dreams and visions I've had, I'm confident that the eye is about to twinkle, and I don't mean the mythical Eye of Horus. I mean that twinkling of an eye that the Apostle Paul wrote of in first Thessalonians, chapter four."

An adult female voice rose from the congregation, asking "what's the Church Age?"

In the silent seconds that followed, Jesse felt no compulsion to answer the woman's question. Pastor Matt stared at Jesse for a moment, and in that quick period of time felt ashamed that a regular attendee of his church needed to ask that question. He then smiled at Jesse, drew in a deep breath through his nose, and looked up toward the arched, cream-colored ceiling. Indeed, it was now so quiet in the sanctuary that one could hear an ant pass gas.

The preacher looked back down at the congregation. His piercing blue eyes were shooting invisible daggers as he opened his tightly-pursed lips to continue speaking. He began by sarcastically offering a question:

"No sir, we don't need any young men seeing visions or old men dreaming dreams, do we?"

The preacher's tone became increasingly agitated and sarcastic as he continued: "We don't want to be upset by any sons and daughters prophesying - we'd need to get them psychiatric help, wouldn't we? Boy, the last thing that we would want is for some Elvis impersonator who lacks a degree from a renowned seminary to come in here and remind us that our priorities are all screwed up, right!?"

Pastor Matt was now preaching with the fire of an old-school southern Baptist:

"No, brothers and sisters, we know not the day or the hour, but Jesus said that it would be as in the days of Noah! To quote Jesus from the Gospel of Matthew, chapter 24, verses 38 through 44, which I have committed to memory:

*"For as in the days before the flood, they were eating and drinking, marrying and giving in marriage, until the day that Noah entered the ark, and did not know until the flood came and took them all away, so also will the coming of the Son of Man be. Then two men will be in the field: one will be taken and the other left. Two women will be grinding at the mill: one will be taken and the other left. Watch therefore, for you do not know what hour your Lord is coming. But know this, that if the master of the house had known what hour the thief would come, he would have watched and not allowed his house to be broken into. Therefore you also be ready, for the Son of Man is coming at an hour you do not expect..."*

"I say be ready! Look around you... Jesus is coming! Do you hear me? Jesus could come at any time! We are living in days like those of Noah! We are eating and drinking, marrying and giving unto marriage... we are chasing material prosperity while not keeping our eyes on what is happening in the world around us! Are you paying attention to Israel, folks!?"

"Israel? What do the Jews got to do with anything?" a 30-something housewife asked aloud.

It was then that elder John McMurtry interrupted with "Matt, this is not the sermon series you are to be preaching on. This deviation is uncalled for! You're fired and take that crazy man in back out the door with you!"

Pastor Matt retorted with venom as he walked up the center aisle toward the exit doors of the sanctuary: "Fired? Thank you! Oh, and by the way John, the Lumina that your son recently sold to my daughter is headed into the repair shop tomorrow for the third time this month!"

When the pastor reached the last row of seats, he turned and faced the congregation as they gawked back at him. Before he spoke, he overheard McMurtry responding to a heavyset bald man in a grey suit who sat next to him, saying "that's nonsense, Jack. How can you say that about my son? My son is a very honest and honorable man!"

As he stood next to Jesse, behind the last row of seats, Matt Carrier spoke one final time to the congregation of Four Corners Community Church: "Ladies and Gentlemen, as my last act as pastor of this church, I would like to leave you this passage from the Bible to chew on. It's from the Book of Revelation, chapter 22 and verse 12, and these are the words of Jesus Christ the Lord:

*"Behold, I am coming quickly, and My reward is with Me, to render to every man according to what he has done."*

As they walked through the double doors that led to the foyer and the exit, Matt Carrier turned toward the murmuring congregation and announced with a self-satisfied smirk: "Ladies and gentlemen, your former pastor and the guy who impersonates Elvis have left the building."

# 7

# The Groundhog and the Ant

As Eileen Sandifer sat in quiet, cozy comfort with her laptop on her lap, reading the headlines on the Drudge Report, she was startled by a loud rapping on the front door. Only trouble would come calling at 7:00 on on a Monday morning, so she pushed aside the computer and grabbed the Ruger LCR .38 revolver from the drawer of the chocolate brown Parson's table that sat next to the linen sofa of similar brown shade. As she made the short, barefoot walk from the living room couch to the front door, she worked the gun between the buttons of her denim shirt and into her Flashbang bra holster, concealing it below her bosom. Mrs. Sandifer fully trusted the safety button on the firearm, as its barrel was pointed directly at her heart. But, her husband was currently "indisposed", so if the enemy was on the other side of the door, she would be forced into being an army of one until he finished his business and could come as her reinforcement.

Eileen peered through the peephole and saw standing on the porch a stocky man with thinning brown hair, dressed in jeans, white sneakers, and a royal blue hooded sweatshirt adorned with the NFL's Los Angeles Riptides logo. Recognizing that the man wasn't a "hostile" but in fact Matt Carrier, her stress was diminished as he was not a process server, FBI agent, or even that fat cop Brostic from the local force. She slid free the chain lock, turned the knob on the keyless deadbolt, and pulled open the heavy white wooden front door. Next, she pushed open the storm door, and as it squeaked she said "good morning, Matt - what's going on? Well, don't just stand there, come on in!"

At 45 years of age, Eileen was 20 years younger than her husband Steve. Like her husband, Eileen had spent time in the U.S. Armed Forces; she having joined the Army in 1983 at the age of nineteen. After serving ten years active duty in the Army - including time in Iraq during Desert Storm - she put in four more years as a reservist in the Army National Guard. Whenever she'd talk about the "old days" she would always say "it was great being in Ronald Reagan's army, still good serving under daddy Bush, but then the world started to change when Slick Willy was elected so I knew it was time to get out."

Steve and Eileen had been married for five years; meeting on Match.com after having both been previously divorced. Like her husband Steve, Eileen looked younger than her biological age. There were faint freckles across the bridge of her thin nose, but virtually no wrinkles on the fair skin of her face. No streaks of grey were visible in her straight, shoulder-length brown hair and just a minor touch of "crow's feet" appeared near her cool blue eyes. Both she and Steve put in 30 minutes running on a treadmill each morning to keep in shape.

In addition to being skilled marksmen, both Steve and Eileen were third-degree black belts in Taekwondo. Steve was also an expert in Krav Maga, a little-known martial art originating from what was now Israel and considered by some to be the most lethal on earth.

To pay the bills - as the militia was a not for profit organization - the Sandifers worked from home operating an honest, legitimate, and successful online affiliate marketing program that only involved 25 hours a week worth of labor. The business centered on pay-per-click Google ads, online coupon downloads, and YouTube video promotion.

Matt was seated at a round, antique oak table in the kitchen and his eyes were drawn to the numerous jars of spices on an oak shelf that lined the cream-colored wall opposite the white Kenmore electric stove and the cupboards and counter that were done in teal green. While Eileen poured a home-ground, freshly-brewed cup of Paul deLima coffee for Matt, she observed his fascination with the spices and remarked with a smile "we use some of them for cooking, but most are up there for decoration."

"Hi Matt, would you like some pancakes? We ate a little while ago, but there's plenty of batter left over" was the question asked by Steve, his warm, radio announcer-quality voice startling Matt as he did not hear him entering the kitchen from the hallway. As pleasant as Steve sounded and as affable a personality as he was, he was also a trained killer whose hands could be registered as lethal weapons.

"Oh, hey Steve, uh…no thanks, I pigged out on Cheerios before I came over" was Matt's response, his bright blue eyes seemingly lighting up as he responded with a chuckle to Steve's offer.

"Yeah, the breakfast of champions, right? Uh, no, that's Wheaties!" Steve answered with a hearty laugh, before becoming solemn as he and Eileen sat down at the table:

"So, Matt, what brings you here this morning?" was Steve's question as he cocked his head slightly to his right and looked quizzically at the unemployed pastor.

"I've been thinking about your invitation to join the North Madison Militia. When we were talking that afternoon when I ran into you and Eileen walking on the canal towpath, I thought you were maybe a little crazy. But, the way things are going in this country and in the world, I can envision a need for something like a militia in this area - especially if there is some sort of Martial Law or complete governmental takeover. I mean, what if there is a total economic meltdown and people are rioting in the streets? Something like what you and Galen have started may be the last line of defense, so to speak. I don't like to curse, but what if the shit does hit the fan? As every day passes I believe it's a likely scenario" was Matt's forthright answer, as his eyes met with Steve's as though they were having a staring contest.

"That's great, Matt, and we'd love to have you, but isn't your 'Rapture' gonna come along and whisk you off to Heaven before the real bad stuff comes? I mean, isn't that what you believe?" Steve asked, at first humorless but then glancing at Eileen while raising his eyebrows and snickering.

"You can laugh if you want, Steve - but the Rapture comes before the start of the Great Tribulation. One of the hallmarks of the Great Tribulation is the one world system and government, run by the Anti-Christ. We've seen Jomo Omondi, in less than one year in office; systematically undermine America's economy and sovereignty while the sheeple ignorantly and blissfully go along with it. America has to fall for the new one world system to come to full power - and it's falling! Plus, there is something about the Italian ambassador to the U.N., I think Chobani is his name - he's making a lot of noise on behalf of a new world economy and system while cutting down Christianity, and because he's good-looking and articulate, all the right people are listening. So, I think that if Jesus tarries any longer, the supernatural storm is going to intensify. It won't be the Tribulation until after the Rapture - but things may get so bad that some people will think it is the Tribulation. So, if your invite is still open, you can count me in."

"Wow, that's heavy, - 'supernatural storm.' Hmm..." Steve replied, stroking his salt and pepper goatee with his right hand while running his left hand across the top of his buzz cut. "But your church can't find out that their pastor is involved in something like a militia. How would you keep it quiet?"

“The top elder fired me yesterday for changing the topic of the sermon from feel-good prosperity and social gospel teaching to Biblical truth - right in the middle of the sermon” Matt answered with simmering anger coloring the tone of his voice and his countenance.

“Prosperity gospel - is that like if you put enough five-spots in the collection plate, Jesus will drop a bank bag full of cash on your front porch as a reward?” Eileen asked with a smirk and a shake of her head.

“And all of those five-spots will buy the preacher a new Cadillac!” Steve cut in before Matt could answer.

Matt laughed at Steve’s Cadillac quip and then said “well, I was able to buy a blue Dodge Ram pickup - but that came from my salary!”

“And mine is the same year and color, but mine is better - it’s a quad cab! And, I didn’t buy it from that shyster Joe McMurtry” Steve answered waggishly.

“Yeah, the son of that good Christian man John McMurtry. John’s the old fart that fired me” Matt spoke with dripping sarcasm, before becoming more conciliatory: “Well, at least I got a good deal and a good vehicle from him; unlike many other customers of his…”

“…John has Joe running the two auto malls while he sits in the counting room adding the wads. John says that God gave him this success as a reward for his faith, positive attitude, and the fact that he donates large sums of money to World Vision International. He says he visualized his dealerships and within a couple of years they happened; that he more or less spoke them into existence. John says if humans have faith in God, He is contractually obligated to deliver on His promises of security and prosperity. If you confess that God is to reward you richly in the material sense and sincerely believe that He will, God will do it. More or less, God exists as a genie to grant our wishes. The whole thing is based on a twisting of scriptures, especially those from the Book of Malachi, which is the last book of the Old Testament. John accuses those at Four Corners Community Church who aren't doing well financially of lacking sufficient faith. That is the Prosperity Gospel in a nutshell and I am ashamed that I allowed them to force me to preach it for so long."

"Wow, it kind of sounds like Jim and Tammy Faye Baker, or that guy with all the teeth, Joel Osteen" Eileen offered.

"It all sounds too good to be true; almost like a scam" was Steve's reply as he nodded his head and glanced out the bay window of the kitchen and toward the back field.

"God loves us, but true faith requires that we carry the cross of His son. Carrying that cross isn't often synonymous with carrying a briefcase full of dead presidents to Oneida Savings for deposit. As I judge the fruit of John McMurtry, I'd say his doesn't carry Christ's cross" Matt answered sternly.

"Fans of the Prosperity Gospel must also like Masonic lodges. I saw McMurtry daddy and son walking into the lodge on Seneca Street in Manlius last Thursday night as I was driving by. I think that's when they have weekly meetings" Eileen chimed in.

"Wow - really!? Well, I guess I shouldn't be surprised to hear this!" Matt exclaimed, and he was in fact surprised.

"The Freemasons are part of the Illuminati; they're one of the smaller groups like Skull and Bones that make up the whole. So, the good church elder John McMurtry may also be a Freemason. No wonder I don't like church" Steve added while shaking his head; a look of consternation manifesting itself through wrinkles around his green eyes and by pulling the skin taught over the high cheek bones on his rugged face.

"Are you absolutely sure it was John and Joe McMurtry?" Matt asked Eileen.

"I'd bet my life it was them. I could see the glow of their perfectly-coiffed white hair and their fake tans even under the streetlights at night. You know - the kind of hair that would stay neat in a hurricane? Even though they're father and son, they look like brothers" she replied affirmatively.

"My number one issue with Freemasonry is its lack of commitment to the real Triune God, which is Father, Son, and Holy Spirit. Instead, they base their philosophy on a 'Great Architect of the Universe', who is a neutral deity that can be in whatever form an individual mason may worship - whether it is Allah, Buddha, the real Holy Triune God, Neptune, or whoever. So, while not being a religion per se, it is a pagan organization with too much power that ultimately ends up with the Illuminati and with Satan himself" Matt pontificated.

"Okay, we're not holding a class in theology here. It's good that we agree that the Freemasons and the Illuminati are tied together. Now, Matt, you understand that we are not an assault force but in fact defenders?" Steve asked with deadly seriousness.

"Yeah, Steve, I've got it. The goal of this militia is to protect the citizens in this area in the event of a cataclysmic breakdown or governmental takeover. We'll be the first line of defense should the government go rogue" Matt replied with equally deadly seriousness.

The conversation continued with Steve explaining: "My home is not a compound like other militias may employ. The members don't live here, we only meet here and train here. I own thirty acres of land out back. It used to be Jed Lathrop's corn field until he passed away ten years ago. His family wanted nothing to do with the farm, so they sold the land to me. Now, it's just a field, but we also target shoot out there to keep up our skills. As you know, the bunker is out below the back yard" Steve spoke gravely, but then chuckled as he said "You remember the stir that it caused with the neighbors - especially Earl Skidmore - when we had it put in!"

"Oh yeah, I remember!" Matt replied with a chuckle of his own. "He accused you of planning to operate a drug-running business out of it. He was fit to be tied when he learned that there was nothing that the Town of Sullivan Code Enforcement could do to stop you."

"Yup, for a redneck, he's quite supportive of Omondi; remember all the signs in his front yard?" Steve asked, still chuckling.

"Yes, I remember" Matt replied, not exhibiting any signs of humor.

Steve continued: "It's probably because he'd been a union employee most of his work life - working at the Budweiser brewery in Baldwinsville. You remember two years ago when he messed up his back trying to pull his Harley 1200 out of the mud in his back yard? He was in agony that whole evening, and yet he was able to go to work the next morning and fake that he hurt his back on the bottle line. Now he's on permanent disability by perpetrating a fraud! And while he tried to accuse me of being a drug runner, it's him who is addicted to Oxycontin and has two different doctors writing prescriptions for it so he has enough to overindulge."

"It's unbelievable. The guy abuses Oxycontin and yet he's out with his buddies every evening slamming beers at the Ten Pin. I continue to pray for Earl and I've tried to intervene, but he's told me I can stuff it - but in more profane terminology. I've been trying to find out who his doctors are, but so far I've hit a brick wall. I've told the Chittenango Police about him, but they seem disinterested in doing anything until there is a tragedy" Matt offered.

"I just hope the guy drops dead. Sorry pastor - er, former pastor, for feeling that way. I know that you Jesus people look at things differently" Steve said sheepishly as he stood up from his chair.

"He's a lost soul who needs the saving grace of Christ, just as we all do" was Matt's earnest rebuttal.

Steve steered the subject matter in a different direction as he zipped up his camouflage hunting parka with quilted lining and retrieved a black knit hat from the right side pocket: "So, uh…what do you say I show you the bunker?" As he said this, Eileen handed him her black leather purse.

"Yeah, sure, let's check it out" Matt replied and began to follow Steve through the kitchen door that led out to the back yard and the chilly morning air. After a short walk they stood at the top of a small hill; the bottom of which leveled into a small field that was the home to the Sandifer's vegetable garden during the warm weather months. Beyond the garden was a much larger field, and in that was a shooting range that was kept rather non-descript.

"It's best to install these bunkers on a slope or gradual incline of a hill, which is why it's in this spot. It helps to keep the structure dry and to achieve natural air flow" Steve said, his breath visible in the cold as they now stood next to the locked entrance that would take them down inside.

Matt watched with keen interest as Steve squatted down and began to dig through his wife's purse. "We alternate - she's the key holder today" Steve said, seemingly embarrassed as he began to dig through the purse. "Let's see, lipstick, pepper spray, tampon, sunglasses, truck keys…ah, here it is, the key to the Land of Oz!" He pulled a single gold-colored key from Eileen's purse and then inserted it into the lock mechanism on top of the steel hatch. With a twist of the key the grey airtight lid to the entryway lifted open with a "whoosh."

Before they descended the ladder and entered the bunker, Steve said "one way nature protects its creatures when trouble comes is to get them under ground. The ground hog and the ant are great examples, Matt. When the brown stuff impacts the air cooling device, we'll have to be like ground hogs and ants. As much as we prepare, we hope the day that we need to take up residence down here never comes."

Once inside, the 27 foot long, 8 foot diameter shelter immediately reminded Matt of a submarine. Although the interior was grey and white, he heard for just a moment in his mind the Beatles singing a rousing chorus of "we all live in a Yellow Submarine, Yellow Submarine, Yellow Submarine." The majority of the structure was reinforced steel, and yet a carpeted wood floor ran down the middle. Five cots were interspersed between metal shelves loaded with canned food, bottled water, and all manner of "doomsday prepper" survival supplies including several M16A2 rifles with cartridges inserted. There was a large kitchen area which included a double stainless steel sink. A flush toilet and a shower made the post-doomsday abode more civilized. There were LED overhead lights and an emergency exit separate from the entrance. A hard wired electrical connection was attached - if there would be any juice during a time of cataclysmic breakdown. Additionally, there were two electric generators, two water tanks and a fuel tank. "Wow, almost all of the comforts of home" Matt remarked as he surveyed the premises.

"The maximum amount of people that could live down here is fifteen. So far, including you, there would be twelve if the entire group was to stay in here. Because there are only 5 cots, we would sleep in shifts of five" Steve spoke as he walked ahead of Matt, seemingly acting as a tour guide - his radio announcer-style voice only serving to reinforce that notion in Matt's mind.

“We’ve got three rifles down here, but all of the other armaments are stored in my basement. If we get to the point to where we need to live down here, it’s not likely that we’d need any weapons. There could be a zombie apocalypse up top, but it’s not likely that they’d be able to penetrate this fortress. But, we would only take up residence down here as a last resort, and it’s only available to members of the North Madison Militia” Steve added gravely.

“I pray that we never need to live down here” Matt added solemnly.

“I’m not a religious man, Matt - but I pray the same thing” Steve replied while looking down at the floor. He then looked up, smiled, and said “let’s get back up top. Today there is still a semi-sane America and my beautiful wife up there.”

# 8

# Gold Soup

It was a cool, breezeless, sunny early afternoon on Thursday, November 12th, 2009. There were just a few cumulous clouds painted on the baby blue sky and the forecast high temperature for the day in Central New York was 52 degrees. *Our Misunderstanding*, the eighth track from the 2006 album "Keep Your Wig On" by the band Fastball began to play in Jesse's headphones as he walked northeast on Genesee Street, through the crosswalk at Rouse Street. The lyric line "rip out the trees and plant your flag, now I know just where you stand" was sung in harmony by Tony Scalzo and Miles Zuniga, and Jesse loved the heartbroken feel of the ballad's vocal melody and the chord changes, and the simple production of strumming acoustic and clean electric guitars laid over a deep, throbbing bass and driving percussion.

The destination of the "dead-ringer" was the Dollar Tree, a little further down on Genesee Street. Every item was a dollar at the store, and Jesse needed to pick up toothpaste, deodorant, and Barbasol shaving cream without paying a princely sum. Jesse's sleep the previous night seemed to be devoid of dreams - well, at least dreams that he could remember. He was feeling unburdened and enjoying both the music in his headphones and his walk to the store.

“Hey, wait up! Hey, it’s me - remember me!?” a woman’s excited voice cut through the hardly impenetrable wall of sound created by his cheap Sony headphones and pushed Fastball to the background. As a befuddled Jesse stopped and turned in her direction, the running woman slammed into him with a bear hug and a happy moan as she stuck her lips on his right cheek for several seconds before pulling away.

“Whoa, what the…?” was all Jesse could say as he regained his balance, wondering if he was actually dreaming now. As the ecstatic 32 year old mother of two stared at him while clutching the arms of his green hoodie, he endeavored to gather and restack the bowled-over Legos of his mind and remember how he knew this woman.

“I won the jackpot! I won the jackpot! Because of you, I won last night’s Powerball jackpot!” she exclaimed with shrieking joy as she jumped up and down on the sidewalk, still clinging to Jesse’s arms and nearly tearing the hoodie off of him.

“Well, congratul…” was all a still reeling Jesse could utter before she interrupted him.

“Thirty-seven million big ones! Ooooo I’m gonna take care of you, you wonderful man! If you’ve got a girlfriend, you tell her to take a hike! I wanna marry you, Mister Number Picker!!!”

As the woman seemed on the verge of hyperventilation, the mental Legos were again forming a structure and Jesse recognized who she was…

…It was yesterday at 11:15 a.m. and he was waiting in line at the Byrne Dairy just a couple of blocks behind where he and the woman stood on Genesee Street. Jesse the connoisseur of fine chocolate milk was waiting to purchase a half gallon in a glass jug, as glass allowed for the best flavor he believed. Chocolate milk was the best way to wash down a delicious peanut butter and banana sandwich on white bread, and Jesse was anxious to get the milk, get home, and dig in.

Erica Cox was at the checkout ahead of Jesse, paying ironically enough for a loaf of white bread, a 16.3 ounce jar of Peter Pan peanut butter, and chocolate milk; but in a quart-sized cardboard carton. Michael the affable cashier handed her the small key pad so she could type in the pin number to her EBT card. Erica was a petite, comely blond who was intelligent and hardworking, but life had dealt her a series of hard blows in recent months - some due to her own poor choices.

"Phew…I had just enough in my food benefits account to cover that" Erica spoke with relief as she took the receipt from Michael.

"Hey, it'll get better if you can catch up with the jerk that ditched you and left you with nothing" was Michael's attempt to be encouraging - and in that, it was though neither he nor Erica knew that anyone else was in the store.

Erica shared her litany of miseries: "No new job, no prospects for one, unemployment about to run out, a cold drafty rental house with two boys with bad colds that I can hardly feed, and a mountain of credit card debt I can't pay. I'm suing my ex-husband for more child support and that should help, but I've had to use the credit cards to help make ends meet, and that's just the tip of the iceberg. I can't pay the emergency room bill from when the boyfriend beat me that last time before he took off with the $1,300.00 I had stashed in an envelope. No, I can't find that jerk Eddie and my free lawyer does virtually nothing to help track him down. That's what I get for having a relationship with an ex-con who is old enough to be my father and behaves just like him!"

“Yeah, that scumbag should rot in hell! You aren’t the only woman he’s screwed over. He dated my aunt a few years ago and killed her poodle because it was always yipping! He took its head and twisted it until the neck broke. I hated the obnoxious little dog too, but I’d never kill it! That’s why he spent time in jail before you met him. I don’t get it, ya know? He has a way of charming the socks off of you women. I wish I could get chicks like he does, but I would treat them good” Michael pontificated, tilting his head sideways and making a skewed face to demonstrate both his befuddlement and his empathy.

“Eddie the turtle killer?” Jesse wondered to himself and almost jumped into the conversation, but decided to remain unnoticed.

“I’m out of food benefits until Monday, so we’re gonna be eating peanut butter sandwiches for dinner until then. At least the boys have free lunch at school” Erica lamented, with moistening eyes.

“Well hey, you wanna hear a joke? It might cheer you up!” Michael asked, as he always tried to be upbeat.

“Sure, anything at all. I’m so depressed I could kill myself, but I have to keep on for my boys” she answered, tears and mascara now streaming down her face.

“Okay” Michael said with an impish grin, “what do you use to make gold soup?”

Erica sniffed and shuddered as she replied “I don’t know.”

“Fourteen carrots! Get it? Fourteen carrots!”

The corny joke brought a smile to Erica’s reddened tear-streaked face. Even Jesse got a chuckle out of the joke, but it was still as if no one knew he was there.

It was then that Jesse saw a too familiar sight. It was one of L. Frank Baum's flying monkeys - translucent of course - and he was certain that the other two could not see it. It had a hand around Erica's throat, and Jesse had the immediate notion that it had been on her for months. It turned toward Jesse as it hovered with wings flapping, and on its bellhop's hat were the glowing arched-block letters that spelled POVERTY. On the left side of its vest was the word LACK in the same font and on the right side of the vest was LOSS. As it locked eyes with Jesse, a white angelic hand appeared - looking as though it came from an open-faced cooler next to the checkout line. While the unsuspecting demon silently laughed at Jesse, the hand grabbed it by its left-side wing and pulled it back toward the cooler. The demon in the guise of a silly flying monkey began to thrash in panic, and then it was gone.

As Jesse saw the demon, Erica said to Michael "you know - I've got a dollar in my pocket and not much to lose. I want to buy a Powerball ticket as it draws tonight and the jackpot is over 30 million."

"A quick-pick?" Michael asked.

"No, let me see, its five numbers plus an extra number, uh…let me think…"

It was then that Jesse was moved to speak up: "you should play 4-11-17-20-39, and a Powerball number of 32." Those were the numbers - originally quick-picks - that were on Ronny's ticket on Halloween.

"What?" Erica asked with a smile as she looked over her shoulder; being startled by Jesse as she didn't know he was behind her.

"4-11-17-20-39 and then 32" Jesse repeated, to which Michael answered "yeah, try those, they sound good. If you win, you can make a tanker truck of gold soup with real gold karats!"

“Uh…okay, whoever you are. I’ll try those numbers because I can’t think of my own” Erica said while glancing at Jesse over her shoulder, the tears having ceased their flow and a dazzling smile lighting up her lovely face. “Oh, by the way, I’m Erica”

“My name is Jesse - Jesse Same” he replied with a grin of his own.

“I didn’t hear you come in, man! Yeah, Jesse’s a cool dude” Michael offered with a smile and a nod.

As she watched Michael punch the series of numbers into the lottery computer, Erica thought to herself “wow, he’s a stud-bagel and he’s a dead-ringer for Elvis Presley! I wonder if he’s single?”

Erica grabbed her bag of groceries, dropped her dollar bill on the counter and took the Powerball ticket from Michael. As she turned and walked past Jesse, she said “well, thank you Jesse Same. You are a kind gentleman and if I win, I’ll be sure to look you up!”

As Erica’s high heels click-clacked toward the exit - she having just interviewed for a job as a receptionist in a Fayetteville accountant’s office - she turned and glanced at Jesse as she pushed open the door. Suddenly, she felt as if there was hope as she walked into the parking lot and toward her black 2007 Subaru Outback that was on the verge of repossession. Indeed, she had the feeling that something dark and sinister had just been lifted off of her…

…So, now as they stood on the sidewalk on Thursday, Jesse finally recognized the woman and asked incredulously “Erica, you’re really the winner? Whoa! Wow! I’d heard on the radio this morning that someone from upstate New York was the lone winner of the Powerball jackpot, but no… really!?”

Motorists on Genesee Street were noticing the animated exchange taking place on the sidewalk in front of the Ten Pin Restaurant & Tavern; a few even slowing down to make sure that a petite 30-

something woman that could be "the mom next door" was not being accosted by a thug in a green hoodie. But, if anything, it was the mom who was doing the accosting!

The Sandifer's neighbor Earl Skidmore noticed the interaction through the bar's front windows as he sat and consumed Budweiser drafts with his nephew Randall Jacobs, and his good friends Jay Jensen, Bart "Murf" Murphy, and Robert the midget. Earl stood up, wobbled a bit, and announced "Well, I think that woman is being mugged by Elvis Presley. We gotta go help 'er!"

As per usual, Randall was too intoxicated to stand up, and his answer to his Uncle Earl's call to heroism was to mumble "yeah, I bought dog food yester-night."

Jay's alcohol-influenced response was "just sit down Earl and don't worry about it - he's only an Elvis impersonator, not the real one!"

Robert "the midget" Bartkowski was afflicted with dwarfism, but he could drink as much as a man two and a half times his size. His rejoinder was "ah…that's Eddie's old girlfriend. She prolly has it comin'. Sit the hell down Earl and finish yer beer!"

Only Murf was eager to accompany Earl outside. After he quickly drained the last swallow from his fourth mug of beer, he offered loudly "faggot prob'ly only fights with girls. We need to get all the gays and all the Jews outta the freakin' country. Let's go kick some ass, Earl! Oh, wait a minute; can we have some of those rubber gloves ya got behind the bar, Sandy? That guy out there prob'ly has AIDS 'er somethin'".

Earl's response to his beer-muscled redneck friend was "well, you ain't got time, Murf. You gotta drive school bus in a few minutes! I can handle this!"

"Yer right, Earl - I better just slam another beer and git to the bus garage, and you better put some gloves on before you go punch that queer" Murf admonished.

"Well, don't assume he's gay or got AIDS, Murf! He don't look gay, ya know? My only issue is that he should be at work somewhere at this time of day, unless he's out on disability" Earl replied.

"Well, of course YOU wouldn't think he was gay; you the stupid Democrat that voted for Omondi! YOU think everybody should be out on disability!" was Murf's incensed reply, as the alcohol was fueling the flames of his already short temper.

"Well, (by habit, Earl began most every statement with the word 'well') Omondi and the Democrats care about the unions and the workin' man, ya know? McCann and the ditzy broad that ran with him, you know the one that can see Japan from her house…"

"That's Russia, not Japan!" was Murf's testy correction of Earl.

"Well, wherever da hell it was! Anyway, all you Republicans care about are the rich management types who make big profits on the backs of us workin' people! You're a workin' man Murf, I don't how you can be so dumb and vote for those Republican slave masters!" was Earl's irate retort.

"Yeah, well at least us Republicans don't illegally collect workman's compensation because we get hurt on our motorcycles, you lazy, liberal, insubordinate, unproductive, overly-coddled, over-paid union lackey! No wonder my damn Bud twelve-packs are so expensive!"

"Well, I can be pretty productive in breakin' yer overly-coddled face!" Earl proclaimed as he delivered a knuckle sandwich straight to Murf's mouth. As Earl's right fist connected with Murf's lips, it was he and not Murf that screamed in pain. Murf was 6'2" tall and weighed 245 muscular pounds; whereas Earl Skidmore was only 5' 6" tall, small-framed, and tougher in his soused imagination than in sobering reality. The impact with Murf's mouth only served to jar Earl's body, causing the lower back that had been injured two years ago to flare in excruciating, burning pain. As Robert and Jay squatted down next to Earl and tried to comfort him as he lay on the floor in agony, Murf wiped a trickle of blood from his lower lip and stated cockily "you yip-yapping liberal French Poodles shouldn't try to take on us Republican big dogs. We're takin' back America in twenty-ten, oh yeah!"

As Murf left the building, Sandy the bartender shook her head in amazement watching Earl, who was now sitting up on the floor, swallowing two Oxycontin tablets with a gulp of beer.

Meanwhile, outside on the sidewalk, Erica asked Jesse "can I at least take you to lunch?"

Jesse answered amiably: "Sure, that would be great, but like I just said, I don't want any money from you, Erica. I'm hardly rich, but I do have some money in the bank and a small stock portfolio, and I make enough from my Elvis impersonation gigs to pay the bills and cover the health insurance."

Just as they had talked outside while the scene inside the Ten Pin unfolded, they continued to chatter as they walked back in the opposite direction on Genesee Street. They passed Jesse's flat and arrived at the popular Donna and Sam's Coffee Shop, which was next to the Byrne Dairy store where Erica had purchased the Powerball ticket bearing the winning numbers that Jesse had given her.

Though called "Coffee Shop", husband Sam, wife Donna, their daughter Christine and Donna's sister Diane together ran a cozy, diner-style eatery that served breakfast and lunch, seven days a week. The food was good, the portions were generous, and the business survived on local repeat customers.

There were two booths along the front window that faced Genesee Street, and being that the one closest to the entry doors was occupied, they sat in the second near the corner. The L-shaped, white linoleum-covered counter was off to the side and on the round-topped stools covered with red vinyl sat mostly overweight men and women in their sixties and seventies who discussed their physical ailments and how there were still plenty of "jabs out der (sic)" if "yooz" (sic) just get out der and put yer name in, ya know! Da new President Omondi is turnin' tings around! Tank gad and da mudder Mary we gat rid 'a dat Bush! (sic)"

As he and Erica ceased chattering long enough to peruse the menu, Jesse snickered to himself as he listened to the cacophony at the counter and found humor in the fact that so many older Central New Yorkers sounded as though they were born and raised in Chicago - pronouncing the short "o" like a short "a", the letter combination of "th" as "d" and "t", and so on.

Galen Moss, co-founder of the North Madison Militia, sat at the counter, finishing off a delicious plate of the day's lunch special which was meatloaf and mashed potatoes smothered in beef gravy, and a generous side of corn. At 32, Galen was half the age of Steve Sandifer, but like Steve and Eileen he had served in the armed forces, including stints in Iraq and Afghanistan with the U.S. Army 3rd Infantry Division. In May of 2007, after nine years, Galen's service to his country was over. Unfortunately, he'd had a difficult time maintaining gainful employment since coming home to Chittenango. At this time, he was collecting unemployment; having recently been laid off by a construction company whose demand for building new homes had severely dropped off as in reality, the U.S. economy was deteriorating steadily under the new president.

While considered a "good guy" by those who knew him, the "G-Man" could be a bit testy and impatient; these traits being exacerbated by the difficult times he was facing as of late. And, as he was by no means a shy man, he was always prepared to speak his mind should the forum be open to him. On this Thursday at Donna and Sam's, circumstance gave the floor to Galen Moss.

A rotund 68 year old man wearing a white cap with the *NYSUT - a union of professionals* logo in blue lettering above the bill, blue winter vest and brown and black checkered flannel shirt was holding court, speaking loudly above the din:

"Da classifieds are full 'a jabs! Fer chrissakes, if yooz gatta work at da Burger King yooz work der, ya know? Even da Dollar Tree is hirin' fer da holidays! Da problem is deez damn people don't wanna work! Hell, if yooz gatta work tree (sic) minimum wage jabs you do dat! Ya do what ya gotta do, ya know? Fer chrissakes!"

Galen had been listening to this man blather on about how good the "ecannamy" was and how good "tings" were in America for the past twenty minutes. And, when the man did take a quick break from yammering to chew his food, he smacked his lips uncouthly. Being a bit testy and impatient these days, Galen had heard enough:

"Hey, fat ass, why don't you stop blathering, eat your lunch, and chew with your mouth closed, alright? I'm sick of listening to you flap your gums about how good things are out there! What, has cholesterol clogged the arteries to your brain? By the looks of you, I'd say you never miss dessert let alone a meal! And speaking of 'jaaaaaaabs' (Galen exaggerated the man's colloquialism) I'll bet you don't even work!

There was a brief moment of quiet, where all that could be heard was Jesse's snickering and the sound of a teaspoon dropped by a shocked patron hitting the grey-tiled floor with a "clink". Then, as if a switch was thrown, there were gasps of "oh my gad" "how rude" "who is dat guy" and various other murmurings before that fat man dropped his fork on his plate spoke in rebuttal:

“Hey now, listen der fella! I worked turty-tree (sic) years for da Chittenango school district as a custodian…”

“Yeah, you tell ‘em Ray!” a female voice coarsened by too many packs of Basic full-flavor and too much Genesee beer interrupted from somewhere along the counter.

The fat man named Ray continued: “I did what I had ta do, ya know? I retired at da age of 67 after workin’ Mondee troo Fridee, second shift tree a clack (sic) ta eleven a clack fer turty-tree years. Because I got a good jab dat paid me twunny (sic) six bucks pen-hour (sic), tree fifteen minute breaks and an hour paid lunch wid six weeks paid vacation, I gat a good pension now from da school distreect. (sic) So no, ace-hole (sic), I ain’t gatta work no more!

“Interesting” Galen replied coolly, sounding like Jack Nicholson, before continuing: “well, gosh, by the looks of you Tubby, you didn’t work too hard pushing that mop bucket along for twenty-six dollars PER HOUR, not PEN-HOUR! Maybe you should have sat in on some English as a second language classes while you busted your considerable pooter for the school DISTRICT!”

Moss drew a breath and then continued, silencing the coarse-voiced woman who was starting to again speak in support of Ray:

“Now, let me set you straight in some things. It’s the taxpayer that pays your pension, so maybe you should give some props to those that enable you to eat like a pig! And the next thing, there aren’t a lot of jaaaaaaaaaaaaaaaaaaaaaaabs (again exaggerating Ray’s colloquialism) out there, you ignorant moron!

“Donna, throw him out! Ray, break his jaw for him!” the woman with the coarsened voice that time getting a few words in.

“Shut up lizard woman! Between your tattoos and your overly-tanned skin, you look like something that would be found in the dumpster of a Holiday Inn after a Hell's Angel's convention, and you've got a voice that sounds like the inside of a saw mill!" Galen shouted across the counter before continuing in a quieter, cooler, Jack Nicholson-esque tone:

"Sweet baby Ray, while you were being overly-compensated for your cushy JOB, that's spelled j-o-b and not j-a-b, pushing a squeaky mop bucket and taking more than three 15 minute breaks and a lunch break I'm sure, I was firing an M4A1 at terrorists in Afghanistan and Iraq. While in Iraq, I got to see my best friend get his legs blown off by an IED.  I got to hear him scream in pain until he died a few minutes later after the shock hit him of realizing that most of his lower torso was fifteen feet away from his upper torso. And I know that what I saw over there is coming here soon, and not to a theater but to the real American homeland. And when it hits, guys like you will be dropping dead from stress and trauma-induced heart attacks."

"Folks, my name is Galen Moss, and I'm not looking for sympathy from any one of you in here, and I would do it all again if I had to. But, what I have come home to are ignorant, pacified sheeple who have let their guard down since 9/11, an economy on the verge of collapse and high unemployment. Since I came home from Iraq, I've been able to find two jobs and both were in home construction. I have been laid off from both and I currently collect unemployment insurance while trying to find another job. Do you hear me Ray? I said I am trying to find another job and there's nothing for me, not even at the Dollar Tree! I wanted to be a police officer but because I have a bad right knee and I don't even know how it went bad, but I can't pass the physical."

Now the entire eatery was focused on the interplay between Ray and Galen. Donna had at first considered throwing Galen out, but now even she was listening intently while preparing plates of the meatloaf special for Jesse and Erica.

While he spoke with the cool tones of a young Jack Nicholson, Galen Moss did not bear a physical resemblance to him. The erstwhile infantryman stood 5' 11" tall and weighed 177 lbs. He wore his brown hair close-cropped but not buzzed, and since finishing his Army hitch he sported a thin mustache and beard trimmed tight to his jaw line. Galen was always considered to be handsome by the worldly women he had known; they finding much to like in his build, his emerald green eyes and his chiseled facial features.

On that day, Galen wore a black t-shirt with the phrase SIGN UP ironed onto the chest in white lettering, all upper-case. He didn't know what the shirt would encourage one to sign-up for, but it caught his eye as he was perusing men's shirts in the Chittenango Salvation Army thrift store shortly after arriving home from Iraq in 2007. It was a Wednesday, and on that day of the week all green-tagged items were 50 percent off, so Galen got the shirt for $1.00. The lettering evidenced pilling after having been laundered many times over the last couple of years, but Galen loved to wear the garment nonetheless. That day, the shirt was underneath a navy blue fleece zip-up hoodie also acquired from the same thrift store for $4.00. His ensemble was completed with grey cargo pants - purchased from the Oneida Wal-Mart - and Wolverine Men's Potomac English Moc Work Boots that came from the East Syracuse Rescue Mission Thrifty Shopper store. Brand new, the boots would retail for $69.99, but in used but good condition Galen got the pair for $7.00. Indeed, he like Jesse had mastered the art of living on a budget.

It was Ray's turn to respond:

"Yeah, well, you were over der fightin' dat Bush's war so he and dat Cheney could make money fer dat Haliburton. Dem guys is oil men, and dose was just wars fer oil and to make Cheney's Haliburton more millions! Well, now Omondi is gonna pull all our boys outta der because he ain't all about oil and money, you know? And hey, I'm sorry fer givin' you a tough time. It's turnin' around out der and you'll get a good jab. Yer a hero der buddy for servin' our country, even if it was a war fer oil. You jus' did what you had ta do, you know? Hey Donna, I wanna pay for dat guy's lunch so gimme his check!"

"Look Ray, it's kind of you to pay for my meal, and I thank you. And I apologize for insulting you, it was uncalled for" Galen said conciliatorily; the embers having cooled in his speech. But, as he had the rapt attention of the eatery, he took a deep breath and continued:

"You people have to understand that the old America is over. There are wealthy elites who run the Federal Reserve and the big banks of the world. Some of these elites are involved in the entertainment industry, politics, the news media, technology sectors, Big Oil - which I know that you have no trouble believing - and foreign governments. They manipulate the world economy and the American politic. Many of these elites have names you are familiar with and they are creating a single world economy and system that they believe will increase their wealth and control. Omondi is their 'Manchurian Candidate' so to speak - but I doubt that most of you are familiar with that movie or that phrase. They believed correctly that his charm, charisma, and the whole 'first black president' angle would win over Americans and that his radical Marxist belief system will deteriorate America to the point that it will be a quasi-third world nation ready to be absorbed into a new North American Union. Once America loses her power, they can fully control the world. It's coming at us like a runaway freight train, and we have to get ready. Now, here's a newsflash for all of you, are you ready?"

There was two seconds of silence before a male patron at a back table yelled "what's the newsflash - that you're a freakin' nut-job?" which elicited hearty laughter from the three buddies who sat at his table and a few other patrons scattered about the eatery.

Galen ignored the stab of the verbal shiv and waited for the laughter to end before continuing; his phizog as grim as the voice the carried the dramatic anger of Jack Nicholson's "you can't handle the truth" moment in the movie A Few Good Men:

"The Pentagon will deny this because they've been told to by the current presidential administration and the one before it. Likewise, those in the mainstream media who know this truth have been threatened with imprisonment or worse if they report it. The soldiers who were there when it happened have been threatened with their lives if they open their mouths. But, I can't sit on this any longer and I don't care if anything will happen to me. Folks…I will say on the record that Osama Bin Laden has been dead since December 12, 2001, and I'm the one who blew his brains out in a cave at Tora Bora."

Strangely enough, only a few of the patrons laughed this time, while the "lizard woman" proclaimed "this guy should be committed. I'm serious, somebody call 911! I don't have my phone with me."

Galen noticed that many were not even sipping their beverages as they were still rapt; either placing credence in what he said or merely finding him entertaining:

"It wouldn't have fit into the 'War on Terror' narrative to have Bin Laden dead that soon. I was actually threatened with a court martial for shooting him without trying to take him alive first. But, as a good soldier, I didn't have much of a choice as he and a group of four or five scraggily bodyguards were shooting at us at close range. We took out his wimpy-assed security contingent quickly enough while most of the Taliban fighters in the area were running for their lives from oppressive coalition firepower. Yeah, it almost seemed too easy, like it was a damn set-up, and maybe it was…"

"Sergeant Leon Bootblack, who was my commander, shouted 'don't waste him Galen' as Bin Laden, out of ammo, sat there on the floor of the cave smirking through his filthy, bug-infested beard. It was then that things got weird…"

"Even though his accent was heavy, Bin Laden himself spoke clear English and looked right at me and said 'you are not to shoot me. You are to let me escape so this charade can carry on. That's the deal that King Abdullah has made with Mr. Rothschild, Mr. Rockefeller, and Mr. Clinton. They have told your President Bush that he must comply. So, pull the clip out of your carbine, cowboy.' Well, I did pull out my clip…after I emptied it into his body at a range of four feet! By the time the clip was kissed, there really wasn't anything left of him but shit, piss, hair, bone fragments, and blood - so there will never be a real 'body' to parade in front of the cameras. Even my good friend Leon changed his tune and said 'nice work, Cowboy!'"

Ray sat silently and listened, but the gentleman who had just a few minutes prior referred to Galen as a "nut-job" now called him "delusional", saying "if you really were in the military, you'd be a 4F! What's next, you gonna tell us that the government has a cure for Cancer that they're holding back?"

"Well, actually…" before Galen could finish his response, he stopped as he recognized a terribly unforgettable voice from his childhood.

The blue-haired, hunch-backed Doris Mathias retired from teaching at Button Road Elementary School in 1996 to the relief of all future fourth graders. Adjectives like "strict" "miserable" and "mean" were used to describe the spinster Miss Mathias by students, their parents, and other staffers of the school. As she was headed for the exit after paying her check she spoke out dramatically "well, we here in the idyllic American village of Chittenango, New York are indeed blessed to have in our presence a former straight 'A' student of mine who went terribly astray. Galen Moss is now a career lunatic who thinks he killed Osama Bin Laden. Will we be known for both that particular fairy tale as well as for the Wonderful Wizard of Oz? God help us and Lord save us! I'm going to the Ten Pin for a healthy dosage of Scotch!"

The erstwhile teacher and current alcoholic's quip elicited a round of laughs from some of the patrons - a few offering support in the form of statements like "yeah, Doris, I wish I could go have a few shots with ya!" and "why don't ya take the storyteller with ya and get him good and liquored-up and see what kind of B.S. he has then!"

Moss the "cowboy" was staid and again he sat and waited for the din to die down before continuing:

"The government has been feeding you the myth that Bin Laden is still alive. 'Dubya' towed the line and followed orders by telling the Pentagon to be quiet, but he agonized over doing so. If this country holds together long enough, before his term is up the current occupant of the White House will announce one morning on national television that Navy SEALS killed Bin Laden 'overnight'. And the thing is the SEALS may actually kill one of his look-alikes. There will be videos of a quote-unquote body that will appear on Drudge and YouTube. The puppet masters will decide when the time is right, and their obliging arrogant marionette president will be maneuvered flawlessly. The trouble is that I screwed up their initial plan by wasting their real boogeyman."

It was Ray, Jesse, and Erica that were listening most intently. As Galen took a few seconds to collect his thoughts, it was Ray who spoke up and announced "hey, I believe da guy", which brought a retort from somewhere within the eatery of "then you're both whackos!" Ray then asked "Hey Galen, do youse tink dat 911 was an inside jab?"

Galen knew the answer but did not respond to Ray's question. Instead, he behaved as though he did not hear and carried on with his story:

"The longer that Bin Laden the figurehead stayed alive, the bigger the profit the elites could generate from the perceived 'war on terror.' It's complex and convoluted how this whole thing works, but I will say that the fall of the Twin Towers was used to send a subliminal yet powerful message to the American sheeple that their Capitalist society was being slowly but deliberately destroyed to make way for something new. Bin Laden was the boogeyman that could serve as both the mastermind of that terrible act and and as a distraction…"

"But that's the thing, ladies and gentlemen; yes, he was a terror mastermind but not as powerfully or effectively as he has been portrayed. He was just one piece - albeit a big piece - of an extensive and yet disjointed jigsaw puzzle…"

"He would say 'poop' and all of the junior jihadists would ask 'how high' - but once I took him down there was an immediate replacement for him - an entire cabal mind you - that's even more ruthless and more effective. You see, Osama Bin Laden was on the Saudi payroll as well as that of the Illuminati - but the Saudi royal family doesn't always play nice with the Illuminati elite. Bin Laden was a figurehead for all sides. The Bin Laden family is extremely wealthy, and Osama liked the Dollar - despite being an anti-American Islamic cave-dwelling terrorist. He was extremely valuable and I forced them all into a Plan B by offing him. But man, I fear that Plan B is more terrible than Plan A…"

"It's a mafia for want of a better term; the Taliban, Al-Qaeda, Hamas, Hezbollah, Islamic Jihad- they're all gangster families in the Islamic terror syndicate. Right now, it looks like Al-Qaeda has the strongest infrastructure and leadership - new leadership that would make Bin Laden look like a Boy Scout. Because Bin Laden was so loved and respected despite his relative impotence, he controlled the tempo of the terror threat to America. While all of America and much of the world thinks he's alive, his death has cleared soil for other members of the mafia to extend their root structure. He was the big finger in the dyke and now that dyke is leaking. I would not be surprised if the elites see opportunity knocking as the new 'dons' with America's destruction in their sites whip their wise-guys into shape. I would not be surprised to see a terrible event take place soon - a really terrible event that could quickly further the goals of the elite's desire for a one world system. It's a Plan B that could turn out better than Plan A…"

"I thought I did a good thing by killing Bin Laden. My brothers and sisters in arms thought I was a hero. But, it was not what the elites wanted and my remaining six years of service were made difficult. I couldn't get promotions that I was entitled to, as paperwork was always 'lost'. But now, they may think I did them a big favor. They can continue to hold up Bin Laden as the face of something more sinister than they can even understand and yet ultimately, they will get everything they want."

Donna was about the ask Galen to leave, but he got up from the counter on his own. As he headed to the door he again said "thank you" to Ray. Ray was then heard to say "poor guy, he's lost his whole life. Dat Bush and Cheney and der blood for oil really screwed him up - damn Republicans!"

Indeed, while Ray heard everything that Galen said, it was though he didn't really listen. It was all too scary and complex to try to understand. Such was the case for most at Donna and Sam's that afternoon - simple American sheeple, ignorant by choice, only caring about the basic things that directly impacted their own personal spheres and believing everything the government-controlled mainstream media told them.

"Hmm…Galen Moss - I thought that name sounded familiar. My lead guitarist Trey knows that guy. There in some sort of 'militia' type thing" Jesse said to Erica as he popped a forkful of meatloaf into his mouth.

“Wow…do you believe his story?” Erica asked Jesse, her brows furrowed as she stared at her half-eaten lunch, as if there would be some sort of clarity in the meatloaf and potatoes.

As the patrons of Donna and Sam’s began to filter out as it would soon be 3:00 p.m. and closing time for the day, they laughed amongst themselves and wondered what “tomorrow’s entertainment will be.” Segments of his dreams and visions began to play in his mind like a movie trailer, and Erica could see the look of discomfort etched into Jesse’s face as he answered her:

“Yes, I am inclined to believe him,” he said.

“Jesse, I’ve got a 3:30 appointment with my new lawyer and then a 4:30 with a financial advisor. My babysitter can only stay until six. Tomorrow, the local media outlets all want time with me. Winning all this money creates some complicated issues, but I am so happy! I’ll have a new life now; a good life! Can I call you sometime soon? You know, just a date, not to be your sugar momma! But, if it wasn’t for you I wouldn’t have anything,” Erica declared joyfully.

“That would be fun, Erica,” was Jesse’s distracted reply.

Erica was nice woman and attractive to Jesse’s eye, but he had bigger concerns than dating. In the sea of thoughts that spun through his head, he had the notion that Erica’s new dollars would not be valuable for long, but if it helped her in the short term that would be wonderful. But what about her “new life”?

Indeed, Jesse was a man wearing an invisible backpack filled with startling dreams, frightening visions, and heavy concerns…

# 9

# Radio Salad

It was a quiet time when Jesse laid his head down for bed on Wednesday, November 25th. It was the night before Thanksgiving when all through the house not a creature was stirring - well, not since he had trapped and released unharmed a mouse. Dean and Cassandra had left that afternoon to spend the holiday with her parents in Ogdensburg, so there were no X-rated sounds coming up from downstairs through the floor.

Jesse had not seen Erica Cox in person (only over Skype) since their lunch at Donna and Sam's thirteen days prior. Still, in the course of their animated conversation in front of the Ten Pin that day before lunch, they had exchanged phone numbers, Skype I.D., and e-mail addresses. Likewise, Erica had "liked" the Facebook page *Jesse Same - Elvis Impersonator* although she had yet to see him perform; as the two gigs the act was booked for since Jesse and Erica had met were private corporate events not open to the public. While still using the social media monolith as a promotional tool for his act, Jesse had made his personal Facebook page inactive in September, believing that as a whole, the site was just a gathering place for narcissists and psychopaths and invasive to one's cyber-privacy.

By phone, Skype, and e-mail, Erica was keeping Jesse up to date with events transpiring in her "new life" as a multi-millionaire. After a matter of days she received her lump sum payment, and after having paid taxes she had just that day settled up all of her delinquent credit accounts; per the advice of her lawyer and her financial advisor. The day before, she had treated herself to a brand-new 2010 Cadillac Escalade with a deep purple paint job, purchased with cash from those shysters at the McMurtry Auto Mall in Oneida. She had been shopping for clothes for her sons and planned to buy a "reasonable" house in Manlius after Christmas. There was so much to do, but she assured Jesse that she would be "frugal and responsible." Her financial adviser was handling her investments and encouraging her to save, and after her long bout of unemployment she would never again have to worry about job hunting as long as she was careful.

Strangely enough - or perhaps not, based on your viewpoint - the sudden acquisition of a huge sum of money paved the way into a relapse of former vices. In the miniscule period of time since "getting paid" Erica had again taken up smoking cigarettes and consuming alcohol; she telling Jesse that it helped to "ease the stress of her transition." No matter what the nomenclature or rationale she used to qualify the resumption of old habits it concerned Jesse; and not only because of her two young sons.

As Jesse was falling asleep at 11:03 this night he had his radio on at low volume. Lately, he would listen to one of two conservative talkers that aired in the 9:00 p.m. to 12:00 p.m. time slot; either new local talk radio host John Alvares live on WFBL-AM 1390 or the nationally-syndicated Michael Savage on three hour tape delay over WSYR-AM 57. Who to listen to was always a tough decision for Jesse to make as he enjoyed the work of both men immensely. As it would turn out, Alvares would receive more listens because he was "live" in the Central New York broadcast region and not on delay. And, Jesse knew that Alvares may not be on the air much longer as the more well-known Savage was beating him in the local ratings and WFBL might be forced to take on a nationally-syndicated conservative talker to better compete with WSYR in this time slot.

But, on this particular night it was Christmas music that Jesse was falling asleep to; WYYY-FM 94.5 having begun its annual play of nothing but holiday music. Indeed, the station had been spinning nothing but Christmas recordings since Sunday the 22nd, and although he didn't mind, it seemed to Jesse that it started earlier every year.

It was the Beach Boys rendition of *Frosty the Snowman* that was playing as Jesse was drifting into a warm, welcoming sleep. After Mike Love sang the line "he led them down the streets of town, right to the traffic cop" there was a crackling interruption that sounded like a citizen's band or EMS radio transmission. At first it didn't alarm Jesse, as on occasion quick bursts of these communications would cut through the FM frequency. But, as Jesse could understand clearly the two words that were spoken - they being "police state" - he didn't think it was his imagination making a pun on the lyric of that particular part of the song.

The song's broadcast resumed for a few more seconds unfettered. Then, the song was again interrupted after the line "paused a moment when he heard him holler stop" by that same crackling voice that Jesse was now sure he recognized. The voice spoke "we won't have an effective police state with an armed citizenry - especially the rural hicks that cling to those guns and their Bibles. We have to seize this opportunity and go take the rural guns. I believe that the weapons in the inner cities will actually help us."

He was sure he was hearing this, and while feeling awake he had the concurrent sense that he was asleep. While his awake brain issued the command to "sit up", his sleeping body would not respond. As *Frosty the Snowman* bounced jauntily to its conclusion, there was a simultaneous static sound that had submerged in its background a conversation between the familiar voice and another one or two male voices. Jesse's brain interpreted this as the radio salad that often occurred at night; where distant radio broadcasts would creep into those of a more local origin.

The voice Jesse had been hearing was not the supernatural male voice that had spoken to him in other dreams and visions. Likewise, this was not the voice of the individual who resembled the Rasta-styled Morgan Freeman. Jesse's brain now knew the voice crackling through the radio belonged to Jomo Omondi, the current President of the United States.

The level of static was now equal to the volume of the broadcast coming from WYYY. As a jingle for McMurtry's Auto Mall - *you'll always go far in a McMurtry car - Cadillac, Pontiac, Chevrolet, get our best deal every single day* played during the commercial break after Frosty the Snowman, a different male voice crackled ominously through the static:

"So, Mr. President, we have reason to believe that there will be some manner of nuclear device, albeit small, in New York. It's not enough to destroy the city, but it'll still cause a big scare and certainly irradiate a number of blocks and likely kill some people in the immediate blast zone. The terror it sends through the city will do more damage and kill more citizens than the actual device. There may be a larger nuclear bomb in Miami, if we can believe the chatter. Additionally, we have more intelligence that indicates they have different events in motion involving fuel tankers, suicide bombers and chem/bio agents. These appear to be concentrated on the East Coast and also in Los Angeles and Las Vegas. This looks to be a well-orchestrated and meticulously-planned series of simultaneous attacks which was initially drawn up in Pakistan..." the voice said.

"Yeah, but Bin Laden's been dead since December of oh-one" the President's voice interrupted.

"Be serious, Jomo. He was the key player, but the infrastructure he put in place operates very well without him. And it continues to be financed every time a stupid, self-centered U.S. consumer swipes a credit card issued by Bank of America or Chase. Now, just picture the TV commercial during a football game… ah, let's see, the Alabama Blazers are playing the Tampa Bay Buccaneers. Okay, here it is: Vera Bradley purse, $99.00. Alexander Wang knee-high boots, $625.00, financing the collapse of America and the start of the One World Corporation: Priceless! There is nothing that the Rothschilds and Soros can't buy. For everything else, well, there's nothing else!"

The second voice sounded as if he enjoyed reciting his parody, but then turned humorless as he continued:

"But, Bin Laden being dead has made this more difficult, especially from the perspective of public relations, so to speak. We've had to use his look-alikes for all of the tapes that have been periodically sent to the media. We've had to contrive the messages, not that it takes much imagination. And honestly, he was a tremendous help in keeping those who would do our dirty work fired-up. If anything, he was a motivational speaker to those foul-smelling jihadists. While there are others with his skills in the plotting and planning department, there are few that could inspire like he did. The soldier who defied orders and killed him lives somewhere in upstate New York. He's been out of the Army for a couple of years, but we're concerned that he won't keep his mouth shut forever. If there ever was a time he needed to be quiet, it would be now. We've got to find him and eliminate him."

"Okay, I see the humor in the parody of the MasterCard commercial, and yeah, that pinhead soldier needs to be offed, but are these events gonna further our goal?" was the voice of the President.

"Yes, these events will allow you to implement Martial Law and go for the redneck guns. You know that the U.N. has already advised the Pentagon to prep the National Guard and that all police forces in the target areas have been issued bulletins and advisories as to how to train their officers to start controlling the streets when this all goes down. After that, everything else will fall nicely into place" the second voice answered.

"Okay, so what do we do?" the President's voice asked, and to Jesse it sounded like it was spoken through a smiling face.

"You order your generals not to attack the sites they have targeted in Pakistan. Likewise, you tell the FBI to refrain from arresting anyone in this country on their list who they feel may be a threat until we give you the 'OK' to do so. An arrest or two will be good for keeping the Great Unwashed pacified - but not until just before we believe the fireworks are about to start. We will get you, the Veep, your families, and everyone important in this government out of town just before it happens" the second voice said. It was then that a third male voice - sounding gravelly and old with a heavy European accent spoke slowly and evenly "we always knew you would play ball, Omondi."

"So, when do you see these events going into motion?" Omondi's voice asked with obvious glee.

It was the second voice who answered: "based on intelligence, it'll be in the middle part of De…"

Jesse was awakened by the sound of someone rapping on the back door at the bottom of the stairs that led to his apartment. He was blasted from sleep before he could hear the last sentence of the dream or whatever it was in total, but he was certain that it was the word "December" that was being spoken. Disoriented, his feet hit the floor as WYYY played Elvis's *If Every Day Was Like Christmas Time* with the static and interrupting voices now gone. As he pulled on his sweatpants, Jesse was lucid enough to say to himself "I need to work that into the repertoire…oh wait, it already is."

The rapping on the door continued as Jesse headed down the stairs. When he reached the bottom, he asked "who is it" as there was no peephole on the door to look through.

"It's meeeee, lemme in!" Erica yelled, making Buddha, the pint-sized, pug-faced mutt next door start yapping. As soon as he heard Erica's voice Jesse could tell she had been drinking. As he had already asked who was there, he could not pretend he wasn't home or still asleep. He had no choice but to open the door.

Indeed, the 5' 4" tall blond was petite and very fair; some would even use the adjective "beautiful." At 32 years of age, she still looked the part of the all-American blue-eyed girl next door. Her hair was parted center-left, being full and straight and hanging over her shoulders. Her nose was small and her lips thin but wide, and when she smiled the grin went seemingly ear to ear, revealing teeth that were perfect. The last time Jesse saw her over Skype she wore little makeup save for a touch of eye shadow, but tonight the naturally pleasing face was veneered with eyeliner, mascara, and red lipstick.

When Jesse had lunch with Erica, she was dressed modestly in Lee jeans, black sneakers, and a light blue sweatshirt under a utile black trench coat. As she stood at his door, she wore the same trench coat unbuttoned, but instead of jeans and sneakers there was a tight black Lycra miniskirt, black nude pantyhose, and black heels. In place of the blue sweatshirt was a satiny purple low-cut shirt. Her fingernails were painted in a shade of purple that matched the shirt.

"Hey handsome…I've called you three times but you haven't answered your phone" she said, and as she spoke she wobbled just a bit. "Nicholas and Christopher are staying with my sister overnight, so I've got time to spend with you…unless you've got one of your groupies up there" she continued, and as Jesse was once again disoriented and trying to rebut her, she continued, proclaiming "yeah, but none of your groupies could ever make love to you like I can!"

It was then that the Legos in Jesse's mind were immediately re-stacked, and he replied with "make love? We're not married! Actually, we're not even dating!"

"Oh, listen to you Mr. Christian man, needing to be married before sex! Well, you know that I offered to marry you! Then, we could…"

As Jesse stared at her dumbfounded, she stopped mid-sentence, wobbled a bit more, and then leaned with her left shoulder against the white door case for support. She looked as though she regretted the statement she he just made as she then continued on:

"Jesse, I'm really, really, really sorry. I've had a bit too much to drink tonight…you must think that I'm some kind of tramp." As she said this, she fumbled through her black leather purse and retrieved a Marlboro 100 full-flavor and a white Bic lighter.

"Yes, Erica, I am a Christian man. Because I am a Christian man, I'd marry a woman who likewise shares my faith in Christ. And, while you are a beautiful woman, I'm going to - with the help of the Holy Spirit - fight my sinful desire to take you up on your little offer. I mean, we aren't even dating let alone married. But, when you finish your stogie, we can go upstairs and I'll make us some coffee and we can chat" Jesse offered.

"Thank you, Jesse. That would be really nice" she said, her speech ever so slightly slurred but her desire to be sober and coherent very strong.

They were quiet as she finished her smoke and then tossed the butt into a puddle that had formed in the yard behind the house from the rain that had fallen over the past two days. Jesse heard a "plink" and then a "ssssss" sound as the burning butt hit the water, and with its considerable volume he came to the sudden realization that he was again experiencing an intensified sense of hearing. He now heard laughter and murmuring voices as he and Erica stood outside, and yet there were no other people as far as he could see in any direction. These voices had to be coming from nearby cars, neighboring houses and from the Ten Pin - but normally they would not be audible outside; save for summertime's open windows.

He heard clearly the forceful *lub-dub lub-dub* of a rapidly-pounding heart, but as he placed his right hand on his chest he felt that his own worked at its usual slow pace. The heartbeat that he heard intermixed with the other sounds belonged to Erica as it worked hard under the influences of nervousness, anxiety, alcohol, and nicotine. And, even now, he could faintly hear Amy Grant's version of *Hark, The Herald Angels Sing* on the radio that played at a low volume upstairs in his bedroom.

While none of the sounds were at an overpowering volume, the mishmash of colliding noises was in a sense its own "radio salad." And yet, while in this state, Jesse was to be able to discern certain sounds as they would increase in volume as though he was meant to hear them. Obviously, he was appointed to hear the conversation between the president and two other men, but how did it get picked up by his cheap clock radio? Why was this conversation taking place on the night before Thanksgiving? Was it a conference call that was somehow, someway picked up by other radios, or was it an act of the supernatural that piped the call into his radio while he slept? Jesse was inclined to believe the latter.

"Earth to Jesse, come in Jesse" Erica giggled before looking at him with a solemnity that belied the titter as she then asked "are you alright?" To Jesse it sounded like she spoke through a hollow tube as there was still a cacophony around him. She leaned into him and he could hear her lungs fill with air as she breathed as well as the beating of her heart; albeit slower now as she was becoming relaxed.

The Chittenango Police Station was two blocks away, and despite the distance Jesse could hear two officers who stood in the parking lot talking about what one of them referred to as "Martial Law Enforcement Training with some soldiers coming down from Fort Drum." The officer lamented that he was supposed to be off the entire week next week, but now he had to attend two eight hour "mandatory emergency training sessions" at the Air National Guard base at Hancock Field with the Fort Drum soldiers. The second cop shared a similar lament, saying "yup, I've gotta go to the same dang thing. I mean, this thing just came down tonight! I just called my buddy Brad Ducey, who's a deputy with Onondaga County…"

The first cop interrupted with "yeah, I know Brad; we went through the academy together. He's a good man."

The second cop continued: "well, anyway, Brad said that they got the notice just a little while ago as well. But, because he was in the military, he only has to go to the first eight hour session and not both. He said that obviously every cop can't go, so the Feds instructed the State to notify every department to send just a few of their officers with the idea that they could help prepare the others in their respective departments. You and I are the only two going from the 'Nango."

The first cop then said: "I wonder why this has gotta happen all of a sudden, you know? This came down at 11:15 tonight, but it sounds like the wheels have been in motion for a while. And now, these emergency training sessions have to happen right away. But, how did this get coordinated with the Feds so fast? And, we can't discuss this with anyone in the civilian populace. We have to tell our families that it's just a mandatory training that is overdue and needs to get done before Christmas…"

"Jesse, you're freaking me out! Are you a zombie?" Erica asked in a near panic as she shook him. He continued to hear the cacophony; part of which was her heartbeat that was once again pounding as she was stressed about his seeming lack of consciousness.

“Oh…yeah…I’m alright…sorry, I just thought I heard something strange” was his absent-minded reply to her as his attention was again in the here and now, while concurrently his hyper-acute hearing returned to normal like a sound engineer quickly pulling down a volume fader on a mixing board.

Erica was nonplussed: “Wow, it’s almost like you’re the one who’s been drinking, buddy boy! You were standing there for about thirty seconds just teetering like you were about to fall over. But, you had this intense look of concentration on your face as you were looking down the street toward the police station. I’ve gotta say, I feel pretty sober now, but you…are you sure you’re alright?”

“I’m fine, I’m fine…really” was Jesse’s unconvincing reply.

“I don’t believe you” she said in a scolding, motherly way as she lit another Marlboro. “I’m gonna suck this ciggie down quick and then we’re going to go in and make that coffee and maybe you’ll tell me what’s going on with you!”

“You know, smoking is bad for your heart” Jesse replied, sounding himself like a nagging parent.

Erica blew smoke in his face and then retorted with a smirk: “So is drinking, but like I told you on the phone a few days ago, it helps me to deal with the stress of my new life. I started smoking when I was 12, and kicked the habit cold turkey just about a year ago. After we left Donna and Sam’s that day, I walked next door to Byrne Dairy and bought a pack of ‘Reds.’ Being that I smoked for 19 years before quitting, I got hooked again almost immediately.”

“That’s quite an achievement” Jesse said condescendingly. Erica was seemingly unfazed by his remark as she continued:

"I used to drink as much as anyone else, and quite a bit when I was going through my divorce. After my divorce, I was dating this fellow Dan and he liked his Labatt's and I liked to help him with it! But, he dropped me when his ex-wife decided that they should reconcile. After Dan, I quit when I got together with old man Eddie because he was a recovering alcoholic and it was torture for him to have alcohol around. But now he's out of my life and millions of dollars are in, and that brings pressure."

"Is Eddie's last name Ramsden?" Jesse asked.

"Yes, it is, why do you ask? Do you know him?" she responded, sounding nasally as she blew smoke out as she spoke.

"He was my mother's boyfriend for a short while when I was a kid. You did say he was twice your age, and for some reason it just clicked that he was the same 'Eddie'. He lived with us for a couple of months and he often hit my mother. He was a mean drunk and I was terrified of him. He killed my two pet turtles by throwing them against a wall."

"Oh my gosh, Jesse, that's awful" Erica exclaimed as she tossed the second butt into the puddle to join the first. "And, he's mean when he's sober, too. What a small, small, world, and your poor mother! Please give her my condolences…I mean, if I don't meet her first."

"She passed away ten years ago; died of a heart attack at the age of 44 while walking home after finishing her shift at Dave's Diner. She was a heavy smoker. When the paramedics arrived she was already gone. They said that she was lying on the sidewalk with a cigarette still burning in her fingers" Jesse answered solemnly.

"Oh, Jesse, I'm really sorry, that is so young" Erica offered with true sincerity while giving him a quick hug.

"She was a wonderful woman, and she did it on her own because I didn't have a father around" Jesse said as Erica pulled away; wobbling as she was still slightly tipsy.

"No wonder you reminded me that smoking is bad for my heart. Well, don't you worry! I had a physical yesterday - now that I can afford to see my doctor - and she said my heart is as 'fit as a fiddle.' So, if I need a few Marlboros and a few whiskeys or hard lemonades to keep me calm while I get all this money stuff straightened out, I am going to indulge" Erica spoke affirmatively through a 1000 kilowatt smile.

"Or overindulge while dressing like a call girl" Jesse rebutted.

Then, the 1000 kilowatt smile morphed into a scorching visage of anger that could have incinerated Jesse as she shot back: "Hey, I'm a grown-up who doesn't need another grown-up to tell me when to say 'when' and how to dress, okay? As if anybody would really be concerned about what happens to me anyway! That little 'fit as a fiddle' heart of mine has been broken one too many times! I've lost everything in this life except for my sons - and now that I have money at least I won't lose them! Do you think that being a mega-million schmillion zillionaire is gonna make anybody love me!? Huh!? Screw you, Jesse SAME, I thought that you were DIFFERENT, no pun intended!"

Her brand-new purple Escalade was parked in the back lot off of Rouse Street, next to Jesse's Grand Cherokee. Her heels went click-clack on the pavement as she stomped away toward her vehicle while she cried with heaving sobs. Jesse was frozen in time, regretting the "call girl" remark, and not knowing what to do, as the Legos in his mind had been scattered again.

When she reached the door of the Escalade, she turned toward Jesse and under the street light he could see the make-up smeared on her face from the hot tears that steamed in the chilly night air. Thoughts were jumping and bucking through his mind; kicking up the loose Legos like a rampaging bronco. He thought she was still drunk; and overall in her life a little unstable and a bit floozy. But the horse quickly settled down as he focused in on her face, and she stared back at him.

The Legos quickly restacked as the nature of her condition crystalized for him: she was a beautiful, heartbroken, frightened, traumatized woman in pain.

She wanted someone to love her, be faithful to her, and to be her friend. Once the shards of her broken heart were filed down and glued back together, she would love that man back with a deep, dedicated, unbreakable, and permanent bond. While she would come off as a bit too forward - maybe "floozy" - it was really just an act. Maybe that behavior would attract the man that would love her, she thought.

She was afraid for herself and her sons. Before winning the Powerball jackpot, she had feared that her boys would have been taken away from her by their father because of her deteriorated financial condition that did not allow her to care for them as well as she wanted to. Stephen Cox informed her days after now five year old Christopher was born that he was divorcing her, as he had found a "sugar momma" to marry that would allow him to leave his backbreaking, on-again off-again job working for a landscaping company. The new wife was an orthopedic surgeon residing in a 1.5 million dollar home in "The Preserve", a gated community in Manlius. Stephen met 46 year old Dr. Esha Kodali while installing a koi pond and rock garden with multiple waterfalls in her backyard. The new boy-toy husband could now pursue his desires to be a science fiction novelist without having to "bust his ass anymore in the hot summer sun."

Erica and the boys stayed in Chittenango, remaining in the small yellow ranch that she rented on Lake Street, kitty-corner from the entrance to Sullivan Park. When Stephen filed the divorce, she was earning more money than he; although it wasn't a lot. While

Stephen's landscaping work was inconsistent and subject to seasonal layoffs, Erica had a full-time, Monday through Friday job as the receptionist for WNRS-AM and WTTY-FM in Oneida. Being that the staff was small and frequently changing, she occasionally had to "in a pinch" read the news and weather on the FM side, and did so with a natural ability that others would have to learn in college. *I'm Erica Cox, and that's your weather on the fifteens from FM 98 WTTY!*

When declining advertiser revenue forced the struggling pair of stations off of the air in early 2008, Erica could not secure another job. She tried to land work as a receptionist, in retail, and also on air, using a recording of one of her occasional readings of news and weather as a demo to pitch to other stations. She came close to landing a job with WSYR-AM in July of 2009, but as station manager Joel Bianchi was preparing to offer her work doing voice-overs for ads and as a reader of news and weather during afternoon drive, the station's parent company Clear Channel forced Bianchi into laying off a number of staffers; thereby eliminating her chance to get hired.

Now her misfortune had become a financial fortune. But, as she opened the door to the Escalade, she yelled through her tears "thanks Jesse, for the six numbers that completed the destruction of my life!" She climbed in, slammed the door shut, and started the Escalade and with that music began to blast. It didn't require hyper-sensitive hearing on Jesse's part to know it was the song *Ava Adore* by the Smashing Pumpkins blaring through the vehicle's speakers. Even through closed windows he could hear Billy Corgan singing *Lovely girl you're the beauty in my world, without you there aren't reasons left to find.* She backed out and then drove past Jesse and into the parking lot of the Ten Pen.

Jesse saw her enter the bar and was undecided what to do. "I don't need this in my life so I think I'll just go back to bed" he said to himself, and with that he headed up the back stairs to his apartment. Despite being conflicted and agitated concerning Erica and still having the memory of the radio transmission on his mind, he laid down on his bed as was asleep in less than 60 seconds.

Jesse was exhausted and the sleep was deep and dreamless. When the LED numerals on his clock radio showed 1:45 on Thanksgiving morning, he didn't see as he was out cold. But, at 1:46 he was startled awake by the familiar supernatural voice that had spoken in his dreams as it shouted SHE NEEDS YOU NOW!

He sat up on his bed and was wide awake. The voice echoed in his head like digital delay as he had the overwhelming feeling that Erica was in danger. He had fallen asleep with his sweatpants, t-shirt, and green hoodie on, so all he needed to do was to pull on his Cross Trekkers and like it was instinct he was running down the back stairs.

He burst through the door at the bottom, across the small backyard and through the puddle where her two cigarette butts still floated. His sneakers and the bottoms of his sweats were now wet, but he didn't feel the icy cold water.

He was nearly struck by a green Volkswagen Beetle that was headed toward Genesee on the one way Rouse Street, but as the male driver roared "watch out jerk" through his opened window, Jesse did not hear.

He ran past the dark, wood shingle façade of the front of the Ten Pin and into the side parking lot. There were only two vehicles parked there: Erica's Escalade and a black Ford pickup belonging to Eddie Ramsden.

Eddie had Erica pinned against the driver's side door of the truck, and as she screamed "let me go you dirt bag" he laughed in a hoarse, gravelly fashion that sounded as though it came from the pits of Hell as he proclaimed "you're still hot, baby!". As Jesse got closer, Eddie began to kiss Erica's neck while rubbing his crotch against her. She kicked his shins and tried to scream, but Eddie now had his right hand over her mouth.

Shirley Parks, the 75 year old widower that lived in the little white ranch house on Seneca Street next to the parking lot heard the ruckus, as did her King St. Charles Cavalier Spaniel named “Cecelia”, who barked frantically and ran in a tight circle on the floor near the foot of Shirley’s bed. “It’s just the normal noises over there, so shut the hell up! And don’t pee on the floor again or I’ll feed you to Earl Skidmore’s Dobermans!” she hollered at the nervous little dog that unbeknownst to her was indeed urinating as it barked and spun.

“Back off, Eddie, or I’ll cripple you” Jesse commanded as he stood a few feet away.

The smaller but still remarkably handsome man with tanned skin and full hair - only now the hair was white and and the once taught belly was loose - did as he was told and took his hands off of Erica. As she struggled to catch her breath, Eddie turned toward Jesse, cocked his head, and again laughed in that same hoarse, gravelly manner that used to give him chills as a boy.

“Hey, it’s Jesse the turtle boy! Long time, no see! You still look like a pansy! Uh…your mommy ain’t here to protect you from me now, and this ditzy whore ain’t gonna do it, so why don’t you get outta here before I really mess you up.”

“Run, Erica!” Jesse ordered her, but being semi-paralyzed with fear, she couldn’t move fast enough, and Eddie grabbed her shoulders and again pinned her to his truck door.

“Ya know, I killed his gay little turtles because I wanted him to be a man ‘cuz he had no dad in his life. His mom didn’t like that, so she hit me with a beer stein and put me in the hospital. I wound up in jail for the first time after that. I guess I didn’t keep that bitch in line as well as I should have. Well, I’m gonna keep you in line

Erica, 'cuz I like the idea of you bein' my sugar momma, Miss Moneybags! Now gimme some love or else!" While Eddie verbalized the phrase "or else" he pushed his torso into Erica, causing her to gasp in pain.

A rage arose in Jesse like none he had ever experienced. With that fury, it seemed as though everything was in slow motion as his right fist exploded into the right side of Eddie's face.

As the man who used to smack Tammy Jo Same around staggered in stunned disbelief, blood trickling from his mouth and his right ear, Jesse asked him with a cool fury "or else what?"

The cocaine in Eddie's system temporarily dulled the severe pain from the cracked cheekbone and three broken molars. Still, the right side of his face was swelling black and blue, causing a partial closure of his right eye. The blow should have knocked Eddie unconscious, but he was as resilient as he was evil.

Erica stood quivering as Eddie regained some of his balance by leaning against the bed of his truck, his eyes glaring with rage under the parking lot's floodlight. As Jesse watched the man, ready to strike him again, he saw the rage suddenly vanish as if a dimmer switch in his brain had been dialed down. As the metaphorical molten lava ceased flowing in his eyes, his legs began shaking and his hands trembled. Himself seething, Jesse again posed the question "or else what?"

Eddie's swelling face and brain caused his speech to slur as he answered with a high, thin voice absent all the former bravado:

"Uh…I dunno…nuthin' I guess. Uh…I'm really bleedin' and I don't feel good. We ain't gotta fight Jesse, okay? I gotta bad heart anyways, ya know?"

"That one was for Erica, now this one is for my mom and my turtles" was Jesse's response; sounding as cool as Clint

Eastwood's character Dirty Harry when he spoke the inimitable "go ahead, make my day."

Before Jesse could drive his potent right fist into the now defenseless man's face a second time, Eddie's eyes rolled up as his brain shut down, and he collapsed to the asphalt in a motionless, pathetic heap.

Dan Furman was the first cop to arrive on the scene. Jesse had "overheard" his conversation with another cop in the police station parking lot a couple of hours before.

The first thing that Officer Furman saw was Jesse holding the traumatized Erica tightly; stroking her hair and telling her that "she was going to be okay, that he wouldn't let anyone else hurt her or her sons." The good cop thought he heard the sobbing woman tell Jesse that she loved him and would do anything for her 'hero' - but he wasn't completely sure of what she said as her face was buried in Jesse's chest.

But there was one thing that Dan Furman was sure of. He was certain there was a fourth person on the scene, a mysterious witness that he would never divulge. This witness looked like actor Morgan Freeman only with cornrows in his hair. "Weird" was all the cop could say to himself as he saw the man standing with his left hand on Erica's back and his face close to her head while Jesse comforted her. It was "weird" that the man was crying and seemed desperate. Yes, it was "weird" that the man was saying something to the woman - pleading with her - but considering the gravity of the situation she did not listen, or perhaps she couldn't hear him?

After the mess was cleaned up, Jesse would face no charges. Eddie had to be resuscitated in the ambulance, as his "bad heart" wasn't "fit as a fiddle" like Erica's. His unhealthy ticker was over-stressed by cocaine and by the hemorrhaging and cerebral swelling resulting from the powerful blow to his head. When Eddie emerged from a coma four days later, he was charged with attempted rape. Having already served prison time for Second Degree Assault in the 1980's and 1st degree rape in the mid 1990's, Eddie would be headed "up-north" to Clinton Correctional Facility at Dannemora as soon as he was released from SUNY Upstate Hospital.

Two days after Thanksgiving, Town of Sullivan Justice Peter Hence would refer to Erica as a "lucky woman" and likewise to Jesse as a "hero." But, despite the accolades, the memory of that Thanksgiving's early morning hour would not leave Jesse's mind. No, Jesse would not forget the bizarre image that only he and the "mysterious witness" saw under the parking lot's flood lights. What they saw were a pasty-skinned boy and girl looking to be in their early teens - and they appeared to be administering cardiopulmonary resuscitation to Eddie.

Indeed, they looked like normal kids who maybe didn't get out into the sun often enough or eat quite enough. The boy had straight but tousled brown hair that hung over his forehead and ears. He wore an unbuttoned navy pea coat under which was a gray pullover hoodie with *WOW* printed across the chest in black lettering. Faded blue jeans and red Keds Royal Hi sneakers completed his ensemble. The girl wore a black knit hat that sat loosely on her thick red-streaked brown hair that was stylishly close-cropped, cut above her shoulders and sweeping across her forehead. She sported a zipped-up black hoodie sans any graphics or logos, and baggy gray sweatpants with CHITTENANGO running vertically down the right leg in black lettering and BEARS in the same style down the left. On her feet she wore white Nike sneakers bearing the black "swoosh".

Everything about this pair of teens looked normal - except for their eyes. The boy and girl each possessed solid-black eyeballs showing no color or light and seemingly lacking pupils and irises. When they looked up from Eddie and met gazes with the mysterious witness that resembled a Rasta-styled Morgan Freeman, they became "spooked." The two teens abandoned the

CPR effort and ran across the parking lot toward a steeply-banked wooded hill where they disappeared into the dark.

# 10

# Underdog and Auld Hornie

Jeremy spent the Friday and Saturday following Thanksgiving with Jesse, and the father and son had a marvelous time just "hanging out." Jesse couldn't tell Jeremy the true reason why he slept through Thanksgiving Day and didn't have a turkey dinner - other than to say that "nobody invited me over for Thanksgiving, so I just caught up on my sleep."

No one did invite Jesse to Thanksgiving dinner, and it made the six year old boy cry when Jesse gave his son the half-true alibi while they sat on the couch that Friday evening watching *The Marvelous Misadventures of Flapjack* on Cartoon Network. Jeremy was a loving and sensitive boy, and he was brokenhearted that his dad didn't have a turkey dinner with all of the trimmings.

"It's so mean that nobody invited you to dinner. I hate that mom made you go away! Sometimes she's like the wicked witch of the east in the Wizard of Oz and I want to pour water on her! And I don't like Dennis! He buys me and her lots of stuff, but he doesn't love me like you do! You're my dad and I wanna be with you! I wanna be with you and sing 'Teddy Bear' in your Elvis band. I wanna be with you and go fishing in the pond where the silver carp lives." As Jeremy shuddered and began to weep, his father was likewise teary-eyed as he held his son and tried to console him.

"I love you too Jeremy and one day soon we'll be together forever. We'll be together in a place where there are ponds full of shiny silver carp and streams filled with the most beautiful rainbow trout that you've ever seen" Jesse whispered to his son.

"Heaven is a lot nicer than Stormalong, right?" Jeremy asked.

"Yes" was Jesse's answer.

"And nicer than Candied Island?" was the boy's follow-up

"Oh, there's much better treats to eat than candy!" was Jesse's emphatic reply.

"Is Heaven as beautiful as the Emerald City where the Wizard lived?" Jeremy asked, switching his geographic point of reference, but still shuddering as his tears of heartbreak were slowly abating.

"The Emerald City and the entire Land of Oz were beautiful, just like you've seen in the movie. But Heaven is way more beautiful than Oz" Jesse answered with bright eyes and a smile, his tears likewise having ceased their flow.

"Is Jesus more powerful than the Wizard?" Jeremy asked; his face still wet with tears but his eyes now wide and beaming.

"Well, one day all the world's wizards and witches will kneel before Jesus and call Him 'Lord.' Does that answer your question?" Jesse answered with a smile, his left eyebrow raised quizzically.

"Yessss!" was Jeremy's excited response.

They sat quietly and heavy-lidded for a few minutes before they both drifted off to sleep, as Doctor Barber uttered his patented phrase "hmm, yes" to young Flapjack.

This time, it was young Jeremy who dreamed vividly…

He and his dad were fishing in the aforementioned pond in Sullivan Park on a sunny, late afternoon in summer. They stood on the rocks at his dad's favorite spot where the outlet brook began its journey from the pond - flowing under the wooden bridge on the path behind them, and down through the woods and then under a culvert at Tuscarora Road. From there, it peacefully meandered within a farm field before finally reaching its destination; passing under the towpath then feeding the Erie Canal.

There were lots of frogs that lived along the banks and in the murky water of Sullivan Park Pond. Not far to the right of where Jeremy and his dad fished, two males, one being nineteen years old and the other twenty suddenly appeared. Both men wore oversized jeans, baggy black t-shirts, and black flat-brimmed, sideways-facing caps with the phrase *OBEY* sewn above the bill in white lettering. Each of the young men kept his jeans from falling by clutching them with his left hand. In this dream, Jeremy said to his father "dad, those guys are bad men. They live right here in the 'Nango. You dreamed about them once, remember?"

"Yeah, Jeremy, I did dream about them and now you are too, son. They are very dangerous but there are millions just like them. Stay over here and don't even look at them" Jesse warned his son as he cast his bread ball-baited line into the pond and then rested his fishing rod on a large rock.

"Dad, I'm afraid" Jeremy moaned as he started to quiver fearfully.

"Don't be afraid, son. We're not alone, see over there? Help is coming" Jesse said calmly while pointing across the pond where two men walked along the path toward the thugs. Both men were dressed in camouflage t-shirts and BDU pants, and wore black, lace-up boots. Each man wore a Kevlar vest on his chest. What Jeremy couldn't have known in this dream was that the two approaching men were Steve Sandifer and Galen Moss.

As Jeremy looked toward Sandifer and Moss, he also met gazes with the twenty year old, dark-haired thug. The thug inquired belligerently "yo, punk-ass, ya'll wanna see us cap some frogs?" And with that, both of the scofflaws pulled Beretta 9 mm semi-automatics from inside the waists of their jeans and began firing into the water while laughing with sinister glee.

As frog entrails and dead sunfish began to float on the reddening water, Jeremy screamed "dad, make them stop!" But, Jesse's only answer was "fish on" as he instead picked up his rod from the rock it rested on and set the hook into something large.

Sandifer and Moss were now standing next to the thugs, and it was Sandifer who yelled authoritatively "drop the guns you animated hunks of human feces!"

While his friend blew the head off of a snapping turtle that had aimlessly wandered in close to shore, the nineteen year old stopped firing and challenged Sandifer:

"What you gonna do old man? Huh? The government took all the guns from you law-abiding Ward Cleavers, yo! I guess your little militia ain't 'well-regulated' now, is it Homes? I think that used to be part of the second amendment er somethin'. Ya'll the reason why they took the guns away! It ain't 'cuz of the terrorists yo, it's 'cuz of rednecks like ya'll! They think ya'lls more of a threat than them A-rabs or playas like us! Remember how jus' before all the shit went boom that those militia dudes shot up that school? That's why they took your guns, Rambo! But playas like us still have our nines. And yo, looky-look, I'm 'a settin' fire to this old piece of paper called the constipation!"

As the thug held the document and placed the flame of a red Bic lighter against the bottom left corner, Galen Moss corrected him with a voice reminiscent of Jack Nicholson that seethed "it's the U.S. Constitution you idiot!"

This was the most terrible dream that young Jeremy had ever had. Jeremy tried to scream, but he couldn't. And how could his father be so intent on reeling in a fish at a time like this?

Sandifer and Moss stood motionless, as suddenly they were handcuffed, ankle-chained, and clothed in orange prison jumpsuits. Next, each of the thugs turned grinning and faced the dad and his son. Jeremy recognized the large graphic of the Seal of the President of the United States printed on the chest of the t-shirt worn by the nineteen year old. Encompassing the chest of the black t-shirt worn by the twenty year old was a graphic that Jeremy didn't recognize - that being the Illuminati symbol of the All-Seeing Eye and triangle. The boy was as much frightened by the images on the shirts as he was by the two who wore them.

The thugs began to walk closer, turning their "nines" sideways and pointing them at Jesse and Jeremy. It was then that Jeremy heard splashing and his attention was drawn from the thugs to a large silver carp that his dad was pulling from the water.

As Jesse dropped his fishing rod and hoisted the thirty pound fish from the water by using one hand on each gill cover, he scolded Jeremy, saying "I told you not to look at them! Now, look here!"

Though silver, the huge fish was likewise iridescent and reflected the colors of the rainbow on scales that possessed mirror-like qualities. As the fish thrashed it freed itself and from Jesse's grasp and instantly grew to about six feet tall. It was now bright blue and surrounded by gorgeous multi-colored light as it assumed the shape of a man with outstretched arms but no discernible facial or bodily features. As Jeremy stood stunned with a gaping mouth, Jesse smiled and said "that's the Holy Spirit son, praise the Lord!"

The Spirit spoke in a virile voice, saying "don't be given over to a spirit of fear, Jeremy" and as it did so, dozens of silver carp leaped and splashed on the surface of the pond - seemingly filled with joy.

Next, the Spirit's head turned toward the thugs that continued to evince malicious grins as each pointed his 9 mm in the direction of Him, Jeremy, and Jesse. At the same time, an African-American man who appeared to be in his mid-fifties bedecked in U.S. Marines dress blue and white had appeared out of nowhere. The cocky, self-assured demeanor of the thugs vanished as the Marine screamed into the face of the one wearing the Presidential seal "I fought to preserve your integrity and you who is not even a citizen of this nation became an interloper president. Now get down and give me fifty!"

Next, the Marine screamed into the face of the thug who wore the All-Seeing Eye and triangle on his shirt, saying "you are the puppet masters who control the arrogant marionette in chief. You have no idea that your syndicate will soon be owned by a single man! But in the meantime, get down and give me fifty!"

After issuing his orders, the Marine disappeared, as did Moss and Sandifer. Left on the bank of the pond in a pile was the Marine's dress uniform, next to one empty orange jumpsuit and one set of unshackled chains.

Then, the Holy Spirit was metamorphosed into a lion and roared "ABOMINATION" - the sound of it echoed through the pines, oaks, and birches that shrouded the pond. With that potent declaration, the two thugs were floating face down in the pond that was now totally placid as the carp had ceased leaping and the air temperature was dropping. After a moment, the spirit vanished in a bright flash and what were once the thugs were instead two pine boughs floating on the still water.

“He makes all things new” Jesse said to Jeremy, and as he spoke the temperature dropped further and snowflakes began tumbling and swirling from the sky. Now, the pond was covered by a thin layer of ice and six inches of pure white snow covered the ground.

“It’s good news, right dad?” Jeremy asked before trying to catch a snowflake on his tongue.

“It’s the best news in the universe for those who believe and the worst for those who don’t” Jesse said while making a snowball, and then Jeremy popped awake, understanding much of what he had dreamed, but not all of it.

Simultaneously, Jesse had been dreaming as well…

He and Jeremy were fishing at the same spot on the pond on the same late afternoon that summer - and Jesse had the knowledge it was August 2009. There were others enjoying what Sullivan Park had to offer, but he and Jeremy were the only anglers on the pond. Across the pond and beyond the wooden pavilion near the parking lot, a group of teenage boys played 3 on 3 half-court basketball.

Jeremy stood patiently on the rocks while a fat, juicy nightcrawler was looped around his hook that was cast about 10 feet from shore. Thus far, the bait had not enticed any fish.

Jesse was using one of Aunt Berta’s bread balls, but the carp didn’t seem to be interested on this late afternoon as evening approached. Jesse was thinking that perhaps he should switch to a jointed Rapala plug to see if he could interest any of the bass that finned in the shallow pond.

As he set his fishing rod down and began to reach for his tackle box, Jesse was startled by a raspy voice that asked from about six feet to the right “how’s the fishin’?”

Jesse and Jeremy both turned in the direction of the voice. Jesse saw three figures standing there; two that were somehow familiar. Dressed in denim shorts, tie-dyed t-shirts and leather sandals were the teenage boy and girl with the coal-black eyes. And even though it was summer, it appeared by their pasty white skin that neither of them got out into the sun very often. "Those kids were giving Eddie CPR" Jesse said, but no one heard him.

The third individual was the man who inquired as to the quality of the fishing, and he was unfamiliar to Jesse. The skinny, sickly-looking man with hunched shoulders stood about 5' 10" tall. The old man smiled ear to ear; revealing a mouth that was absent most of it front teeth. Tobacco juice dribbled form the left side of his mouth. The man's head was shaved and his face was gaunt, with high cheekbones. His ears seemed a little too big for his head and they stuck out nearly straight and Jesse thought he looked as comical as he did scary. His nose was long and pointed – as was his jaw - and his neck was thin with cartilage and veins easily visible under his wrinkled skin.

The man wore a white t-shirt under faded denim overalls. The shirt was stained by chewing tobacco spit on the left shoulder and around the collar. On the man's feet were dirty green rubber boots that extended to just below his knees.

"Wow, you startled me! I didn't hear you walk up! My name is Jesse and that's Jeremy"

"Yup, them kids there already told me what yer names were. Them's smart kids, alright - better than my Ouija board sometimes! Aw dang, hold on a minute, I got another tooth comin' out" the old man said, and with that he spit out a stained molar and with it went a wad of tobacco with a "plink" into the water. As Jesse and Jeremy stood aghast, the man continued while the kids with the black eyeballs sat down on the bank and cast out their fishing lines:

"My name is Josiah, but you can call me 'the Eel.' I was a New York State champeen (sic) wrassler (sic) here at Chittenango High in 1942, or was it 1842, aw hell, I cain't (sic) remember! Nobody could ever pin me 'cuz I was tooooooo slithery, so that's why they called me 'the Eel'. You git it, there Messy - oh, I mean Jesse, ha ha!"

"Uh…sure, Josiah, I get it" was Jesse's confused reply.

"You said you wrestled for West Genesee, not Chittenango" the girl butted in, her voice monotone and void of expression.

"West Genesee, Chittenango - it's all the same, ain't it? What gives - you callin' me a liar?" Josiah answered back red-faced, the veins in his neck looking as though they would explode.

"We're here to fish, not to tell stories" the boy with the black eyeballs interjected, in a voice as equally monotone and expressionless as that of the girl.

"Well, lemme tell you hip-cats and kittens a story anyhoo! It's a hell of a fish story and all my stories are true! I've been alive so long I cain't even remember my birthday!" Josiah exclaimed.

"So, what's this fish story you want to tell us - is that it?" Jesse asked, sounding confused as though there was a punch line he was supposed to get and missed.

"Why dontcha' shaddup n' listen" Josiah fired back, his face again red and the veins in his neck bulging. Before continuing, Josiah spit a stained, rotted molar at Jesse, who was now wearing his white jumpsuit normally reserved for Elvis impersonation.

"Auld Hornie cured my cancer, yep he did. I had the Big C in my stomach and up my ass, and he came to my house out in Warners…"

"You said you live in Chittenango" the girl interrupted in monotone.

"I got a summer home in Warners, okay? Now, shut the hell up and lemme tell my fish story" Josiah answered angrily, before turning back toward Jesse and continuing on in a calmer manner:

"So, I was ridin' the porcelain bus and jus' got done bustin' a move. The water was all red with blood, jus' like what's gonna happen ev'rywhere in a few years, and my skinny little deformed turds was a' floatin' in it. And man, my stomach was achin' like usual! Yup, everything I ate at that time come right back out as skinny, deformed turds or bloody barf!" Josiah paused for effect, his bony, wrinkled face revealing a wide smile missing many teeth. Then, he continued:

"My wife was always sayin' I needed ta' git ta' the doc, but that sumbitch was too expensive and we didn't have the free healthcare that the one world corporation is gonna make ev'rybody have before the water turns ta' blood. So, I jus' drank Pepto-Bismol like it was water, but it did no good. Whiskey was one hell of a lot better, but it didn't cure my ills, no sirree. Nope, all it did was take away my amiable temperament and turn me into one mean-ass drunk!"

"So, there I was, wipin' my bloody bee-hind - and lemme tell ya there Elvis, I went through a lot a' Cottonelle! I looked at the toilet paper to see what the poopy to blood ratio was, and as I dropped the wad down in ta' the bowl, I looked up and he was jus' standin' there! He was a wearing a Scottish kilt and over top a' that a white doc's coat. He spoke in a brogue n' said, 'I'm Doctor Auld Hornie and I kin take away your cancer.'"

"Next thing ya know, the Big C came a' buzzin' and flyin' outta me as big 'ol five inch long bugs! They looked just like some sorta grasshopper-hornet-scorpion hybrids with funny little human heads. Them there heads had angry faces and long blond hair, uh-huh! They looked kinda like my bitchy wife after she used the Clairol! They was a buzzin' around my loo and bouncin' off the walls! Then, Doctor Auld Hornie said 'aye, they will be flyin' around the whole world and stingin' ev'rybody before the water turns to blood like in your commode. But, you are cured because I am the world's greatest doctor. I can cure any disease!'"

"Then a black hole about the size of a basketball jus' formed where my medicine cabinet was, and all a' them cute little buggers jus' flew through it and they was gone! I thanked the doc because I felt good and for turnin' my medicine cabinet back ta' normal! He told me all I had ta' do ta' stay cured was ta' use my Ouija board every mornin' ta' see iffin he had any messages fer me."

"Show him the leg" the boy with the black eyeballs interrupted, needless to say speaking in monotone.

"Stop interruptin' Aliah, that's rude! I was gonna show 'em" Josiah retorted and then turned back toward Jesse and spoke "now look at this Elvis. A back leg fell offin' one of 'em as it was bouncin' against the wall."

From out of the bib pocket of his overalls Josiah retrieved what appeared to be the hind leg of a grasshopper, only larger. If pulled straight from its contracted position, the leg would be 7 inches long. The exoskeleton was light brown in color and 11 spines ran the length of the tibia. As Josiah held the leg by the femur between his forefinger and thumb, Jesse could tell that the spines were sharp enough to pierce human flesh in the same manner that a thorn from a rose bush would. The claw at the end of the leg was bent in a semi-circle and looked metallic, resembling a tiny scythe.

Jeremy turned from his intense concentration on fishing and looked at the leg. As Jesse was temporarily speechless in his dream state, it was Jeremy that remarked "that thing is scary and gross! I'm glad I won't be here on earth when those locusts are stinging all the people that won't believe in Jesus!"

Josiah was sincerely compelling as he rebuffed Jeremy:

"You don't believe that silly rapture story, do you Jeremy? You know that's a whole buncha bull-hockey! Jesus is just a pansy who couldn't pull himself down from that cross, so how can he come and get you if he's dead? Come over here and do some fishin' wit Grampa Josiah and I'll tell you a really great story about the real god, the one that is gonna rise to power really soon and fix all the world's problems! The whole world will believe in him and it will be Utopia here on earth!"

"Come fish with us Jeremy. We can catch all the fish we want and so will you. Come, right now" the girl with the black eyeballs spoke hypnotically.

"Jeremy, stay here with me! Josiah is not your grandfather and Aliah and Lilitu are evil kids" Jesse commanded his son. He didn't know how he knew the girl's name, but anything is possible in dreams, eh?

"How do you know I ain't his grandfather when you don't even know who your daddy is?" Josiah snapped; his face again flushed and the veins again bulging from his neck.

"Yeah dad, who is my grandfather?" Jeremy asked innocently

Jesse's head was spinning as he groped for answers that he did not possess. Before he could offer some manner of reply, it was an incensed Josiah who spoke next:

"So, ya ain't gonna let your precious little brat fish with us? And, you call Aliah and Lilitu evil? You think yer all that 'cuz you get blessed with hyper-sensitive hearin' and you can hear people's heartbeats? You know what Messy, yer stressin' me out! You won't need no hyper-sensitive hearin' to hear my overwrought heart!"

With that, Josiah drove his right fist through his overalls, causing blood and a few bone fragments to splatter into the pond. The old man then ripped his beating heart out from behind his breastbone and held it in his right hand in front of Jesse's face. Jesse could see and hear the sloppy-looking organ beating rapidly and with an irregular rhythm, reminding him of a red and gray bag filled with Mexican jumping beans.

"Yeah, you've caused me to have a heart attack and you broke poor Erica's heart. And tonight, for the first time she's putting cocaine up her pretty little nose and right now her heart sounds a lot like mine! It's that whole nearly gettin' raped by Eddie thing, ya know? She needed you to comfort her tonight but instead yer sleepin' on the couch wit yer punk brat! Well, I really ain't got the heart ta do this, but I guess I gotta give you guys a little preview of Revelation sixteen-twelve, bein' that you think that yer little Jesus is gonna come and take ya home before it comes t' pass. Let's pretend that this pond is the Euphrates River!"

Josiah placed his heart back into his chest and all the gore was gone. Next, he bent down and swept a large clear glass bowl through the water and the pond began to drain out through the outlet brook with a powerful torrent. As Josiah laughed and Jeremy cried, the pond was dry after a matter of ten seconds. Hundreds of fish flopped on the mud bottom, and Aliah and Lilitu laughed and walked hand in hand amongst them. Jesse saw Aliah kick the small silver carp that he had caught during the summer of 2006 and unhooked with care.

Josiah was now dressed head to toe in black; including a clergy shirt and collar and wide-brimmed Amish-style hat. He held a black-covered New King James Version bible in his left hand and was flipping through the pages near the back of the book with his right. It was then that he spoke mockingly in an exaggerated southern drawl:

"People, please open yuh Buh-hybles to the book of Revelation, Chapter sixteen, and 'ah' will read verse twelve, and it goes like this: *'Then the sixth angel poured out his bowl on the great river Euphrates, and its water was dried up, so that the way of the kings from the east might be prepared.'"*

After finishing his reading, he closed the bible and looked up toward the clear blue sky and chortled. Concurrently, Aliah and Lilitu had assumed the culturally-accepted form of naked green space aliens with frog-like skin, large heads, and those same coal-black eyes - only larger. They were now hovering on either side of Josiah, and Aliah held the silver carp in his long-fingered hands. The head was still fully intact - albeit crawling with maggots - but all that was left of the rest of the fish's body was its skeleton.

A frightened Jeremy was clutching Jesse's waist with his right arm while sucking his left thumb like he did as a toddler. Jesse repeated the words of the Holy Spirit from his son's dream as he said "don't be given over to a spirit of fear, Jeremy." While he spoke those words, he snatched the bible away from Josiah and opened it to the second chapter of the second book of Thessalonians.

"That was a convincing act of drying up water, Josiah" Jesse spoke firmly, "but you and I both know that Sullivan Park Pond is not the Euphrates and you and your demon kids here are not the Kings of the East. So, why don't you two E.T's go phone home while I share some more of God's word with Reverend Josiah." Jesse paused for a second to draw a breath before continuing:

"The second book of Thessalonians, chapter two, verses eight through twelve say: *'And then the lawless one will be revealed, whom the Lord will consume with the breath of His mouth and destroy with the brightness of His coming. The coming of the lawless one is according to the working of Satan, with all power, signs, and lying wonders, and with all unrighteous deception among those who perish, because they did not receive the love of the truth, that they might be saved. And for this reason God will send them strong delusion, that they should believe the lie, that they all may be condemned who did not believe the truth but had pleasure in unrighteousness.'"*

After reading the passage, Jesse said: "You know, Josiah, you stand in the accordance of the workings of Satan, but you are not the 'lawless one' that the apostle Paul wrote about. Let's face it buddy, you're a piece of work! The lawless one will be handsome, articulate, and beguiling. You're ugly, inarticulate, and frightening as opposed to beguiling. Yeah, I've got to hand to to you, emptying out the pond like you did requires supernatural ability, but bro, the lawless one is going to school your skinny evil keister in the wonders and deceptions department. Lies and wonders in the guises of Aliah and Lilitu will create more deception than you do…"

Josiah fired back red-faced: "Big talk from a third-rate bible-thumpin' Elvis-impersonator who ain't got the guts to quit doin' that and write his own songs! Yeah, you got some mysterious grampa named Richard who gave you lots a' cashola but you ain't got no daddy and yer momma was a whore! She ain't in Heaven with your dead Jesus; she's in Hell copulatin' with Auld Hornie!"

He was still dressed in the preacher's garb and as he hurled his invective at Jesse spittle flew from his mouth, as well as another molar. He wasn't finished, and as Jesse could only listen and Jeremy sucked his thumb, Josiah flourished in his diatribe:

"Oh, your little dead Jesus might win the war, but we gonna win a whole lotta battles, Jesse! We gonna take a whole lotta those lazy, ignorant, pacified, narcissistic sheeple souls down with us, uh-huh! Yeah, you might have some kinda prophetic gift, but you ain't got the balls ta' use it! You better get on yer face and pray to your little bloody dead man on the cross, 'cuz Auld Hornie knows there ain't much time left. He knows he's in the fourth quarter and can't come back and win, but he's gonna score as many touchdowns as he can to make the score close! Yup, ya better hope yer little dead Jesus comes with His trumpet and angels and raptures yer asses home. Toot-toot-toot, yeah right! Yeah, Jesse…uh…damn…here comes Underdog to save the day…"

Josiah instantly lost all of his zest as he lapsed into a poor impersonation of Wally Cox, the *Underdog* cartoon character's voice as his next statement was "there's no need to fear, Underdog is here…aw shit."

Josiah was once again dressed in overalls as he sat down on the bank of the pond and rested his face on his bony knees. Now, standing next to him was the man who resembled a Rasta-styled Morgan Freeman. He wore a green hooded parka with fur-lined hood, blue jeans, and black lace-up boots on is feet. Immediately, the pond was refilled with water and covered with a thin layer of ice. Suddenly, the trees were bare and there was six inches of snow on the ground as well as on the sitting Josiah.

The friendly man that Jesse had become familiar with in his dreams who was likewise the mysterious witness from the parking lot of the Ten Pen quoted Luke chapter 21, verse 28, as he said:

*"Now when these things begin to happen, look up and lift up your heads, because your redemption draws near."*

And then the dream was over and Jesse was awake…

"Dad, are you okay?" Jeremy asked his father anxiously.

"Yeah, I was just having a really weird dream about the pond, a good guy, a bad guy, and some strange kids" Jesse replied as he shook the cobwebs from his head.

"You were moaning in your sleep, but just before you woke up, you had a huge smile on your face" Jeremy said excitedly, before his visage turned two shades of dismal as he followed up with "I had a really strange dream about the pond, some bad guys, a silver carp that you caught, and the Holy Spirit. I think we need to tell people about our dreams dad, because they mean something is gonna happen."

"Have you been having other dreams similar to the one you just had?" a now wide-awake and fully cognizant Jesse asked his son.

"Yeah…well…sorta" was Jeremy's disconnected reply as he focused on another episode of The Marvelous Misadventures of Flapjack that was on TV.

# 11

# Memphis Blues

The last days of November were restless for Jesse. The dreams that had been invading his slumber were now keeping him from getting a good night's sleep.

There was indeed too much on his mind and the metaphorical Legos would not stay stacked in any manner of structure. While driving Jeremy home Saturday night, Jesse asked him to talk more about the dreams he'd been having. It truly bothered the loving dad that the dreams seemed to be so unsettling to his son. Jeremy would only say "they're dreams about God being mad at the world and devil-people trying to hurt you and me and other people I don't know who love Jesus. I told mom about them, but she said that if God is really real, he wouldn't get mad because he'd want everybody to be happy. She said there is no such thing as the devil and that you believe in weird stuff and I shouldn't listen when you talk about it. But I like the stuff you believe in because I love Jesus."

To spend some time decompressing after her terrible ordeal, Erica had taken Nicholas and Christopher to Williamsville, a suburb of Buffalo. The three of them shared a belated Thanksgiving dinner and spent "downtime" with her cousin Carrie Westervelt, who attended Buffalo State and had graduated that past June. Carrie was the daughter of Erica's father's younger brother, making 'Westervelt' Erica's maiden name before marrying Stephen Cox. The two cousins who could pass for sisters consoled each other; Carrie having just had her heart broken by a handsome lawyer named Gavin and Erica nearly having her heart permanently stopped by the evil Eddie Ramsden. And, despite what Josiah had said in Jesse's recent dream, Erica was not putting anything up her nose. But, after the boys went to sleep each night, Carrie put plenty of alcohol into her body while Erica refrained and instead drank coffee and chain-smoked as they sat in the living room of Carrie's apartment watching movies and commiserating.

Erica offered to buy her younger cousin a "reasonable house" like that which she was going to purchase for herself very soon. Carrie was thankful, but told her to "hold off for now" as she was going to be serving "for a while" in the President's "new civilian security force" and would be spending time training in a "boot camp" at Buffalo State starting on January 3rd.

When she arrived back in Chittenango at 7:15 a.m. on Sunday, November 29th, Erica stopped by Jesse's apartment before heading home. While Jesse had fallen into the first restful sleep he'd had in days just an hour before, she quietly walked up the back stairs while the boys waited in the Escalade. When reaching the door that led into his kitchen, she slipped under it a tri-folded note inside of a white letter-sized envelope with "Jesse" written on the front in blue ink and neat, cursive lettering. Quietly and carefully she stepped back down the stairs, clutching tightly to the varnished wooden railing as her vision was blurred by hot tears.

While Erica was surreptitiously ascending and descending his stairs, Jesse was dreaming about her…

In the dream, he was sitting up on his bed, watching *The Polar Express* on his bedroom television; specifically the scene where

Santa gives Hero Boy the sleigh bell as the first gift of Christmas. Jesse loved the movie and counted it as among his favorites. It was an evening near Christmas, and Jesse should have been performing a special "Christmas Tribute to Elvis Presley" at the Turning Stone Casino, but he was sick with the flu. Even in the dream state, Jesse truly felt feverish and achy as he realized that he had a thermometer in his mouth.

He could hear the voices of three young boys laughing happily as the sounds emanated from the living room and slipped underneath his closed bedroom door. He knew the voices belonged to Nicholas, Christopher, and Jeremy. They were playing some manner of Wii game and were having metaphorical barrels full of fun. Jesse hadn't met Erica's sons, but he had the knowledge in this dream that it was the voice of Nicholas who yelled from the living room "mom, can Jeremy stay overnight on New Year's Eve and watch the 2010 ball drop with us?"

"Yes, if they still do it" Erica called out her response out from the bedroom as the boys resumed making their gleeful sounds.

Erica was sitting on the edge of the bed, facing Jesse. She was not "dressed to kill" like the last time he saw her, but instead wore white ankle socks, black sweatpants and a grey sweatshirt with *PROPERTY OF MEMPHIS BLUES* screen-printed in royal blue block lettering across the chest. Above the lettering was a small NFL EQUIPMENT shield logo near the collar. She wore no makeup on her face, and her blond hair was pulled into a white scrunchy and piled on top of her head.

Her face was careworn as she pulled the thermometer from Jesse's mouth and gazed at it with brows furrowed. "Hmm, you're still at one-oh-one. It's time for more aspirin, fever-boy" she said with an impish grin before setting the thermometer down on the lampstand and grabbing the bottle of Bayer.

“Thank you, Erica” Jesse spoke with a hoarse albeit sincere voice that was not much more than a whisper. He took two aspirin tablets from her opened hand and washed them down with water from a clear plastic tumbler bearing the Coca-Cola logo.

As he swallowed the aspirin and water, Erica turned toward the TV and remarked “this is the last time it’ll be on television.”

“Yeah, probably the last time this year” Jesse replied hoarsely.

She turned back to him and with a grave mien coloring her face she said “no, the last time ever.”

Before Jesse could ask her to qualify what she meant about “the last time”, she began speaking again as she pulled the blankets over his shoulders:

“You’ve been exposed to poison Jesse, possibly bubonic plague, and that’s why you’re so sick. There were Al Qaeda agents in this area testing to see how it could be spread through an aerosol-based delivery system, and they’ve got mustard gas, too. So far it seems that the boys and I have been spared. Just relax honey and let me take care for you. Remember, I was a nurse before I worked in radio.”

After speaking, she smiled and then gave him a quick peck on the lips. As she drew her face away from his he experienced a relaxed, soothing feeling that was akin to having his body filled with warm bath water.

“That’s what love is like” she whispered to him as they met eyes, and in that moment he thought to himself that she was the most beautiful thing he had ever seen in this world…

…and then he was awake.

It was 7:25 a.m. and he pulled on a pair of sweatpants and headed for the kitchen. The envelope was on the floor in front of the door, and while scratching his head with his left hand he bent down and retrieved it with his right. The envelope wasn't sealed, so the letter pulled free easily and as he stood there shirtless and with bed-head, he began to read:

*Dear Jessie,*

*After the incident with Eddie, I wanted to get away for a few days, so the boys and I went out to visit my cousin Carrie who lives near Buffalo. We had a belated Thanksgiving dinner with her and just generally chilled out. Though she's my cousin, Carrie is like the younger sister that I never had. We even look a lot alike! She is my father's brother's daughter so you have a point of reference. Carrie is joining that new civilian security force that Omondi is rolling out. It's the one that he mentioned in his campaign as being as powerful as the actual military. I always thought that Carrie was politically conservative like I am...well, at least she used to be. Unfortunately, Omondi has worked his mojo on her.*

*While visiting Carrie, I got an e-mail from an old friend from college named Kate Sims. She now lives in Memphis Tennessee because her husband works as the equipment manager for the Memphis Blues. Wasn't there some famous singer that you impersonate who lived in Memphis? LOL!*

*Anyway, over the course of a couple of e-mails she's convinced me to relocate there, and I'm going. Gosh, I've already got the sweatshirt! The boys and I will stay with Kate and her husband for a while, and if I like it down there I'll buy a house. But, either way, I'm getting the "hell outta Dodge" Jesse, and I'm leaving tomorrow. I have 3 months on my current house lease and I'm going to pay off the landlord before I leave. I've already arranged for movers to come and haul my furniture and I'll keep it in storage until I settle in. I'll have Button Road Elementary send*

*Chris and Nick's school records so I can register them in Memphis.*

*Living here is just too painful. And after what happened with Eddie, I'm a little bit scared because he has some crazy friends. There are too many failures and bad memories and I need to start over. But, I do have one good memory and that is the memory of knowing you.*

*Because of six numbers that you gave me that were originally quick-picked for someone else, I'll never have to worry about money again. I can have the best of everything if I choose to - well, not everything, because I won't have my hero named Jesse.*

*Jesse, I hope that someday really soon I rediscover your Jesus. I know all about him, but I have a tough time believing in him anymore. My Uncle Craig, Carrie's father, is the pastor of that little Baptist church on the main drag in Kirkville. I reached out to him when things got really tough after I lost my job at the radio station and there were no prospects. He just said to me "You gotta do what you gotta do" and told me that there were government programs that could help. After that, he wouldn't return my phone calls. But you know what's funny, Jessie? He called Carrie yesterday and asked to speak to me! He wanted to know if I would be interested in helping to finance a new building for his church! Can you believe that!? Even Carrie is appalled that her father would do such a thing after refusing to help me through his church when I was broke and struggling. And then there are those money-hungry shysters the McMurtry's. I got a good car, but after doing some research I see that they way overcharged me and took advantage of me being a "dumb blond." Wow, so these are the followers of Jesus, huh? Do all Christians other than you wear pins with the Freemasons logo on their collars?*

*If there were more Christians like you Jesse, I'd believe what you believe because I really want to again! I am going to miss you and I'm crying right now as I write this. I came to your door the night before Thanksgiving with the intent of seducing you and you wouldn't give in, as much as you wanted to. Wow, I can't believe I did that and I'm very ashamed. I need to cut down on the drinking. But, the point is, you were true to your faith and that is so commendable.*

*You are the best guy I have ever known. And you saved my life because Eddie would have killed me. Although we've only known each other a very short time, I truly am in love with you. But, despite how I feel about you I need to go away. It's as much for my sons as it is for me.*

*Please don't try to contact me today or tomorrow and please don't try to locate me in Memphis because it will cause me too much pain.*

*All of my love,*

*Erica*

He folded the letter and it set on the counter next to the coffee maker. This bit of news did not surprise Jesse considering all that Erica had been through, but it hurt nonetheless. It was in that instant that he stepped off of the ship named *Denial* and set foot onto the pier of acknowledgment. Indeed, in that moment he came to grips with the fact that his feelings for Erica were strong and he would likewise miss her. He was forced to admit to himself that he would worry about her. As he leaned on the counter in a daze, the dream he had just had minutes before began to replay in his mind as tears rolled down his cheeks.

It was a chance to start a new life and leave behind the pain of the former existence, so she was headed to Memphis at the behest of an old friend whose husband worked for the Blues. In the dream she was wearing a Memphis Blues sweatshirt. She told Jesse over the phone a week or so ago that she loved football and was a cheerleader in high school, but that the Buffalo Bills were her favorite team.

Over the last few weeks Jesse had learned there was no irony in his dreams, and likewise he did not believe in coincidences. Planted into his recent dreams were both biblically-related and personal prophecies - from the subtle to the blatant. It did not faze him that he dreamed of her wearing a Memphis Blues sweatshirt before reading her letter. But, what did she mean when she said that The Polar Express was being televised for the last time ever, and what about terrorists and the plague?

He would honor her request and not attempt to make contact. Instead, he would pray fervently for her and leave it in God's hands. She was leaving and it would be better for all parties involved, he thought to himself as he scooped ground Maxwell House into the filter that rested in the basket of his white Proctor Silex 12-cup coffee maker.

As Jesse leaned against his kitchen counter and stared out the window that overlooked a quiet Rouse Street, Jeremy, Allison, and Dennis were spending the early morning decorating the Christmas tree in the house that Jesse once lived in. As Jeremy sipped a cup of hot chocolate, Dennis hung in the center of the 6 foot tall artificial pine a 3 inch in diameter plastic ornament with colorful stars around the trim and the Freemasons square and compass symbol in the center.

"Hey, that's the Freemasons. Dad said that you guys are Universalists and you are trying to control the whole world. I don't think that we should have that on a Christmas tree" Jeremy spoke adamantly.

While Allison shook her head and said "I wish your father would learn to keep his thoughts to himself" Dennis laughed good-naturedly and remarked:

"If your dad joined us, he might actually be inspired to do something with his life other than make believe he's Elvis Presley. We're a group of successful, hard-working men who love the Great Architect of the Universe. That's who God is, Jeremy. There's only one God but he has different names. He can be Buddha, or Allah, or even have horns like what my friend Geoff the Wiccan believes. If you want to believe in Jesus that's okay, but to believe that Jesus is the only way to God is wrong, Jeremy. We all go to Heaven if we do good things to help society and work hard to make ourselves better people. Remember to live by the Golden Rule Jeremy, 'do unto others as you would have them do unto you.' If you believe in God, you have to believe that he's too big to fit inside of one religion, don't you think? There are so many good and godly men who are freemasons but aren't stuck on Jesus as their savior. He was very special, but mostly a good teacher who was killed by bad Jewish people."

Jeremy was furiously impassioned as he screamed "you're a liar, Dennis! You're a liar! God does not have those other names and Jesus is Lord of all and one day even all of the witches and wizards will know it's true! And my dad told me that Israel is special to God! I hate it here and I wanna go live with my dad!"

As Jeremy ran crying to his bedroom, Dennis looked somberly at Allison and asked "do you think that maybe he should see less of Jesse?"

"You know I'm already creating reasons for them not to be together as much" Allison replied sharply, biting her lower lip while staring at the hardwood living room floor.

As the overcast, 53 degree late Sunday afternoon bled into early evening, Jesse lay on the living room couch seeing the Kansas City Chiefs battle the San Diego Chargers in NFL action but not really watching, as his mind was elsewhere. The preceding game at 1:00 featured the Portland Tritons visiting the Buffalo Bills, but he couldn't recall who had won. The Memphis Blues were the NFL team on his mind. As he lay on the couch, The Smithereens cover of the Beatles track *Don't Bother Me* played on Jesse's mental radio. As Jesse saw football with his eyes, lead singer Pat DiNizio sang "I know I'll never be the same, if I don't get her back again, because I know she'll always be, the only girl for me."

Yes, his brain had always been figuratively wired for multi-media spanning the generations. While "Don't Bother Me" played on the abstract AM-FM radio in his head, there were other things that occupied megabytes worth of space on his cerebral hard drive. One of the files taking up space was the perceptual MPEG-4 of Galen Moss sitting at the counter at Donna and Sam's. The memory of him gesturing with his hands while he made his compelling case to the eatery's patrons that he had killed Osama Bin Laden was now playing silently in Jesse's mind as the Smithereens provided the musical backdrop. As the song finished, looping into the mix came the voice that had crackled over his radio on the night before Thanksgiving; the voice that stated "if there ever was a time he needed to be quiet, it would be now. We've got to find him and eliminate him."

Jesse needed to find Galen Moss and alert him that the government was planning his assassination. But would the co-founder of the North Madison Militia think that he was a lunatic when he told him how he knew what the President and his manipulators were planning?

He picked up his cellphone from the coffee table and scrolled through the alphabetized contact list. As he reached "Erica" he almost pushed the SEND button but stopped himself. All the psychological media had cleared from his head except for "Don't

Bother Me" which began to play again. Jesse took a deep breath, moaned, and then scrolled again until he reached "Trey" and then pushed the button to send.

His band mate wasn't answering his phone and the call went straight to voicemail, where Jesse left the message "hey Trey, it's Jesse. I need to get Galen Moss's phone number. Please call me ASAP - thanks, bro."

He set the phone back on the coffee table and changed from a sitting position to a reclining one as he was still tired from a lack of sleep and the Chiefs and Chargers weren't exciting enough to keep him stimulated. His eyelids were heavy and he fought to keep them open, but as a Coors Light commercial promoting their "silver ticket promotion" and featuring a mock press conference with former NFL coach Herm Edwards telling a group of obnoxious men-children that "you play to win" was running, sleep won the tussle and Jesse was lights-out.

By 7:37 pm Jesse was in a dream state. How bizarre it was that he was riding in the passenger's seat of the black 2008 GMC Acadia driven by Jeremy's stepfather Dennis. In the dream they were headed westerly on East Seneca Turnpike-Route 173 from Chittenango toward the village of Manlius. Jesse had the knowledge that their destination was the Masonic hall on Seneca Street, and he was confused as to why he was in the vehicle with Dennis and why he would be going to a lodge meeting. It was then that he saw that his wrists were tied together with rope, as where his ankles. Seemingly, he had been abducted.

Next, he realized that John and Joe McMurtry were sitting in the back seat, laughing over some manner of inside joke that revolved around Jesse. It was now that Jesse realized how much of a physical resemblance Dennis bore to the McMurtry father and son. The high cheek bones, thick wind-proof hair, fake tans; the appearance being very preppy and blueblood. The difference was that Dennis was younger and so most of his hair was still a light shade of brown with just a few streaks of grey.

While he had of course known that Dennis's surname was Dalton, Jesse was now being imparted knowledge through this dream that Dennis's mother Joan had the maiden name McMurtry. Joan was John's younger sister, making John the uncle of Dennis.

While the father and son continued to giggle like school children in the back seat, Dennis took it upon himself to lecture Jesse:

"I had to kidnap you to get your attention, Jesse. You need to understand that Allison and I are not messing around. We are tired of you skewing Jeremy's perception of Great Architect of the Universe. We'll take legal action to prevent you from seeing him if that's what it takes. You've got him thinking that the Bible is the only truth concerning God, and we're trying to get him to understand that yeah, there is one God, but he goes by many names and is too big to fit into one religion. You need to stop trying to Southern Baptist-ize the kid. God is Allah, he's Buddha, he's…"

Before Dennis could complete his pontification, Jesse felt his hands and feet become unbound as he was pulled from the Acadia by a pair of hands that glowed a bright white and radiated color in a prism-like manner. As the hands released him, they morphed into a brilliantly-white dove that winged for a moment facing Jesse before disappearing, leaving him to gasp in astonishment as he could barely whisper the words "oh my…how beautiful."

He now floated above the north shoulder of East Seneca Turnpike where Enders Road went south from the left. As it approached the intersection with Enders Road, he saw the black Acadia that a moment before he was riding in. All action now was at half-speed…

It was nearly dusk and Jesse knew it was a day in late autumn, but the seasonal setting was not important. He could see a vivid sunset straight ahead to the west; resplendently hued in orange, pink, and purple as “Old Sol” sank below the horizon. Above were streaky purple and grey stratus clouds as the sky grew darker higher up.

“Look and listen” spoke the voice that had uttered the same command in previous dreams, and Jesse’s gaze left the captivating sunset and focused on the intersection that was bordered by bare trees and a grassy field on the east side and on the west by split-level and raised ranch houses lacking as much noteworthiness as the mundane upper-middle class families that lived in them.

Although the action was at half-speed, Jesse could tell that the yellow New York State D.O.T. dump truck that was approaching East Seneca Turnpike from Enders was travelling at a high rate of speed. Like looking through a zoom lens, he had a clear view of the inside of the cab of the truck and saw a panicked driver pumping the brake pedal, but there was zero air pressure. As the Acadia entered the intersection, Jesse heard the voice of John McMurtry as he said “Dennis, you’ll be a responsible father to that boy, not like this low-life musician here.”

Jesse tried to avert his gaze but could not. Instead, he screamed out a desperate warning of “look out” as the large International truck chassis with winch on the front bumper slammed into the driver’s side of the Acadia at 45 miles per hour.

Still in slow motion, Jesse saw the airbag pop like a child’s balloon as the collapsing driver’s-side door became like an oversized axe blade, cutting Dennis in two, just below the abdominal region. Jesse saw Dennis’s upper body shatter the windshield as it passed though it; a string of small intestine unraveling like a red, bloody, and feces and food-laden kite string. Jesse saw the lower body smash through the window of the front passenger’s side where he had been sitting, before the dump truck rolled the Acadia over the lower torso and squashed it.

On impact, the dump truck veered to the right and came to a stop in the center of East Seneca Turnpike, facing east. As several other drivers were slamming on their brakes to avoid being part of the wreckage, the Acadia rolled a total of three and a half times, finally coming to rest in roadside brush on the north side of the intersection below where Jesse hovered. Jesse saw Dennis's gory upper torso lying face up in the intersection with one eye missing and the other bulging in fright. Jesse was paralyzed and could not move from the scene as the Acadia burst into flames below him. He could smell the sickening stench of John and Joe McMurtry's flesh burning inside the vehicle.

Suddenly, Jesse was surrounded by darkness. He was no longer floating but instead the lone patron in an IMAX theater, seated comfortably, and yet his immediate sense was what he was about to see would not be entertaining or relaxing.

In 3-D on the screen he saw Dennis and the two McMurtrys rising toward a tunnel of bright blue and white light that emerged from utter blackness. He could recognize the faces of their unclothed, pellucid bodies, and he had the immediate knowledge that what he saw in this graphic and lifelike "movie" was their souls.

Jesse knew Jesus in faith, but now it was though he saw Him in ultra-high definition. He sat on a brilliant white throne in the tunnel of light and Jesse could see that He was likewise the source of that light.

Although he sat, Jesse could tell that Jesus stood at over six feet tall. His hair was thick, wavy and shoulder length; being colored brown and yet having streaks of silver and gold that seemed to change depending on the angle; almost as though the hair had a luminescent quality to it. His eyes were brown but very bright and luminous and for a few seconds seemed to possess an emerald pigment. His brown beard was neat but rugged and his cheekbones were high and his nose was thin, as were his lips. His skin was "tanned" so to speak; and it emitted a warm glow.

Not only did He emit the light the filled the tunnel but likewise He was surrounded by brilliant white, gold, and silver light. Jesus was resplendent in a white robe that sparkled with gold, silver, red, and emerald. Diagonally across his chest was a sash of purple bearing the phrase KING OF KINGS AND LORD OF LORDS - the lettering made out of glittering gold. On his feet were sandals made of pure gold.

Jesse could only gasp in astonishment and wanted to reach out and touch Jesus but again it was though the Lord was on a movie screen. It was the souls of the three men killed in the horrific wreck that instead walked close, but they were halted by a seven foot tall male angel with long, flowing brown hair. He was clothed in white with a silver breastplate that was form-fitting to his muscular chest and had a long silver sash tied to his waist. His magnificent silver wings were twice as tall as he was and reflected the surrounding light.

Three three souls stood at a distance of seven feet from Jesus, with the angel standing to the Lord's immediate right. Behind Jesus, Jesse could see a multitude of angels as well as balls of white light that he knew were the souls of other believers who had recently gone to Heaven. There was much joy and magnificent music in the scene behind Jesus, but where the souls of Dennis and the McMurtrys stood there was an aura of heartbreak so strong that even Jesse could feel it, see it, and be touched by it.

The face of Jesus registered an amalgam of sadness, disappointment, and righteous anger. The three souls appeared to be afraid of the angel who nudged Dennis ahead to stand before the Lord with his left hand while holding John and Joe McMurtry back with this right.

As Jesse saw Dennis now standing before Jesus, the marvelous light that shined and radiated seemed to be hurting the eyes of the man's soul as he raised his pellucid left hand in an effort to shield those eyes. It was then that Jesus spoke, in a voice that was equal parts kindly, warm, angry, and sad; or to be described in a single word - heartbroken:

"Who am I, Dennis?"

"Well, you must be Jesus" replied the soul of Dennis Dalton, the sales manager of McMurtry Auto Mall's North Syracuse dealership - lacking his usual guile, bravado, and confidence.

"Who am I, Dennis?"

"Well, certainly, the Bible refers to you as Lord and Savior, Son of God, Son of Man, and the Great I Am amongst other things. I know that because I've read the Bible" the soul of Dennis answered with a quavering voice.

"Yes, that's what the Bible refers to me as, but your heart does not! You have made the false god of the crescent, the false god of Siddhartha Gautama Buddha, the false god and goddess of the pentacle, and other lying spirits equals to me" Jesus replied with sorrow, but then that sorrow turned to anger as he continued:

"You have served as the leader of the home where my young servant Jeremy lives. You have been purposeful in your attempts to dissuade him from knowing me as the Alpha and Omega, the Beginning and the End. You have been deliberate in your efforts to mislead him with heresies and apostasy while you falsely enlighten yourself under the oracle of Hall and Pike while ignoring my word. Dennis Dalton, your attempts to push my beloved Jeremy away from me have failed! I am the LAMB OF GOD!"

Jeremy could now see Dennis in full naked physicality and no longer in a spiritual state. The confidant, cocky, and shrewd sales manager was now trembling and attempting to speak in self-defense, but no sounds came from his mouth as his lower lip trembled.

Jesus lifted his hands chest high and opened them so they faced Dennis. Jesse saw what he knew that Dennis could certainly see, and that was the hole in the palm of each of the Lamb of God's hands. While they no longer bled, the holes were stained with blood to forever bear testament to a debt of sin paid in full for those who would merely believe. While Jesse could only smile joyously when considering what Jesus did for him, the image of Dennis turning his head away was confirmation that he saw the hands as well.

"Dennis, I was there when you were born as your mother Joan struggled through a dangerous labor that caused her heart to cease beating as you were pulled from her womb. As the physician yelled for a crash cart, I reached into her chest and sparked her auricles and ventricles back into a normal rhythm that still beats to this day. And while I did that with my left hand, I untied the umbilical cord that was wrapped around your neck with my right as a nurse groped for forceps. I had prepared a path for you Dennis but out of love I gave you free will, and with that free will you chose not to follow the path or me."

"You had the opportunity to do great things in my name, but instead you chose to be the god of your own life and attempted to be the god of those around you. You chose tyranny and the pursuit of power and wealth. Through your lust for power and control you have ruined the lives of some others around you. And because of your uncontrolled carnal lust, you fired salesperson Kayleigh Ralston because she would not accede to your demands that she wear skirts above her knees. She cannot find another job and her unemployment benefits have run out, but she has sought me through faith and prayer and she will find provision. Yes, you have ruined the lives of other adults but you will not ruin the life of my beloved little one, Jeremy."

Now, Jesus sounded truly grief-stricken as he spoke:

"Dennis, if you would have made me your Savior and Lord, you would have been forgiven all of those trespasses, and as you grew closer to me in repentance, you would no longer have committed them. I bled and died because I love you, Dennis, but I and my father are one and cannot have unrighteousness in our presence. Had you come to me in faith Dennis, you would have been made righteous through my shed blood. My father's Kingdom would have been shared with you and a royal inheritance would have been yours for eternity. "

The grief then manifested itself in a roar from the Lion of Judah:

"I and my father are one! I am the Word and I am the Truth! Your foul works and your deliberate rejection of me have sealed your eternity. Depart from me Dennis Dalton, for I know you not!"

If the feeling of rejection could manifest itself through facial expression, the countenance of Jesus showed it as Dennis fell backward away from him. Indeed, it was Jesus who was rejected and not the hard-charging Dennis Dalton. Through the free will given to him out of love by his creator, he chose in his earthly life not to accept Jesus' gift of salvation and now found himself falling backward into the pits of Hell.

On the screen in 3-D Jesse watched Dennis fall as John McMurtry was nudged forward by the angel. As Dennis screamed while the tunnel moved away, Jesse could hear in the distance the voice of John McMurtry saying "I'm the most influential elder at Four Corners Community Church. I control the direction of the church and help to maintain a professional yet family-centric façade. Being a Freemason helps me to carry out the works of the Great Architect of…"

As Jesse strained to hear the case that the elder McMurtry made to Jesus, his attention in the IMAX Theater of his dreams was instead forced back to Dennis and the dark, cavernous, reeking place where he now stood.

"You'll have an eternity to thank me for stitching your pieces back together, Dennis" the doctor said with a grin as Dennis peered around confused with a wide-eyed (again with two eyes) look of panic on his face that would never again leave.

"Who are you? Jesus is Lord! Jesus is Lord! I know that now! Let me out of here, please" Dennis cried as he walked in a circle in the dark room, stepping on other souls that were lying on the sticky floor and causing them to remonstrate profanely. All around were moans juxtaposed with cackling laughter and the smell was akin to raw sewage. Indeed, the landscape here was similar to a big city's underground sewer system.

The doctor answered: "Who am I? I'm renowned surgeon Doctor Akbar, but this obviously isn't Jannah! On behalf of Hamas I martyred myself on a bus in Tel Aviv and this is where I am. Something is wrong!"

As a torch mounted on the stone wall flashed to life providing flickering light, Jesse could see as Dennis did the man with a gaunt, gray-tinted face that looked skeletal. His head evidenced tufts of thick, dark hair that looked as though it was once full. His hands were likewise gray-tinted and were more bone than skin. Essentially, he appeared to be an animated dead man in the middle stages of decomposition. His grey legs were bare and covered with unraveling stitches; appearing as though he had been put hastily back together. There was a Littman stethoscope hung around his neck and he wore a white physician's coat covered with blood stains. On the blood stains maggots crawled and fed.

"Where's Allison…oh my god, where is she!?" Dennis asked as he continued to panic.

"Ah yes, Allison. She's not here but in a matter of hours she will be copulating joyously with her ex-husband Jesse, so I heard the Great Architect say" the Doctor answered.

"You mean The Great Architect of the Universe?" Dennis asked hopefully, disregarding the doctor's comment concerning Allison.

"What you thought was G-A-O-T-U was really the G-A-O-T-V which is the acronym for the Great Architect of the Void. Somewhere through the decades, the letter 'U' was confused for a letter 'V' and all of you Masons ran with it. The premise of the lie completed the deception. This is Hell - the great void that will one day be the lake of fire for all eternity. It's void because Jesus isn't here. Wherever Jesus is absent there is void. Jesus is fullness and evil is emptiness. So, this is Satan's world, you get it? He is the great architect of the void. Evil fills this void, allowing it to remain a void. Zero plus zero equals zero. Zero is eternal death while God is spirit and through Jesus' sacrifice is fullness and eternal life in paradise. We both know that now."

"Please, please, I don't deserve this…I did a lot of great things in my life…I…"

As Dennis' soul beseeched whoever or whatever would listen, there was a sudden increase in the moans and cackles and in the fetid odor. Likewise there was an increase in light, and Jesse could see that the soul of Dennis stood in a large circular room with the floor covered with wailing, writhing individuals that could pass for zombies from the film *The Night of the Living Dead* - but zombies they were not. They were tortured souls who had refused to accept the saving grace of Jesus Christ. Those that were newer to Hell still had the energy to run like beheaded chickens while the veterans of the void were too drained to do anything but lay, wail, and scratch each other. The walls of the room of what Jesse now knew served as a receiving portal were stone and on them were strange symbols and hieroglyphics, including an image of the "all-seeing eye". Extending from the room were four arched hallways that resembled sewer tunnels.

Then the light increased and assumed an orange-red hue, and the heat intensified as well - Jesse sensing the rise in temperature but not actually feeling it. As two new arrivals in the form of John and Joe McMurtry ran by screaming in agony, the doctor said "you shouldn't have complained about what you don't deserve. The Great Architect, or should I say Satan - you know, the devil - heard you and is coming to set you straight. I'm going to lie on the floor and lament the 72 virgins that I never got. He gets a kick out of me doing that and who knows - maybe he'll go easy on you?"

The light became intense as Jesse watched in 3-D and he could tell by the steam that was wafting through the room that the temperature had become exceedingly hot. As the shadow of a large, winged entity swooped in on Dennis as his soul let forth an agonized and haunting howl; Jesse was anguished and driven to tremors by the terrible, painful sound. The sound was such a torment to Jesse's soul that he vomited on the floor in front of his theater seat…

…and as he was jarred awake and out of the dream by the buzzing of his cellphone, his olfactory tract was assaulted by the putrid aroma of the hot, fresh vomit that had just been spewed onto his sweatpants.

"Ugh…hello Trey" was Jesse's greeting to his friend as he answered is cell.

"Ugh? Is that any way to answer when I call?" was Trey's retort.

"Sorry, man. It's just that I threw up on my sweatpants in my sleep and it's vile. The buzzing of my phone is what woke me up to this."

"Are you sick? I mean, that's a dumb question right?" Trey answered, sounding concerned.

"Uh…yeah, I'm sick, and no, it's not a dumb question" was Jesse's response, and it wasn't truthful as what he heard and saw in the dream was the catalyst for the reverse peristalsis, not illness.

"Well, you picked a good time to be sick as we don't have any Elvis gigs until a few days before Christmas. You know, Jesse Same - Elvis impersonator isn't working much lately. Are you doing okay financially?"

"Yup, I still have most of my inheritance" Jesse replied straightforwardly.

"Good, man. Between the Nozeloids and Sexxxy Sounds, I'm paying the bills. I can't wait to get the Nozeloids record out because that's really what I wanna do. But anyway, why do you want to get a hold of Galen?"

"Trey, the President and his men are going to try to assassinate him. You know he killed Bin Laden, right?"

"Yeah Jesse, all of us in the militia know, but how do you know? And, what's this crap about the the prez wanting to kill him?"

"He told a bunch of us at Donna and Sam's. And as far as Omondi wanting him dead, I got the information through a supernatural occurrence. I overheard a conference call between Omondi and two other men on my clock radio on the night before Thanksgiving."

Trey answered with a chortle: "Yeah, he shouldn't have run his mouth at the diner, but I'm sure that none of the morons that live in the 'Nango would believe him anyway. They believe everything that the mainstream media feeds them. But hey man, let's not get too crazy with these dreams and visions of yours, okay? You have a vivid imagination, man, and I think you have too much spare time on your hands. Maybe you need to spend more time with that hot little blond that's been stalking you? I mean, she's loaded and could show you a good time!"

"Erica is not stalking me, and I know that you don't put much credence into my dreams, visions, and supernatural occurrences, but I believe they are driven by the Holy Spirit that you also don't put much credence in. Look Trey, I feel strongly about this, so if it's all the same to you, could I have his cell number? There's paper and a pencil here on my coffee table, so I'm ready."

"Okay man, as you wish. If anything, he'll probably get a kick out of your call before he accuses you of being deranged and tells you to get stuffed. His number is 222-5104, got it?"

"Thanks, Trey, I'm scribbling it down right now. Now, if you don't mind, I'm going to toss these sweats into the kitchen trash and then take it outside. Well, take it outside after I put some different pants on. Bye."

As Jesse pushed END on his phone, he found himself worrying about Erica and truly missing her. And now, not only did he have to contact Galen Moss, but he was compelled to deliver a message to Dennis Dalton as well.

# 12

# Secrets

Erica had planned to spend Sunday the 29th packing, but that never happened. The boys were not excited about leaving upstate New York, and as dreadful as life had become for her there, she likewise was not eager to go.

But life for her was changing for the better, wasn't it? Now, she was wealthy. Now, she could buy a house and not worry about having a mortgage. Indeed, she now provided for her sons without food stamps, unemployment insurance, or any other manner of government assistance. Now maybe her sons could find as much joy in their own home as they did in their dad's.

Now, she would no longer have to hear her sons lament "I wish we had as much money as Dad and Esha. Everything they have is better."

One immediate goal of Erica's was to instill into Chris and Nick the virtue that money wasn't everything and that it could be a dangerous thing. Yes, life in the material world was becoming a hundred times better than before, but everything in that world has a spiritual cost as well as a monetary one.

The decision had already been made as she walked out onto the back sun porch of the yellow rented ranch; going outside so she could smoke while she used her new iPhone. There was a rain and snow mix that was falling at 6:56 a.m., and as she sent the call to her old friend Kate she wished she had put a jacket on over her long-sleeved purple t-shirt.

"Hey Erica, what's up honey?" Kate answered pleasantly. Erica could tell that her friend was developing a 'Tennessee Twang', having now lived in Memphis for a little over a year.

"Good morning, Kate, I hope I didn't wake you up" Erica's voice sounded nasally as she inhaled a drag of her Marlboro 100 as she spoke, and then Kate could hear her exhale it - making a sound like a gust of wind blowing across the phone.

"Nah, Mark has to be at team headquarters at 5:00 a.m. during the season after a home game. You know, they've got to sort out uniforms that need to go to the tailor for repairs, get helmets cleaned up, listen to prima donna players complain that their jerseys sleeves ain't short enough, that kind' thing. So, long story short, I've been up for a while! So, you all ready for your flight?"

There was a pause before the nervous Erica answered, as she took a long drag from her cigarette and inhaled deeply before speaking:

"Kate, I've been thinking that this move is being made in haste. Nick and Chris aren't happy about it and honestly, I just want to stay put. I appreciate you…"

Before Erica could finish, Kate interrupted: "Say no more, honey. I understand and I think that you're making the right decision. Now that you won't be struggling anymore, your life up there will get better, you know that. But hey, I need to share something with you."

A feeling of relief swept over Erica as she answered "I'm glad you understand, Kate. And okay, so you need to share something with me?"

"Well, yeah. So this guy you're all crazy over, his name is Jesse Same, right? And he's probably a little teensy-weensy part of the reason why you don't want to… um…how did you put it 'get the hell out of Dodge' after all, right?"

"Wow, I'm amazed that you remember his name! And well, yeah…I kind of hope that maybe he'll fall in love with me. A girl can have dreams, can't she?'

"Sure she can, honey. Now, you said he looks a lot like Elvis Presley and he's a terrific Elvis impersonator and that's how he makes his living, right?"

"Yes. That's how he makes his living, but he would rather write and record his own songs and do something with a different sound. That's one of the things that I want to encourage him to do. I've only known him for a short time but I love him and I want him to be happy in his life. He doesn't need to worry about money because I would make sure…"

Kate interrupted again: "I know you love him, Erica. He sounds like a terrific and talented man, just like his father was."

As Kate and Erica shared a friendly chat over the phone, Jesse's cheap cellphone buzzed with a return call from Galen Moss:

"Hello?" Jesse answered, having woken up just five minutes before.

"Jesse? This is Galen Moss returning your call."

"Hey Galen, thanks for calling me back. I'm sure Trey filled you in on why I wanted to talk to you."

"So you're 'Jesse Same - Elvis Impersonator'. You're the reason why some of the dimwits here in Chittenango have sworn that they've seen Elvis alive and walking the streets! What are they gonna see next, flying monkeys? The residents of this one-horse town need to lay off the sauce…but anyway, sir, you've got this notion that the government wants to rub me out? You heard something over your radio? Are you one of the aforementioned dimwits?" As Galen spoke, he at first chuckled but then sounded stone-cold serious as he asked Jesse if he was one of the "dimwits."

"Galen, I was sitting at a booth next to the counter at Donna and Sam's where you sat. I heard you say that you killed Osama Bin Laden and I believe you. You seem to know what's…"

Moss interrupted: "You know I did see a guy that could pass for a young Elvis. Yeah, sure, I remember you being there with an attractive blond woman. Is she your wife?"

"No, she's not my wife, and yeah, she's certainly attractive. But look Galen, you can consider me crazy if you like, but I won't rest until I tell you about my supernatural occurrence. I heard Omondi and two other men…"

Moss interrupted again: "Look Jesse, I don't want to be rude and I appreciate you watching my back. You might be gifted with the prophetic or something, I don't know. I didn't mean to refer to you as a 'dimwit' either and I apologize, but it does seem mighty strange sir, not WHAT you heard but HOW you claim to have heard it. I know those bastards want to kill me. They're conspiring…"

This time it was Jesse who interrupted: "They've already conspired, Galen. They're coming for you and it is imminent. They need to propagate the myth that Bin Laden is alive and they fear that you won't keep a secret and guess what - you didn't! Like you said, you messed up their globalist plans by going against orders and killing him."

"Alright, Jesse, fair enough - you've got my attention. You know the pastor that just got fired from Four Corners Community Church, a guy named Matt Carrier?"

Jesse answered: "I used to attend there until they started straying too much from the meat of God's word. That's why Matt got fired, because he was convicted by the Holy Spirit to stop preaching a feel-good prosperity gospel. There has been a Satanist agenda pushed into that church by one of the elders, John McMurtry. He's a freemason and I've had a dream about him as well, and it didn't end well."

"Matt said that the Holy Spirit used you to convict him. But look, Jesse, Matt has joined us in the North Madison Militia. I used to go to church with my parents when I was a kid, but I kind of lost my faith - especially after what I saw happen in Afghanistan and Iraq. Matt and I have talked and he is getting me to reconnect with Jesus and some of the others to come to faith. Some are receptive but Trey in particular doesn't want to know. But Matt is one amazing dude and he's making me believe again…"

As Galen spoke the words "making me believe again" Jesse could tell that the tough, intelligent, hard-as-nails former soldier was choking up.

"So, Matt has joined up with your militia and he drives a blue Dodge Ram pickup like I dreamed about. Trey is with you…"

"What's that, Jesse? I didn't hear you" Galen cut in.

"Oh, nothing Galen - I was thinking out loud" was Jesse's cursory response.

"Jesse, I want to talk to you more. What do you say that we have lunch today at the the Ten Pin? It's not just a bar, the food is actually good and I don't think I can go into Donna and Sam's ever again."

Meanwhile, on a roofed porch in another part of Chittenango, a telephone conversation continued:

"Just like his father was? He doesn't even know who his father is or was" Erica giggled.

"You told me that his mother would only tell him that his grandfather lived in a little town near Memphis. Well, I know who his father was" Kate spoke proudly.

Erica felt her heart start to pound erratically as she asked "who" through a constricted throat.

"There is a gentleman down here named Roscoe Same. He's a Blues season ticket holder and has a luxury box for him and his family and friends…"

"Roscoe Same? Is he Jessie's father? Oh my god" Erica interrupted excitedly.

"No he's not. Now let me finish my story, okay?" Kate answered with her own giggle.

"Okay! I'm all ears!" Erica voiced impatiently.

"So, Roscoe owns a chain of barbeque joints in this area called 'Rockin' Roscoe's'. It's really delicious food and if you ever come down here to visit, being that you're not gonna move down here, we'll take you the one near the Liberty Bowl. The pulled pork sandwiches and the spicy baked beans are mm…mm…awesome! They have got ribs that are to die for! They just fall off the bone they are so…"

"Will you get to the point!?" Erica replied breathlessly, cutting-off Kate.

"Okay…okay, just sayin.' But anyway, you know that our starting quarterback is Justin Rossington. Well, we were having dinner on Friday night and Roscoe was there and knew that Mark worked for the team, so he came out to tell us that our dinners were on the house. Roscoe then said that he wished that the Blues made their game-worn jerseys available to the public, because his grandson really wanted one worn by Jared Rossington. Mark, being the Head Equipment Manager told Roscoe that he'd give him one after the game on Sunday, that he'd make sure that it he was 'taken care of.'"

"It was then that I spoke up and asked 'hey Roscoe, are you related to a Jesse Same that lives up in New York State?' He rubbed his chin for a moment and then looked around to see if anyone was listening. Then, he looked at me and said 'we share a surname, so we must be relatives right?' Then he asked me how I knew this Jesse, and I told Roscoe that he was a 'friend of a friend.' He looked around again and rubbed his chin some more. Then he told Mark that it was very kind of him to get a Rossington game jersey for his grandson. He looked around again and whispered 'if y'all can keep a secret, follow me back to my office and I'll share something with y'all - but you can't tell anybody!'"

"So, Mark and I followed him through the kitchen and into his little office that seemed like more of a closet. Up on the wall above his computer was a framed black and white picture of him, a man that looked a lot like him, and Elvis Presley - the three of them standing and smiling and looking like they were sharing a happy time."

“Roscoe pointed to the photo and said that it was taken over at Graceland in 1969. His older brother Richard - but everybody knew him as ‘Dicky’ - was high up in what they affectionately called the Memphis Mafia. He pointed and said ‘that’s him standin’ to the right of the King and me on the left.’ We could tell that he was so proud and his eyes were getting misty. He said Dicky was head of the King’s security contingent and one of his preferred bodyguards. They were close friends and Elvis loved him like a brother.’”

“Roscoe went on to say that when the photo was taken, he too was a junior member of the Memphis Mafia, working as a ‘gopher’ more or less, but he loved it just the same. He said that Elvis affectionately referred to him as ‘Rockin’ Roscoe.’ That’s how he came up with the name for his barbeque joints.

“It was then that he stopped smiling and told us that his niece, Tammy Jo - who you said was Jesse’s mom - had a little tryst with Elvis in 1973. Although Dicky had been working for him for years, she was finally introduced to Elvis by her father when she was eighteen. She was mad crazy about the King of Rock-n-Roll and he being separated from ‘Prissy’ as Roscoe referred to her, and soon to be officially divorced, was overcome with lust one night when they were alone. It wasn’t rape as it was totally consensual on her part, she even admitting that she teased and coaxed him. He was grief-stricken over his mistake and knew that he could not be associated with an 18 year old woman. To this day, even though he’s dead and gone, ‘Prissy’ has never found out. Dicky was upset and to his dying day never came to grips with the fact that his daughter gave birth to Elvis’ son and that there could be no ‘trail’ so to speak. Dicky wanted to get to know his grandson and help to take care of him, but again there could be no ‘connection.’ Roscoe said that only a few surviving members of the Memphis Mafia know, but he felt moved to tell us - that ‘something just made him do it’ he said.”

"Abortion was never a consideration for Elvis as he was dead set against it, so Tammy Jo was 'hid out' while she was pregnant. As soon as baby Jesse was able to travel - and I think it was on Tammy Jo's nineteenth birthday, Roscoe said - they were sent up to 'a town near Syracuse, New York' where Dicky knew someone that could get the baby and mother started on a new life. Paternity could never be established and Tammy Jo swore she would never force the issue, but Roscoe said there were times when she almost reconsidered and threatened to go after the estate. Either way, it would have been settled and taken care of 'all hush hush' he said. And oh, by the way, that Gibson acoustic guitar that Jesse plays belonged to Elvis. Elvis gave it to Dicky not long before he died, and told him 'make sure that one day my son gets this. I wish I could have done more.' At that time Elvis believed that his death was imminent, Roscoe said. The awful thing is was that he was right."

There were four seconds of silence before Kate asked "are you still there?"

Erica was light-headed and needed to sit down, and the cold wooden floor of the porch was all that was available. It felt for a moment like the earth had moved sideways, but it was only the after-effects of the shock of what she had just heard from Kate. But was it really shocking? Was this news truly a surprise?

"Um…wow, Kate. Common sense would tell me to think that you were either fed a load of crap or that you are feeding me one, but seeing, hearing, and knowing Jesse makes me believe you. This is totally out of left field! I'm stunned and yet, why should I be? I mean, after all Jesse's told me this story adds up."

"And he has no idea, does he?" Kate responded somberly.

"No Kate, he doesn't. Tammy Jo told him that his father disappeared when he was a baby and that he was probably dead. Whenever he'd ask about Grampa Richard, she told him that they'd go visit him some day, where he lived in a little town near Memphis. For years, he lost interest in trying to figure out his ancestry but he says that just recently the desire to know who his father and grandfather were has been re-awakened. It's partly because his son Jeremy wants to know too."

"Well, Tammy Jo was telling the truth about his father being dead" Kate still sounded somber, but then there was a lilt in her voice as she then said "so how does it feel to be hooked-up with the son of Elvis Presley? Mm-hmm, good catch girl!"

Erica's head had cleared enough now to where she could stand up off of the cold porch floor. There was no lilt in her rejoinder to Kate:

"I'm not hooked-up with him, Kate! As far as he knows, I'm heading to Memphis today. I wrote him a note telling him I was going and in it I asked him not to contact me and he hasn't. Yeah, it hurts a little that he hasn't but that's what I wanted, right? If he had contacted me it would have hurt even more. And as far as being the offspring of Elvis Presley, well that doesn't make him any more appealing to me. Yes, Elvis was a handsome man and Jesse looks a lot like his father and is drop-dead gorgeous, but I wouldn't care if his father was a railroad bum. Jesse is Jesse and he is amazing."

"Okay, 'hooked-up' was a poor choice of words and I'm sorry. So, the the question is, how are you gonna tell him?' Kate countered.

"I don't know, Kate. I guess first I'd have to eat crow and tell him how I changed my mind about going to Memphis. But, I just don't know. I'm not in a hurry to tell him; it won't be today. I can't just show up at his door and say 'hey, baby, I decided to stay in town because I don't want to be without you.' I need to let today slip away, Kate, and then I'll go see him because I want to and I miss him. As far as telling him that Elvis is his dad, I wonder if he'd be better off not knowing."

"You two haven't known each other long. I can tell that you're concerned that it's all you with the strong feelings and you don't want to be rejected" Kate sympathized.

"I know that he likes me, sure, but I think that at this point my feelings are stronger than his. No matter what I know about him now, he's still a mystery in some ways. He's a strong Christian and that directs everything in his life, and while I'm all mixed up about God right now, his strong faith is part of the attraction for me. He's such a good and kind man and I know he's a good father, even though I've yet to meet his son Jeremy. And, you know he's my hero because he saved my life. My boys really want to meet him…he'd be such a great father figure to them…Oh, Kate…I love him…"

And with that, Erica's dam broke as she was overcome with emotion. She hung up on her friend as it was too difficult to speak while shedding melancholy, forlorn, heartbroken tears. In her mind, if she hypothetically had to choose between her new found millions and Jesse that choice would be oh, so easy to make.

At 12:02 p.m., Galen Moss was seated at a small, square-topped table with four chairs inside the wood-paneled walls of the Tin Pin Restaurant & Tavern's dining room. The bar itself was busy with patrons including Earl Skidmore, Randall Jacobs, Jay Jensen, Murf Murphy, and Robert the midget - but only one other table was occupied in the dining room, so Galen was free to choose his preferred seating next to the window.

Galen preferred the window seating because he felt safer being able to see the comings and goings outside and who might be approaching. As he saw Jesse walk up to the dining room entrance, he heard a harsh-voiced woman shriek from the barroom din "Robert, stop touching me you little pervert!" Her indelicate reproach elicited a hearty burst of laughter from the fifteen or so male patrons who were drinking nearby.

"Hello, Galen" Jesse said as he approached the table with his right hand extended. "Hey Jesse, nice to officially meet you" the former soldier replied as he stood and shook Jesse's hand. As the two men sat down, they couldn't help but overhear a woman in her seventies seated with the other party of diners proclaim "oh my god, he looks just like Elvis before he got fat!" As the one other woman and the two men in her party - all in their seventies - smiled and murmured in agreement, Jesse could only purse his lips and shake his head while Galen chuckled.

Regular bartender Sandy had the day off, so it was Mary Ann who was serving double-duty as waitress and bartender. As she emerged from the barroom to take their order she addressed them with "hi guys, can I get…hey, you're Jesse Same! I saw your show at the Turning Stone a few weeks ago. You do an awesome Elvis, man, and your band was amazing! I took my mom to the show for her birthday, and she actually got to be in the audience out in California when Elvis was being filmed for his Comeback Special in 1968. She is such a huuuge Elvis fan and she said that you're a dead-ringer for him! Yeah, she said that seeing you in concert was the next best thing to seeing the King! Wow, you know, you should use that as your slogan - 'the next best thing to seeing the King' - that rhymes! And you live right here in Chittenango, don't you? Wow, we have two famous people connected to Chittenango - that guy that wrote the Wizard of Oz, um…what's his name…"

"L. Frank Baum" Jesse answered in embarrassment.

"Yeah, him, and Jesse Same the Elvis dead-ringer! Oh, I'm sorry guys, uh…whatever you want to order is on the house" the 44 year old Mary Ann offered, still sounding like a 16 year old teeny-bopper.

The "Garbage Plate" was the day's lunch special, and both men decided to try it. What the Ten Pin served was a variant of the original dish served by Nick Tahou Hots, a Rochester-based restaurant that owned the rights to the "Garbage Plate" name.

Similar to the originator, the Ten Pin's variant of the Garbage Plate was a combination of foodstuffs cooked on the grill. It was comprised of portions of Italian sausage, cheeseburger, hamburger, red hots, white hots, chicken tender, haddock, fried ham, grilled cheese, or eggs - eggs being what was available that Monday - and two sides of either home fries, French fries, baked beans, or macaroni salad. To go on top of the main ingredients were the options of mustard or onions, and both Jesse and Galen opted for the latter. While the Nick Tahou original used its own patented hot sauce as a topping, the Ten Pin piled on a version of Texas hot dog sauce that was similarly spicy and savory. The plates were served with Italian toast on the side.

Jesse chose a glass of Fanta orange soda as his beverage while Galen went with A & W root beer. Mary Ann brought the drinks right away, and as she placed them on the table Earl Skidmore complained loudly enough for both the dining area and bar to hear "well, am I gonna get another beer today, or should me and my buddies just go down to the Red Wood, huh Mary Ann?"

Mary Ann smiled embarrassingly before hurrying back to the bar, but stopping before going through the entryway to say "I'll have your food up in a couple of minutes, guys. Thanks for being so polite, unlike others here!"

The two men had been yakking about the weather and the NFL season, but it was time to swing the conversation from the safe harbor of idle chitchat out into the turbulent sea of dreams, visions, supernatural occurrences, individual safety, and future security.

"Galen, you might think that I'm a crackpot, but I heard what I heard and I know that I was meant to hear it. That's why I needed to tell you."

Galen's answer was to passionately lay out his case:

"Jesse, I don't doubt your sincerity, man. As Matt and I have talked, I've started to believe that there are people in this world that are gifted with the prophetic. I prayed and re-committed to Christ on Saturday night when I went over to Matt's place for coffee. I was raised as a church goer and I accepted Him as Lord when I was eight, but instead of drawing closer to Him, I fell away and forgot about Jesus as life began to eat me up…"

"I joined the Army in 1998 to escape life in this lousy town. I was 20 years old, living at home, and working part-time at the Burger King after dropping out of community college. My father died when I was 17 and my mother gave up on life and was addicted to sleeping pills. My former school mates, some of whom were my co-workers at Whopper World, were all burnouts and I couldn't stand to be around them, so I faced a choice of living a life of depression and failure or joining the military and doing something that would potentially be positive."

"I excelled at being an infantryman and was eager to be where the action was, so my rewards for that were to fight in both of Bush's wars. I've killed more than a handful of men, not including everyone's favorite terror mastermind Osama Bin Laden. Yeah, I was ordered to let him run and if he didn't smirk at me with that cocky-assed, pompous, 'I'm more valuable than you are' smile and tell me that I was supposed to let him go, well maybe I would have followed orders. But, there was something so inherently evil about not just him, but the entire operation and system. It was like the whole dang thing was a stage show and both wars were made-for-TV events. Valiant soldiers with honorable intentions were and are just meat puppets for the puppet masters that control the media, the presidency, the world economy and many world events…"

"Man, it's though the sociopath puppet masters have released a metaphorical vial of parasitical bio-toxin that is slowly but steadily creeping and eating along the edges of what the sheeple know and understand, and the more that it consumes the less they know and understand, and with it is devoured their desire for truth. They're doped with drugs, sex, false religion, technology and television, and they are fed convincing lies through the media and through the entertainment industry that soften their hearts and minds and prepare them to OBEY - like those stupid black hats that you see some young people wear and they have absolutely no idea what it means!"

"It's happening slowly but deliberately so as to keep people pacified, but ultimately there will be rioting and extreme civil disobedience when the puppet masters like Soros, Rockefeller, and all of the banksters decide it's time. And, with the U.S. and European economies in shambles and the Middle East on the precipice of the worst war yet, and with the threat of terror over here, they have all the pieces in place for the fall of America and the rise of the singular system. I know, it seems impossible for most people to believe that anyone would want to install a global dictatorship, but genuinely sociopathic people in positions of great power do exist. Brother, they are very well-organized, and have seized power quietly but very effectively -- particularly in the US, UK, Germany, France and Italy. And it's no coincidence that those nations are G5. But, in order to bring down their largest obstacle which is America, they will need to disarm the population, and that is one of the reasons why Steve Sandifer and I founded the North Madison Militia."

"Trey has told me that you guys are heavily armed and that you get target practice in Steve's back yard and also at the rod and gun club. He also said that you have an underground bunker loaded with survival supplies. What exactly do you guys aim to do?" As Jesse asked this, he recalled the dream of militia members in the blue Dodge Ram shooting a police officer and then destroying a police vehicle with an anti-tank gun.

"The Feds will find a reason to suspend the Constitution and implement Martial Law. As you know, Jesse, it'll probably be served to them a silver platter, so to speak. So, while this is only Chittenango and the town of Sullivan in poverty-ridden Madison County, there needs to be a true line of defense for that time when those who are sworn to defend instead turn into the offenders" Galen answered with a total lack of levity.

Jesse asked "the North Madison Militia isn't totally unknown. Some people around are aware of you. Do you get grief for it?"

"We don't flash it around, but we are open to having a larger membership. We even have a website, North Madison Militia dot net. We explain on the site that we are a 'don't tread on me' organization and not a group of vigilantes. But yeah, the local constabulary checks up on us as well as the fibbies. They both have searched us but thus far, they can't find a reason to shut us down" Galen answered.

"Some of my dreams would seem like they're related to a pre-trib storm, Galen. It's very strange and there is a supernatural element because Satan is the one who is driving not the dreams, but the events. And in the conference call that I heard over my clock radio, you know - the one where they state that they are going to eliminate the soldier who killed Bin Laden? Well, they also talked about standing down and letting some terrible event take place, something that they already have intelligence on. It involves cities on the East Coast, plus L.A. and Las Vegas. It's something that will accelerate their timetable by badly damaging America. It would allow for the implementation of Martial Law. That damage would allow for the rapid acceleration of the one world government, and it's the Anti-Christ that will run that. I was awakened from sleep while they were talking, but I could almost swear that one of them said 'December' in regards to the 'events.'

It's weird because it was though they spoke through my clock radio and yet I was dreaming" Jesse explained.

"Well, I'm not worried about what happens to me Jesse because I know the Lord as you do. The one world government is right out of the Book of Revelation. Do you think that what is happening behind the scenes is leading up to something biblical?" Galen asked with the enthusiasm of a child.

Jesse answered unequivocally: "Galen, I'm gonna tell you more in a minute, but yeah, I can't help but think any other way and most of all its what I feel in my spirit. It's the dreams and visions combined by what I see on the ground that make me feel so convinced that the world is entering into a very prophetic time and the Great Tribulation can't be far off - especially considering how quickly the one world government or 'corporation' is coming together. What you tell me only furthers my belief. But, before the Tribulation begins the Rapture will happen."

Galen followed with: "Yes, and Matt was talking to me about a 'pre-Tribulation storm period' that he feels we are entering into now. He believes that the longer that Jesus tarries, the worse it's going to get here and some Christians will think that the Tribulation has already started. He feels that this supernatural storm period is already blowing into the natural with an increase in demonic activity, which will make people start to 'act up' so to speak. So, if the 'storm' blows in hard before Christ returns for us, we may very well need that bunker. Trey said that you're not interested in becoming a member, but bro, if you change your mind you are welcome to join up."

"Rapture?" Mary Ann interrupted as she delivered the Garbage Plates to their table. "That's like in the movie *Knowing* with Nicolas Cage. Have you guys seen it? The 'Whisper People' are aliens that come in spaceships and take the kids to a new place like Heaven before solar flares destroy the earth. I bet it really does happen like that!"

"I saw it in March when it was released. It's a terrific film but no, the Rapture won't be like that" Jesse responded with a chuckle.

"I didn't see it. I don't support the entertainment culture" Galen answered politely as he stared down at the plate that Mary Ann had just set before him.

Mary Ann cocked her head to the side and looked at Jesse quizzically as she asked "well, how is it going to happen, then?"

"Jesus is the one that returns and not any kind of space aliens. A trumpet will sound and those who have accepted Him as Lord and Savior will be called up into the air to be with Him forever in eternity" Jesse answered with a smile.

"Oh, you're one of those" Mary Ann replied red-faced, with an uncomfortable smile. "Enjoy your food guys, and please don't leave one of those little tracts as my tip. If you need anything else, I'll be around."

"Not a believer" Galen said with a smirk as he shoved his fork into the mix of grill offerings that comprised his Garbage Plate.

"It seems that more aren't than are. It's one thing to not believe that Christ will return for His bride in a pre-tribulation Rapture, but to not have Him in faith is to rot in despair and desperation in a dark, dank, foul-smelling sewer tunnel with no way out" Jesse mused before putting a fork-full of food in his mouth.

"That sounds like Hell. I'll bet you saw it that way in one of your dreams" Galen said with a grimness that matched his mien.

"Yes - Hell before it becomes the lake of fire as described in Revelation" Jesse replied with dismalness on level pegging to that of Galen.

As Jesse spoke, Galen noticed through the Ten Pin's dining room window a black 2009 Chevy Express cargo van pulling up on the southwest side of Genesee Street along Dr. West Memorial Park, within feet of the intersection with Arch St.

"Impressive - they've got some brand-new vans it looks like, the filthy bastards! They really need to brush up on how to operate covertly in the States" Galen groused as he motioned with his head for Jesse to look out the window.

"Hmm…who's that, the CIA?" Jesse asked as he leaned closer to the window in an effort to get a better view.

"Lean back out of the window, man. Don't let them get you printed" Galen spoke abruptly, and as Jesse leaned back he could see the tinted driver's side window go down halfway and two hands holding a Sony digital camera aimed at the Ten Pin.

"In answer to your question, yes, that's the CIA. They generally don't operate domestically as that's the job of the FBI, but I must really be special to deserve such attention! I'm obviously a significant threat to homeland insecurity…oh, did I say that? I mean SECURITY, THOSE LOW-LIFE PIGS!" As Galen emphasized those words in anger, Jesse was amused at how much the man naturally sounded like Jack Nicholson.

"They're going to try to kill you, man!" Jesse spoke quietly but intensely.

"I've known that for a while, Jesse, but this is the first time I've been tracked by the Company or anyone else associated with the government. I need to get a new phone and keep the Kevlar on under my clothes. I'm always packing and you know what, you should too. You wouldn't happen to have a pistol permit, would you?"

"No, I don't have one" Jesse answered flatly.

"Oh, you'll never be able to get one now. But in case they saw you with me, you've really got to watch your back. It looks like they're planning to rub me out imminently like you said, but they'll be careful about how they do it. My goal is to bring failure to their plans but my immediate goal is to finish this delicious grub."

Though they kept their heads back from the window, they could both see the van drive away. But what Jesse could see that Galen couldn't was the pellucid flying monkey that was crouched on the roof of the vehicle and pointing at the window where they sat.

As they both made an effort to clean their plates, they didn't hear Earl Skidmore approach from the barroom - that is, until he stood next to their table and spoke:

"So, you're the Elvis-impersonatin' Jesus boy that thinks that some Rapture is gonna come and take you away, huh? Well, listen jack-wagon, I think you got too much spare time on yer hands. You know that the asbestos removal place up the street is hirin', right? Why don't you get your 'Love Me Tender' singin' ass up there and apply fer a real jab (sic)" and with that Earl burst into cynical laughter.

Galen fired back in Jesse's defense: "Hey Earl, first and foremost, my friend here doesn't need a real 'jab.' Secondly, why don't you stop eating Oxycontin like its candy and get back into the bar with your idiotic drunken friends before I either break your jaw or report you to the New York Compensation Board for committing fraud and for doctor shopping. Remember, it was me that helped you pull your Harley out of the mud and I saw you strain your back! It was me that offered to drive you to the hospital but you refused, and we both know why. You didn't hurt your back on your brewery job!"

"So what - New York State would never believe a right-wing militia freak like you" Earl muttered under his breath as he began his retreat.

"What did you say, Earl?" Galen asked.

"Oh, uh, I'm sorry fer interrupting yer lunch and fer giving Mr. Sideburns there a tough time."

"That's better, Earl. Now get lost!"

Jesse was laughing as he inquired of Galen "are you full?"

"In more ways than one" Galen answered, shaking his head.

"Alright G-Man, I'm going to leave Mary Ann a cash tip. Now I hate to be anti-social, but I think you'd agree that maybe I shouldn't be in your company for a while."

"Be careful, Jesse. It's me that they're after, but they may use you as a way to get to me if they I.D'd you through the window."

Jesse was concerned for the safety of his new friend, but it was after all in God's hands. And while he had just met Galen, he felt a comfort around him that would be more akin to a friendship that had been built over years. It was not unlike the feeling that he had with Erica; only different in obvious ways. And after he and Galen shook hands and headed off in separate directions on that final day of November, Erica was on his mind.

# 13

# Shiners

The first day of December brought a continued mix of snow and rain to Chittenango and all of Central New York. It was that type of miserable weather that made Jesse desire to hunker down, but instead he spent the hours between 11:00 a.m. and 1:00 p.m. rehearsing with the band at Trey's house; and to say that his heart wasn't in it would be an understatement.

Trey quizzed Jesse about his conversations with Galen Moss, and was quite astonished to hear that Jesse's dreams and visions weren't rejected as the delusions of a mad man. "Since Galen's been spending time with Matt Carrier, our new unofficial Militia chaplain, he's been turning into a Jesus freak like you, pal. Seems like he'll be new your new best buddy, huh? So far, I think he's the only one who's getting religious, but I'm wondering about Steve and Eileen Sandifer lately, too. I'm concerned that we're going to turn into Waco North, if you know what I mean." Trey's quips may have appeared jocose, but everyone in the room could tell there was a firm, underlying bitterness in his comments.

Ian LeBeouf immediately piped in: "Geez, Trey, I've gotta say it makes me a little nervous to play in a band with a gun-crazy guy in a militia you know? You just seem like you're too into it. I mean - what if you have a bad day and go postal and shoot us all?"

As Mickey Starnes laughed at the comment, Trey could only smirk and respond "you're kidding, right?"

"No, I'm not man" was Ian's stone-faced reply.

"Well, listen Gear Fab Beatle Paul, you may end up having to play 'Happiness is a Warm Gun' in your new act - you know, the one that is touring the world and being billed as *the most accurate and life-like Beatles tribute ever - even more so than Beatlemania.* I know it's hard for a liberal like you to understand, but peace is achieved through strength. You ought to be damn glad that there are a few militias in this country to protect the asses of pretty little idealists like you. There should be more militias, and you insult me by thinking that I would 'go postal' and pull a gun on anyone in this room! You're an idiot, man" a hotheaded Trey shot back with righteous indignation.

Ian rebutted; equally as incensed: "You gun-loving NRA types are the reason so many children are shot in this country. Fewer guns would mean fewer deaths, get it? I mean, really - who needs assault weapons, you know? It's Americans with guns that put this entire planet in danger. Are guns what you guys use as your penis extensions? I mean, really!"

In a flash, Trey pulled off his Telecaster and placed it in its stand before stomping across the basement rehearsal room toward Ian with his right hand balled in a fist - only to have Jesse step in between them.

"Calm down both of you" Jesse shouted, before quietly commanding "Trey, go back to your guitar and let's get some Christmas songs down!"

"Get out of my way, Jesse" Trey snarled.

Jesse put his face close to Trey's and snapped "no! Now please get back over there so we can get some work done!"

"Screw you too, best friend" Trey growled before punching Jesse in the right eye.

The punch didn't knock Jesse down, but it did stun him - especially since it was thrown by his childhood best friend and first musical partner. Jesse wouldn't retaliate against his friend, but Tony Zonnerville did.

Tony was an affable and good-natured guy who was liked by most everyone he met. He loved to play music and was thrilled that he was eeking out his living by being a keyboardist for hire, record producer and recording engineer on the upstate New York music scene. Tony had recently finished the production and engineering of the debut album by Pie Kite, the aforementioned band that Trey's younger brother Seth played keyboards for.

As musically gifted as he was, it wasn't "T.Z's" only talent. He was an athlete as well; having played safety and wide receiver for Fayetteville-Manlius High School's varsity football team. Then, as a Music Industry/Sound Engineering major at Ithaca College, he was a football "walk on" and by his junior year had become the team's starting strong safety. Although overlooked by the NFL, his play was solid enough that he was invited to training camp with the Canadian Football League's Edmonton Eskimos after graduation in January of 2002. The Eskimos converted him to outside linebacker and he showed well in camp, but ultimately did not make the squad after the final cut-down. Instead of pursuing another shot at pro football, Tony returned home to Fayetteville and quickly found work as a recording engineer and producer in upstate New York studios and also plenty of gigs as a mercantile tickler of the ivories.

As Trey turned from Jesse and prepared to slug the shocked and horrified Ian, Tony raced out from behind his Yamaha keyboard and wrapped the guitarist in a form tackle that would have met the high standards of legendary NFL coach Vince Lombardi, driving him into the tan carpeting. As Trey lie dazed and wide-eyed with rug-burned arms, Tony knelt beside him and shook a finger in his face while angrily admonishing "cut the crap you idiot! What the hell is wrong with you, are you on Crack or something?" The erstwhile football player then stood up and quickly backed away, making a scrunched face that would indicate that he was repulsed by something unseen.

Mickey sat dumbfounded behind his drum kit; wondering if had imagined the scene that had just played out before him. Jesse was developing a shiner around his eye, but he alone had no trouble seeing and hearing the gargoyle-esque demon that hovered over the prone Trey. The entity was a smaller version - approximately four feet tall - of that which in his dream stood atop the First Presbyterian Church and gave birth to flying monkeys. Its man-like facial features could be described as "chiseled" and its grey complexion was craggy and weathered. The hair on its head was straight and black and fell across the shoulders and muscular chest to just above the waist. While the sinewy arms and defined upper torso resembled that of an athletic man, the legs were scaly and reptilian with three claws on each foot.

As it squatted down and bent toward Trey's left ear, its mouth was moving frantically as there was a discordance of sound emanating from it. To Jesse's ears it was if the thing was speaking with a multiplicity of utterances. At a lower volume was a number of voices bathed in reverb; in essence the sound of a cavernous, high-ceilinged room filled with people in distress. Some of the voices only murmured, while some moaned and others wailed. But the voice that spoke most loudly and clearly was directed at Trey as it said "these musicians disrespect you and mock you behind your back. They deserve to be injured and Steve Sandifer deserves to be killed because you should run the militia. Now get up off the floor and relieve yourself of these infidels!"

The voice that spoke directly to Trey did not fit the masculine entity it came from. The voice was male no doubt, but was strident and lisped in a stereotypically gay manner. When it finished speaking it looked up and as its pale orange eyes devoid of pupils met Jesse's, the entity spread its chiropteran wings and vanished.

Without conscious realization, Trey heard the demon in his spirit. He was furious and embarrassed as he quickly stood up and bellowed "everybody get the hell out of here now! Take your instruments and leave my house. I'm quitting this freakin' band and you can all drop dead!"

As Ian, Mickey, and Tony were in that moment too shocked to move, and as Jesse stood still while trying to process the supernatural occurrence that he had just witnessed, Trey roared "Jesse, I thought you were my friend" as he marched the short distance across the room, grabbed the Gibson J-200 from the stand behind the bewildered Jesse, and swung the old instrument onto the floor where it smashed into numerous pieces in a manner that would have made Pete Townshend envious.

"You're out of your freakin' mind! You better replace that guitar, you lunatic" Tony shouted as he desired to go after Trey again but was strangely fearful of doing so.

"Call the cops, Jesse - and I'm outta here" Ian proclaimed as he struggled to carry toward the door his bass case in his right hand and his Ampeg BA-115 amp in his left. The look of terror was palpable in the bassist's eyes and Jesse noticed a large wet spot on the front of his jeans.

Mickey lamented as he began tearing down his red 5-piece Ludwig drum kit: "this is unbelievable, just unbelievable! This may not be the time or place to say it, but we still ought to play the Christmas show at the Turning Stone. If Trey won't play, we need to get someone who will, and fast! And oh, by the way Trey, you're an asshole!"

"Get out now, all of you" Trey bellowed as he walked up the stairs that led from the basement to the kitchen.

Jesse didn't chime in. Instead, he stared at the pieces of the ruined J-200; they appearing blurry through his tear-filled eyes. Mickey stopped the packing of his drum kit and walked over to Jesse and put his right arm around the shoulders of his friend. When Mickey did this, Jesse began to cry in shuddering weeps while Tony joined the gathering and said "I'm sorry that he did that, Jesse. That was a cool old guitar. You'll never find another one like that one."

As Jesse could only cry harder while Tony and Mickey tried to console him, it wasn't so much the instrument that he wept over, but what it represented. It represented his loving mom who was so excited for him the day that it was delivered and she instructed him to take it from the closet where she hid it. He missed her because she was kind and caring and her smile could light up the darkest, most gloomy room. It represented the beginning of his musical journey and the old Trey, the friend who wasn't angry and bitter but who was a fun-loving, caring, rock-n-rolling brother in arms who would be there through thick and thin. It represented Jeremy, who as a toddler would pluck its strings and make up silly songs sung discordantly until Allison would complain "knock it off, Jeremy - that's really annoying." It represented the disappointed face of his toddling son when his mother disapproved at his innocent attempts to play and sing like the dad he loved so dearly…

…And it represented the mysterious Grandpa Richard that Jesse to this day could never track down the heritage of and who, like his mom, had years ago passed away. It represented the turtles that Eddie Ramsden so viciously killed, sweet innocent little turtles that would never harm a soul…

…But in the pain and heartbreak there was something else represented: a sort of familial connection that Jesse could not put his finger on. Indeed, it was a heritage and a 'somebody' that Jesse never knew. There was a sorrowful could-have-been and a well-concealed mystery; and as the metaphorical stage was bare and Jesse stood there with emptiness all around, the answer to that mystery wouldn't come and pull that curtain down…

The pieces of the guitar were placed inside its case and Jesse didn't know what to do with the carnage other than to take it home and hide it in a closet. He would need to purchase a new six-string, but not that day. There was no desire on his part to go after Trey legally, as he knew that the apparition that he saw hovering over his old friend had much to do with the hostile, erratic behavior. Indeed, a supernatural storm was blowing in and it explained the behavior of so many people that Jesse saw in Chittenango and elsewhere. Jesse would pray for Trey. Likewise, he desired to speak with Matt Carrier and Galen Moss.

Calls rarely came to the house phone as he used his cell for most of his telephony. Still, as the traumatized Jesse arrived home from Trey's house at 1:55 p.m., he saw the red light flashing on his answering machine indicating that a message had been left. After getting a wash cloth filled with ice to hold over his black and blue eye, he pressed the "play" button with his left index finger and heard:

"Hello, Jesse, this is Dennis. Hey, listen, I was wondering if you might like to come to a lodge meeting with me on Thursday night. You're a guy who worships God, and we are, you know, an organization that does God's work. It would be good for you, Jesse, because you'd see God at work through all kinds of good men who pursue our great architect along different paths. I don't know, it might just expand your horizons a little and maybe motivate and inspire you some. And not to say that you're not a good father, but it would help you to be a better one for Jeremy. Anyway, give me a call on my cell at 222-9601. Thanks, bye."

Jesse was a boiling disharmonious stew of sadness, anger, and shock as a result of the events that had transpired at Trey's house. Being in no mood to be on the phone with an arrogant jackass like Dennis Dalton, he still thought it better to return the call and get it over with:

"This is Dennis Dalton, can I help you?" was the answer, the sales manager being on the job, saying whatever and doing whatever it took to blow-out those 2009 model year vehicles and hype the twenty-tens.

"Hi Dennis, this is Jesse returning your call."

"Hey Jesse, good timing - I was just sitting down at my desk to catch up on some computer stuff. Hey, hold on one second."

As Jesse "held on" while Dennis pulled the phone away from his face, he could hear him speaking to someone who had walked into the office. He barked at the salesman "I don't really care what you tell her. She doesn't know shit about cars, right? It should be an easy sale, Jeff. You've been here long enough now that your numbers should be higher. You're on really thin ice, just so you know!"

"Sorry Jesse, I'm back."

"Okay Dennis. I'm going to have to pass on your invite…"

Dennis interrupted again: "Sorry Jesse, hold on a second" and again it didn't take an episode of hyper-sensitive hearing for him to hear Dennis speak to the salesman Jeff:

"So she doesn't want a brand-new car? Well, you told her about the great pre-owned vehicles that we have right? There's that blue

2001 Impala that we got yesterday in trade. Push her toward that one so we can get rid of it. Just don't tell her about the bent frame. Let her test drive it and you ride along and tell her how you drove it yesterday and loved it! What!? I don't give a shit if you didn't really drive it, you tell her that you did and you sell that effing car or else John will fire you himself, got it? You better remember Jeff, you've got a three year old and a baby on the way and you need to be a responsible father. You need this job buddy, so use that power of persuasion that I demonstrated for you and get your ass out there and sell that car right now!"

Jesse was appalled but not at all surprised by what he heard come from the mouth of Dennis, who switched from being intimidating to affable as he returned to the call: "Sorry Jesse, so you were saying that you couldn't come? Well, I guess I'll have to kidnap you and bring you against your will…ha ha, just kidding!"

"No, Dennis. I'm not interested in being a Freemason. I don't believe in a mere supreme being that could fit into any religion and make me 'regular.' I don't partake of religiosity at all, Dennis. I believe in the God of the Bible who is the God of Abraham, Isaac, and Jacob, who begot His only son Jesus to take my place on the cross and die for my sins. Yes, God is the greatest of architects and He did create the universe through the most intelligent design, but there is only one path to Him and it's through the blood of Jesus Christ, Savior and Lord, who came to earth as God in the skin of man."

Dennis' response was restrained yet seething:

"Hmm…Jesse, Jesse, Jesse, you really trouble me I'm so sorry to say. You've got Jeremy convinced that there's only one way and you've sewed his young, open mind completely shut! He even told the six year old son of one our members that Allah is not God! This is the son of a third degree Mason who worships god through Islam! And you're gonna tell me that his god is not the same

Supreme Being as yours!? I almost slapped Jeremy because of his disrespect but because I am a godly man I held back!"

"My second piece of advice to you, Dennis, is to never, ever, ever lay a hand on my son, get it? However; my first and foremost piece of advice to you is to know Jesus as your all in all. Trust me when I say that, because there may not be much time for you. I would encourage those fine churchgoing and 'regular' lodge members John and Joe McMurtry to do the same." Jesse's tone became less forceful and more pleading as he then said "Please, Dennis, I implore you not to delay. I'll come over and pray with you if you like."

In response, Dennis barked at Jesse in the same 'big dog' manner that he did to Jeff moments before:

"Look, Jesse, Allison and I are thinking about changing the terms of your joint custody of Jeremy. I know we can get a great lawyer and just by using your own words and actions against you; we could convince a judge to no longer allow joint custody and only supervised visitation. I mean, really - anyone can see how you've screwed poor Jeremy up. That way, you couldn't fill his head with any more of your Christian extremist bullshit. And the fact that you're a musician for a living that has to rely on an inheritance to help make ends meet would only further our case!"

"I'm not worried about losing joint custody of my son, Dennis, because it's not going to happen. No sir, I'm more concerned with your eternity. Jesus is the way, so don't you delay, because a McMurtry's management shakeup is only days away - and I didn't mean for that to sound like a song lyric" was Jesse's unruffled reply.

"I gotta go" was all Dennis said before terminating the call.

Jesse shoved his phone into his right side jeans pocket with his left hand as he held the ice pack over his eye with his right. "I can't keep this thing on forever" he muttered to himself as he walked into the bathroom to look at his black eye. As he let the wash cloth fall open and drop the ice cubes into the sink, he looked into the mirror on the medicine cabinet and inspected the damage.

"Ah…I've seen worse" he spoke aloud to no one as he tilted his head to the left in order to fully view the contusion. The majority of the swelling was directly below his right eye; represented in a jagged semi-circle colored purple, black, green, and pink, with the darkest of the coloring bordering the bridge of his nose.

Indeed, Jesse had seen worse when he was a boy of seven. Eddie Ramsden provided Tammy Jo with a shiner that swelled so bad that her left eye was partially closed for a week. Filled with temporary guilt, the angry abusive man held Jesse's terrified mother while applying ice to her eye and lamenting "I'm so sorry baby, I'm so sorry, I lost my head. It'll never happen again, you have my word." Being psychotic, his remorseful, caring display instantly turned menacing as he warned "but you better not tell anybody I hit you, alright? I'm serious Tammy Jo and that goes for you too, Jesse. I ain't afraid to bust your face up if I gotta, you little punk!"

As Jesse relived the terrible scene through memory, he recalled how after Eddie issued his warning, the mood swung back to a more remorseful yet unrepentant place as the man said "I'm sorry honey, I really am, but if you weren't so friendly to other guys then I wouldn't have to hit you, baby."

Despite being prone to melancholy, Tammy Jo was "friendly" to everyone; whether working as a waitress or walking down the street. It didn't matter if it was a man, woman, or child, she was always quick with a "hello" and a smile and would enjoy small talk about the weather, current events, or most any topic. Tammy Jo honestly cared about people and desired to encourage them. While she and Jesse never had much money, she would still give the proverbial shirt off of her back to anyone that needed it. These were traits that the possessive yet hardly faithful Eddie could not stand.

Though upscale in its rustic quaintness, not everyone that lived in Manlius had money - not in 2009, and not when Jesse was a child. As he stood in the bathroom while concurrently walking down a memory lane strewn with broken glass and jagged shards of wood from a smashed Gibson J-200, he suddenly recalled an instance of his mother's generosity.

It was a blustery, cold afternoon in early December of 1998. Jesse had an hour lunch break from P & C which was in the same shopping center - just kitty-corner across the parking lot - from Dave's Diner. Jesse would sometimes have lunch at Dave's when his mother was working; she at that time was the most senior waitress on the staff. Being that Jesse now lived on his own and was soon to be married to Allison, he didn't see his mom as much and this gave them time to catch up if the diner wasn't extremely busy.

Being that he as solo, Jesse chose to sit at the counter as opposed to taking a booth. There was a stool available, down one spot from the corner, and Jesse took it. Tammy Jo came around the corner and walked behind the counter where she beamed as she said to Jesse "hi honey, the burger and fries today?"

"Yeah, mom, and just a glass of water, because I've had enough caffeine for now" Jesse laughed. As he finished speaking, he turned to his right and noticed the man sitting next to him on the end stool. He had just finished eating a club sandwich and potato chips, leaving the two dill pickle spears that came with the meal on the plate. As Jesse met eyes with the man, the kindly fellow smiled and said, "I'm in no position to be fussy, but I never did like pickles."

It was then that Tammy Jo hustled by, setting a glass of ice water in front of Jesse and a check in front of the gentlemen who had ordered the club sandwich plate and coffee. Before the smiling waitress could rush away, the gentlemen said "I'll pay right now, Tammy Jo."

His mom would tell Jesse the following day that she didn't know how the fellow knew her name, as she didn't wear a nametag and being busy had forgotten to share with him what it was. He recalled the man pulling a tattered black wallet held together with duct tape from the back pocket of his heavily-faded blue jeans. The man opened the wallet and then remarked solemnly: "oh dear, I hadn't realized that I didn't have any more cash with me. I am very sorry and quite embarrassed." And though the man was dark skinned and wore a goatee, Jesse could tell that he was blushing and as well his eyes were beginning to tear.

"I'll wash dishes, I'll sweep and mop, I'll do whatever I need to do to make this right" the man spoke humbly and yet in a deep, warm, articulate manner that would indicate intelligence, compassion, and leadership.

Tammy Jo's mouth showed a smile, but her eyes could not hide her heartbreak as she said "I don't think you've had anything in that old wallet for a long time, sir. And honestly, we have more than enough helping hands around here these days. But don't worry sir; your lunch is on me. And if there is anything else I could ever do to help you, you just come back and see me, okay?"

The man smiled and said "God's richest blessings on you, Tammy Jo. I sense you too have struggled very hard and yet you are a bright light that won't dim. Can I give you this before I leave? It's all I have."

She said "thank you" as she accepted from him the 3" by 3" tract booklet that on its white cover had a gold, embossed cross that glowed - almost as though it had its own source of light. Jesse was amazed and speechless as he saw the glowing cross and the words printed in golden cursive font below it that read *Jesus loves you.*

Jesse remembered his mother holding the tract tightly in her right hand as her face beamed and her eyes misted. And now, all those years later as the memory returned while he stood in the bathroom looking at his shiner, Jesse gasped as he realized that the man was the very one he'd dreamed of; the one who could be best described as a Rasta-styled Morgan Freeman.

As he rested his hands on the sink to help keep his balance, Jesse recalled Allison clutching his left arm tightly as he stood in the receiving line of Tammy Jo's wake on Tuesday, February 9th, 1999. The receiving line was small, comprised of Jesse, Allison, and Dave Kowalski, the owner of the diner. But what struck Jesse was the size of the crowd that came to his mother's calling hours. Seemingly, they were all the people that Tammy Jo had said "hello" to. Many were regular customers of Dave's Diner. Others were people that she had met along the sidewalk as she would walk to and from work. Others worked with Jesse at P & C, not knowing that one day he would be able to leave the employ of the grocer and be an Elvis impersonator full-time. What amazed Jesse even to that day in 2009 was that his mom had enough of a life insurance policy to cover the cost of her burial.

He recalled Allison whispering into his ear, "don't be sad, Jesse. Your mom was a good person. Look at all of the people that came to pay their respects. You know that a good person like her has gone to a really good place." Jesse hadn't come to faith in Christ yet, but what he didn't know was that his mother had renewed her faith after receiving the tract from that unusual man. She had mentioned to Jesse when they had Christmas dinner that she had started attending the Baptist church on North Street. She'd said that she believed as a little girl, but her faith grew weak as a teenager and she fell away - but she had that man who couldn't pay for his lunch to thank for giving her "the little booklet that got me thinking about the Lord again and I reconnected."

Jesse had quickly forgotten that conversation from eleven years prior, but as he leaned against the bathroom sink he believed that it was the sight of that beautiful little tract in 1998 that planted the seed that made the writings of Hal Lindsey come alive for him and lead him to faith in Christ in 2004. And it brought a reassuring smile to his face to know that his mom was indeed in that better place - that place with the Lord.

The J-200 was wrecked beyond repair, and after leaving the bathroom Jesse put the case inside of the living room coat closet that was not unlike the one in his childhood flat on East Pleasant Street in Manlius. He thought it to be a bit ironic that the guitar was in essence leaving his life in the same manner that it entered it; via a closet. He likewise sensed that for whatever the reason, he was reaching the end of his career as an Elvis Presley impersonator. He believed that he could rally the troops sans Trey to play the Christmas Tribute scheduled for Thursday the 17th, but after that he himself would walk away from the enterprise known as *Jesse Same - Elvis Impersonator*.

Since late October, life had become markedly taxing for Jesse and he was mentally, physically, and emotionally fatigued. On one hand, he had felt immensely blessed that he was gifted the dreams and visions and in that he was confident that they were prophetic. But those dreams and visions also brought care and concern and it was a heavy load to carry. While he did not know the day or the hour, Jesse had the knowledge and discernment that the sands in the bulb labeled *The Church Age* were nearly run out.

While he did not like Dennis Dalton, he was called to love him in the way that Jesus would, and because of his recent dream he feared the worst for him. He did like Trey and loved him like a brother, and was grieving for him as the smashed J-200 that represented so many things was representative of his childhood best friend's current spiritual condition. There were so many people that swirled in Jesse's mind, including a man he hadn't met named Steve Sandifer. Because Trey's soul was without the Holy

Spirit and therefore a stronghold for all manner of demonic parasites, Jesse feared that the words of the entity that hovered over Trey would appeal to his heart and in that Steve's life was in danger.

Yes, there were so many and so very much. A checklist of people and a climactic change as truly there was a pre-tribulation storm blowing in from the supernatural. There was Allison, who he could not reach and who viewed Jesse as damaged goods. There was Jeremy, but Jesse knew he did not need to worry over his son. And there was Erica…

Despite the trauma and the fatigue Jesse needed to press on. Rest would come, but not in this hour. So, while he only desired to take a nap, he instead found Galen's number in his contact list and pressed the send button.

Galen's voicemail greeting indicated that he would be "out of town" until Wednesday, December 2nd, and that if the caller would leave their name, number, and a brief message, he would return their call then. Jesse left the message: "Hey Galen, it's Jesse. After a peculiar episode at rehearsal today, I'm a little concerned about Trey doing something stupid as in possibly attempting to take Steve Sandifer's life. It's a supernatural thing and I think you'd understand. Please give me a call or have Steve Sandifer call me as soon as you can. Thanks bro, bye."

Jesse didn't have Matt Carrier's cell number and the unemployed pastor kept his home phone unlisted. If he couldn't reach Galen right away, Matt would be the next choice. As Jesse sat on the couch with his laptop, he visited the Four Corners Community Church website, hoping that the webmaster was slow to make updates and Matt's e-mail address would still be posted on the "Contact" page. Jesse was disappointed to discover that all traces of the church's former preacher had been eliminated and that associate pastor Dan Duncan had already been promoted to replace him.

On the “News” page of the site was a collection of photos of Dan Duncan’s dedication ceremony with the balding, grey-goateed 50 year old man smiling joyfully with eyes beaming behind round glasses. “The guy’s a dead-ringer for Dave Ramsey” Jesse chuckled to himself. The church elders were part of all of the photos, and it amused Jesse as it appeared that each of them was taking part in a contest to see whose grim visage could most starkly contrast that of the new head pastor - with John McMurtry being the winner by a nose.

# 14

# The Wayfarer (part 1)

Meteorologist Gordon Johnston forecast "warm weather for the second of December" as Jeremy laid on his bed listening to "Oldies 92" WSEN-FM 92.1. It was 12:03 p.m. on that Wednesday, and Jeremy had "faked an ache" - telling Allison that he was too sick to go to school that day. While he wasn't physically sick despite his claims, the six year old first grader was depressed and with that came malaise and overall disquiet that would make anyone feel rotten; especially a little boy who was living in unhappy surroundings.

What came next over the airwaves brought a weak smile to the little boy's face; a face that bore a resemblance to his dad's and yet carried the brown eyes and light freckling of his mother. While both parents had naturally brown hair that they passed on to their son, Jeremy's was fine and wispy like his mother's and not thick like his dad's and hung in bangs over his forehead and partially over his ears. Jeremy would frustrate himself as he would try to pile his hair into a pompadour like his dad did and because of its wispiness it wouldn't stay!

As *Blue Christmas* played as a background to the ad, the sonorous male voiceover announced "Don't miss the Turning Stone Casino's Christmas Tribute to Elvis Presley, featuring Jesse Same - Elvis Impersonator and his band on Thursday, December 17th, at 8:00 p.m. Mark Bialczak of the Syracuse Post-Standard says 'Jesse Same is a dead-ringer for the King of Rock-n-Roll.' Elaine Musgrave of the Rochester Democrat and Chronicle says "Elvis Presley was the King and Jesse Same is the crowned prince.' Tickets on sale now at…" and the rest of the commercial spot was blah-blah to Jeremy's ears.

Jeremy had few opportunities to see his dad's shows because they were private corporate events or in nightclubs and other rooms where alcohol consumption was a big part of what the audience partook of. The little boy did get to see his dad and band play an outdoor show for all ages at the Manlius Amphitheater adjacent to the Swan Pond in September, and was awestruck as the band played his favorite song *Hound Dog* and his dad shook his hips and the microphone stand as he sang - all while snapping his fingers with his left hand and seemingly gliding on his feet like the stage was air.

"That's my dad" Jeremy spoke softly yet proudly to himself and in that moment the pride became awash in melancholy as he missed his father and looked forward to talking to him later on the phone. Still, the daily phone calls and two weekends a month visits were not enough for Jeremy or Jesse. His father was so much that his mother wasn't: patient, kind, humorous, easy-going yet very firm when needed, and a lover of Jesus. Certainly, Allison loved her son and took care of him as a mother should; however she was impatient, manipulative, controlling, selfish, and an accomplished emotional blackmailer. Jeremy recalled as he laid there in bed the time the previous week that he peed his pants because he couldn't get into the bathroom after a long wait. Why couldn't he get in to use the toilet? - Because Allison and Dennis were having one of their increasingly frequent spats and she as she too often did had locked herself into the bathroom sobbing until Dennis would beg enough for her to come out so he could "apologize." Jeremy was the one who begged that time to get in because he had to go. After an hour of his mother's emotionally unstable and manipulative behavior, the little boy could not hold it any longer. Yes, the Dalton's had many fine things in the Manlius house that Jesse used to live in, but one thing they lacked was an auxiliary bathroom. Jeremy recalled crying as his mother scolded him after she emerged, saying "you should have told me you had to go!" The embarrassed, lachrymose little boy defended himself by proclaiming through his tears "I did mom, I did, I did!"

Jeremy shook his head in an effort to rid himself of the embarrassing and traumatic memory, and it did get blotted out - only to be replaced by a sound that he heard "live and in person."

Dennis was using three vacation days and combined with the weekend would be off from berating and intimidating his sales staff until Monday. Because of Dennis' good salary, commissions, and bonuses, they could now afford to have Allison be a stay at home mom running a business on ebay selling used clothing and collectibles acquired from thrift stores and garage sales.

Jeremy's bedroom was on the upper floor of their Washington Street colonial, but as he turned off the radio in an effort to take a catnap, he could hear his mother and stepfather as they sat talking on the couch at the bottom of the stairs in the living room.

Allison: "I shouldn't find it hard to believe that my ex the Elvis-wannabe isn't interested in going to the lodge with you tomorrow night."

Dennis: "No, I guess the transition to manhood is a tough one for him. He's too worried about what his Jesus might think and not too interested in being a responsible father and member of society. And, can you believe this shit? He's trying to tell me that I need to accept Jesus right away and he even wants to pray with me! Not only does he have Elvis fantasies but he's got Billy Graham fantasies too! He's got some sort of mental illness for sure. And then he spoke some silly rhyme about me needing to accept Jesus right away because there was some sort of 'management shakeup' coming to the McMurtry enterprise! I guess he wants to be Eminem too! What a friggin' jackass!"

After a few seconds of giggling in the style of naughty children, Allison lowered her voice to a notch above a whisper and asked "So, are you going to talk to that lawyer that John knows, so we can see about getting the custody and visitation terms changed? It shouldn't be hard because Jesse will indict himself."

As Jeremy heard his stepfather ridicule his dad, a quiet rage welled inside his soul. But then as he heard his mother's murmur of their jiggery-pokery in regards to getting custody and visitation terms changed, fear mixed with that rage to create a most powerful elixir. Jeremy had had enough and it was time to do the only thing he knew that he could.

The six year old climbed out of his bed and pulled on a pair of camouflage BDU-style pants that were "just like the ones the guys in the army wear" he would often exclaim with pride. He rifled through a dresser drawer and first pulled out a green t-shirt bearing the McMurtry Auto Mall with shamrock logo on the chest and the slogan "You'll go far in a McMurtry car" screen-printed on the back in yellow lettering. "I'm not ever wearing this crappy shirt again" he spoke quietly through lips clenched in anger as the balled-up the garment was heaved into the closet. There was another green shirt that was instead suitable; a long-sleeved tee with white NIKE above and swoosh icon below, screen-printed across the chest. Jeremy wrestled with the garment while pulling it on as his head was stuck for a moment in the neck opening.

The temperature was near 60 degrees, but because the breeze could be chilly, and Jeremy had the foresight to know that another layer might be advisable. It was a black short-sleeved t-shirt with the "got milk?" slogan screen-printed in white on the chest that he decided to pull on over the green long-sleeve. "I like it because it's just like the one that Jacob the cool guitar player who lives down the street wears" Jeremy would say of the shirt that was among his favorites.

As he pulled his red and blue Spider-Man backpack bearing three different action images of the superhero out of his narrow and cluttered closet, Jeremy could still hear his mother and stepfather talking on the couch about "sales goals" and the "lodge meeting tomorrow night." Still, hearing the mention of "getting custody and visitation terms changed" was enough to cause a deep unsettling in his spirit. As the little boy unzipped the top of the pack, he shuddered nervously for a moment before taking a deep breath that brought with it a feeling of calm.

On the top of his dresser was a collection of little boy knick-knacks including 7" tall D.C. Universe plastic action figures of Superman, Mr. Miracle, Dr. Impossible, Hawkman, Shazam, and Killer Moth. Additionally, there were miniature green army men and a model of an Apache helicopter.

But the one item that caught the boy's eye like no time before was the 6" by 8" metal-framed photo of a beaming Jesse and Allison huddled together in front of the Christmas tree with the mom cradling baby Jeremy. The mom and dad appeared very happy, and perhaps the dad was content and settled; however the mom was already hoping that soon she could be relieved of the marriage if she could just find a legitimate "out."

Jeremy had heard Dennis call his mom a "bitch" on more than one occasion. Jesse had recently told his son that the word was bad and that he should "never think of any lady or a girl as one, because God doesn't think of his children that way." Still, in this moment of duress, the young boy couldn't help but think of his mother in that derogatory term as he stared at the photo. He needed to summons every ounce of restraint to keep from pulling the photo from the frame, crumpling it up, and tossing it under his bed to live with the dust bunnies.

The six action figures were scooped up and dropped into the bottom of the backpack. In his mind, the presence of Spider-Man on the outside of the pack and Superman, Mr. Miracle, Hawkman, and Shazam down inside it gave Jeremy the courage to do what he was about to do. Though Dr. Impossible and Killer Moth were villains, they had to come along so as to not break up the set.

Next, from the top dresser drawer several pairs each of socks and underwear were thrown in. From the next drawer down, where t-shirts and sweatshirts were neatly folded, Jeremy selected a light blue Old Navy t-shirt and a tan-colored sweatshirt with the images of Captain K'nuckles and Flapjack screen-printed on the front. From the next drawer came a brand-new pair of Lee jeans. Back to the top of the dresser his attention was drawn and his Game Boy Advance was retrieved and dropped into the pack on top of the clothes. Jeremy was a smart boy and knew he had to travel light. Now, if he could just sneak down into the kitchen to grab some snacks and a bottle of water. It had become quiet down in the living room, which could mean that his mother and stepfather had dozed off as they often did if they weren't arguing…

As a Spider-Man backpack was being loaded with mission-critical supplies in Manlius, a cellphone was buzzing and begging to be answered in Chittenango:

"Hello?"

"Jesse, what's up man? It's Galen."

"Galen, I'm glad to hear from you bro - but your name didn't come up on my caller I.D. It was a number I didn't recognize so I almost didn't answer."

“It’s a new TracFone, Jesse. Like I alluded to before, I’m going to be changing phones frequently because of the heat.”

“So, where did you go?”

“Actually bud, I didn’t leave the ‘Nango. After we had lunch on Monday the black van followed me as I drove up Genesee Street toward my trailer on Lakeport Road. I didn’t want to lead them right to my door, so I continued north to Route 31 in Lakeport. They were still tailing me at that point, so I hung a right onto 31 and headed east. I drove seven miles to the intersection of Routes 31 and 13 and pulled into the Sav-On gas station. It must be that the Company fears the Oneida Indian Nation, because they slowed down like they were going to pull in behind me but then sped off eastward, even running the red light at the intersection where they had to swerve to avoid getting hit by a Northeast Motor Freight eighteen wheeler heading north with the green light. They ended up into the guardrail on the north shoulder of 31, but I didn’t hang around to see what developed. I pulled back out onto Route 31 and sped back to Lakeport and then to Chittenango. Since that time, I’ve stayed away from my trailer and hunkered down in the bunker for safekeeping. Of course, I’m not going to say where that’s located, but you know where it is. As a matter of fact, being that the shit has already hit the fan for me, I’m going to be in there for the duration. I’m breaking the crib in so to speak, should the rest of the militia need it! But, I had to come up and out to make this call as you can’t get a connection from inside. And, I’ll still go out and live my life until they find me again.”

“Man, oh man - the way that they tailed you sounds like an episode of Starsky and Hutch or any of those other cop shows from the seventies, but hmm…maybe you shouldn’t mention the naughty “M” word?”

“No worries, bro. They know all about the North Madison Militia. We’ve got a popular website, remember? But, they don’t know about the hidey hole. And, because a poor sucker like me has to buy pre-paid cards, I have to be careful not to be my usual long-winded self. So, what's this about Trey wanting to kill Steve? Did you have another supernatural event?"

"Yeah…I saw and heard a demon whisper in his ear that Steve Sandifer should be killed. This was after he punched me and gave me a shiner and our band mate Tony who is a former football player knocked him on his butt. I'd be careful because he's already filled with rage and I get the sense that he feels that he should have a leadership position in the militia. Trust me when I tell you it's a legit concern."

"Trey gave you a shiner! Did you punch him back?" Galen asked with a chuckle.

"No, because it would have hurt me more spiritually than it would have hurt him physically" Jesse replied, not masking his pity for Trey.

There was a short pause as Galen considered what Jesse said, and then the militiaman answered: "Trey is a hothead and he's a little too gung-ho in the wrong way. Before I called you back I prayed and I'll take what you said on advisement. I believe you, Jesse, and I'll try to talk to Steve, but saying that a friend had a vision of a demon that instructed Trey to etcetera etcetera will be a tough sell…um…uh-oh, gotta go!" And with that the call was abruptly terminated, causing a wave of anxiety to sweep across Jesse's soul like a spilled vial of sulphuric acid. Still, he was blessed with enough discernment to not accede to the impulse to call Galen right back.

Jeremy stood at the top of the stairs and peered over the bannister and saw what he'd hoped he'd see - his mother and Dennis asleep on the couch. The only way to the kitchen and likewise the only way out of the house from upstairs was down the stairs and through the living room.

But what if one or both woke up as he tippy-toed past? What would his answer be if he was asked why he was carrying his backpack loaded with a number of clothing items to the kitchen? What if he was caught in the kitchen putting snacks and a bottle of water inside the pack - what would he say? Jeremy was not a liar and was afraid he'd be put into the position to have to lie to keep from being punished. The little boy had been forced to promise his mother that he would never tell Jesse that there were a few instances where Dennis had smacked him in the face for "not following orders" - but enough was enough and that was one promise that the little boy was going to break when he saw his dad.

Although he was only six, Jeremy knew how the words "custody" and "visitation" applied to his relationship with his father, and despite his nervousness and trembling in this moment, he was not going to allow anything or anyone to keep him from spending time with Jesse.

Allison and Dennis had fallen asleep while talking as on the 44 inch flat-screen ESPN's SportsCenter prattled on at a low volume about the upcoming weekend's NFL action. The window of opportunity was open and it wouldn't stay that way for long. So, despite his fear of being caught, Jeremy carefully placed his stocking feet on the stairs and ever so deftly began his ascent. He carried the backpack by its red top strap in his right hand while holding the varnished maple railing with his left. Slowly now, so as to not cause the steps to creak, slowly…

BUZZ…BUZZ…

Jeremy froze where he stood as Dennis' iPhone, having been set to "vibrate", juddered on the wooden coffee table in front of the couch. It seemed like forever until the phone finally went silent as the incoming call was sent to voicemail. But, did it wake them?

They weren't stirring, but from behind Jeremy had no way of knowing if their eyes were open.

He stood frozen and tense for another minute, watching the tops of their heads to see if there was any sign of movement. "Maybe they're dead" Jeremy thought for several giddy seconds, but the Holy Spirit convicted the young boy that their death would be nothing to find joy in. And with that conviction he knew it was time to finish this leg of the journey; the one that would get him to the bottom of the wooden stairs.

The stair that was two up from the hardwood floor made a cracking noise as he stepped on it, but Jeremy had made it to the floor and was on his tippy-toes before he had time to fret over the noise. He was moving stealthily behind the couch and they were still asleep; as they were tired from being up late and quarreling the night before.

He looked back as he sneaked like a bandit into the dining room, and they hadn't moved an inch. He pictured his feet gliding across the hardwood floor like his dad's did across the stage when he sang Hound Dog, and Jeremy's were in essence skating across grey linoleum tile as he reached the kitchen.

His white Nike sneakers with orange trim were waiting by the door that led to the backyard and his grey zip-up hoodie hung on the knob, but first some comestibles needed to be packed.

After shoving the hoodie inside the top of the Spider-Man backpack, a 16.9 ounce bottle of Poland Spring water was plucked from the fridge and slid into a mesh pocket on the bottom left side. It was an abnormally warm 60 degrees outside at 12:50 in the afternoon, so the water would need to be readily accessible while the hoodie would not have to be, as the young boy with the foresight of someone more than twice his age had already dressed in two shirts - with the top one being easy to remove if he became overheated.

As the backpack rested on the grey and white granite countertop that occupied the center of the kitchen, a package of 6 Keebler cheese and peanut butter crackers were slid into the same mesh pocket as the water. From a side compartment of the fridge was retrieved a 9 oz. package of Polly-O Twist Cheese that was placed into the smaller zippered compartment that displayed the image of the superhero crouched down above the phrase "Spider-Sense" which was in smaller lettering above "Spider-Man." Into that same compartment went a package of Scooby Snacks vanilla wafer cookies and a small but shiny Red Delicious apple.

As he nervously tied his sneakers Jeremy sensed that his mother and Dennis were still conked-out on the couch, and his sense was correct. They were in dreamland and there was no better time for him to slip through the kitchen doors and out onto the patio, and seemingly without conscious thought he grabbed his pack, pulled open the wooden door and then the metal storm door, and stepped out into the warm but breezy air. Once the two doors were quietly shut with his left hand, his arms were run through the backpack's main straps and it was secured onto his shoulders and back.

Hot tears ran from his eyes as he cried just a little, but the little boy was driven to leave this place behind and walk the seven miles to his dad's flat in Chittenango. While his mother and stepfather napped, his feet were hitting the sidewalk on Washington Street and he walked purposefully up the gradual incline that would take him to where Military Way left State Route 92 - which was Washington Street and would become Cazenovia Road at the point where Military intersected. Military Way would twist and wind past colonial and ranch homes and a cemetery before ending at State Route 173 - the road that led to the rustic village where the "Yellow Brick Road" sidewalk ran along both sides of Genesee Street for several blocks.

But first Jeremy would need to cross the busy Route 92 and that would be a daunting task. As he arrived at the point where

Academy Street met Military Way and Military Way ended at Route 92 - Cazenovia Road, the car and truck traffic was heavy and most of the vehicles were travelling at a speed far in excess of the posted 35 MPH limit. He stood at the end of the driveway of a house where a girl named Grace lived. Grace had been his babysitter a few weeks ago when Allison and Dennis went out to dinner with John McMurtry and his wife, and Jeremy remembered her telling him that December 2nd was her birthday and that she was going to be 15 this year. As the little boy waited apprehensively for the traffic that would not break, he hoped that Grace had a great birthday because she was "really, really nice" and let him stay up late.

Jeremy began to worry that the traffic would never clear enough for him to run across the road and that while he stood there he would get caught by his mom and stepfather. It was then that he saw a guy that was in a band that played in the same concert at the Manlius Amphitheater that his dad did in September. They were a band called Pie Kite and they played after his dad was done. The guy's name was Joshua and his older brother was Jacob who had the same "got milk?" t-shirt that he was wearing. They both played in Pie Kite together, and this Joshua was walking along the shoulder toward his house that was just a little way down the street from where Jeremy lived.

As Joshua approached he asked "Hey little dude, you trying to get across the street?"

"Hi Pie Kite guy! Will you help me cross this street, the traffic is crazy!"

"How come you aren't in school - do you do homeschool?"

"Um…yeah, and I'm going to see my friend up on that street over there that does home school too."

"That's a really cool backpack you have and you look like you're loaded for bear! And you know what? My older bro has a shirt just like yours!"

"I know! When I saw you play in the concert by the Swan Pond, he was wearing it. That's why I got one, because I thought it was cool and I really like milk - especially chocolate!"

"Hey, it looks like the traffic might be letting up some - how about if you hold my hand and we'll run across together? Does that sound like a plan, little dude?"

"Yeah, it sounds like a plan, Stan!"

"My name is Josh, not 'Stan'!"

"And my name is Jeremy, not 'little dude'!"

"Okay Jeremy, take my hand, and on the count of three, we're gonna run across, okay? Ready now, one-two-three…"

And instead of having to run across the dangerous section of two lane highway, Jeremy was surprised as he was scooped up by the kindhearted Josh and carried across to Military Way as the driver of an eighteen wheeler that was travelling at 52 MPH downhill around the curve in the posted 35 MPH zone blasted his air horn because he thought that he was going to hit the two pedestrians.

"There you go, Jeremy. Now be careful, and I'll be sure to give you a signed copy of our CD when it comes out in a couple of weeks!"

As Joshua sprinted back across Route 92, Jeremy grinned as he spoke aloud to no one, "Pie Kite is awesome and Josh is so cool!"

A small pang of guilt flashed in Jeremy's soul as he began his trek up Military Way. He had lied to Joshua when asked if he was homeschooled, but he couldn't have told the truth because that could have ended up with him being back home in big trouble. As he took advantage of the short section of sidewalk that ended at the apartment building that was once a military school for boys, there whirled in his soul a tempest of exhilaration, anticipation, remorse, and anxiety. What a surprise it would be for his dad when he arrived at his door, and what a relief it would be for Jeremy to enter into that safe harbor and out of the tumult that was his life with his mother and Dennis. Still, he could get into serious trouble for what he was doing and find himself in precarious situations along the way. And, he had just told a lie. It was a lie that got him safely across the busy Route 92, but a lie is still a lie and he'd told it to someone that he truly admired.

As he passed the green ranch house where his school friend Nathan lived, he whispered a simple prayer:

"Lord, I'm sorry that I lied to Joshua when he asked me if I did homeschool. He was really, really nice and he carried me across that busy road. But I'm a big boy and I could have run across! Hey, he lied to me too! He said that we'd run across the street but he carried me! Please forgive us both for being liars. In the name of Jesus I pray, amen."

An older kid shooting baskets in the driveway of a grey colonial on that abnormally warm day stared at Jeremy as he walked past. "That kid must be homeschooled" he thought to himself as he reached the sidewalk's end, causing him to remember a book full of silly poems called *Where the Sidewalk Ends* written by an eccentric author named Shel Silverstein. His dad had that book and he looked forward to him reading some of the poems from it at bedtime, after a story from the children's illustrated Bible that his mom made his dad take with him when he moved to Chittenango.

The shoulder of Military Way was muddy where the sidewalk ended in front of the long, two story brick structure that formerly housed the St. Johns Military School in the late 1800's but now served as an apartment building. Parked at an angle on the shoulder was a moderately rusted white 1982 Chevy Pro Street pickup truck owned by one of the building's tenants. The tinted back window was laden with stickers, but the three that caught Jeremy's eye and distracted him as he walked around and out into the street were the two-legged "Darwin" fish, a colorful Grateful Dead skull and lightning bolt emblem, and a circle and slash through the word GOD.

As he was being uncharacteristically careless as he circumnavigated the haphazardly-parked pickup, he didn't see the silver 2002 Pontiac Sunfire 4-door that was coming too quickly around the curve toward him. The blast of its horn startled Jeremy into cognizance and as he turned bug-eyed to face it, the car swerved into the opposite lane and stopped on a dime.

As the startled little boy stood motionless against the side of the truck's bed, the front passenger's side window of the Sunfire rolled down and Jeremy's auditory and olfactory senses were immediately assaulted. The skunk-like odor of burning marijuana was foul to his nose and the profane lyrics of *Cold Steel* by rapper Phat Cat playing through the car stereo was abrasive to his ears and soul.

What was worst of all was his recognition of the individual who sat on the passenger's side. It was none other than the freckle-faced thug with the sideways black *OBEY* cap that he'd dreamed about when he fell asleep on his dad's couch on the Friday night after Thanksgiving. But now, as they met eyes, Jeremy realized that this was not a dream but in fact a most distressing reality.

"Yo, little bitch, we almost ran your little punk ass over, right?"

Jeremy felt his courage begin to grow as he replied "my dad says bitch is a bad word and you shouldn't call ladies and girls that. And besides, I'm a boy, so I can't be one anyway, duh!"

As the thug on the passenger side laughed, the other from the dream who was the driver in reality leaned across the lap of his friend and spoke through the window:

“Ya’ll got a smart mouth, you know? I ought a’ take this here nine and smack it across your grill! What ya think a’ my nine, huh?”

Jeremy was unflinching as he answered directly “I think that both of you guys are gonna die really soon. I dreamed that you were floating dead in the pond after you tried to hassle me, my dad, and two other guys I don’t know. Sometimes when I dream stuff it really happens, so I’m sorry you that you guys are gonna die and so is America and the secret bad men that think they’re gonna run the world. That’s because only one bad man is gonna run the world before Jesus takes it back from him.”

“Jesus? You better get down on yer knees and pray to ya little Jesus that we don’t just grab ya and pimp ya out to some old molester that got’s bank, yo” the thug who sat in the passenger seat voiced his threat through a sinister sneer.

Jeremy was now paralyzed with fear and irritated by marijuana smoke as the 19 year old driver who had been leaning across his friend leaned back and chortled “yo Homes, Joe McMurtry would pay good fer this kid and he’d pay even better for us not t’ tell his papa!”

The little boy was of course very familiar with who Joe McMurtry was and as well his father John. As he heard the 19 year old driver mention the name and allude to what awful thing could happen to him; his innocent six year old mind couldn’t understand and yet knew it was bad.

The fear and anxiety tightened his muscles even more, and in that moment Jeremy wanted to run but couldn’t. As the young thug on the passenger’s side opened his door and set his right foot down onto the pavement, he heard clearly inside himself the Holy Spirit speak:

"Don't be given over to a spirit of fear, Jeremy."

As the thug's left Nike Jordan made contact with the pavement, Jeremy was startled by the blast of the horn of a blue Dodge Ram quad cab pickup that was waiting to proceed down Military Way to Route 92 - Cazenovia Road. The residential street was narrow, and the truck was blocked by the Sunfire that occupied the opposite lane, Jeremy, the thug, and the white Chevy pickup that was parked at an angle.

In response to the blast of the horn, the thug that drove the Sunfire stuck his left hand out of the window and raised his middle finger. In the metaphorical sense, it was the finger that pushed the button that caused three of the doors on the quad cab to open and the three occupants of the truck to step out.

"Aw shit" was all the thug who had been sitting on the passenger's side could mutter under his breath as Steve Sandifer stepped out of the driver's side of the Dodge, Galen Moss climbed out of the front passenger's side, and Jerome Wooden climbed out of the rear passenger's seat. As the three militiamen gathered around the Sunfire, the passenger's side thug leaned into the vehicle and pleaded quietly yet fervently "yo D.B., you better get out and help me!"

As Jeremy leaned against the bed of the white Chevy and whispered to himself the word "heroes", it was retired U.S. Marine Sergeant Jerome Wooden, who liked to jokingly refer to himself as "the North Madison Militia's token black" who spoke first:

"Man, you lily white boys have got a lot to learn about being 'gangsta' - I mean really now, a Pontiac Sunfire? Can't your mommas buy you something a little more pimped-out than that?"

"Shut up, Nigga, we jus' givin' da lil' boy a ride home, yo!" the thug on the passenger's side remarked reflexively.

Wooden chuckled as he replied: "Nigga? Jus' da lil' boy? Where did you learn your Ebonics from, MTV and YouTube? What a couple of chumps!"

As Steve Sandifer stood next to the driver's door, D.B. the driver crawled out and pointed his 9 mm at him and proclaimed "ya better step off or I'm gonna put some hot lead in yer belly!"

In a flash, Sandifer's right arm reached forward and he grabbed the 9 mm from D.B. the driver. As cool as cucumber, Sandifer sneered "if you want this back you'll have to take it from me."

As D.B. shivered nervously, Galen, who was standing in front of Jeremy to shield him from any manner of shrapnel that may fly, asked Steve "is it loaded?"

"Yeah, it's got a fully-loaded 10 round magazine. It would be a nice little gun for Eileen, but it's probably stolen, so I'll end up melting it down" Steve answered.

"I paid fitty dollahs (sic) cash money fer dat, yo!" D.B. replied indignantly.

"Alright, alright, I have heard enough!" Jerome groused. "I am sick of listening to you two crackers making a mockery of the way that some - and I don't mean all - of my race speaks. Now, what your name, you here in the co-pilot's seat of this Sunfire?"

"Yo, my name is T-Maz and I…"

"What in God's green earth is your name, plebe?!" Jerome screamed into the face of the one who had occupied the co-pilot's seat, grabbing him by the chest of his black t-shirt with both hands and pressing him against the back passenger's side door of the Sunfire.

"My name is Tommy Mazzini, sir, and my homey is Davey Barnes." As a terrified Tommy answered Jerome, his 9 mm Glock fell from the right-side pocket of his oversized jeans and landed on the asphalt.

"These two dirtballs work for those fine, church-going men John and Joe McMurtry" Galen offered as he walked over and picked up the firearm before retaking his post guarding a stunned-silent Jeremy who was too paralyzed with fear to run.

Wooden commanded: "You, Davey, walk over here right now. If you try to run away, Steve will use your own gun on you."

As a nervous David "Davey" Barnes a.k.a. "D.B." walked over and stood next to Tommy, the retired Marine sergeant continued:

"Okay, I see that your cellphones are on your seats. That's fine, because even though you two are stupider than a pound of smashed cornflakes, I know that you're too smart to call the police, right? And Steve, while you're in there smashing up their brick of weed, could you turn that god-awful music off please?"

"Now, when I say 'go' I want each of you to give me fifty in the middle of the road, and with each pushup you are to shout 'yes sir' like you mean it. And just like your stupid hats say, you are to OBEY me, got it?"

After a few seconds of silence, Jerome barked "go" and the two thugs dropped and went as hard as their skinny arms would allow, proclaiming "yessir" with every agonizing pushup. Even though Military Way was a quiet residential street, it was amazing that no other vehicles had attempted to travel through while the scene ensued.

As Steve and Jerome watched and smirked while the gangstas struggled through their pushups, Galen turned and knelt down to talk to Jeremy, but the little boy no longer stood behind him. As a stiff southerly gust blew two small pine boughs that had been part of a newly-hung Christmas wreath up to where the sidewalk ended, Galen saw Jeremy sprinting away with the wind. The boy ran along the shoulder that paralleled one side of the cemetery that at that point occupied both sides of the street, before another section of sidewalk acted as a separator between the street and a short row of colonials and bungalows

"He makes your feet like a deer, son" Galen spoke softly as he saw the boy racing away, his Spider-Man pack bouncing on his back.

Galen too had noticed the stickers on the back window of the Chevy pickup when he first stood with Jeremy. Now, he was pleasantly dumfounded as he turned and again glanced at the truck's window and as he did so, the circle and slash part of a particular sticker blew off into the street, leaving the word GOD stuck in place.

Once Jeremy reached a new section of sidewalk, he stopped running and looked back to see that the three men who came to his rescue were climbing back into the blue Dodge Ram as the Sunfire in front of it drove away slowly. It was a good thing they were moving, because three cars were turning onto Military Way from Route 173 and would need to pass.

As he walked slowly and caught his breath, Jeremy remembered the three men who came to his rescue being in the dream with the bad men who wore the *OBEY* hats. In the dream, the man who made the bad men do pushups was dressed differently than he was in the reality. And in the dream, two of the men who helped to rescue him had ended up in chains - but in the reality of that day there were no chains. Nor were there the orange suits he'd dreamed of.

All in all, he was glad that those men had showed up and he hoped that they never would be handcuffed or chained. But, there was something extra special about the man who stood in front of him. "He would have died to protect me from those bad men because he knew my body was too scared-stiff to run even though my spirit wasn't afraid" Jeremy thought to himself as he stood resting for a moment in front of a grey bungalow with white trim where Military Way ended at Route 173.

He looked both ways and the crossed Military Way so as to join the sidewalk that bordered Route 173 - addressed as East Seneca Street as it was still within the village line - with the northeasterly traffic. His legs ached just a little as he walked up the incline past the yellow Stick-Eastlake style house built in 1872 that belonged to Marty and Martha Mills. There was a Christmas wreath resplendent with pinecones and red and green balls that hung on the front door and strings of lights all along the porch that would be lit once dusk came. "It doesn't feel like Christmas time today" Jeremy thought to himself, and likewise he hoped that nice lady Mrs. Mills wouldn't see him because she'd ask him where he was going and why he wasn't in school, and he didn't want to lie. Mr. Mills was nice too, and Jeremy didn't like the mean things that Dennis said about him, that he "looked like a hippy dope-smoking college professor."

As Jeremy made his way uphill passed the Mills house, he spied Martha bent over in the yard picking up trash that had blown in on the strong gusts of wind. Martha was no spring chicken, and as she stood up to give her throbbing lower back a rest, she turned and met eyes with Jeremy for a second before being distracted by a brown rabbit that hopped through the yard. The little boy quickly looked away and thought to himself "I hope she didn't recognize me."

As a school bus devoid of passengers passed by heading southwest down the hill, the driver locked eyes with Jeremy for an eternity trapped in a millisecond, and the little boy's level of paranoia was considerable. “Why are there so many cars and trucks going by and why is everybody in them looking at me?” A paranoid Jeremy asked himself this question as he felt like he was wearing an orange prison jumpsuit having just scaled the concrete wall of Sing Sing; and in essence he had indeed.

There was a small grove of trees now where he walked uphill, and while his legs were feeling heavy there was nonetheless brief relief. The small wooded area meant no houses, which meant no windows or driveways from which stoolpigeons could see the six year old fugitive and alert the Fuzz - or even worse, Dennis and Allison. And still, while it wasn’t heavy, the flow of traffic in both directions along East Seneca Street was steady, and anyone in any of those vehicles could be a stoolie, copper, kidnapper - or even worse, Dennis and Allison.

Though the water in the bottle was no longer cold, it was still cool, and Jeremy took a big swallow but had to stop himself from gulping down all 16.9 ounces. As the temperature still hovered at 60 degrees, the hoodie would not need to be retrieved from his backpack. The sky had become partly cloudy since he had scaled the figurative wall of the prison he lived in, and he wondered if the warden and the assistant warden had awakened and realized that he had made a jailbreak.

It was almost two o’clock and soon the high school students would be ending their day, which would mean more buses and cars on the road and more betraying eyes to see him. Conversely, the later the afternoon grew the more natural it would seem for Jeremy to be out and about.

Jeremy loved dogs almost as much as he shared his dad’s love of turtles. But, the big black, tan, and white mutt that was now barking at him was a dog that he wished didn’t exist, as he feared it would bring unwanted attention. The animal was chained to a short railing servicing dilapidated wooden steps; those steps leading to the white door in need of paint of a small ranch with weatherworn grey siding that was the first house after the patch of woods.

Displayed on the front yard of the house was a plastic Santa in his sleigh pulled by two reindeer; the right arm of jolly old Saint Nick being raised above his head but his red right mitten had been broken off, making him appear one-handed. Santa's face was indeed jolly, but Jeremy couldn't see him beaming behind the empty paperboard of a Keystone beer 30 pack that had blown on the day's strong breeze and rested against it. A 45" tall smiling snowman was on its left side next to the sleigh; having been knocked over by a strong gust of wind but still dutifully clutching his broom. An adult with an imagination may have surveyed the scene and concluded that the snowman consumed the Keystone beer and fell over drunk.

The front yard banked upward against the sidewalk, and as Jeremy looked down toward the annoying dog and the bizarre Christmas scene, the front door opened and a fat balding man walked onto the small landing at the top of the steps, dressed in a tight white tank top, red and black plaid shorts, black socks and brown slippers.

"Shut the hell up Trixie, fer chrissakes! It's just some stupid kid walkin' up the street! He ain't gonna hurt our goddam Christmas stuff" the fat man squawked, a Pall Mall non-filter bouncing in the corner of his mouth with every word. Before the man re-entered the house, Jeremy was mortified to see him yank forcefully on Trixie's short chain, pulling the dog sharply sideways and causing her to yelp in pain.

It was hard for Jeremy to quicken his pace while still ascending the hill, but he dug down deep and did so in order to distance himself from the objectionable scene at the grey house. He was operating on equal parts adrenaline, anxiety and desire; and that pie cut into thirds would provide the energy to get him to the top.

After five more minutes and numerous vehicles filled with gawkers had passed, Jeremy reached a flatter landscape as the hill began to top off. On his left was Fayetteville-Manlius High School and the buses were lining up along the front and side of the main campus to begin loading. The two middle schools in the district would dismiss shortly, but Enders Road Elementary where Jeremy attended first grade was an hour away from dismissal. Even though the paranoia that came from being seen out of school was on the wane, the fear of his mother and stepfather tracking him down stuck in his soul like an invisible burdock head.

While the aching in his knees and thighs lessened upon reaching the top of the hill, his calves still protested mildly from what was already becoming a long walk. He uncapped his Poland Spring bottle and took a quick swallow, and wishing to drink more he second-guessed his decision to not bring additional beverage. There were the snacks in backpack, but too many butterflies fluttered in his belly to allow food consumption to be profitable.

He could now see the sign for Enders Road up ahead in the distance and to the right, and he was amazed that he had walked this far. The sidewalk had ended again, but there was a wide enough shoulder paralleling the front yards of split-level, colonial, and ranch homes to make walking a fairly safe endeavor. And, there was a ditch if he needed to duck down and hide!

The sports fields and parking lots belonging to the high school were still on his left, and he could hear the sounds of teenagers yelling and laughing as their school day was over. The traffic on the road ahead was light, but behind him there was much commotion as kids who had cars were recklessly speeding out of the parking lots with windows down and music blaring on this atypically warm day.

As a silver 2009 Lexus GX 470 carrying five high school seniors drove northeasterly past him, a male with disheveled black hair streaked with blond who had just inhaled the gasses of a hot meth pipe screeched with a demented laugh from the back passenger's side "get off the road you little dweeb" as he tossed a half-empty can of Arizona green tea in Jeremy's direction. The can hit the pavement with a smack four feet in front of the little boy, spraying a small amount of tea onto his white sneakers. The sneakers were becoming stained anyway, so a few small tea splatters didn't bother him. But the vicious greeting by the SUV's young passenger combined with the loud impact of the can startled and frightened Jeremy and made him cry.

This was a terrible walk so far and although Jeremy wanted to turn back, he couldn't. There were the 19 and twenty year old thugs, but didn't three heroes arrive in a nick of time and save him? There was the weird fat man with the broken Santa who hurt his annoying dog, but the dog was going to be okay, right? Well, Jeremy didn't know the answer to that question. And then there was that methed-out teenager in the SUV and maybe he was the worst of all? There was something abjectly frightening about the joy in his face as he screeched at Jeremy before tossing the can. He seemed to Jeremy even more dangerous than the thugs or the fat man, and Jeremy may have dreamed about him once, but in his distressed state he couldn't remember for sure.

The little boy was blessed with an amazing sense of purpose and drive, and he pulled a red paisley-patterned bandana from the right pocket of his camo pants and wiped his eyes and his nose. He needed to get to his dad as soon as he could, and if he had planned more carefully he would have called him first to come and get him - no matter what his mother and Dennis said or thought. But, this was no time for second-guessing. Jeremy was a wayfarer, and he needed to push on.

He was walking again, and Enders Road was drawing closer. The road wasn't important other than the fact that his school was located on it and named after it - but in Jeremy's mind the road sign was a landmark and a milepost that could be used to measure progress. While walking again, he felt compelled to look over his shoulder, and in the distance behind him was a man dressed in a grey running suit quickly closing the distance.

Again, Jeremy was afraid; that fear being fueled by what he had already encountered on his journey. As he looked ahead, he didn't see any blue Dodge Ram pickup trucks coming to save the day. A car did pass from the opposite direction, but the old lady that drove it didn't look like she could save anybody from anything, he thought to himself as he began to panic.

The running man was close now, and Jeremy couldn't decide if he too should run, scream, or jump into the ditch and cower. His brain was saying "go", but his legs were saying "please stand by, we are experiencing technical difficulties. We are paralyzed with fear again and we cannot run but only walk slowly at this time." Thud, thud, scrape, scrape, thud - the man was right behind him now and his constricted throat would not allow him to scream while his heart was ready to burst through his breastbone.

The man ran up alongside Jeremy's left and then walked at an even pace on the white line that separated the shoulder from the traffic. As he panted, he said "hi Jeremy" with a smile as contrarily the little boy's eyes bulged with fear.

"I've been trying to catch up with you by running" the man panted, before saying "but golly, I could have gotten here much more quickly if I would have just used the tools that God gives me. I guess I was up for a challenge today!"

As Jeremy saw the man's benevolent, sincere smile, he suddenly felt safe. As he stopped walking to gather his wits, the man stopped as well after walking in front of him and further into the shoulder to get away from the traffic.

"Hey, how did you know my name? You're not gonna try to take me back home, are you?"

As Jeremy fired the two questions in rapid succession, he became uneasy again as he contemplated the possibility that this man would indeed drag him back to his mother and stepfather. The urge to run reared its ugly head, and this time his legs would cooperate, but as the man answered, the unease released its icy grip:

"I've heard your name around here and there, and no, I am not taking you back home. Instead, I was about to inquire as to whether or not you'd like some company to walk with you for a while?"

"Uh…yeah…okay…but both my mom and my dad have told me not to walk or talk with strangers" Jeremy answered, and deep inside he sensed that this man should not be considered your standard, run of the mill evil stranger.

"Well Jeremy, both your mom and your dad agree on that, don't they? But, I've got no candy to offer you and no car to climb inside of, so I hope you trust me when I say that this stranger poses no danger."

As a yellow New York State D.O.T. dump truck that would soon take a left onto North Eagle Village Road passed by with a roar, the two commenced to walking while the man glanced up at the increasing overcast with a look of concern on his face that also indicated a peculiar knowing. After a few seconds past, he looked over his right shoulder at Jeremy and said "I know where you're going Jeremy, and you shouldn't take Route 173 all the way. I'll walk with you far enough to show you a different way to get to your dad's place in Chittenango."

"Well, Route 173 is the only way that I know. What's wrong with going all the way that way?" a confused Jeremy asked.

"There's been a wolf, maybe two or three sighted in the bushes along the road on the big hill that's called Brinkerhoff Hill. These kinds of wolves aren't ordinary, they're very sickly with something worse than rabies and they aren't afraid of people. That's one of the reasons why I want to walk a ways with you."

"Have you seen any of these wolves?" Jeremy then asked wide-eyed, anticipating the answer as a child would who was being told a scary ghost story.

"I've seen them and I know who owns them. They're the kind of wolves that normal wolves are afraid of" the man answered gloomily, and Jeremy sensed that he wasn't kidding and was not interested in inquiring of the man who it was who owned those wolves. Then, in an effort to change the subject and lighten the mood, Jeremy vocalized the observation that he made when he first saw the man:

"Are you the guy who played God in that movie *Evan Almighty*? You could be him except that your hair is longer and funkier. My mother and I watched that movie one night last week when Dennis wasn't home and it was kind of okay. What I liked best was that Noah's Ark was in it!"

The man chuckled as he replied "No, I'm not that guy. That actor's name is Morgan Freeman, and I do bear a resemblance to him, except that my hair is 'longer and funkier' as you say." Then, as they began to cross Enders Road, the man was fiery and impassioned as he continued to speak:

"The problem is that there are too many people playing God in this world, Jeremy. There are too many haughty and headstrong people who think they are Him and try to be the god of their own lives. As scripture says, they have a form of godliness but deny its power. Nobody that you see in a movie or on TV can even come close to portraying Him accurately. He's God and there is no other. Yes Jeremy, He's God and there's none like Him."

Jeremy's faith gave him a basic understanding of what the man had just said, and even as a six year old he comprehended that his mother and Dennis both tried to be gods; gods of their own lives and over the lives of others.

After crossing Enders Road, they rejoined Route 173, which at this spot became addressed as East Seneca Turnpike and not "Street" as they had just crossed the Manlius village line and entered the Town of Manlius.

As they set foot onto East Seneca Turnpike, Jeremy noticed that the man had a tear in each eye, and he sensed that it wasn't because his eyes were irritated by the gusts of wind and the dust and leaves that blew about.

What's wrong, mister, are you crying?" Jeremy asked, his young voice laden with mature concern that belied his age.

"No…um…I was just sad for a moment because something bad is going to happen near here. Something that could end differently if some men weren't trying to be the god of their own lives and other's lives while ignoring the truth and believing in false things" the man answered as he wiped his eyes on the right sleeve of his grey nylon Under Armor running shirt.

The little boy asked "what kind of bad thing? Is somebody gonna die?"

"Time will tell, Jeremy. Right now we need to keep moving" the man answered while forcing a smile and trying to put the subject behind them.

"Can you get my apple out my backpack pocket? I can't reach it because I'm walking" Jeremy asked of the man, and no sooner did he complete his request than the apple was being handed to the hungry boy.

An astounded Jeremy stopped walking as he took the apple from the man's right hand, and as the man stopped with him, the astonished little boy asked “whoa…how did you get that so fast!? You didn’t even reach into my backpack but then the apple was in your hand. Holy hamburgers, Batman! You must be a magician or something!”

“Can I tell you a big secret? Do you promise not to tell anyone?” the man asked with his goateed face filled with a bright smile revealing gleaming white teeth.

“Okay…I can keep a secret” Jeremy replied sheepishly, not knowing if he really could keep a secret as sometimes he had trouble - as any six year old would - with matters of high confidentiality. As Jeremy answered, a Syracuse Haulers trash truck roared by, filling the air with the not wholly unpleasant aroma of diesel fuel.

“I’m an angel. That’s how I was able to get your apple without using my hands” the supernatural man replied, still grinning.

“Are you really, really, really an angel? Have you been to Heaven? Oh wow…have you seen Jesus?!”

“Yes, yes, and yes, Jeremy. I live in Heaven, but I get what you would call ‘assignments’ to carry out missions here on earth. Jesus is my commander. He is the King of all Kings and Lord of all Lords, and He sent me here. I love Him Jeremy, just like you do. He made me, but not in the same way that he made you. Now c’mon, we need to walk but we can talk too.”

As they resumed walking, Jeremy asked “what is your name?”

The angel answered “hmm…my name is something kind of strange, so while I’m here carrying out my mission, why don’t you give me a name that you like?”

The first thing that popped into the little boy’s mind was the name ‘Jack’, but that was not suitable or regal enough for a real, living, breathing angel. It was then that an orange 2002 Dodge Neon drove past, and it had to slow to a stop as the vehicle in front of it was making a left turn into a driveway. As the Neon waited six seconds for the car in front of it to make its turn, it was enough time for Jeremy to spot the Xavier University magnetic decal on the back bumper. The first grader was in his class's advanced reading group, so even though the college's name started with an "X" he was able to read and pronounce the word correctly as well.

"I'll call you Xavier. That's a really special name that's good for an angel" the boy answered proudly.

The angel nodded in approval as he said "You know - that has a nice ring to it. I'll use that from now on if you don't mind."

"It's a deal" Jeremy replied, and a walk that had started out terribly was now becoming quite wonderful.

A strong gust of wind ripped unimpeded across an open field to their right, blowing parts of a newspaper into a copse of shrubs that lined the opposite side of the roadside ditch. A second gust freed the front page of what appeared to be a copy of the Syracuse Post-Standard, and it blew to a rest on the road's shoulder in front of Jeremy.

The curious little boy stopped walking to bend over and pick up the dirty and wet page of the newspaper. Most of what was printed on the page was illegible from looking at though it been out in the elements, but the headline of one story was clear:

*Man Claiming to be Angel Attempts to Abduct 6 Year Old*

The part of the text below the headline that wasn't made indecipherable by the elements read: "the man who refers to himself as Xavier is in Onondaga County lockup in lieu of $100,000 bail after the child's stepfather Dennis Dalton, sales manager of the McMurtry Auto Malls, drove along Route 173 in

Manlius in search of the boy. Dalton said *'When I found my precious Jeremy he ran to me saying daddy, daddy, I love you. That's when I knew that...'*"

Jeremy quivered as he read the small section that wasn't obliterated. Confusion and distrust registered in his brown eyes as he looked up at Xavier and asked "if you're an angel, how come you don't have wings?"

Xavier was deliberate as he answered "first off, the very paper that you are holding is a deception created by Satan. You see right now that it's turning into dust and blowing away as you're holding it." As the angel said this, Jeremy began to wipe his hands on his pants to get the dirty grey dust of the disintegrated paper off his skin. His face now registered bewilderment as he turned back toward Xavier, who continued with his answer:

"Secondly, you know that if Dennis ever referred to you as 'precious' that he would be a lying, right? Unfortunately for him, he doesn't know or care how precious you are. Thirdly, I don't often use my wings on earth, and for this assignment I am human incarnate and don't need them. And fourthly, I'm not here to abduct you or take you anywhere, but I am here to help you get to where you have to go. While that's not what all of my assignments are, most are to help wayfarers get to where they need to go, and then I go home. But every wayfarer has a choice, Jeremy, they can use my direction or disregard it - and that includes you - just like the God who created both of us gave you the free will to accept the grace offered by His son or disregard it. His son who sits at His right hand sent me to help you. You can accept my help or you can disregard it and I will go on my way."

"No, no, no, please walk with me more, Xavier!"

"Okay precious Jeremy - and I mean 'precious' when I say it - let's get moving" the angel replied with a forward nod and a grin.

The little boy was still amazed that an angel came to earth to walk with him, and as they resumed their journey, he gushed "I've never met an angel before, but you have to be the best one of all!"

Xavier chuckled as he replied, saying "you are very flattering Jeremy, but you have yet to meet Michael and Gabriel."

"Hey, I know about those angels 'cuz they're in the Bible! Am I gonna meet them today?"

Still chuckling, Xavier answered "not likely today, Jeremy, but you will meet them. Michael is God's archangel and Gabriel is swift and brave. Michael is the chief of the warriors who fight against the outcast angels who became Satan's demons when God threw Satan out of Heaven. Gabriel is the fearless messenger and it was he who delivered the word to Mary that she would give birth to Jesus. Gabriel said to her, as the scriptures say *'The Holy Spirit will come upon you, and the power of the Most High will overshadow you; therefore the child to be born will be called holy—the Son of God.'*"

"I love the Bible" the little boy said as they made an effort to follow the shoulder tightly as East Seneca Turnpike became curvy. After a moment of silence, save for the passing vehicles, Jeremy asked "so what kind of angel are you?"

"Hmm…well…you could say I'm a 'Jack of all trades' kind of angel. The Lord likes to use me to help people directly. You could say I'm more like Gabriel than Michael. I can battle and I have battled and won, but Michael has gifts and strengths that I don't have. I've battled wicked spirits and demons in this world, but my primary duty is to get the people that God assigns me to into position to finish a journey. I can counsel people and I can protect them, and sometimes I can walk and talk with them like I am with you. God heals sick people through my hands, too. When I'm here on earth, I look and sound like that Morgan Freeman guy because he's a familiar and comforting face to so many - even if only on

TV and in movies. In a nutshell, I'm a multi-tasking guardian angel."

"Where do you go after you finish walking with me" Jeremy inquired.

"I'm off to East Syracuse for another mission. I don't know when I'll get to go home, probably not until specific events take place and people get where they need to be. Now in the meantime, you ought to eat that apple that I worked so hard to pull from your backpack, ha ha!"

Jeremy bit into the apple and juice ran down the sides of his chin. As he started to chew, his eyes grew wide as though he was hit with some sort of revelation, and it was then that he asked with a mouthful of fruit: "do you know when the Rapture is gonna be?"

"No Jeremy, I don't."

"Oh yes you do!" the precocious boy persisted.

While they ascended a small rise, Xavier stared straight ahead, steely-eyed for a few seconds, before answering:

"Jeremy, Jesus said that we would not know the day or hour, but that we would know the season by watching the signs. Even an angel does not know when, but I see the signs in Heaven and on earth and I sense that it is very near. God's angels and Satan's demons sense that something is about to happen. I've had more assignments in the last eight months than in my entire existence; so many people that I've had to spend time with. The pieces seem like they're in place, Jeremy, so stay watchful because Jesus will come like a thief in the night."

"My dad says that Jesus is the bridegroom and everyone who has believes in Him is His bride. He said He's gonna take us to a big wedding feast in Heaven when the Rapture happens. He read it to me from the Bible" Jeremy said straightforwardly, huffing and puffing a bit from exertion.

"Jeremy, written in Matthew chapter 25 is Jesus speaking the parable of the wise and foolish virgins - or wise and foolish young women if that's easier for you to understand. I'll bet your dad might have read this to you, but I think I have it here on the top of my head, ah yes..."

Xavier began to recite:

*"At that time the holy nation of heaven will be like ten women who have never had men. They took their lamps and went out to meet the man soon to be married. Five of them were wise and five were foolish. The foolish women took their lamps but did not take oil with them. The wise women took oil in a jar with their lamps. They all went to sleep because the man to be married did not come for a long time.*

*"At twelve o'clock in the night there was a loud call, 'See! The man soon to be married is coming! Go out to meet him!' Then all the women got up and made their lamps brighter. The foolish women said to the wise women, 'Give us some of your oil because our lamps are going out.' But the wise women said, 'No! There will not be enough for us and you. Go to the store and buy oil for yourselves.' While they were gone to buy oil, the man soon to be married came. Those who were ready went in with him to the marriage. The door was shut.*

*Later the foolish women came. They said, 'Sir, Sir, open the door for us!' But he said to them, 'For sure, I tell you, I do not know you!' So watch! You do not know what day or what hour the Son of Man is coming."*

Jeremy's face indicated knowing as he smiled and said "The Son of Man is Jesus, and the people who have accepted Him as Savior and Lord and are watching for Him with their eyes and their hearts are like those women who have oil in their lamps. The women who don't have the oil are the people who don't believe in Him or have walked away from Him and not kept oil in their lamps and their flame goes out. The people without oil won't be ready for Him when He comes to take us to the wedding feast! We have to be ready with oil in our lamps!"

"That's it in a nutshell, Jeremy. You are a smart kid and yes, people must watch with their eyes AND their hearts" Xavier replied with a wink and affirming nod of his head.

As they ascended a rise in the road, Jeremy inquired of Xavier "do you have the whole Bible committed to memory?"

The angel laughed and replied "goodness, Jeremy, I don't know, and yet whenever I need a scripture it's right there in my noggin!" As he said "noggin" he tapped on the side of his head with his right pointer finger for emphasis.

After crossing Hyde Road, which was a main artery into the Eagle Village housing development, they began to ascend another tree-lined gradient, not steep but with a leftward twist, and at the top on the left was a road that they would soon join.

Xavier pointed and asked "do you see that blue house up there on the left? That's where North Eagle Village Road is, and we're going to go that way."

"I've never been on that road, are you going to stay with me?" Jeremy asked nervously.

"Yes, Jeremy, I'm going to walk with you until we get to Salt Springs Road, which goes into the village of Chittenango, just like East Seneca Turnpike does where it becomes Brinkerhoff Hill Road. You remember what I said about Brinkerhoff Hill Road?"

“Yeah, you said there are sick wolves that regular wolves are afraid of” Jeremy answered.

“Indeed, and besides the wolves, Brinkerhoff Hill Road is dangerous to walk on because it’s steep and twisty and the shoulder is very narrow and people drive very dangerously fast around the curves” Xavier said knowingly and assuredly.

The little boy’s legs hurt and his back was aching from carrying his pack. He had travelled a long way as the minutes of that afternoon fell onto the scrapheap of history. The buses had just left Enders Road School loaded with passengers, which included bus #160 that he would have taken home.

His appetite had been satiated by the mere consumption of an apple. On a normal Wednesday he would be riding the school bus home and be ravenous, but this was not a normal day. This was an uncharacteristically warm day for early December and an unusual day in his life as a whole, and the bright, intelligent, and spiritually-mature six year old realized that he wasn’t the same little boy that woke up in his bed at 5:35 that morning, complaining of a stomach ache that wasn’t really a stomach ache at all but a heartache.

He believed that Xavier was an angel and not merely a man because he too was peculiar. He was sage and thoughtful but his smile was like that of a child. He pulled the aforementioned apple from Jeremy’s backpack without even touching it. And he had an air about him…

Seventeen year old Ali Feinstein didn’t much believe in angels or even God for that matter. The Fayetteville-Manlius High School senior was the god of her own life, with her parents being the well-heeled worshippers who lavished her with gifts like the black 2010 Land Rover LR4 that she had just received for “being a good girl who needed a dependable vehicle.”

The high school's music department would be putting on the musical *42nd Street* in late February and as the school day ended on that abnormally warm Wednesday in December, Ali was notified that she'd won the role of the chorus girl Peggy Sawyer.

"You wouldn't believe it daddy, I was like OH - MY - GOD" she screeched through her Bluetooth into attorney Paul Feinstein's ear as he sat with his feet on his desk while his paralegal Audra massaged his shoulders. "I mean, Katie McClenthen was a close second and would be my fill-in if you know, something happened, but like, as if? She's so thrift store, you know? And her father like works in a gas station or something, like…"

"OH MY GOD" Ali screamed as she hit her brakes, having not seen Xavier and Jeremy crossing East Seneca Turnpike as she chattered away while glancing at the freshly-manicured fingernails on her right hand while steering with her knees. She was literally two feet from hitting them when suddenly they were gone and she was heading into the ditch near the intersection with North Eagle Village Road.

The Bluetooth went flying and the nail polish smeared as the airbags burst open, and despite the damage to the front end of the brand spanking new Land Rover, Ali was uninjured. Jeremy was bewildered however as just seconds before he and Xavier were crossing East Seneca Turnpike and now they were standing on the shoulder of the short downhill gradient on North Eagle Village Road, a short distance from the stop sign at East Seneca Turnpike, next to the blue colonial house.

"Whoa man…how did that happen?" was all a nonplussed Jeremy could ask as he looked back over his shoulder in an effort to measure the distance he just travelled and the time he travelled it in - all while hearing the groaning metal of the Land Rover as it landed in the ditch.

“Faster than me grabbing that apple from your backpack, eh?” the angel chortled, as it took him literally one second to run he and Jeremy forty yards to safety - as only one of God’s angels could.

“So, a car almost hit us?” Jeremy asked, still befuddled.

“An SUV to be specific” Xavier replied as he stared up at the overcast mid-afternoon sky.

“And you carried me across the road and over to here?” Jeremy asked while squinting and rubbing his chin.

“Yes. We were crossing the Turnpike to get over here, but a young lady was distracted by her phone conversation and not paying attention. I scooped you up and moved as fast as I could before we would get hit, and I’m blessed that I was able to move that fast, praise the Lord. We got here more quickly than originally planned. I won’t be able to move that fast again while I’m on this assignment, so we need to be careful.” As the angel was answering Jeremy, he began to wince in pain as his expression revealed a sudden lack of wellness and much of the light in his eyes was gone.

“Do you feel okay?” Jeremy asked with concern.

“I’m suddenly very sore and tired, Jeremy. When an angel is human incarnate, they’re subject to some of the limits of the human body. Even incarnate, we’re stronger than any mortal human, but like a mortal human we can get sapped.”

“Can we stand here and rest for a few minutes? I have some snacks” the young boy offered hopefully.

Xavier’s reply was terse: “You go ahead and have a snack. I think you should eat one of your cheese sticks but I’ll pass, okay?”

“Are you mad? Did I do something wrong?” Jeremy replied, and his face looked as though he had been unexpectedly scolded.

A wan smile appeared on Xavier’s face as a Volkswagen needing a new exhaust passed by while a Manlius Police car chirped its siren as it slowed through the intersection behind them, responding to the Land Rover in the ditch.

“I’m sorry Jeremy, I didn’t mean to sound mad because I certainly am not. But, that maneuver I just made, taking us out of the road and over here - which is about 40 yards - all in the matter of a second’s time took a lot out of me. I can’t do that without suffering, because I’m in human form and God didn’t create human bodies to move that fast. God created physics and I defied the laws of physics and now the body suffers. I can’t go any farther without recharging so to speak, and the kind of recharge I need to repair the damage I did to this human body can’t be done while I’m in human form.”

“Well, how come we had to go 40 yards?” Jeremy asked.

“Pieces flew off of the front of the Land Rover that would have struck us, and anyway when you’re moving that fast you can’t stop on a dime” was the answer as Xavier squatted down.

“So after you change into an angel with wings for a few minutes and get a recharge, you can change back to the way you are now and you’ll be okay to walk more?” Jeremy asked hopefully, and before Xavier could reply, the little boy continued “when we start walking again, I want to tell you about how great my dad is and how I don’t like living with mom and Dennis, and how Dennis hits me and says mean things to my mom and how he makes fun of my dad because he loves Jesus and…”

The little boy ceased chattering when he saw the tears in the angel’s human eyes. In supernatural form, those eyes had seen the smile of Jesus up close and personal, and had so often gazed upon the indescribable wonders and inimitable glories of Heaven. But now, in mortal form, those eyes were heartbreak and physical human pain incarnate. As the tears of sadness flowed like rivulets from Xavier's eyes, his human hips, legs, and lower back were in excruciating pain as muscles and tendons had been pushed beyond human limits and were torn and strained. What the angel did should have been done in supernatural form, but with the Land Rover nearly on top of them there wasn't that extra second to make the metamorphosis. As the angel cried in physical pain and because he had grown so fond Jeremy and desired to go further with him, Jesus smiled as his good and faithful servant and warrior had already gone above and beyond in fulfilling his mission, but there was just a little more to do:

"Jeremy, I need to go and heal so this physical body can be ready for its next mission. I can't go any further my little friend but listen to me carefully, okay?"

Jeremy's face was red as tears streamed from his eyes as being wise for a six year old he understood that it was time, but he didn't want his friend to go.

"Okay, Xavier, I'm listening" he said while sniveling like any sad little boy would.

"Keep walking straight that way, and in a little while you'll come to Salt Springs Road. Go right on Salt Springs Road and you'll get to where you're going, got it? Just be very careful of strangers, okay? Trust the Holy Spirit, Jeremy, and listen to what it says. And oh, I know how great your dad is and he knows how it feels to be told that he looks like somebody famous!"

Xavier moaned and staggered as he stood up, his face contorted in agony. After standing, he quietly bent down and kissed Jeremy on the cheek and then he was gone.

Jeremy stood motionless for a moment, surveying his surroundings. He was sad, but he'd shed enough tears lately and it was time to dig down deep and be strong. When Xavier said "straight that way" he'd pointed directly ahead, so Salt Springs Road wouldn't be too hard to find.

Several cars drove by in either direction and the occupants of each gawked at him like he was a circus freak, but no one stopped to inquire as to why he stood on the narrow shoulder of the road. The wind still blew in occasional gusts, but it wasn't as persistent as it was an hour before. And likewise, the temperature had dropped a couple of degrees, but it was still abnormally warm. However, if the temperature dropped much further the hoodie would need to be retrieved from his backpack.

He took a bite from his cheese stick and began walking. He already missed the angel that he assigned the alias "Xavier" to, but who would ever believe him when he told the story of how the supernatural deity who looked like a Rasta-styled Morgan Freeman walked and talked with him and saved him from being run over by a Land Rover? He wondered if he would ever see Xavier again and he hoped that the angel would get "recharged" quickly.

The houses here were spacious split-levels and Georgian Colonials and set back behind deep front yards and a row of pine trees that bordered the road and ran from one property to the next. As Jeremy gazed at one particular tan Georgian with black trim, he whispered to himself "some of these people that live in these houses must be wealthy" and his observation was spot on. But, despite the houses along North Eagle Village Road and the tract that was fed by a side road, the area was very quiet and rustic.

Before long, Jeremy was looking at a sign for Townsend Road and he could see that farm road heading off to the right, with a big white barn and tall silo near the intersection. "That doesn't say Salt Springs Road, so don't go down that one" Jeremy thought to himself as he drew closer. He snatched his bottle of water from the mesh pocket on the side of his backpack and swallowed down the remaining fluid that was in it. He knew that his dad would have all the water he would need when he arrived there, so even if he got thirsty on the way he would just have to persevere.

As Jeremy approached the spot where Townsend Road angled from North Eagle Village Road to the northeast, a two-tone blue 1979 Ford F-150 pickup that was badly rusted rolled through the stop sign on Townsend and made a left onto North Eagle Village, headed in the direction Jeremy walked from. When the driver was even with Jeremy, he stopped the rusty truck and rolled down the squeaky driver's side window.

The driver was the skinny, sickly-looking man Josiah "the Eel" that Jesse had dreamed about on the Friday night after Thanksgiving. A passenger rode with him, the ashen-skinned black-eyed teenage boy named Aliah that Jesse had dreamed of and also saw in the parking lot of the Ten Pin attempting CPR on Eddie Ramsden. The black-eyed girl Lilitu who was in the same dream and in the parking lot was not present.

"Where ya goin' kid, ya need a ride er somethin'?" Josiah asked with a rasp, as tobacco juice dribbled down his chin and onto the door of the pickup.

"Oh, no, sir, I'm almost there. I'm not supposed to talk to strangers but thanks anyway" Jeremy answered nervously, and he tried to resume walking but his legs were again having technical difficulties.

"Stranger? I ain't no stranger! Gee whiz kid, ya hurt my feelings. I'm Josiah the Eel, 1952 New York State high school wrestlin' champeen from Fayetteville Man-less High Screwl, er was it 1942, aw hell, I cain't remember! But anyhoo…"

Aliah interrupted Josiah's shtick with a monotone "you said you wrestled for West Genesee and Chittenango. You need to get your story…"

Josiah cut Aliah off: "Shut up kid or I'll feed ya t' the wolves on Brinkerhoff Hill! Anyhoo, that's why they call me 'the Eel' - because I was so quick and slippery that nobody could pin me! So, little Spider-Man fan, what's yer name?"

"Sir, I don't want to tell you…"

Josiah roared "listen you little piss-ant, tell me yer cotton-pickin' name, Jeremy!" As he did, a bloody ball of phlegm flew from his mouth and landed in the road while more tobacco juice oozed along his chin.

Jeremy was experiencing the same paralyzing fear that overtook him when he encountered the two thugs on Military Way. There were no signs of a blue Dodge Ram or Xavier, so he was truly alone in the world.

"You already know my name" Jeremy answered in a tight-throated whisper.

"Yeah, I know it 'cuz me and 'Coal Eyes' over here was playin' Ouija and we saw the words 'BOY' and 'JEREMY' spelled out, so we know that Auld Hornie was tellin' us we was gonna meet you, and then the plectrum spelled out 'GIVE HIM A RIDE'. So, when Auld Hornie says t' do somethin' we do it! We brought along a plastic baggie a' some a' them marshmallows from Lucky Charms cereal 'cuz the board said you like 'em. So, ya gonna git in er what?"

"Come ride with us Jeremy. Come tell us about Jesus" Aliah spoke in his usual monotone as he poked his head into the window.

“Jesus is Lord. I like to tell people about Him” Jeremy answered, and now it felt like his legs would work and he’d be able to share the gospel with the two in the truck - even if they were kind of strange.

He looked both ways to make sure that the road was clear to cross. But then, as he put his right foot forward the word “*NO*” welled up in his spirit as a still, soft voice inside of him, and yet there was no mistaking what it said.

Jeremy stopped in his tracks and turned volte-face in the direction he originally was headed, but was startled when Josiah snarled with his raspy, damaged vocal chords “where ya goin’ ya little turd?! Git over here n’ tell us about Jesus so we can believe! You don’t want it t’ be yer fault if we go t’ Hell, right? You don’t want Jesus t’ hate ya, do ya?”

It was Aliah who spoke next; with a face as forlorn as any Jeremy has ever seen in his six years of life:

“Jeremy please…please don’t let us go to Hell. Make us believe. It’s the one thing that Xavier forgot to tell you to do. Come share the gospel with us, Jeremy. Please Jeremy; it will be your fault if we burn in the Lake of Fire…please, make Jesus proud of you!”

Jeremy was terrified and shaking. He didn’t want it to be his fault that they didn’t believe. As he turned back toward the truck, the Holy Spirit spoke again as a lovely, snow white dove landed on a branch that overhung the road where the truck sat idling:

*Run, Jeremy. Aliah is a demon and Josiah is overcome with a demonic spirit. They are deceivers and murderers who will not believe until the White Throne Judgment. Run Jeremy, now!*

His feet were again like those of a deer, running like he did on Military Way. As he ran as fast as he could, he heard the pickup truck peel out and speed away. He then glanced over his shoulder while his legs throbbed in protest and he saw that Josiah and Aliah were gone. As he turned and faced forward while slowing to a steady walk he pressed on because he had too, past the back entrance to the Fayetteville-Manlius High School on his left and the observatory that his first grade class was planning to visit in the spring.

Although his young hips ached like they would if he was an elderly person and his legs and back had lost much of their strength, the little boy knew he had to push onward. He had an idea as to how Xavier felt because he too was in pain and wanted to morph into a supernatural state in order to recharge.

The shoulder was wide again and that gave Jeremy a feeling of safety. After passing a white shotgun-styled house he saw the signs for Salt Springs Road. The abode's large side yard that bordered the intersection was bedecked with a row of six and seven foot tall pines that were strung with Christmas lights waiting for dark to come so they could twinkle and shine. He was glad that he remembered Xavier saying to go right on Salt Springs Road, because here the intersection was "L" shaped; Salt Springs going straight toward Fayetteville and right toward Chittenango.

# 15

# The Wayfarer (part 2)

Jeremy was about to begin his trek along Salt Springs Road, while Dennis and Allison had a while ago awakened from their naps and discovered him AWOL. The stepfather had driven several miles in either direction along Route 92 and around the residential streets of the village of Manlius in search of his stepson, and East Seneca Turnpike would be the next roadway he would search. Allison was combing Mill Run Park, which was one of Jeremy's favorite places, while frantically calling the parents of her son's friends to inquire as to whether or not they'd seen him. She had likewise contacted the Manlius Police, but as it had only been a couple of hours since they'd noticed him missing, there was nothing they could do as far as filing a missing person's report just yet. Still, officers on the street would keep an eye out. Being that his backpack was missing as were some foodstuffs, it appeared that he was a runaway and not an abductee. An Amber Alert could not be filed unless there was evidence of abduction.

Although the paths through Mill Run Park's woods were muddy from recent precipitation, the weather on that uncharacteristically warm December 2nd brought out plenty of the Manlius yuppies and Haut Monde to jog and to walk their designer dogs. None of the snooty partakers of the day's warm weather had seen Jeremy, nor did they have much patience for Allison's frantic inquiries thereof.

After being treated like a piece of gum stuck to the bottom of a particular young Syracuse University professor's $220.00 Ecco Biom running shoes, Allison was finally moved to call Jesse to inform him that their son was missing.

"I don't know where he went, Jesse. His backpack and some of his clothes are gone and so are some snack foods, so he definitely ran away."

"He'll come home, Allison. He can't get too far and he'll be hungry for supper soon. I still think he's in the park somewhere. Just don't panic, he'll be fine, I know he will" Jesse spoke coolly, and for the first time in years Allison was calmed by his voice and was curiously struck with the notion that she missed him.

Dennis had driven East Seneca Turnpike (Route 173) past East Lake Road to where it became Brinkerhoff Hill Road and then recklessly down the high-hilled, curvy stretch of highway into the village of Chittenango. As the conversation between Allison and Jesse was ending, Dennis was slowly driving his black 2008 Acadia along the one way Rouse Street; going behind Delphia's Restaurant, past the dilapidated pink barn and the rear of MGM Auto Parts, and then along a row of small bungalows and modest multi-family houses. When he had arrived at the back of the two-family house that Jesse lived in on Genesee Street, Dennis had hoped to see the Jeep Grand Cherokee parked in its usual spot in the small parking area on Rouse, but the vehicle wasn't present. "Well, the brat probably isn't here" Dennis grumbled to himself before turning left onto Genesee to head back toward the center of town.

Being distracted by a phone call that came in from John McMurtry as he approached the fork where Brinkerhoff Hill Road twisted uphill toward Manlius and Route 5 bent to the right toward Fayetteville, Dennis made the right turn instead of travelling back up the way he came down.

After a short but anxious discussion about the declining sales numbers, Dennis said "No worries" to John McMurtry who was on the other end of his Bluetooth, "I can just take Salt Springs Road back to Manlius." And as he said this, he made the left turn onto the aforementioned road and started up the hill that was not as hazardous as Brinkerhoff but still fairly steep and twisting.

"Joe and I are leaving the Oneida store right now and heading to the lodge with the last burgundy 2010 Equinox. I know it's the one you wanted Dennis, but Bob Sollars is really interested and he doesn't get your employee discount, so my margin will be better! So, you're out looking for Allison's kid?"

"Yeah" Dennis answered, "and when I find him I'm going to beat his ass. I can't stand his father Jesse and…what the hell!?"

The next thing John McMurtry heard was a quick but blood-curdling scream combined with an air horn blast, the screeching of tires, and a rapid series of pops and bangs before the phone went dead.

The speedy succession of horrific sounds through his own Bluetooth so startled and terrified the 82 year old McMurtry that his heart jumped into cardiac arrest, causing him to lose control of the Equinox while his 58 year old son Joe attempted to grab the wheel - but it was all too little too late. The Equinox hit the guardrail at 50 MPH and then scaled it, rolled over three times and came to a rest on the passenger's side in a field before becoming engulfed in flames. As Joe McMurtry shrieked for a few seconds until he quickly burned to death, his father was already plummeting toward the "sewer tunnel."

The last rational thought that Dennis Dalton had as he vocalized "what the hell" was why was there a mangy-looking wolf sitting in the lane in front of him and why wouldn't it move? The answer to the question that Dennis never received was that not all of Chittenango's sickly wolves were roaming the brush along Brinkerhoff Hill Road.

Dennis was in shock, and his blood-deprived brain and misfiring synapses produced other questions: How come the airbag didn't work? Why am I laying on the hood of a NY D.O.T. dump truck? Did somebody call 911? I really think I might be hurt, can somebody help me? Where are my legs? Ugh…did all this blood come out of me? How come only my right arm works? Do I have more intestine hanging out, or did that guy from across the street push it all back in before he puked? Why did that other guy say 'his legs are over there and they're still twitching?' Uh…is my heart still beating because I don't feel it?"

As he stared up in shock at the overcast sky, all became dark and he felt like he was rapidly falling backward. There were voices that moaned, some that screamed, and even some that cackled dementedly. As the feeling of falling stopped, he was standing in a dark room with dimly-lit hallways that led away. At first, he felt better because it seemed that his body was fully intact. But, in his final act of arrogance and indignation he asked "I believe in a higher power, so how did I end up in this stinking sewer tunnel?!"

After he spoke, the moaning became more mournful, the stench more rancid, and the cackling ceased - except for that from the deteriorating individual in the physician's coat that held the suture and needle. Then, a feeling of separation and despair swept over him as he realized he would never know the most royal of royalty. He realized too late that an inheritance worth more than all of the world's gold and silver would have been his for all eternity if he would have just believed in the simple truth of a bloodstained cross. Indeed, he was about to come face to face with a higher power who was not some great architect of the universe but the prince of darkness and destruction.

Passengers in cars that passed Jeremy continued to gawk, but fortunately no one stopped. He'd had enough trouble that day, and he prayed silently that the remainder of his journey would be a safe one. On the surface, he worried a little that when he reached the end of Salt Springs Road that he wouldn't know which way to go, but way down deep inside that worry was abated and confidence arose.

There weren't many houses on this end of Salt Springs Road, but the shoulder was wide and safer to walk than that which he just left on North Eagle Village Road. He was tired and growing hungry for real food and thirsty for fresh cold water, but he had to push on, despite the hilly terrain and the pain in his legs and lower back. He did not second-guess his decision to head for his dad's place, but he did not consider how long and tiring a walk it would be.

In the distance Jeremy heard the sirens of emergency vehicles and the sound came from the direction in which he was headed. He felt a chill like an icy lightning bolt flash through his chest and stomach as the sirens were foreboding in a way that he could not put a finger on. He was both spiritually mature and sensitive for a six year old, and the sound of those distant sirens was causing distress to bubble like magma in the crevices of his soul.

"Something happened to somebody that I know" Jeremy spoke aloud and the sound of his voice surprised him and heightened his anxiety.

He began to worry that something had happened to his father. He thought to himself "what if his apartment caught fire and he was trapped? What if a helicopter crashed into his apartment? What if the whole 'Nango was suddenly on fire?"

He found himself walking more quickly as he was powered by a surge of adrenaline. It was then that he had a vision in his mind of his mother sobbing while his father said "I'm sorry for your loss, Allison" while he held her for a moment but then let go and walked away. In the vision his mom cried "please don't go, Jesse" while his father, now out of view said "I can't stay, Allison. All I can do is pray for your comfort."

Jeremy was just a toddler, but he remembered how his mother hurt his father. As he walked, he remembered his mother saying to his father that he needed to try to do better in his life and that she wanted more. He remembered her saying to his father that for the sake of Jeremy he shouldn't leave right away, but as soon as the divorce was finalized that he had better be gone. He remembered Dennis staying overnight and sleeping in the same spot in his mom's bed that his dad had before she decided to divorce him.
These memories made the mourning in the ocean of Jeremy's soul sink fifty fathoms deep because he not only loved his dad but he liked him too and wanted to be with him. He loved his mother as well, but he did not like her. His dad said that people had to love the way that Jesus did, but he could not love Dennis as much as he tried. Dennis made good money in his job and that made his mom happy, but Dennis was a very bad man who was the god of his own life and tried to the god of many other people.
The breeze was becoming chilly as the afternoon grew later and the sun was getting into position to begin its descent into the western horizon. Jeremy's sadness dissolved like an Alka-Seltzer tablet in his soul's ocean as he stopped walking and pulled the pack from his back and set it on the shoulder of the road. It felt good to have the pack off and Jeremy released an "aah" while stretching his arms.

As he opened his backpack and retrieved his hoodie, an SUV drove past in the direction that he was headed. As he began to pull the garment onto his arms, he saw the vehicle's break lights come on and then its backing lights as it started heading toward him in reverse.

Jeremy froze in fear as he did not know the intention of the driver. He wanted to run, but again his legs experienced temporary technical difficulties. As the SUV backed toward him, a police helicopter circled above, being involved with whatever tragic scene was unfolding further ahead. He wished that the helicopter's occupants would see him and lower down a rope ladder so he could climb to safety.

As the vehicle backed up even with him, he could see two young boys that were close to his age sitting in the bench seats. There was a lady who was the driver, and she lowered the front passenger's side window from where she sat behind the wheel.

"Jeremy?"

His mom and dad and even Dennis had told him not to talk to strangers. Xavier had warned him to be careful of strangers and in that he remembered the demon-possessed Josiah and the demon boy that rode with him. As he looked at this smiling lady and saw the two boys sitting behind her - one of whom offered a friendly wave - he did not sense any stranger danger. But how did the lady know his name?

"Jeremy - is that you?" she inquired of him, having seen a photo in an e-mail that his father had sent her just before that night where she had a bit too much to drink and nearly got killed.

The purple Escalade was sharp looking, and as he thought about how nice it would be to ride in it he answered "yes, I'm Jeremy."

As he answered her, he remembered his father showing him her Facebook profile picture and him saying "that's Erica. I'm not her Facebook friend, but I'm her friend in real life. She has one son who is a year younger than you and one that is a year older than you."

"Honey, you had better get in here right now! I don't know how you got here, but this is no place for you to be walking alone." As he began to climb into the front passenger's seat, Erica grabbed his left hand to help him in and said "I don't have an extra child seat, but that's not anything to worry about."

She took his backpack from him and set it behind her seat, in front of Nicholas, who exclaimed "that's a cool backpack. I think that Spidey is awesome!"

"Buckle your seatbelt, Jeremy. And oh, by the way, my name is Erica, and that's Nicholas who's seven and Christopher who's five."

The boys all exchanged greetings while Erica began to drive forward. Jeremy then asked "so you're the lady that won all the money?"

Before Erica could answer, Nicholas proclaimed with glee "yeah, we're filthy rich, dude! Yee-ha! We have more money than dad's new woman now!"

"Nicholas, that is not appropriate" Erica scolded. "We were very blessed to win a whole lot of money, but we need to do good things with it so it won't be 'filthy', right?"

"Yeah, mom" the embarrassed seven year old replied shamefacedly as his younger brother giggled while watching a SpongeBob SquarePants episode on the DVD player in back.

"Jeremy, it is so nice to meet you. I've heard so much about you" Erica gushed, before a look of grave concern overtook her face as she demanded "but what were you doing walking out here? Does your father or your mother know where you are?"

The cabin seat was comfortable, and as Jeremy sank into it smelling the strawberry-scented air freshener he felt like he could fall asleep. But, he had Erica's question to answer, and he didn't want to lie, even if it meant that she would drive him back to Manlius.

"I ran away from home because my mom and stepfather are gonna talk to a lawyer try to keep my dad from seeing me without someone else being with us. They really don't want me to see him at all, so I'm running away to his place."

"I see; they're trying to get custody terms modified so your visits with your dad would be supervised, if they'd allow them all!" Erica spoke with a sense of knowing, her voice providing an agitated soundtrack to the canvas of consternation that was her face.

As Christopher and Nicholas were immersed in another episode of SpongeBob, Jeremy voiced his greatest fear of all. It was a fear greater than meeting Josiah and Aliah or the two thugs Davey and Tommy. It was a fear greater than having to encounter again that druggy kid who threw the can of Arizona tea.

He held back tears as he beseeched "please, please, please, don't take me back home...please!"

Erica the loving mother was a lioness who would defend her cubs to the death if it came down to it. And the cub that sat next to her in the cabin of the Escalade was the the son of the man that she'd known only a short time and had shared more communications via phone, Skype, and e-mail than in person; but still she loved that man. So in her heart and mind, his cub was her cub too.

She had to keep her eyes on the twisting, dipping road, but she nodded her head as she spoke:

“Jeremy, I am taking you home.”

She paused for a second and as she did a lightning bolt of panic flashed through Jeremy’s chest and stomach before she finished with “I’m taking you home to Chittenango with your dad.”

“Hey, we live in the ‘Nango too!” Christopher pronounced from the rear bench seat.

“Don’t yell while mom is driving - ‘Chrissie!’” Nicholas scolded, calling his brother the feminine version of his name in a facetious, mocking voice that made Jeremy giggle.

“My name is Christopher, not Chrissie, sticky Nicky!” Chris retorted as he smacked his brother’s shoulder as best as he could while being belted into his seat.

“Knock it off you two, or else no television for the rest of the day and no ice cream” Erica fired back without taking her eyes off the road. The two boys were funny, and Jeremy bit his lower lip to help keep back his laughter.

Erica’s eyes were focused on the intersection of Salt Springs Road and Palmer Road. A New York State Trooper had just parked his blue and gold Crown Victoria with red and blue flashing strobe lights in the middle of the intersection, and he climbed out and walked toward the stopping Escalade as he held up a flashlight with a florescent orange cone at the end.

A small feeling of panic rose up in Erica’s chest as she wondered if Jesse’s ex-wife had called the police and reported Jeremy as kidnapped. It wasn’t likely after all, but it was possible she thought to herself as she nervously pushed the button to lower the driver’s side window as the trooper approached.

A curious Christopher asked “Mom, is he gonna put Jeremy in jail for running away?”

“Hi” Erica said as the trooper walked to the window, her heart pounding so hard that she wouldn’t have been surprised if the cop could hear it from a couple of feet away.

The 56 year old trooper with M. DONNELLY on the name bar pinned to his chest pocket peered inside the vehicle for two seconds that seemed like an eternity before saying “mam, I’m about to set up roadblock. There’s been a bad accident further down Salt Springs near Route 5, so you’ll have to take Palmer Road up to Route 173 and go down Brinkerhoff Hill if you’re heading to Chittenango.”

Feeling some relief, she asked “would it be okay to take Gulf Road to Route 5?”

“No m’am, we’re closing Gulf as well. We’re trying to keep traffic off of Route 5 going into Chittenango because it’s near the spot on Salt Springs where the wreck is. Have a good day and drive safe” the trooper said and then backed away from the vehicle while motioning with his flashlight - even though dusk had yet to fall - for her to drive up Palmer Road.

“I wanna be a police man and have a gun” Chris announced, while Nick said “cool. I’d arrest all the people I don’t like - like you Kris Kringle!”

“Mom!” Christopher protested, which elicited the response from Erica of “Nicholas, don’t you talk that way! You love your brother and you like him too. You tell him you’re sorry!”

Nick: “I’m sorry Chris.”

Chris: “Only ‘cuz mom told you to be!”

As Erica drove up Palmer Road, she said with a nervous giggle “he could have given me a ticket Jeremy because you’re in the front and not in a child seat. I guess he was concentrating on getting the road closed."

"And he didn't think you kidnapped me" Jeremy said with a smile, before his visage darkened and he followed with "but maybe we shouldn't go down Brinkerhoff Hill Road."

Erica answered "There's no other way to go, Jeremy, unless we take this road all the way to Route 92 and go into Cazenovia. We'd have to take Route 13 from Cazenovia back to Chittenango. What's the matter with Brinkerhoff Hill Road?"

"Uh…nothing, I guess" was Jeremy's answer, and as he spoke he realized that as long as they were in an SUV they'd be safe.

Palmer was a curvy, hilly country road like others in this area, and while Erica straightened the curves with the skill of an Indy car driver, Jeremy conversed with Nick and Chris about SpongeBob, Power Rangers, Wii, Spider-Man, and Super Mario.

After two minutes time the Escalade had climbed the hill on Palmer Road to the intersection of Route 173 - East Seneca Turnpike, and after waiting at the stop sign for an 18 wheel Sunoco fuel tanker to pass by at a dangerously high rate of speed headed toward Chittenango, she turned left with a sudden feeling of foreboding that could not be overshadowed by the gleeful sounds of the three boys.

Erica wasn't a racist, but she did find it peculiar that as the truck sped by she noticed that it was driven by a young Middle Eastern man wearing a white t-shirt and not a blue Sunoco uniform top. Her younger brother Jeff had driven for Sunoco before going to work as an engineer for the Finger Lakes Railroad in 2008, and he was required to wear the Sunoco uniform when on the job.

As she turned onto East Seneca Turnpike, she saw the trailer fishtail several times as she estimated that the truck was moving at close to 80 MPH on the curvy road. "That's just not right" she said to herself as she headed toward the Madison County line and the town of Sullivan in which Chittenango was part of. Something was wrong with this picture; she didn't know just what, but something was certainly wrong.

Her mind was awash with thoughts as she drove. It had been four hours since she'd had a cigarette and she really needed one, but she would never smoke in the Escalade while children were with her - exposing them to secondhand smoke. She thought about how surprised Jesse was going to be to see his son at his door; courtesy of the woman who was supposed to be in Memphis, Tennessee. She thought about how she believed it would be best for Jesse if he never knew that he was the son of Elvis Presley. Sure, she'd love to deliver the news, but she wouldn't let it slip.

What a busy day it had been as she had gotten the process started to homeschool her sons. They had shopped for clothes and for books, and they'd looked at a house on East Pleasant Street in Manlius. She'd never told her landlord that she was going to buy out her lease, so she didn't have to jump on the first house she saw as there would be time to shop around. She could afford a home in the seven figure range if she so chose to, but that was not how she wanted to live. Her money would not be squandered and in that she desired to do more good with it.

In the hustle and bustle of her day, she had forgotten to get gasoline, even though the Escalade's fuel gauge had indicated the tank was nearing empty. And as she thought again about the fuel tanker that was now at the bottom of Brinkerhoff Hill and running the red light at the intersection with Route 5, the Escalade was stalling as it had run out of gas at the top of the hill, just beyond the intersection of East Lake Road.

As she pulled the rolling vehicle over to the shoulder on the last remotely flat section of road at the top of the hill, Nicholas asked suspiciously "what are we doing, mom?"

"Guys, we've run out of gas. I mistakenly left my cellphone home and I haven't activated my On-Star subscription yet, so we're going to have to walk down the hill and into the village."

As Nicholas and Christopher moaned their discontent, a lump formed in Jeremy's throat as another anxiety-driven bolt of iced lightning flashed through his chest and stomach.

Jeremy was bug-eyed with panic and his voice cracked as he asked "we're going to walk all the way down the hill?"

Erica flipped on the four-way flashers and then pulled the keys from the ignition. As she helped Christopher unbuckle the straps on his child seat, she answered "yes, that's the only way. It's narrow and it's not very straight, so we'll need to walk single-file and be very careful guys. Wait until there's no cars coming then get out on the driver's side so you don't step down into the ditch. When you get out, line up on the side of the road and wait for me to lead. Does everybody understand?"

After a black Kia raced by, straddling both lanes on its way down the hill, Erica commanded "everybody out and get onto the side of the road!"

Nicholas was out first as he sat on the driver's side, and Jeremy was a nanosecond behind, after climbing over the driver's seat. Christopher was scooped out by his mom and they made it to the shoulder, just as a jacked-up red Ford pickup rolled past. The truck slowed as the passenger's side window went down, and a scruffy 30-something construction laborer catcalled "hey baby, you're a hot little MILF!"

Erica was moved to respond back, shouting with intemperate sarcasm and disdain "thanks for stopping to help, renaissance man" as she maneuvered the three boys into single-file while the truck's driver hit the gas, creating a vociferous roar through the vehicle's Cherry Bomb muffler.

Before they commenced to trekking down the hill, Nick inquired innocently "mom, what's a MILF?"

Erica was firm in her response as she explained "it's a very bad word about women, and I don't want any of you boys to ever use it!"

"Really? I didn't think it was bad because once when I was in the lunch line, I heard the principal Mr. Bannister say to the gym teacher Mr. Corbett that my teacher Mrs. Lucio was a MILF, and she's really nice" Nick replied, his seven year old mind not having been tainted with the knowledge of the derogatory nature of the term.

Erica answered resolutely "and that's one of the reasons why you boys are going to be homeschooled from now on. Now, I don't want to hear that word again, so let's walk - and carefully!"

It would be dusk soon, and the lioness desired nothing more in these waning minutes of full daylight than to get her three cubs down off of this treacherous, twisting hill with its narrowing shoulder. She was glad that they were headed downhill and not climbing up, but the descent on foot was nearly as vigorous and precarious as the ascent.

There were some fine homes set back off of the road near the top of Brinkerhoff Hill, but her instinct was not to go calling on any of the residents for help, especially since one of her cubs could be considered a runaway - but was he really? And there was always the burden of putting up with the "new normal" until the hubbub quieted down. There were the encounters with well-meaning yet irritating busybodies who would treat her like a reluctant celebrity as they would ask "hey, ain't you the lady who won the Powerball?

I saw yer pitcher (sic) in the Post-Standard! Boy, if ya ever need any help spendin' all that money, ya lemme know, okay?"

More than ever, she wanted only to keep a low profile. There were letters and e-mails coming from struggling individuals and from numerous charities seeking her help, but she was certain that many were scams. She had already helped two struggling Chittenango families by paying off mortgages on their modest houses before they were foreclosed on - and she desired to help others - but all in time and right now she needed to get all of her own ducks in a row.

The individual that she desired to help the most didn't seem to need it - at least not in the monetary sense. Certainly his parsimonious existence was smart but not truly necessary as he had some money in the bank, courtesy of Dicky Same, who was compensated well by the King of Rock-n-Roll not only for security provided but even more for true, unwavering friendship.

Money didn't matter a whole lot to Jesse, as he seemed to make do with what he had and not complain about what he didn't have. To Erica, Jesse seemed like he really wasn't a part of this world, only a wayfarer on a journey to something and someplace better - and while on the way he would do as he needed to do.

It was Jesse's kind, almost alien-esque quality that attracted her even more than his good looks. In a world of evil he was inherently good. In a world of drunkenness he was the epitome of sobriety. In a world of dishonor and deceit he was honorable. In a world of injustice, he was just. As much as a mortal man could be he was pure. And while he was handsome, in Erica's mind and heart he was truly lovely. The way that he put others before himself and the way that he fathered his son in a world of fathers stuck in perpetual adolescence was commendable. Yes, as a human, mortal man Jesse was excellence personified.

The cubs were quiet, perhaps a bit distracted and overwhelmed as they followed behind her. After passing driveways on either side of the steep hill, Erica stopped abruptly, causing the forward momentum of the cubs to be halted. She knelt down and hugged Chris, then kissed him on the cheek before saying "I love you." She then repeated the act with Nick, saying "I love you my big boy." Then, she looked at Jeremy, who physically took after both his father and his mother, and she saw enough of Jesse to fill her heart with joy as she hugged him, kissed him on the cheek, and said "and I love you just like you're my own." She then stood up and said "now everybody be careful because the traffic is getting heavier and the hill is getting steeper."

As the lioness and her cubs resumed walking, she thought to herself "it's amazing that none of these drivers would stop and see if we needed help." When that discontented thought passed, something from way back in her childhood flashed in her mind as she passed a gorgeous, white split-level house with a long driveway and a huge yard that was surrounded by a cornfield on three sides and woods off in the corner. The home and the property reflected opulence, and after this house was nothing but trees, brush, and sharp curves. The home had nothing to do with what was in her mind, but it did bring to mind her church teen group and reading the scripture from John chapter 14 where Jesus said that in His father's house were many mansions and that He was going to prepare a place there. It hit her that Jesse had that quiet knowledge that Jesus was the one who would get him to that better place, that mansion in Heaven when his time on earth was finished. And as that comforting thought floated through her busy brain, a scripture returned after having been locked out of her life for so many years, and she remembered it as one of her favorites, and it warmed her heart as it returned home. It was Philippians chapter 4, verse 8:

*Finally, brothers, whatever is true, whatever is honorable, whatever is just, whatever is pure, whatever is lovely, whatever is commendable, if there is any excellence, if there is anything worthy of praise, think about these things.*

It was those very things that she could easily ascribe to Jesse, and in that she realized that he was the man that he was because of His love of and faith in Jesus. As they passed the magnificent house and its sprawling property, she was moved to speak aloud "Jesus is Lord!"

Jeremy was only six years old, but his cognizance of the Lordship of Jesus was more mature than that of many adult Christians. As Nick and Chris had walked quietly and Erica had been reviewing the essence of John 14 and recalling Philippians 4:8, Jeremy had prayed silently:

"Lord, I know that this nice lady Erica believed in you once but ran away. She's being like a mom to me and my dad really likes her, I can tell. Please Lord; let her remember you, in the name of Jesus I pray, amen."

After Erica's pronouncement of her faith, Jeremy spoke up and said "Lord Jesus, please protect us from the wolves."

"Are there wolves here?" Christopher asked nervously.

"Yeah, werewolves" Nicholas answered with a smirk, and then turned to his brother who walked directly behind him and in front of Jeremy and affected a howling sound - "barr-ooooo!"

The grade was steepening, which increased gravity's pull on them as they walked downhill. At this point there was nothing on either side of Brinkerhoff Hill Road but brush and trees, save for the shallow ditches paralleling both lanes. The shoulder was narrow and a pewter-hued 2007 Chevy Silverado pickup that was travelling at an unsafe speed down the hill blasted its horn at them as they maneuvered around a dead raccoon that had been crushed by a vehicle earlier that day.

"Ugh, that's gross" was all Erica could say as Nicholas offered his analysis: "it's road pizza, look at the sausage and pepperoni!"

“That’s not sausage and pepperoni, that’s guts” Christopher corrected his brother, not understanding the humor implied.

“Your brain is sausage and pepperoni” was Nick’s caustic reply, feeling embarrassed by his little brother’s admonishment.

It was then that Erica intervened with “okay guys, forget the road pizza and pay attention to where you are walking, please!”

A little further down the hill was a sharp curve that was marked with three yellow signs, each bearing a black arrow pointing in the direction that the road followed the curve. Attached to the yellow sign that was furthest to the left was a green metal sign with VILLAGE OF CHITTENANGO applied in white reflective lettering.

Jeremy had been silent during the “road pizza” debate, and that was because his insides were throbbing with the sensation that danger lurked near. He couldn’t and wouldn’t put out of his mind the warning that Xavier had issued to him, and now there he was, walking Brinkerhoff Hill Road as daylight was starting to slip into dusk. He’d taken his hoodie back off when inside of the Escalade, and now he wished that he hadn’t left it in the vehicle with his backpack as the temperature was falling further. Nick and Chris each wore a hooded windbreaker - Nick’s being light blue and Chris’ navy blue. Erica wore a grey Carhartt hoodie with a quarter-length zipper, and Jeremy imagined that each of them were warm as the temperature was dropping through the fifties. It could have been even chillier for Jeremy if he didn’t have the foresight to dress in two shirts.

Erica was mentally kicking herself for not fueling up when prompted to. Having struggled financially for so many months, she had developed a habit of “running on fumes” with the hope of making it until there was cash for more gas. Wasn’t it fitting that it was now when she could afford to keep her vehicle sufficiently fueled that the fumes would actually run out!

It would have been worse if she had run out of gas while descending the grade, but the top of Brinkerhoff Hill was bad enough. She was fortunate that the shoulder was wide enough there that the Escalade was out of the flow of traffic - however barely - but her concern that the disabled SUV would be hit by a reckless driver was plausible. The four-way flashers were on, but dusk was nearly upon them and Brinkerhoff Hill Road was a treacherous place to drive - and to walk - in low light conditions. Vapors of anxiety were beginning to creep in through the cracks in the walls of her mind and it inspired images of a terrible wreck where someone is killed - all because she made the absent-minded decision to run on empty.

Christopher's voice startled her out of her anxious obsession as he asked fretfully "what was that, mommy?"

As they approached the sharp curve, there was rapid snapping and swift rustling in the trees and brush that bordered the road, and they were separated from whatever made that sound only by a ditch strewn with rocks, roots, and discarded food wrappers and beverage bottles and cans whose colorful labels had been faded by the elements.

They all heard it, even as several vehicles passed in either direction. As the vapors of her anxiety became more of a heavy fog, Erica began to second-guess not going to the door of one of the houses back behind them in an effort to get help.

"That's it guys, I need a cigarette. We're outside so the smoke won't bother you" Erica snapped as she pulled her pack of "Cowboy Killers" and her yellow Bic lighter from the right pocket of her hoodie. She was glad that she didn't leave the smokes back in her purse locked in the Escalade.

“It’s a wolf” Jeremy elucidated as he stared at the brush, “maybe even more than one.”

“A wolf? Wolves don’t live around here!” Erica said with equal parts surprise and confusion as she drew a refreshing drag of Marlboro smoke deep into her lungs. Before anyone could say anything else, she offered a useful bit of advice: “No matter what it is, we need to be walking away from here toot-sweet!”

As they began to walk with new-found energy, Jeremy illuminated further: “they are wolves, and they’re sick with something worse than rabies. It’s something supernatural.”

“Is supernatural a superhero that will come and save us?” Christopher asked, and the sweet little boy was starting to shed tears of genuine fear as he walked.

“They’re paralleling us, almost like it or they is trying to taunt us. Just keep walking everybody, keep on walking” the lioness instructed her cubs.

“Mommy, I just saw the eyes on one of them and they were orange” Nicholas declared fretfully. For the seven year old to refer to his mother as “mommy” and not “mom” indicated a considerable level of duress.

“Don’t look in their direction, just keep walking” Erica ordered.

“I heard a growl”

“So did I”

“Me too”

“Once we get around this curve and the next one, there is a house across the road and Crouse Gravel Company on this side. We are going to one of the two for help. Pray guys, silently to yourselves.

The Lord will protect us. He didn't bring us all this way just to get ripped up by demonic wolves" Erica spoke with a confidence fueled by her reignited faith in Jesus, and as the boys started to pray while they walked, she spoke again:

"Careful, there's one in the ditch over there…Oh no, no, no, it's walking toward us but it has a limp…"

She extended her right arm behind her back in an effort to halt the boys as she spoke rapidly "now there are two in the ditch and they both seem injured but they're coming toward us and…"

"Mommy, mommy, mommy" Chris screamed as he grabbed Erica by the waist as his brother Nick's lower lip quivered while his legs froze in panic. Nick heard Jeremy whispering silently behind him in a language he did not understand; that language being Hebrew. Jeremy had never prayed in tongues before but he did now, led by the Holy Spirit. Suddenly, the wolves limped into an unsteady about-face as their attention was drawn to the vehicle that was coming up the hill and around the curve while slowing to a stop.

The driver blasted his horn in staccato as he halted his Grand Cherokee. The sound of the horn snapped the four of them out of their fear-induced inertia as Jeremy cried out "it's my dad!"

Jesse yelled "c'mon, get in" through his lowered driver's side window. "Hurry up, boys - get in back!" They all ran across the road with only a cursory glance to make sure the way was clear. As the three boys climbed into the back bench seat, Erica grabbed the handle of the front passenger's side door and pulled it open, seeing from the corner of her eye that one of the wolves had crossed the road and was able-bodied enough to rapidly close the gap. As Jesse grabbed her left hand and pulled her, she yanked the door with her right and as it was about to close something jammed it.

The door bounced back open, and the sound of agonized yelping and screeching filled the interior of the Jeep as the wolf writhed on the narrow shoulder of the road before rolling into the ditch. While attempting a second time to close the door, a mortified Erica saw lying on the floor runner next to the seat the bloody amputated paw of the animal. Its right front leg was the obstruction that initially prevented the door from closing as the creature had attempted to climb into the Jeep after her. As a moan of revulsion was expelled from her throat, Erica kicked the paw out of the Grand Cherokee and successfully closed the door.

From the back seat, Jeremy yelled "hurry up dad, go!" as Chris urged "go Jeremy's dad!" Nick leaned on the front passenger's seat and asked in a near panic "are you okay mom?"

"Yes…yes…I'm fine" she answered before saying "thank you again, Jesse."

His unemotional, straightforward reply was "wolves…why not, considering everything else that is happening lately?"

Jesse accelerated the Grand Cherokee up the hill, and with that came questions asked in a less than good-natured manner:

"Jeremy, why didn't you call me before you ran away and Erica, I thought you were in Memphis? Jeremy, you go first!"

"Dad, I couldn't take it anymore" Jeremy began and then on this day when he had never cried so much, the tears started to flow as he spoke through shuddering breaths:

"They were gonna talk to some lawyer about making it so we couldn't spend time alone anymore. And Dennis has been hitting me lately and they make fun of the way that you and I believe in Jesus. They are always saying mean things about you, saying that you're a loser. So, I just ran away."

Jesse kept his eyes on the road while answering "you're safe with me now, Jeremy, but running away was a very bad idea. Your mother is worried sick about you but she's got another problem to deal with; Dennis was killed in a car accident a little while ago on Salt Springs Road."

Three seconds of stunned silence elapsed before Jeremy answered with "he deserved to die! I hated him!"

Erica had never met Jeremy's stepfather or Allison, but she was struck by the news and knew now that Dennis was in the wreck that had created the detour. And Jesse was moved to rebuke his son:

"Jeremy, he didn't deserve to die. What happened is a tragedy and you should feel sympathy for your mother. She loved Dennis and he did help to provide a home for you. Yeah, I know son, that it wasn't the home that you wanted nor was it the home I wanted for you, but that is going to change. What happened to Dennis is very sad. I had a feeling that he may have hit you and I know that he and your mom didn't like your faith in the Lord, but your mom and I will discuss this at length once her grieving is over. As for now, you need to pray for your mom."

"I'm sorry, dad."

"I know you are, Jeremy."

Before the information-gathering session could continue, it was Erica who interrupted with "that's my Escalade. It's out of gas."

Jesse was facetious as he replied: "oh, hi, Erica - nice to see you! Did you run out of gas driving back from Tennessee? Let me get turned around here in the intersection and we'll head back into town and fill up a can."

"I never went, Jesse. The boys didn't want to go and something told me that I needed to stay around. I was going to call you but I wasn't sure you'd want to hear from me."

"Well, I have to admit that I would have liked to have heard from you, but I honored your request to not contact you" Jesse asserted while maintaining his focus while doing a three-point turn the darkening roadway.

"Sometimes you're too honorable, Jesse Same" Erica countered with a roguish grin, and then the smiling face gave way to a more diffident appearance as she said "you're a lot of the reason why I didn't go."

He glanced at her quickly and grinned crookedly as he remarked "I'm glad you stayed" before returning his attention to the road.

As they came back upon the spot where Jesse had unwittingly rescued the four, they saw skinny, sickly Josiah struggling as he lifted the injured wolf sans right paw into the bed of his pickup as it was parked blocking the southwestward lane.

"Dad, he's evil" Jeremy said with a quiver in his voice.

"I know, Jeremy - I dreamed about him" was Jesse's aloof, detached reply.

As they drove down the winding hill to the village where they would purchase gas to able the disabled Escalade, there was the frenetic chatter of three young boys discussing their shared adventure on the hill. Two of the boys had never seen anything like the redoubtable wolves. The third one had experienced more than enough of both the natural and the supernatural for one day, and his exhausted body would win out over his stunned, overtaxed mind and sleep would quickly come.

Despite the hubbub created by the intimates inside his dad's Jeep Grand Cherokee, Jeremy slipped into a slumber more peaceful than any available in the comfortable bed that occupied his room in the turbulent, discord-laden house in Manlius.

# 16

# Dupes and Sin-Sniffers

To be expected, the loss of Dennis was devastating to Allison. He was her security blanket, her confidant, her metaphorical partner in crime, and she loved him almost as much as she loved herself.

But, Dennis was so much like Allison that too often they clashed. On one hand, he was the helium that filled her balloon of narcissism, but at the drop of a hat was would become the pin that would burst that balloon. On one hand, he was easy to schedule, to manipulate, and to control, and then on no notice he would become defiant, disobedient, and abusive. They were both arrogant know-it-alls, and trouble would start when one would claim to know more than the other. Indeed, they were both the gods of their respective lives, and things would become heated when Allison's overinflated view of her own self-importance would stand in the way of Dennis being the great architect of her universe…

…And too often, young Jeremy was caught in the center of the maelstrom.

Jeremy had been in his father's care since December 2nd, and would be staying with his dad for the time being. A week after

Dennis's passing, Allison's life was a shambles, and in her mind it was everyone else's fault. It was Jeremy's fault for running away and forcing Dennis to go out driving in an effort to find him. But some of the blame was posthumously heaped on Dennis as well, as he should have been paying more attention to his driving and less attention to the phone conversation with the boss that seemed have more of a life with him than she did!

The 40 mg daily dosage of Prozac wasn't helping to relieve the depression and anxiety. So, on the morning of December 9th, Allison swiped the grey ceramic cremation urn emblazoned with the Freemason's angle and compass logo off of the coffee table and smashed it on the living room's hardwood floor. In her strung-out rage she screamed "I hope you rot in Hell you son of a bitch!"

After kicking two of the larger ceramic shards across the floor as the ashes wafted about, Allison stomped up the stairs and into Jeremy's bedroom, where she grabbed some of the various little boy gewgaws that remained on the top of his dresser and from a white wooden shelf next to the closet and chucked them with all of her might out into the hallway; causing most of the items to break.

As her tirade continued, she spotted the green McMurtry Auto Mall t-shirt that was wadded up on the floor of the closet and grabbed it. She ran back downstairs into the living room and through the ashes - tracking a considerable amount into the dining room - and then into the kitchen. After turning the front right burner to "high" on the gas stove, she dipped the bottom of the t-shirt into the flame until the garment was alight. The burning shirt was quickly tossed into the sink, and as the kitchen smoke alarm began to sound she screamed "I'm glad you two filthy bastards are dead too!"

As quickly as her physically-fit legs and cardiovascular system would take her, she was back upstairs in Jeremy's bedroom, reaching for the framed 6 x 8 photo of her, Jesse, and baby Jeremy in front of the Christmas tree. But before she could do any damage to the photo, she stopped and stared at it for nearly 30 seconds as she gasped for breath. Overcome by sorrow, she dropped to her knees and screamed hysterically "Jesse, I'm sorry I listened to my mother and divorced you. It's all her fault!"

But no one in the natural heard Allison's remorseful, self-pitying cry.

Erica and Jesse had seen each other every day over the weeks' time. They prayed together as she had recommitted to the faith in Jesus that she had abandoned as a teenager. They read scripture together and just generally hung out when she wasn't homeschooling Chris and Nick. On a few of the days, Jesse brought Jeremy to her Lake Street rental after picking him up from Enders Road School, and on the other days she would bring her boys over to his place. Indeed, Jesse and Erica hadn't known each other long, but his feelings for her were strong and growing and reaching the level of love that she felt for him.

Jesse had described his dreams and visions to Erica, and she did not find them to be the delusions of an insane man. As they read scripture together and watched the world together, she understood that there could be something prophetic in what he had dreamed and seen; especially considering that he had dreamed that Dennis and the McMurtrys would die in a car wreck - although in reality it was two separate crashes that day and not at the intersection of Enders Road and East Seneca Turnpike.

Erica had not consumed a drop of alcohol since the night that Eddie Ramsden attempted to rape her. Her life was put in peril that night because alcohol influenced her thoughts while a demon in the guise of a pseudo-comical flying monkey in bellhop's uniform whispered in her ear. But, pseudo-comical the supernatural was not, as Satan and his demonic hoards were stepping up their attacks on the armored and unarmored alike. The Prince of the Air sensed that great change was afoot which would give him freer rein to be that roaring lion seeking whom he might devour - and devour he would. But Erica again dwelt in the shelter of the Most High and abided in the shadow of the Almighty. And for Nick and Chris faith was easy, especially now with zealous Jeremy being a regular part of their lives.

Temperatures had remained unseasonably warm during the first nine days of December, though not again reaching 60 degrees as they did on the 2nd. Still, for the first time since his divorce Jesse was moved to put up a Christmas tree and decorations, and Erica insisted that they go to the Hobby Lobby store in DeWitt and acquire a 6 1/2 foot tall artificial Blue Spruce as well as strings of lights and garland, a variety of ornaments, and a silver star topper adorned with colored twinkle lights. The boys had a blast decorating the tree that night, and it gave Jeremy great joy to hang the brand-new ball with the red and green gradient finish and phrase *Jesus - The Reason for the Season* adorning its perimeter in white and silver glittered Harlow Solid font.

And as every day passed, Erica found it easier not to share the secret of Jesse's lineage. In her spirit she knew that if there was ever to be a time that time was not now. Jesse was happier now with Jeremy staying with him and she couldn't help but think that she, Nick, and Chris contributed to the lifting of his spirit - and she was right. But while he seemed less weighed down by the invisible burden that he carried on his back, there was still something out of sight that caused discomfort. It was something akin to the wash care tag of a new t-shirt that irritatingly rubbed against the back of his neck. While he was buoyed by joy seen and unseen, his mood would suddenly darken as if he had been the recipient of bad news outside of the deaths of Dennis and the McMurtrys. He would become fretful and agitated as though he needed to take care of a pressing issue that did not present itself in the natural.

And on the evening of December 9th as the boys finished decorating the tree, Erica sat next to Jesse on the couch and messaged his tight shoulders and upper back. As the three joyful chattering boys flicked the switch on the multi-outlet bar that brought the strings of lights to life, she spoke softly and said "I know you feel something is wrong out there, Jesse. I feel it too, there's something happening, and your dreams and visions were sneak previews and warnings." She then laid her head on this left shoulder and spoke words that comforted him: "fear not, because he's with us, even until the end of the age."

As a Christmas tree became illuminated in an upstairs flat on Genesee Street, a tense meeting was taking place in the living room of Steve and Eileen Sandifer's home on Lakeport Road, where a fractious Trey Emerson was voicing his concerns:

"All I'm saying Steve, is don't get too soft with the Jesus stuff, okay? It's fine if you, Eileen, Jerome, and Galen want to smell what the the good pastor is cooking over here, but let's not become the Branch Davidians, alright?"

Steve's voice rose above the din of all those who at once responded: "That was a cult, and we are not a cult, Trey. There are few of us here who now believe in the Way, the Truth, and the Life, and that's Jesus…"

Trey interrupted Steve with "truth? I'll tell you the truth, Steve! You saw the report on YNN News a little while ago. So far this week, three Sunoco tanker trucks have turned up missing from the depot out on Pottery Road in Warners. Nobody seems to know what happened! And, you heard that Omondi's civilian military has been training out in Buffalo and on some college campuses out west. You know - that mysterious little civilian outfit that he spoke about in his campaign? And why are so many National Guard members being called up to report for 'special training' and why does it include police officers here and around the country? And you see that the Dollar is steadily slipping just like the Euro is and it seems to be a deliberate manipulation to bring it down. What I'm trying to tell you guys is that the shit is about to hit the fan and we as the only militia in the area need to be ready! We can't be getting swallowed up in 'Kumbaya' Jesus stuff!"

There was silence as Trey paused to catch his breath as he was close to hyperventilation. As Galen was about to chime in, Trey was reinvigorated and continued passionately as he spoke while gesturing wildly with his hands:

"Look, people, the enemy is as much within as without. I don't think that Jesus is gonna sweep in and save us! We need to be ready for war!"

Jerry Walters, who had been a member of the militia since its 2008 inception, spoke up in support of Trey:

"You tell 'em Trey! And maybe a little bit of separation between church and state would be a good idea here in the NMM, guys. It's all good if Steve, Eileen, Galen, Jerome, and Matt wanna pray and such, but not on our time, okay? Now, some of us still have contacts on the inside and we're getting little bits of intelligence from them. My brother in the Air Force says there are targets that they could and should hit but aren't allowed to, just like Moss was told not to shoot that bastard Bin Laden. We all see the stuff that gets leaked. So screw religion 'cuz religion creates fundamentalist extremists like Al Qaeda and we need to protect the people from them and from the commies in our own friggin' government!"

"Ironically enough, commies controlled by very wealthy men no less" Andy Dudzinski chimed in. At 23, Dudzinski was the youngest of the militia's members and likewise the most technically savvy; serving as the IT tech for the NMM. Andy Dudzinski had more to say:

"I've been monitoring our website traffic through open tracker dot net. We are getting an increasing number of visits from the

Department of Defense and the FBI. Also, we're being visited like crazy by an anonymous proxy that appears to be from Bulgaria. I've bulked up our server capacity and put in all of the safeguards that I can, but our site has been taken down twice this month by denial of service attacks. Usually, it's the government that gets DOS attacks, but they're instead doing it to us, I believe."

Dudzinski paused for a moment as he opened his laptop and then continued speaking:

"Now, when it comes to communicating with each other, we should abandon all land lines. The Feds have been tapping mine I can tell. We should be using Skype to contact each other because it's as close to being bedrock secure as anything online can be.

"Steve, most of the guys in this room think that they run this militia, but I respect you and Galen as leaders here and oh by the by, it's you two that aren't running your mouths like jackasses! So, I recently started a hacktivism group called 'Vapor' with some guys from college and incorporating some crack hackers from Germany and Japan. We're like that group 'Anonymous', only brand new and therefore extremely low profile. Anyway, we can start initiating some DOS attacks on the Pentagon, the Department of Defense, and even the White House. We've already gotten into those systems through breaches…"

Steve Sandifer would no longer allow anyone to talk over him as he interrupted Dudzinski mid-sentence:

"Andy, don't let me find out that you hacked anybody on behalf of the North Madison Militia, or I will take these two hands of mine and tear you into six pieces, do you understand? Now, don't test me on this! I appreciate you keeping our website up and maintaining our cyber-security, but we are not to initiate anything - whether it's physical or virtual. We are defenders of freedom, not initiators of acts of war."

Andy Dudzinski was a prideful, hot-headed young man who hadn't often been told "no" in his life, and he responded accordingly:

"What? You don't think my plan is good? Well, I guess you take that whole 'blessed are the peacemakers' thing from the Bible a bit too seriously! I say go to the root of the problem and destroy it!"

Trey jumped in on Andy's side: "yeah, Steve, what the hell? The kid is brilliant and he could pull it off! Start hacking into their sites and you could seriously cripple their operations. Talk about defending freedom!"

Andy's head quickly cooled; realizing that over-reacting would not help him to make his case:

"Steve, sorry I flashed, dude. Anyway, Vapor has someone inside of the White House - a friend of mine from college who worked on Omondi's election campaign, even though he's a staunch conservative who hoped he could commit some sabotage from the inside. He was one of two friends of mine from school who faked their way in, hee-hee! But because he could convincingly mimic the behavior of a radical lefty he got a job in what amounts to be their IT department. He was able to forward me a couple of e-mails that he was able to decrypt. After I read them I was to delete them and empty my trash, which was part of the deal. But, he didn't say I couldn't keep notes on my laptop!"

As he sat on the couch, there was a pause of a few seconds while Andy opened a notepad file from an icon on his laptop's desktop. Once the rudimentary file was opened, he continued:

"The one that was the most eye-opening was sent to Omondi in November from a guy named Renaud Littler, who is high up in the CIA. It was copied to Vice President Beckmann, Chief of Staff Piniella and some other guy who goes by the moniker "Bee-Zee". Littler said in the e-mail that he knew the 'day and the hour that the Al Qaeda attacks would begin' and that they would be 'sensationally shocking and superbly awesome.' The only part that can't be encrypted is 2009Dec77HA77, which appears to be a date this December. Littler went on to say something to the effect of 'don't let those assholes at the Pentagon read this e-mail' and 'we can trust DHS to carry our water.'

"Well there's your answer, Andy" Galen jumped in and replied solemnly. "It appears that if that purported e-mail was legit that Al Qaeda is going to strike America this month on some day, and there is an effort to keep the Pentagon from taking preemptive measures. And, if this far-fetched story of yours is true, the Department of Homeland Security may be aware that it's coming and be non-reactive. So it seems that hacking any sites would be a waste of time as the wheels are already in motion for a terrible attack or attacks. If you were able to hack Al Qaeda it wouldn't matter because they can operate primitively. The American sheeple would laugh this off and go grab another beer from the fridge, but considering my past experience it seems more than plausible."

It was Steve who spoke next:

"Alright everybody, we're nine days in and it hasn't happened yet, but a big part of the reason I chartered this militia on September 1st, 2008 was because I knew once that radical Omondi got the Democratic nomination that the government would take the next level in going rogue. These United States are as much threatened by the enemy within as the enemy without, and both enemies are now partners in crime. We have been under attack economically, and I have expected that we would be attacked physically and worse than 9/11. So if we are to believe this information that Andy has gotten access to, at some point over the next three weeks we are going to be hit with something nightmarish.

"Galen has a friend that had some manner of inexplicable supernatural occurrence where he heard over his clock radio Omondi and others talking about allowing an impending attack to happen. This friend also heard them say that they needed to kill

Galen before he talked too much about having assassinated Bin Laden. Well, Galen is being followed by what appears to be the CIA operating domestically, so there is something to this all. That's why Galen has been living in the bunker."

Trey interjected with a sneer: "That friend of Galen's is Jesse Same, the Elvis impersonator that I just quit working with. The guy used to be my best friend, but he's gone off the deep end so I don't know if I'd believe much of what he says. He's a real loony tune with his crackpot dreams and visions"

"I believe him because he's been gifted with the prophetic" Galen replied staidly.

"And you're just as much of a loony tune as he is, Moss" Trey answered with an arrogant smirk.

Before the tit for tat could escalate, Steve intervened:

"Trey, why don't you head home? Galen, I believe your friend Jesse as well. Um, as a matter of fact, this meeting is adjourned. My Skype I.D. is steve dot sandifer, all lower case. If you don't have it yet, Skype is a free download. I am doing away with my landline, effective immediately. If nothing happens over the next several days, meet me here Saturday morning for some target shooting and some prep and planning. If something does happen, plan A will go into effect, so goodnight, everybody."

After all but Galen, Eileen, Jerome, Steve, and Matt had quickly filed out; Steve said to Galen "I believe your friend Jesse is right about Trey. Maybe a demon did tell him to kill me, I don't know, but I have a bad feeling in my spirit about Trey."

Matt made a suggestion, but it was more like a command: "There is something coming and it is triple-pronged like a pitchfork. But the sharpest of the prongs is gold, while the other two are rusted. I dreamed this last night and I think the five of us should pray right now."

Thursday the 10th was sunny with a mile-high sky and temperatures hovering in the low thirties; and it began at 6:00 a.m. as a quiet day in the life of Jesse Same. He had driven Jeremy to school in Manlius, and his son would continue to remain in his residential custody as Allison was staying with her parents while she recovered from the shock of Dennis' death and the subsequent trauma that it brought her. "I hope I never have to live with her again dad" Jeremy remarked as they drove along Enders Road and prepared to pull into the school's entry drive. "Time will tell, Jeremy, but right now you need to pray for your mother because she is very sick" Jesse advised his son.

Jeremy asked with the utmost sincerity "Do you pray for her even though you're divorced and she says bad things about you?"

"Yes, I do son" Jesse answered earnestly.

Jeremy's follow-up query was "even though you have Erica now?" as they pulled up to the sidewalk near the main entrance to the brick; single-level school building that resembled thousands of others in America.

Jesse could only chuckle as Jeremy opened the back passenger-side door, telling his son "have a great day and I love you. See you this afternoon."

Later that morning Jesse communicated with Ian, Mickey, and Tony and they all were committed to playing the "Christmas Tribute to Elvis Presley" show at the Turning Stone Casino on Thursday the 17th. A lead guitarist named Scott Seals who worked with the upstate New York oldies band "Retro Ricky and the Eight Track Players" would fill the spot abandoned by Trey. Scott was thrilled to be offered the gig as Elvis Presley was his all-time favorite artist and he could play all of the lead guitar parts to a "T." Jesse e-mailed him the list of Elvis Christmas songs they would play, and wrote in the message that "you're on your own Scott, as we won't have the opportunity to rehearse." The confident and comical reply from Mr. Seals, parodying the oft-misquoted line from *The Treasure of Sierra Madre* was "rehearsal? We don't need no stinking rehearsal!"

He had been dancing on the edge of it since the time they sat having lunch at Donna and Sam's, but on that morning after dropping off Jeremy at school Jesse finally admitted to himself that he was deeply in love with Erica. The renewal of her faith in Jesus as her Lord and Savior was what pushed him over the aforementioned edge, as they now shared the most important thing in the universe. Likewise, he had grown very fond of Nick and Chris, and they adored him and were already starting to see him as a father figure. Jeremy was developing a fast and firm friendship with the two boys and in essence he was becoming their brother.

Jesse had begun to feel a heavy fatigue on Tuesday and it still lingered that Thursday, even after getting nine hours of dreamless sleep on Wednesday night. At 11:49 a.m. he laid down on the couch for a nap, hoping that a few winks would relieve the fatigue. FOX News was on the television with the sound muted, and the last thing Jesse saw before he fell asleep was a live cut-in of President Omondi speaking in a Brooklyn, New York elementary school auditorium packed with star-struck students and sycophantic teachers and administrators. Though there was no sound, the President appeared pompous, smug and snug behind his Teleprompters and seemed caught up in the wave of adoration that lifted him.

At 12:21 p.m. the buzzing of his cellphone jarred Jesse awake, and the first thought that popped into his mind as it scrambled to stack his mental Legos was "Erica calling." When he grabbed the phone he instead saw a number from the upstate New York 315 area code that he did not recognize. When he answered, it was a robo-call from Fayette-Manlius school district superintendent Corinne Kiernan. The recorded message that Jesse heard sent metaphorical shards of broken glass flying into his mind, heart, and soul:

*All schools in the Fayetteville-Manlius district are on lockdown until further notice, due to an emergency situation involving security at Enders Road Elementary. I repeat - all schools in the Fayetteville-Manlius district are on lockdown due to an emergency situation involving security at Enders Road Elementary. Parents are ordered by Manlius Police to not attempt to pick-up their children until the situation is resolved. Please stay near your phones and tune into local news radio and television for further updates. Thank you.*

As the shards of glass raced around his body, tearing the internal threading of his very existence, his mind raced in an effort to collect its Lego pieces and build a wall to defend itself. Before Jesse could react, his phone rang again and this time it was indeed Erica.

“Honey, turn on YNN News. Me and the boys are on the way over right now. I love you Jesse, and don’t worry.”

“I love you, too” was all he could mutter as she ended the call while he grabbed the remote and switched to channel 10 WYNN, the 24 hour local news network serving upstate New York.

As the President climbed into his limousine parked in front of the Brooklyn school, “Bee-Zee” who was his confidante and factotum, sat down next to him in the back seat and uncapped a bottle of Dasani water while staring at his Blackberry as secret service cleared the vehicle to make the drive to LaGuardia airport where Air Force One waited.

"Gimme an update Bee" the President ordered while quickly scanning messages on his own Blackberry.

"So far so good, Jomo" Bee-Zee answered after swallowing a gulp of water with a satisfied "aah." "Our hired help got the two dupes into the school's cafeteria and each of them has an AR-15. They got Mrs. Clock the cafeteria monitor gagged and tied to a chair; which the kids are probably thrilled about because she's quite a mean bitch, I hear. We told the dupes that if they could pull this off without shooting anybody we'd give 'em each 10 G's in cash plus 50 pounds of Sour Aliens for their own smoking enjoyment."

"You didn't offer them any of the smoke from my private stash did you?" the President asked tautly as he was finally compelled to look away from his Blackberry as the limo began to move.

"Relax Jomo, nobody touches your dope! And seriously, you need to give that shit up before somebody like Breitbart catches on. I mean, he's already looking into your old boyfriend..."

"We need to eliminate Andrew Breitbart" the President snapped as he checked something else on his Blackberry.

"And we need to forge some sort of credible Hawaiian birth certificate for you too, but all in time. Right now we have an American public that by and large is happy to let us sodomize them, so we have the luxury of time" Bee-Zee answered as he stared steely-eyed into the eyes of the President. After looking away and quickly checking something else on his Blackberry, Bee-Zee continued speaking:

"Now, as I was going to say, our hired help told the dupes that if they have to shoot anybody only do it as a last resort. Certainly some dead six year olds would help make your gun ban an easier sell, but honestly I don't think it will have to come to that. What we're looking for here is the fear factor. After one of our police plants shoots the two shitbags in the head, you, Schumer,

Feinstein, and all the rest go on TV and get the rednecks ready to lose their guns, because we can't have any more situations like this on our schools again."

Omondi smiled and waved in the window at the adoring fans lining the street to see his motorcade as he asked "so why was a school in that particular town selected?"

"Manlius, New York is for the most part liberal and wealthy - save for a few small pockets of conservatism. The town's wheels are rolled by residents who are trial lawyers, doctors, and Syracuse University professors that give big cash to the Democrats. And, there's quite a Green movement there. It's your people, Jomo, it's not the type of place where two crazed young men would take assault rifles into a school and threaten to shoot it up. And hell, we could get all the Sour Aliens we would need from Fayetteville-Manlius High School to give to the shooters, but like I said, they ain't gonna live long enough to smoke any of it!"

Omondi chortled as he then asked Bee-Zee "do the high school students share any of that good smoke with their parents?"

Bee-Zee cackled with glee as he answered "You got it backwards, Jomo. The kids steal it from their parents!"

As the President flipped on the TV monitor in back of the limo to MSNBC who was just breaking the story nationally from the wire, Bee-Zee explained "the hired help had a tough time convincing the dupes to take off their Hip Hop clothes and dress up in camo to look the part. But, the allure of loads of cash and dope was too much for the two addicted, mind-controlled shitbags to resist."

There was drama inside the cafeteria of Enders Road Elementary while the President, Bee-Zee, Erica, Jesse, and others across the nation took in coverage from various television news outlets. The

President and Bee-Zee were hopeful that this incident - and the events that were coming - would be the straws that broke the camel's back and would make their seizure of firearms from the U.S. citizenry go that much more smoothly.

The plan was for a thirty-day taxpayer-funded gun buy-back to be offered in all fifty states. After 31 days from enactment, local police, National Guard, and the brand-new civilian security force would begin going door to door to collect all registered guns that weren't turned in and likewise search for unregistered weapons. But, the implementation and subsequent success of this dissolution of the Second Amendment was heavily dependent on what they were reasonably sure Al Qaeda was going to do in a matter of days.

If Al Qaeda did as intelligence reports indicated they would, the President could then issue the order of Martial Law that he had already prepared; being that the quiet maneuvering of its chess pieces was already underway under the noses of a pacified sheeple. But in the end, Omondi was himself only a proverbial plastic king on this chessboard, as the elitist secret society game masters moved bishops, knights, rooks, and pawns over black and white squares toward the eventual checkmate. But even they in their arrogance would ultimately have to reckon with the chess master that would prove them to be the same manner of "dupes" that were currently holding an elementary school under siege.

Erica had to convince Jesse to not go to the school in an attempt to rescue his son. "You won't get near it and you'll only get yourself arrested or worse, killed; and that won't help Jeremy. We need to pray and wait for God to act" she admonished him.

The careworn face of Nicholas was tear-streaked as he asked "mom, is Jeremy gonna get shot?"

"No honey, he is not. You and Chris should pray with us that everyone comes out okay."

“When this is over, I am going to make sure that he is homeschooled and his mother better be onboard” Jesse spoke acerbically. But, Allison was unaware of the peril that her son was in that afternoon as she was heavily sedated.

ஜஜஜஜஜஜ

Inside the cafeteria, Davy Barnes and Tommy Mazzini were convinced that they enjoyed the role that the guys who dressed up as ATF asked them to play just the day before. They were assured that they wouldn’t get hurt, they were getting paid 10 Large each, and the “digity dank” was going to be “transcendent.”

Neither of the young men had ever fired an AR-15, but they were given a quick lesson by one of the ATF plants on how to shoot it if it turned out to be necessary. “Just think of it as a big, fancy-ass nine millimeter” one of the plants instructed them.

And as it was at 1:15 that afternoon, they kept their rifles trained on the 41 first graders, two teachers, and bound and gagged Althea Clock who all sat terrified in the cafeteria while out in the hall Manlius Police, Onondaga County Sheriff’s SWAT members, and FBI who had no clue that this was a staged event kept their arms trained on the two camo-clad thugs.

Inside the doorway that led to the food line, ATF agent and “director” Wolf Biden watched the flow of the event, and with a headset microphone he could whisper instructions into the tiny earpieces that Barnes and Mazzini wore. The food service staff had already been “rescued” by “heroic” ATF agents so they would not be able to witness the maneuverings from the inside.

“Hey, mister repressed man with a firearm, I need to urinate really bad” 6 year old Hunter Hollister, son of Syracuse University Cultural Anthropology professor Star Hollister bellowed from the quiet, mortified group, which elicited a response from Tommy Mazzini:

"Yo, then piss yo pants you little punk-ass mutha…"

Before Mazzini could complete his diatribe, he was interrupted as his earpiece screamed with the voice of Wolf Biden:

"Hey you idiot, you're a redneck, not some humpy-bumpy hip hop speaking Eminem wannabe! Now start speaking correctly or you don't get paid! Don't forget, we're on national television so speak your damn parts you pathetic pant-load!"

"No, you gotta pee yer pants or hold it er somethin'. Now shut up or else we'll shoot all of you heathen non-Christians" was Mazzini's forced, corrected reply.

"That's much better, Tommy. That's good, push the heathen thing. Remember, you're an intolerant, rightwing Christian gun-lover, so give me an academy award performance" Biden's voice spoke softly into Tommy's earpiece, but loudly enough that Althea Clock who was a foot away heard it. Mrs. Clock began to cry "this is all a setup! The government is behind this" but from behind the duct tape over her mouth it came out muffled and indecipherable. Davey then stuck the business end of his AR-15 against the side of her head and she knew enough to shut up.

Erica was right in that Jesse wouldn't have gotten within a mile of the school. But trucks from FOX and the alphabet affiliates from upstate New York occupied any empty spots along Enders Road that EMS, police, fire, ATF, and FBI didn't. As several helicopters circled overhead, it was a tense and gripping scene and it was a miracle that up to that point no one had been hurt.

Jeremy's class was one of the two that had been having lunch in the cafeteria when the pair of gunmen burst in and seized control. While he was as frightened as his classmates were, Jeremy's attention was also drawn by the seeming familiarity of the two young men who toted the AR-15's. The sound of Tommy's voice shouting gutturally at Hunter began to bring it home, and it was after the muffled voice of Mrs. Clock - who despite her undeserved reputation was always kind to Jeremy - that it all clicked in the six year old's head.

Just as the room had grown quiet again, save for the panicked whimpering of some of the children, Jeremy stood up. As he took his feet, the brave little boy pointed and shouted "I know who those guys are! Their names are Tommy and Davey and they don't want to be bad! Somebody is making them do this!"

As Jeremy's proclamation ended, Tommy screamed "no, no, no, please turn off the voices in my head, I don't want to hurt anybody!" The dupe then dropped his AR-15 and grabbed his head while moaning in a terrible anguish. The assault rifle fired several rounds aimlessly and harmlessly when it hit the floor while Tommy fell to his knees, gripping his head with his left hand while ripping out the earpiece with his right.

The response to Tommy's action was a rapid and varied series of shots that rang out; causing the cafeteria to be filled with the acrid smells of sulfur and cordite, the wail of terrified children, and the frenzied shouts of real cops, real government agents, and a few imposters who played those roles.

The shooting lasted a matter of seconds, but the hysteria continued. While children screamed, cried, vomited, and fainted - the skull fragments, hair, blood, and brain matter of Davey Barnes and Tommy Mazzini were but a gory spectacle splattered on the wall and floor near the food line hallway. Some of the young men's gore fell on Althea Clock who passed out from shock but would recover and then retire two days after the traumatic event from her part-time job with the F-M school district at the age of 61.

The dupes were in effect two sick dogs that had been put out of their misery by men playing god. But, the terrible truth was that it was men playing god that had infected the two young men and made them terminally ill.

The relatively short-lived event was over, and the only two casualties were the dupes Davey Barnes and Tommy Mazzini. Jeremy was a truth-teller when he had prophesied to them the week before "I think that both of you guys are gonna die really soon."

No, the cafeteria of Enders Road Elementary wasn't a pond and they weren't floating as pine boughs, but despite that awful reality, such is the nature of dreams, eh?

Heaven is filled with gorgeous stately pines of many shades of green and other colors. And the souls who love Jesus and have accepted his gift of salvation are in a sense metaphorical pine boughs - each beautiful grafted into the stateliest of trees where He was nailed and gave his blood for their sins.

Tommy and Davey gave their blood that day because they were dupes who had been drugged and manipulated by men playing god. They lived that last year of their lives under the influence of both legal and experimental toxins administered by elites who would use them as mules in much the same way that a kingpin cocaine dealer would use mules to run his wares.

The dupes were picked out by the McMurtrys and offered up as sacrificial lambs so to speak, and being young men from fatherless homes where mothers on government assistance had struggled to provide the basics, they were as fruit ripe for the picking. But there was a moment for each dear friend - moments of silent lucidity over the prior two days where they could separately hear a voice that wasn't in their heads or ears but in their souls. It was a voice that reminded them that even though they were young, to remember the former things of old.

It was a voice that said “I am He…”

…In quiet moments separately, when the government-administered drugs had been urinated from their bodies before the “doctor” would visit and give them a fresh jab; in a quiet sober moment each said “thank you Jesus, I believe.”

By 6:00 p.m., the scene had been given the “all clear” and the authorities - both real and imposters - continued to investigate and clean up. The television news media maintained its vigil and reported on how “it could have been so much worse if the FBI and ATF did not act so effectively.” Over America’s boob tubes the back stories of Davey Barnes and Tommy Mazzini were being told, and little of what the Omondi-compliant media reported was actually true.

Some of the misdirection and deception was carried out by crisis actors who played the roles of parents of terrified students and of local residents who were “witnesses” to the tragic event that could have turned out so much worse. Marc Dressler, who played the role of Enders Road homeowner “Charles Kubiak”, talked to reporter Kristin Davis of Syracuse’s NBC affiliate WSTM as they stood in the parking lot of Eastside Bible Church, which being an eighth of a mile down the road was a convenient staging area. As the 26 year old Davis did her live stand-up outfitted in a white knit hat, matching scarf, and tan trench coat, the “witness” said:

“Well, I saw the two shooters enter the school through the side entrance that faces my house. It’s right over there - well, uh, I mean you can’t see it from here, right?”

Davis interrupted: “I must have misunderstood you, sir. I thought you said before we went live that you lived behind the school and you saw them enter through a back entrance?”

Dressler as Charles Kubiak continued: "no, no, side entrance. In all the stress and confusion of this day I was mistaken…wow! I live next to the school and it was the side entrance. So anyway, I saw them enter and immediately called 911. The thing is I recognized them right away. They're in that militia over in Chittenango that I've seen online. It's the North Madison Militia and I've seen them in their group photo. I've been researching militias and rightwing extremist groups because I'm very concerned about them proliferating in our nice area here. So, man, wow…I mean now they've touched our beautiful town of Manlius! I always thought we were safe here. My wife and I have a baby girl on the way and now I fear for my baby's future!" Then, for dramatic effect, the Juilliard graduate Dressler made his lower lip tremble as he shed forced tears and turned away from the camera.

Andy Dudzinski's concerns about the North Madison Militia website were legitimate. Hackers working on behalf of the Omondi administration had that morning added a photo of Davey and Tommy dressed in camouflage to the site; expertly Photoshopped to appear nothing short of convincing, to back up the false statements that "Charles Kubiak" was making.

Kristin Davis was only 26 years old, but she was an old-school style reporter as her father Jack Davis was in Topeka, Kansas where she grew up before attending Syracuse University's Newhouse School of Public Communications. Something about Charles Kubiak didn't jive, and in the maelstrom of the event she was covering - a maelstrom being energized by her reporting being broadcast nationally via MSNBC, she couldn't vet him like she desired to.

As the reporting was tossed back to New York City and the cameraman on scene relaxed while the local WSTM feed went to commercial, Davis with suspicious eyes followed "Charles Kubiak" as he walked across the parking lot in a direction that would be opposite of where he claimed to live. As producer Tyler Franks handed her a Styrofoam cup of coffee and an already lit

Virginia Slims menthol to quickly ingest before the next report, she saw two middle-aged men sporting black trench coats emerge from under mercury light. One patted a smirking Dressler on the back while the other said with a snigger "nice work, Marco. The President is pleased and will talk to his pals in Hollywood about getting you some first-rate movie gigs!"

The young woman's memory was as sharp as her attention to detail. As she swallowed a gulp of flavorful black coffee acquired from the nearby Nice-N-Easy Grocery Shoppe, it hit her that this so-called "Charles Kubiak" was also an actor in a Miller Light commercial that she and her fiancé had seen several times that past Sunday while watching NFL football. Mark Dressler, who had just duped her while in the role of Charles Kubiak, also played a convincing frat boy type so common to those insipid beer ads that appealed to a large segment of the American man-child population.

She had been duped and so had the sheeple viewing her reporting, and Miss Davis took it personally. "Hey, get back here you lying bastard" she yelled as she turned to start running after him, but Tyler Franks grabbed her right arm and spun her about-face.

Franks, who had graduated from the Newhouse School in 2007, was a diminutive young man who carried himself in a manner much larger than his physical stature. As he warned Kristin that "this is Big Brother's media now, so you go along or else you'll be selling coffee and cigarettes in a convenience market" she had to place the utmost credence in what he said.

While the President was pleased by the performances of his various crisis actors such Mark Dressler, he was not fully satisfied by the outcome of the day's school shooting. As he sat in the Oval Office switching between FOX, CNN, and MSNBC with Vice President Beckmann, Bee-Zee, and several others in the inner circle, he stared off into space as he remarked "I still wish a few kids would have been killed because it would make the gun ban a little easier for those on the other side of the aisle to swallow. Why didn't any of our plants pick off a few of 'em?"

While Bee-Zee snickered and the others in the room only shuffled their feet uncomfortably, it was Beckmann who spoke up: "look, Jomo, it's gonna happen anyway because you'll circumvent Congress, so it's good that only the two dirtballs that we've been drugging up died and not anybody's kids! What the hell is wrong with you? I mean, heaven forbid, but what if it was your kids?"

Jeremy was safely at home by 7:10 p.m., and was understandably shaken and morose. Considering all the he had been through not only that day but over recent days and weeks, it was amazing that he hadn't become catatonic. The distress of the children and the scene around him would have been enough to inflict serious mental trauma, but strangely it was the vision and memory of Tommy and Davey that haunted and saddened him most.

Jesse had turned off the television coverage, but in the process of watching and learning the names of the perpetrators, one name was a shock to him but not a surprise. And as Jeremy expressed his sadness for the shooters - shooters who didn't seem to understand what they were doing or why they were there - Jesse explained:

"Davey Barnes was your cousin, Jeremy. He was the son of your Aunt Pamela, your mom's older sister. He was at your grandparent's house one Thanksgiving when you were a baby, but that was the only time you ever had contact with him or your aunt. After your mom married Dennis, he hired Davey and his friend Tommy Mazzini to run parts and clean cars for the McMurtry Auto Malls. But, there were other things that they got involved in too - obviously some very bad things. John and Joe McMurtry were bad men, Jeremy, and we may never know just how bad they were."

"Yeah, but didn't the McMurtrys go to that church you took me to a couple of times, dad? Doesn't that mean that they believed in Jesus?"

Jesse answered as delicately and directly as he could:

"Not everyone who goes to church believes in Jesus, son. And not everyone who believes in Jesus goes to church. What's important is that Jesus is always in your heart and on your mind. Jesus is angry at a lot of churches and what the people who lead them and attend them do."

"Dad, do the followers of Jesus sometimes make other people not want to believe in Him?"

"Yes, Jeremy, many of Jesus' followers represent him very poorly. They're too busy pointing out everyone else's sin while not looking at their own. They're what I call 'sin-sniffers' and they're one reason why I haven't gone to any church lately. And, they're a big reason why people who don't believe don't want to come to faith. Too often, the lost see the found as too self-righteous, self-anointed, and self-appointed. And very often, sin-sniffers have a lot of sin in their own lives that they're trying to hide. Does this make any sense, son?"

"I smell what your cooking, dad" Jeremy answered, and even if he didn't know the meaning of all the phrases Jesse used, he did get the gist of them and he did know what sin was.

Jesse then picked up the black leatherette-covered Bible from the coffee table as Erica snuggled in close to he and Jeremy; Chris and Nick having dozed off on Jesse's bed. He flipped to the Gospel of Matthew and turned the pages to chapter 7. "Look here" he said to Jeremy as he placed his finger on verse 3 and read aloud through verse five:

*And why do you look at the speck in your brother's eye, but do not consider the plank in your own eye? Or how can you say to your brother, 'Let me remove the speck from your eye'; and look, a plank is in your own eye? Hypocrite! First remove the plank from your own eye, and then you will see clearly to remove the speck from your brother's eye.*

After reading, Jesse said "I think if more followers of Jesus actually took that passage to heart and lived it out, there would be more new followers of Jesus."

There was a few seconds of pondering silence before Jesse spoke again:

"But many people go to church for the sake of appearance. John McMurtry was a man who went to church because it looked good for him to be there and it was good for his business. He was one of the founders of Four Corners Community Church and it elevated him, not Jesus, in other people's eyes. John McMurtry believed that many paths, not just Jesus, brought people to God and that in his own mind he was a god too. But ultimately it was Satan that he followed. John McMurtry led a lot of people astray because he was so well respected."

"Dad, do you think that we'll ever go to church again?"

Before Jesse answered Jeremy, he shut his eyes and prayed silently. Erica took his right hand in hers and closed her eyes as well, and in that moment they were two gathered in the name of Jesus, seeking His help in providing the answer to Jeremy's innocently simple question.

After ten or so seconds passed, Jesse opened his eyes and began to speak:

"Jeremy, we are in a very special time in history, and too many churches don't care to acknowledge it. I believe that we are going to be a small church on our own - me, you, Erica, Chris, and Nick. Others may come and join us and they will be welcome. We are to be a church of watchers on the wall, because Jesus said we would not know the day or the hour of His return, but we would see the signs…

…Some of us in these last days have been blessed with the ability not only to see, but to touch, taste, hear, and smell the signs. And like the scripture from Joel says, let's see, it's right here:"

*Then you shall know that I am in the midst of Israel:*

*I am the Lord your God*

*And there is no other.*

*My people shall never be put to shame.*

*"And it shall come to pass afterward*

*That I will pour out My Spirit on all flesh;*

*Your sons and your daughters shall prophesy,*

*Your old men shall dream dreams,*

*Your young men shall see visions.*

After Jesse read the passage, he smiled at his son and said "I know that you have had dreams and visions too, Jeremy."

"Yeah, dad, I dreamed about Davey Barnes and Tommy Mazzini and then I met them in real life, and they were bad on the outside because something was really wrong with them. I think that a man from the government was giving them marijuana that was poisoned. They were being used as guinea pigs" Jeremy spoke and his countenance revealed true sadness and compassion.

"And they were used as pawns in a very evil chess game, and America is at least half of the proverbial game board" Erica replied astutely, he face revealing a similar sadness and compassion as that of Jeremy.

Then, Jeremy's mood shifted and his face brightened as he asked "do you remember that angel that I told you about that walked with me part of the way here?"

Jesse spoke with the glee and enthusiasm of a child of Jeremy's age:

"In a dream I had, where I was sitting on a bench by the pond, that very same angel that you met sat down next to me and showed me a newspaper where the lead story told a lie about people disappearing in a massive UFO abduction, but in truth it was the Rapture that really took them. And it was though we had already been raptured and he was asking me if it was done by UFO, and I said no, but he already knew the answer anyway and was just testing me!"

"Do you think that the Rapture is gonna be soon, dad?"

"I dreamed about hourglasses and the bulb on one of them that was representative of the Church Age was practically empty of sand. I've been seeing demons; they're somewhat translucent but I see them, and what is so strange is that some look like flying monkeys from the Wizard of Oz. I don't know if they are only here in Chittenango and I have to wonder if L. Frank Baum might have seen them as well. I've also seen scarecrows, but they weren't friendly! I've seen things like gargoyles and things that looked part human and part reptile, too. I know in my spirit that these things are demonic and I'm really seeing them."

"I've had a vision that I know was from the Great Tribulation, where the Mississippi River was red and filled with dead, stinking fish. In that dream, I saw members of the civilian security force that Omondi wants to implement, the one that your cousin is taking part in, Erica.

I've heard conversations over my radio and I've seen black-eyed children that I know were demons. Erica, I saw them the night that Eddie Ramsden got to you. They gave him CPR and it may have worked!

I believe that Trey is going to try to kill Steve Sandifer, but Steve is aware and being watchful. I'm glad that I've gotten to become friends with Galen Moss and I'm really glad that Matt Carrier has joined the North Madison Militia as their de facto chaplain, but I would never want to be a part of the militia...

...there's more, Jeremy, but long story short, between what I feel in my spirit and what I see, and when I see Israel surrounded by her enemies like she is, and as I see America and her sheeple as apathetic and deceived as they are, and I see the organized Christian church as soft as it is, and when I recall my dream about the Wal-Mart Christmas shoppers and the warning I heard in it, I will say to you my dear Jeremy and Erica that we are deep, deep, deep into the 11th hour and midnight could be a heartbeat away."

"I'm not afraid dad. Now, I just want to go to sleep."

A very short time later, Nick and Chris were yawning and putting on their sneakers as they prepared to go home for the night. As Jesse tucked his son into bed while Erica looked over his shoulder and smiled, the last words Jeremy heard before the book was closed on that awful day and his eyes fell shut were "sweet dreams, my son."

# 17

# Drones

The Omondi administration didn't have prior intelligence regarding the event that took place on Wednesday, December 16th at the Motel 6 on Carrier Circle near the village of East Syracuse. Nothing was supposed to happen there, but a vigilante named John Bonstable - who had recently been denied membership in the North Madison Militia - couldn't help but act on behalf of the people of the United States of America. As a result, heavy weapons were fired, windows were shattered, and Al Qaeda lieutenant Abdul Saleem Mohkendeem was taken into custody and two of his subordinates were killed.

And on that day - prior to the shooting spree and as the snow began to fall lightly before the winds increased and the storm intensified, a bomb threat had been phoned into the National Grid building in downtown Syracuse. The threat called into the electricity and natural gas provider caused a virtual gridlock on Erie Boulevard East and other main streets during rush hour and into the late evening as authorities shut the area down. It was Mohkendeem's subordinates who were responsible for phoning in the hoax as they were testing the response of police, EMS, and the FBI.

"I wonder what they were doing in the area…um…well, maybe I don't wonder at all" Jesse remarked as he laid on the couch watching all of the breaking developments on FOX News as Erica, Nick, and Chris came in the front entrance of his flat with a large pepperoni pie from Pizza Hut. Jeremy was sitting on the living room floor watching the news coverage with his father that early evening, and as the mouthwatering aroma of pizza began to waft across the room, he asked "dad is Carrier Circle near here?"

"It's about 14 miles away, so it's not far, but it's too close if Al Qaeda terrorists are involved" Jesse answered directly, while smiling at the woman he loved as she set the pizza and some paper plates on the coffee table while the boys that were becoming like his stepsons flopped down on the floor next to Jeremy.

As Erica began to serve pizza to the boys, she stared at Jesse quizzically for a second before in her perplexity she announced "your muttonchops and pompadour are gone! Wow, what gives with the short hairstyle?"

"Do you like it?" Jesse asked as he lay on the couch inert, seemingly unwilling to move.

Erica's answer was sincere: "I think you're handsome in short hair, but you don't have Elvis hair and sideburns anymore. Are you going to wear a wig?"

"The Elvis impersonation act is over" Jesse answered as he sat up, and his face was pallid except for the bags under his eyes.

"Are you feeling okay?" Erica inquired with heavy concern coloring the tone of her voice.

Jesse explained: "Well, I feel like I'm coming down with the flu. I'm achy and very tired. Earlier today I called Mike Wickert and told him that I couldn't do the Christmas show because I was sick. He got mad and began hurling F-Bombs at me, so in my own righteous indignation I told him it was over, as our contract was set to expire after the Christmas show anyway and we needed to find a new lead guitarist and bass player. I called Tony, Mickey, and Ian, and they were relieved on one hand and disappointed on the other. When I called Scott Seals, he was disappointed because he was looking forward to filling in, but he's a busy guy and he'll get over it. So, after calling everybody, I walked over to Pasquale's barber shop and got trimmed and shaved as a way to break the chains of all that bondage. Jesse Same the Elvis impersonator has left the building!"

Erica's face glowed with delight as she replied "well, you wanted to do something new musically and I've encouraged you to, so I'm glad." Her lovely face then evidenced distress as she finished by saying "but you look like you're ailing. You just lie back down and I'll take care of everything, and the first thing is to get some Tylenol into you."

The boys chattered happily as they sat on the the floor eating pizza while Erica was getting Tylenol from the bathroom and orange juice from the fridge. A warmth akin to that generated by a loving family filled Jesse's apartment, and in that moment he realized that this woman that he had known for only a month or so would make a wonderful wife.

Over the chatter of the boys and as Jesse swallowed two Tylenol caplets, FOX anchor Shepard Smith broke into the coverage of the scene at the Motel 6 with the surprise announcement from the Vatican that Pope Lucius Grimaldi IV would be stepping down effective immediately. Smith - bedecked in a pinstriped charcoal grey suit, white shirt, and patterned purple tie reported:

"There is still much to learn in regards to what could be considered a shocking development, but sources close to the Vatican say that the Pope's deteriorating health is a concern, and he is finding it increasingly difficult to quote 'fulfill the obligations of the ministry entrusted to him.' Sources go on to say that 85 year old

Pope Lucius had been considering stepping down for weeks but has found it nearly impossible to carry out his duties any longer. The Pope is not expected to take part in the conclave that will choose his successor, but is said to be strongly in favor of Cardinal Peter D'Cici, who insiders consider to be the heir apparent. We will have updates on this breaking news story as more information becomes available."

"Hmm, that could be significant, considering all that is going on in the world right now. Grimaldi is the one hundred and eleventh Pope, and some prophecy experts contend through study that the one hundred and twelfth will be the last" Jesse commented languidly as he lay back down.

"That's strange, alright. We saw him on TV just a few days ago speaking out against abortion and he seemed to be in robust good health for a man his age. And, he's been quite active on Twitter lately, too" Erica offered, sounding skeptical.

"There's more here than meets the undiscerning eye. I believe he's being pushed out" Jesse said softly as he closed his own eyes.

"Yes, there is more here than meets the undiscerning eye, and you need to get some rest" Erica voiced with a roguish grin before she quickly kissed Jesse's lips as he dozed off.

Jesse awoke two hours later, feeling refreshed but still very woozy. He got up off of the couch and kissed Erica goodnight as she was preparing to head home with Nick and Chris. "I just tucked Jeremy into bed and there's a slice of pizza in the fridge if you feel up to it. I'll see you tomorrow" she said with a wink and a grin as she stepped out into the stairway after the boys.

"Lord, thank you for her" were the words Jesse spoke just above a whisper - with a voice that was marginally hoarse - as he turned away from the door. He walked into the kitchen for a drink of water and as he peered through the window that looked out over the small parking area on Arch Street, he saw her brushing several inches of snow off of the Escalade while a cigarette dangled from her mouth. A blast of wind blew up and caused her black trench coat to ripple and her red scarf to wave like a flag behind her head, while snow swirled on the narrow street like little white tornadoes.

Nick and Chris were already snug inside of the vehicle, and as he saw her climb in after tossing the cigarette that may have been impossible to smoke in the bitter breeze, Jesse was struck with the notion that he would not want to be out walking on a night like this because the wind and the snow were only a part of the peril.

Concurrently, as Jeremy slept, he dreamed of Xavier cloaked in a green parka and walking on a snowy night with a man wearing an orange knit hat and a small black dog. As they walked in the dream, Jeremy saw a wolf shadowing them, sneaking along the front lawns of houses strung with beautiful twinkling Christmas lights and arrays of plastic and inflatable Santa Clauses and snowmen. A couple of the properties even had illuminated Nativity scenes on the front lawns. As Xavier, the man, and the dog walked by one such wooden Nativity scene illuminated by a spotlight, the wolf that they did not see stopped long enough to lift its leg and urinate on the babe in the manger. After the wolf committed its spectral act of desecration, Jeremy moaned, awoke for a few seconds, and then rolled over and fell back asleep.

While snow fell and a bitter wind wailed on that Wednesday night, there was a pitched supernatural battle taking place. As Jeremy slept and Jesse prepared to, both felt the disturbances in their souls. Evil mortals high on the gas of their over-inflated view of their own power were reviewing the latest CIA intelligence reports and conspiring to bring down a nation, while demons attacked angels in a misguided effort to derail God's plan.

Jesse's agitation increased as the muffled squeaking of Dean and Cassandra's bed, combined with the groans and laughter of their uninhibited passion was audible through his bedroom floor. He had never been forced to listen to them sound so ecstatic and yet so iniquitous at the same time, and his spirit shuddered as he wished he was in another place with Jeremy, Erica, Nick and Chris.

Even though she lived only a mile away, Jesse was then compelled to call Erica to make sure that she and the boys made it home safely.

"Yes, Jesse, we made it okay. The hill on Russell Street was slick because the sanding trucks haven't been out yet, but we got up it. Are you feeling any better?"

"My headache is gone but my throat is sore and I'm still very logy. We've been hearing that a bad strain of flu is going around and I hope I'm not getting it" was his answer.

"Well, take more Tylenol and get into bed and I'll see you in the morning" she replied sweetly.

There were a few seconds of silence where they both searched for something to say as they didn't want the conversation to end. It was Jesse who broke that silence:

"If you were here right now, I'd ask you to marry me."

"Oh, really" she answered with a surprised, delighted giggle before continuing with "well, ask me anyway."

"Erica, will you marry me?"

"Yes I will Jesse, because I love you and want to spend the rest of my life with you. See you tomorrow."

He was too worn out to be excited, as he had the confidence of knowing that she was meant to be with him anyway. They would likely plan a simple wedding even though with Erica's wealth they could stage an extravagant event. But, he wouldn't care if she still lived in poverty, he would feel exactly the same about her. And she didn't care that he was the secret son of the King of Rock-n-Roll; and she loved him enough and already knew him well enough to know that it would be better if he never discovered who his father and his mother's father were.

Jesse wore only a pair of orange mesh athletic shorts with the intertwined "SU" Syracuse University logo in blue near the bottom of each leg as he collapsed onto his bed and was quickly asleep, despite the muted orgasmic shrieks that arose from his floor. The infection was marauding through his body and sleep was the best weapon to retaliate with.

The clock radio showed 2:03 and sounded like a waterfall as the station that he had been listening to as he fell asleep had fallen out of range. He was awake because he had the sensation that something was on the bed with him. His first response as he began to grasp the straws of cognizance was to ask "Jeremy?"

"Our son, Jesse, and he so wonderfully takes after his dad" was the answer from the woman who sat twelve inches away on the left side of his bed, wearing a black negligée and black thigh-high stockings.

"Allison?"

"I miss you, Jesse, and you know that little blond bimbo is no good for you" she admonished with a sneer as she swung her legs up onto the bed and then straddled his mid-section. As he was confused by what exactly was transpiring and struggled to hold the straws of cognizance, she placed her hands on either side of his chest and bent close to his face and whispered coyly "let's make love like we used to. Maybe we'll make another baby?"

It sure looked and sounded like Allison. Her brown hair was pulled back and piled on top of her head, and in the light that spilled in from the hallway he could see the faint freckling across the bridge of her nose and the cola brown irises of her eyes. And certainly, he could smell the Chanel No. 5 that she often wore. "Jesse, I never stopped loving you" she whispered in his right ear and as he pushed back on her chest in an effort to remove her body from his, he felt her heartbeat thudding against the palm of this right hand.

"Don't reject me Jesse, please" she begged as he pushed and she started to slide off of his abdomen. "You, me, and Jeremy back together in Manlius. Doesn't that sound awesome?"

As she spoke the word "awesome" Jesse was able to see a stream of the hall light shine through her head, and then it all became crystal clear what this was in his bed. "Father God, I rebuke this succubus in the name of Jesus, amen" he prayed with a quiet fury.

It was then that the face morphed into that of a demented scarecrow, and the voice that had been a dead-ringer for Allison's now rattled with phlegm as it threatened "don't make me lock myself in the bathroom Jesse! I'll die in there and it will be all your fault!"

The face shriveled and then the demonic presence was gone. Though Jesse was perplexed, he was able to say "thank you, Lord" as he realized the succubus was gone and that likewise Dean and Cassandra were now quiet. His head was again aching from the infection that was assaulting him, but despite that and the bizarre interaction that just occurred his body began to relax and a peace was settling in on his bedroom. He breathed in deeply then rolled over on his left side and fell back asleep.

Jeremy would not be returning to school at Enders Road, and the plan was to begin homeschool after Christmas. And it was Jeremy that shook Jesse awake at 7:30 a.m. that Thursday the 17th, five and a half hours after the encounter with the demon that mimicked Allison.

"Dad, look out the window, a lot of snow fell last night! Now it really looks like Christmas!" The little boy was excited, but in his ailing condition Jesse could not share in the excitement.

"That's wonderful Jeremy, but I need to sleep a little while longer, okay? I'm feeling pretty awful" Jesse moaned. "Maybe when Erica gets here she'll take you three boys outside for a while."

Enders Road School had just reopened after the shooting incident, but that morning it and most of the schools in central New York were closed because of the snow and high winds that had impacted the area that previous night and into the early morning hours. But while kids were rejoicing, the general feeling in upstate New York and around America to anyone who was at all sensitive to the unseen was one of turmoil and danger. Something was off, and that disturbance was manifesting itself physically in Jesse and exacerbating his flu-like symptoms.

And while something was "off" - the White House knew something was coming, and directives and bulletins had already been passed down through the chain of command and had reached even the smallest of police departments. The National Guard was on alert and standing by, having been prepped over the last 30 days to be ready on short notice to undertake a "police action."

But your friendly neighborhood cop on the street wouldn't talk about it, and to be fair not all police officers had been brought fully up to speed. Likewise, if a National Guard member that you knew was suddenly called up, he or she would only say it was for a "mandatory training mission."

When Erica arrived at a few minutes after 8:00 a.m. - replete with books for Nick and Chris' school lessons - Jesse asked her to stay over that night as he felt like she and the boys would be "safer."

At 10:00 a.m. Galen called to see how his friend Jesse was doing, and asked him if he'd noticed military helicopters flying over Chittenango.

"Yeah, Galen, we've heard a couple fly over this morning. Something is definitely up" was Jesse's answer.

"Well get this, man, not only have the copters been busy, but we shot down a funny little surveillance drone a little while ago that was hovering over the area where the bunker is buried!"

"A drone ? Why am I not surprised?" Jesse answered, sounding hoarse and congested.

"Yup - it looks like your typical helicopter only unmanned, of course. It reminds us of those radio-controlled models that you see for sale in the mall; only bigger - about six feet long. It's not a Predator Drone like we used in Iraq and Afghanistan. This thing is painted white and had a camera attached to the landing gear. We pulled the SD card out of the camera and it's got pictures of where we are here and of the Town of Sullivan Rod and Gun club. There was a transmitter on the camera which we disabled with a hammer, and while we were at it we smashed its GPS box as well. While the camera stored images, it was also transmitting video at the same time. But you would think that Big Brother with all the technology available to him would come up with something a little more stealth and sturdy than this! Steve took it down with a couple three and a half inch Magnums fired from a 12 gauge!"

Jesse inquired "hmm…do you think that it was operated by someone locally?"

"Well, it appears to be a Federal Government aircraft and not a police thing, but yeah, the operators can't be too far away" Galen answered.

"I haven't talked with you in days, bro. Are they still tailing you?"

"That's what's strange; 'they' seem to have backed off - weird, eh? But there's more, no one has seen Trey or his buddy Jerry Walters in a week, and the rest of us are glad in a way. Have you seen Trey?"

"Since Trey and I had our falling out, we've been out of touch. The Elvis band is over now" Jesse answered and then coughed harshly.

"You sound sick. Are you alright?" Galen asked with concern.

"I've got the flu, I think. I have a fever that comes and goes, a cough, congestion, chills, episodes of shortness of breath, and I'm very fatigued. All I want to do is sleep. Basically, I feel like death warmed over."

"No way…uh…when did these symptoms begin?" As Galen asked, the urgency was palpable in his voice.

"I've been tired for days, but I think that is a physical manifestation of what I'm sensing in the supernatural and the stress of what has been going on in general. But this actual flu-like feeling started yesterday. What are you getting at? I can tell there's something" Jesse replied, with a flourish of vigor and a hint of suspicion.

Osama Bin Laden's assassinator drew in a deep breath and then elaborated: "I'm a multi-tasker, bud. As I've been talking to you I've been scanning some of the online prepper and militia forums to see if anyone else has been encountering the drones. First off, the helicopter types and also some that look more like an airplane have been spotted near a militia encampment outside of Ocala, Florida. There was one just like the one we have here that was shot down yesterday by a guy that has what he calls an 'unofficial volunteer militia' outside of Charlotte, North Carolina. There are posts from folks in Massachusetts that say they've seen them over the last few days and even a guy from North Syracuse that says he saw one just a little while ago."

Despite the cheap cell phones that both men used, Jesse could hear the scrolling of Galen's computer mouse during a six second pause in the conversation. Then Galen continued:

"Hmm…what is really interesting is that there are posts from towns around Syracuse and around Boston that are describing your exact symptoms and it all started two days ago. These people are posting that they're concerned that it might be some sort of low-scale CBNR event, which is an acronym for Chemical, Biological, Radiological, Nuclear. Now, considering what went down at the Motel 6 yesterday that's quite plausible. There's even a post from a user who goes by the I.D. 'Osama Been Trodden' that claims to have a quote-unquote inside military source that tells him or her that a few days ago members of Al Qaeda did some 'test runs' near Syracuse and near Boston to see how certain biological agents would travel on the breeze."

"Do you believe that's possible?" Jesse asked.

"If we are to believe what is being reported, four members of Al Qaeda were in that shootout at Motel 6 yesterday, but we can't get near the place to verify - which in itself may be the proof. Two were killed, one was taken into custody, and one is still on the loose. So, it sounds like they are in the neighborhood" Galen answered.

"But Galen, do YOU believe that these test runs may have happened?" Jesse persisted.

"Yeah, Jesse, I believe they happened and they're precursors to something bigger."

# 18

# Peace in the Valley

Friday the 19th of December came, and as the sun rose in a clear, mile-high sky its light made the tiny ice crystals in the snow on the grounds of Dr. West Memorial Park glitter like miniature diamonds.

At 7:30 that morning Jesse walked the sidewalk that bisected the park in the 27 degree chill despite the fact that he felt sick as the proverbial dog. He was suitably outfitted - wearing his black leather jacket over his favorite green hoodie; with a black knit hat on his head. He sported a white scarf around his neck and black Isotoner gloves on his hands. Blue jeans and his black Cross Trekkers completed the ensemble.

His fever that morning had rekindled and burned at 101 degrees after having cooled to 99 the previous night through the loving care of Erica, who nursed him as he watched The Polar Express on TV and made sure that he had regular doses of good old fashioned Bayer Aspirin and ice cold water after deciding that Tylenol wasn't doing the trick.

And in the wee hours of the morning when he awoke briefly, he burned for her as well. She was asleep on the living room couch, and likewise in her brief waking moments she knew that he was a short distance away in the bedroom and she longed to be sharing that bed with him - but, as followers of Christ that would need to wait until marriage.

It took the boys a long time to settle down, but by midnight they were asleep; Chris in Jeremy's bed and Jeremy and Nick pretending they were "camping out" in sleeping bags on the floor. At 7:30 the boys were still asleep, while Erica had been up since 5:00. She had showered, put on her makeup, and dressed for the day, and had likewise attempted without success to dissuade Jesse from going out for a walk. But, as unwell as he felt, the agitation and stress that seeped like an invisible bio-toxin through the cracks in the wall between the natural and the supernatural was more discomfiting. Walking was the way that he relieved his stress, and as he walked he prayed silently for strength, discernment, protection, and healing.

As he reached the end of the bisecting sidewalk where it met Russell Street, he took a left and headed toward the Creek Walk. He continued to pray while he walked, and was so deeply locked in his mobile prayer closet that the sounds of the village's morning rush hour traffic were impervious to its invisible door. As he crossed Arch Street, he did not see the baby blue 2009 Chrysler 300 driven by 84 year old Madge Tilley that was turning left onto Arch Street as he stepped into the intersection. Even though the elderly woman who could barely see over the steering wheel was in no danger of hitting Jesse, she overcompensated and gave him a wide birth as she made her turn. As she engineered the turn, Mrs. Tilley was unaware that she struck a trash can belonging to the First Presbyterian Church and sent garbage spilling onto the sidewalk in front of the edifice. She was instead concentrating more on rolling down her window and yelling with her rough yet whiny voice "get the hell outta the way you stupid ass" while Burl

Ives sang "say hello to friends you know and ev'ryone you meet" as *Holly Jolly Christmas* blared over her car radio.

Jesse was oblivious as he proceeded westward on Russell Street with the old church on his left. He was deep in prayer and the Holy Spirit had a substantial list for him. He was praying for mercy for Ronny and Eddie Ramsden; two brothers in the grips of the demons known as drug addiction and alcoholism - but in his spirit he felt a move that indicated that there could be hope for the passionate Philadelphia Eagles fan Ronny who had since recovered from the mild heart attack that he suffered on Halloween.

He lifted up the former Chittenango cop William Brostic, whose weight was as much a threat to his life as his drinking. Brostic had been an angry, desperate, and incompetent cop on the dole, who was that very morning on his knees and weeping with guilt over young boys that on two separate occasions in October he had delivered to the pedophile Joe McMurtry. And as Jesse prayed for the man, he too shed tears in his spirit. Jesse also was led to pray for the two victims he'd not been acquainted with, but in his spirit knew that total and complete healing would soon be theirs.

Jesse's head was down as he walked, and he did not see the tall, lean seventeen year old baggy-clothed male with shaved head and 41 mm "propaganda fist" double-flare gauges in his ear lobes. The young man seemingly had to exert considerable effort to walk and tipped side to side while he moved in his outsized black hoodie, baggy jeans that hung from his waist, and oversized tan work boots. While not seeing the lad, Jesse bumped into his left arm as he passed, causing the lost soul to shove Jesse sideways, while taunting "c'mon bitch, ya wanna piece a' me?"

Jesse was still oblivious as he continued on, but the young scofflaw pulled a Buck knife from his hoodie pocket, flipped it open, and began to follow Jesse, continuing to taunt him with "yo, c'mon bitch, let's play!"

“Forget it, Teddy, he ain’t nothin.’ We gotta hurry up and get to the dude in the suit and get our Sour Aliens before he bails” the young man’s tattoo-faced girlfriend instructed him as he turned from Jesse’s direction and continued to wobble along on his way. “He must be from like a foreign country er something ‘cause he was like talkin’ to himself in a weird language” she then said, appearing uncomprehending. Likewise she would not comprehend and could not see the invisible bevy of flying monkeys and winged half-anthropomorphic, half-reptilian deities that swarmed around her and Teddy, whispering in their ears and directing their thoughts and actions.

As he crossed Race Street, he lifted up Dean and Cassandra and prayed that they would turn from their pursuit of the dark things of the occult and seek the Day Star. Wittingly or not, they had opened a door in the house on Genesee Street to demonic activity and offered it a stronghold, and it had manifested itself on both floors.

After crossing Race Street, Jesse was forced to walk along the snowy shoulder of Russell Street as the sidewalk on that side had ended. As he passed the unusually long blue ranch house that appeared to be two double-wides combined into one and approached the Chittenango Center for Rehabilitation and Healthcare, he lifted Trey up in prayer and asked Jesus to please draw him into faith. In his mind he saw Trey as a silhouette holding a handgun and engulfed in swirling shadows, and his spirit groaned on behalf of his former best friend since childhood.

Jesse turned left into the entrance of the CCRH building, as that was a shortcut to the Creek Walk. He prayed for Allison as he approached the path that was covered in a layer of snow and overlapping tracks from other walkers.

Even though her relationship with Jeremy had been fractured, Jesse prayed that there could be healing. And when it came to healing, his spirit groaned on his ex-wife’s behalf - that she would allow in the Great Physician who persistently knocked at her door as He made a house call. And like a most royal of dinner guests who knocked at her door and only desired to dine with her and to have her dine with Him, that she would extend her empty cup to the Cleansing Fountain who would fill it with Living Water.

Galen Moss, Steve and Eileen Sandifer, Jerome Wooden, and Matt Carrier; three of these five people he had never met but still they were five that gathered in the Name Above All Names and had prayed for Jesse, and he would lift them up and say "thank you for them, Lord Most High." In his spirit he now knew that three of these had come to the aid of Jeremy; not knowing whose little boy he was but doing what few men would do in the current day but what many would have done in a bygone era. And they were prepared to fight to preserve what was left of America but deep in their hearts knew she was gone forever. Still, they knew that peace that transcended all understanding and with that they would declare "amen!"

Jeremy, his precious son - what a wonderful blessing from God he was and oh, how his son loved the Son of Righteousness with Healing in His Wings. "Blessings for Him Lord, please" and in his heart Jesse knew that they were poured out like the purest snowflakes to be caught on his tongue. "Thank you for Nicholas and Christopher, Lord, that those little boys are like mine but are truly yours."

He lifted up Erica and said "thank you Lord that she loves you again and thank you for the blessing of her love for me. Please Father; if it is your will may I take her hand in marriage?" It was then that just like in the dream, Jesse saw in his mind the hourglass that bore the inscription "The Church Age" and it appeared to be empty. A joy rose in his spirit as he said "thank you Lord that she knows you and will be at your wedding feast."

The prayer was now over and as Jesse had treaded a short distance along Chittenango Creek, he needed to stop and leaned into the trunk of what was left of a two hundred and fifty year old

American elm that stood next to the path and at one time offered shade over the creek. The trunk alone was so large that Jesse would not be able to reach his arms around if he tried. In his compromised physical condition, he was light-headed and his body ached as though he had actually been hit by Madge Tilley's Chrysler. Indeed, the sunlight sparkled on the creek's rivulets and off of the snow, but despite the scene worthy of a calendar or Christmas card, Jesse was far from picture-perfect.

He slumped down and sat on a section of the grand old tree's root structure that was dry and absent snow. His head was spinning and he was thirsty, and he wondered why he didn't possess Jeremy's foresight to know to bring water as he put a handful of clean snow into his mouth. He wanted to call Erica to tell her where he was, but he also neglected to bring his phone as he didn't think he'd be gone too long.

The cold air was making him feel weaker, but staying put there for a while would be the best course of action. After a minute of sitting with his face in his hands while the sound of the rushing creek served as white noise, he began to nod off.

"Hey there, pal, ya'll need a hand er somethin'?" was the croaky voice that startled Jesse awake before he fell too deeply into slumber. As he opened his eyes he saw chewing tobacco spittle on the snow near his feet. As he looked up and focused in on the gaunt, sickly-looking figure that smiled at him with a maw that dribbled brown juice and lacked most of its teeth, there was an air of familiarity as the Legos in his brain scrambled to stack themselves while he grasped the straws of cognizance.

"I been working part-time over there t' the rehab place. I clean the poopy and pee-pee out the toilets n' mop up the puke. Then I mop the floors and make nicety-nice in there. They call me a cuss-stodian 'cause I curse up a storm while I work, ha ha ha!" As the man laughed his chest rattled with congestion before he spit out a bloody ball of catarrh into the snow to join the tobacco spittle.

It was then that Jesse remembered dreaming about this man Josiah, who appeared with two black-eyed teens at Sullivan Park Pond. He likewise recalled seeing him in real-life loading an injured wolf into the back of a pickup truck on Brinkerhoff Hill Road. His brain wanted to get up and walk away, but his legs were like rubber. It was then that Josiah continued with his narrative:

"So I get a little break and I like t' walk out here on the path. There's fun stuff t' do like shush, wait a minute…"

A small brown rabbit was hopping in the snow behind Josiah, and he turned around with speed and alacrity that defied his sickly appearance and dove on the little animal, trapping it against his chest. Just as quickly he jumped back to his feet and faced Jesse with snow pasted to his overalls, holding the squirming bunny by its ears.

With a smirk akin to that of a mischievous child he said "now be quiet and you'll be able to hear the little bastard's neck break!" As Jesse was too mortified to react, Josiah twisted the rabbit's head with his emaciated yet strong right hand as he secured the animal against his chest with his left. To his distress, Jesse was able to hear several popping noises as the animal's vertebra broke and its spinal cord severed.

"Here, take it home to that little trollop Erica and tell her to make ya some rabbit stew" Josiah said with a snigger as he dropped the dead rabbit at Jesse's feet, before explaining "that's why they call me Josiah the Lion, 'cause I'm so quick and powerful that my prey can't escape!"

"You're Josiah the Eel, and Jesus is the Lion. I rebuke you in the name of Jesus" Jesse corrected him - albeit weakly - as he struggled to keep from passing out.

"You ain't rebukin' nothin' 'cause I ain't no demon! What ya need t' do is cast the demon out that's inside me, Jesse! Ain't ya read Acts chapter sixteen verse eighteen or Mark chapter sixteen verse seventeen? But, I don't think ya got it in ya t' cast out nothin' 'cuz ya been made sick by those nice little A-rab fellas and their biological agents!"

Jesse was feverish and weak and desired to stand up and with authority given him by faith in Christ, cast out Josiah's demon. But Josiah was a conscientious worshiper of Satan and hater of Jesus. The wicked man would hold onto the teachings of Anton LaVey through the *Satanic Bible* and would never be free because he did not desire the freedom that the truth would give him. Josiah was flesh and bones with a beating heart but was equally an empty shell used as a vessel and a vehicle for the demonic. With the Satanic Bible and through diligent reading of the works of Aleister Crowley and daily usage of an Ouija board, Josiah had knowingly opened himself up to a level of demonic possession that would make modern Goth-styled teenagers seem as choir boys and girls by comparison.

Jesse continued to sit on the tree root after he had quickly prayed for strength. It was then that he demanded, albeit feebly "demon, what is your name?"

The voice that came out of Josiah's mouth sounded rougher yet possessed more vitality than before. And as it spoke, blood hemorrhaged from Josiah's nostrils like he had been punched. "Eat shit and die, Jesse Same" the demon answered, and as it did, Josiah reached down inside of his overalls and into his underwear, where he retrieved a handful of stinking, steaming feces and heaved it at Jesse. Fortunately for Jesse, the excrement landed 12 inches to his left, but unfortunately the malodorous scent still found its way to his nostrils.

As Jesse rolled slightly to his right to be sure to avoid the splatter, he heard a familiar voice say "don't bother, Jesse. The demon has legal rights to him and to cast it out would have it return with seven others that are even more wicked."

As Jesse looked toward the path, he was surprised by who he saw, and spoke croakily "Matt, fancy seeing you here!"

"Jesse, I was meditating on Matthew chapter 12 earlier this morning. Then I felt moved to drive down and park by the the kiosk and stroll the Creek Walk. And now as I see this man who loves the evil that has overtaken him, I feel pity and verses forty-three to forty-five of that chapter apply here, and I think I have them committed to memory:

*"When an unclean spirit goes out of a man, he goes through dry places, seeking rest, and finds none. Then he says, 'I will return to my house from which I came.' And when he comes, he finds it empty, swept, and put in order. Then he goes and takes with him seven other spirits more wicked than himself, and they enter and dwell there; and the last state of that man is worse than the first. So shall it also be with this wicked generation."*

"Because we should pity this man, we wouldn't want his last state to be worse than his first. My advice would be to let him go on his way."

Matt Carrier then knelt down next to Jesse and laid his left hand on the feverish man's shoulder. Josiah at first looked angrily upon them as he wiped blood from below his nose with the same hand that he'd used to toss excrement, but then he turned in the opposite direction and began staggering toward the Rehab Center while whistling the theme to the Andy Griffith Show.

Before Jesse could say anything, Matt said "Eileen Sandifer and a couple of the guys from the militia are sick with the bubonic plague, as are the kids that live next door to me. It blew through Chittenango at some point inside of the last week, and I'd guess that the test runs have infected others around this area."

Jesse's fever had spiked to a temperature of 104 degrees Fahrenheit and he needed medical attention. While his head ached and burned, the rest of his body was stricken with the chills and he shivered uncontrollably. In a state now of semi-consciousness he heard the former pastor of Four Corners Community Church speaking, but the voice was merely a soundtrack to the hallucinations - albeit pleasant ones.

The clear, rustling waters of Chittenango Creek that flowed behind him were fine for fishing, but Jesse saw himself standing with Jeremy at the outlet brook of Sullivan Park Pond. It was a sunny, warm, late afternoon in summer, and there was the man and his 11 year old daughter from previous dreams he'd had fishing directly across the pond where the spring-fed inlet brook flowed in. The daughter was pulling small sunfish from the water - one after the other - as her dad unhooked them and carefully set them free. It was a peaceful, pleasant and happy scene; save for the weeping of Jeremy.

"No dad, don't go without me, please, please" the crying boy pled with his father, but all Jesse could say was "goodbye Jeremy, I love you and we'll be together again soon."

Jesse felt himself begin to rise up over the water, and as he looked down a school of silver carp leapt from the middle of the pond, their scales glinting in the sunlight. He saw the father and the daughter pointing at the fish and heard them "ooh" and "aah" at the marvelous sight that lasted mere seconds.

As Jesse looked toward the sky, there was a shimmering ball of light that was not the sun but the Son, and as the dead-ringer floated closer, he saw two hands held up with the pierced palms facing forward as if to indicate he should stop. Jesse could not see His face, but the words spoken in the warmest of vocal tones said "don't let go, Jesse, it is not time. I have more I would like you to do."

Then, as he felt himself falling backward, he realized that he was being shaken. As the pleasant summer warmth faded and the cold of December and the fever chills slapped his face and crawled on this skin, he heard Matt Carrier speaking with exigency "stay with me Jesse, c'mon buddy, stay with me!"

Jesse gasped and drew his arms tightly to his chest as he shook and shivered. The hallucination was over - if it was a hallucination at all. Clearly and cognitively now he felt the uncomfortable elm root beneath him and the odd mix of heat and cold he heard Matt praying:

"Father God, I lay hands on your servant and my friend Jesse, and I pray for his full healing, recovery and strength. I renounce, sever, and break the spirit of illness in Jesse and I know that he prays in agreement in the glorious name of Jesus, amen."

Matt stood up and then reached down and slipped his right arm under Jesse's right armpit and began to lift him. Jesse used the elm tree for support and was quickly on his feet.

"Feeling better, eh?" Matt commented assuredly with a cocked left eyebrow.

"I felt the poison flow out through my feet as I joined you in prayer, bro" Jesse answered, and to offer some visible evidence he pointed to where the snow had melted from the area where his feet had rested on the path.

God had brought healing and recovery to Jesse and both men were joyful but with their faith they were not at all surprised. But while they both thanked the Lord and praised His name, Trey had hotwired Matt's blue Dodge Ram pickup and was pulling away from the parking area where the yellow kiosk marked the start of the Creek Walk and was squealing left onto Genesee Street across from the white-pillared and brown brick facade of the Sullivan

Free Library. As he floored the gas pedal and sped past a patrol car that was leaving the police station parking lot, Officer Ryan McMaster was oblivious to the recklessly-driven pickup as he focused intently on his radio for a "special emergency preparedness announcement" coming in "5-4-3-2-1."

Matt Carrier walked with Jesse back to Russell Street and would not know for a little while that his truck had been stolen. Before arriving at the end of the Creek Walk - or beginning, depending on your perspective - he agreed to marry Jesse and Erica after Christmas. As Jesse extended his right hand to the unemployed preacher, Matt instead bear-hugged the erstwhile Elvis impersonator and said "thank you for making me speak the truth. It got me fired, but it led me to a small group of individuals in the North Madison Militia that were hungry for God's word and are now feasting on it."

As the quick embrace ended, Jesse said "it was a Holy Spirit thing, Matt."

"Yeah, Jesse, but He called on you and you answered and it shook me into repentance. And it may sound awful, but now that John McMurtry is gone and his wife moved away, Four Corners Community Church may become a true house of the Lord."

Jesse continued along Russell Street while the frosty air stung his face. An hour before this he had never felt so sick and now he was purged of a plague that would have killed him. He recalled the demon-possessed Josiah staggering away whistling the theme tune to the Andy Griffith Show, and he wondered how such a happy tune could be carried by someone so evil.

While Jesse did indeed feel physically renewed, the feeling that up was now down and wrong was now right gnawed at his insides like a starved pitbull on a human arm slathered with bloody au jus. So many of the houses around the village of Chittenango were decorated with Christmas regalia, yet when he thought of the

Christmas day that was a week away he envisioned it not as a day of celebration but of mourning. America and the world had been on a path of self-destruction for years, but in this moment as Jesse walked and his recent dreams and visions flashed in his mind like a film trailer, he knew that very day would be like no other, and he wanted to get back to his apartment with his fiancé and the three boys.

Indeed, in his spirit he knew that this would be a day of infamy…

A forty-something woman with close-cropped grey-streaked hair and black-rimmed glasses approached from the opposite direction and as she walked briskly she barked into her Bluetooth "look, your job depends on it! We have six shopping days left and you had better do what you need to do to get those numbers up and that means no day off tomorrow! Do you understand where I'm coming from?"

"Please ma'am, Jesus is Lord" Jesse spoke with quiet urgency as he passed her, to which she screeched in reply "why don't you drop dead, asshole" as she spun to face him.

The woman's words did not hurt him as instead he felt pity for her. As he approached the sidewalk that cut through Dr. West Park, Jesse's entire soul ached with an overwhelming sadness like he had never felt in his life. He was sad for people he never knew and the tears began to flow in a hot, steaming torrent as his entire body trembled. As he stopped and stood on the sidewalk just off of the street, a tender voice graced his spirit and it comforted him as it said "there is no shame in your tears, Jesse. There is no selfishness in them as they are the tears of a heart that is broken by a world that has rejected my love."

Indeed, it was a strikingly beautiful sunny morning. It was cold but this was December, after all. The sun was smeared in the tears in his eyes but through Jesse's spirit the Son spoke the words of scripture that brought peace and comfort:

*"The Spirit of the Lord is upon Me, Because He has anointed Me to preach the gospel to the poor; He has sent Me to heal the brokenhearted, To proclaim liberty to the captives And recovery of sight to the blind, To set at liberty those who are oppressed; To proclaim the acceptable year of the Lord."*

Jesse needed to get home as Erica and the boys were concerned as to his whereabouts. But he was moved to walk into the park and sit in the first bench he happened upon. From the bench he could see the house he lived in on Genesee Street and he knew all was well on the upper floor.

He would linger there for a while as his tears dried and survey a landscape that he now had the knowledge was going to change in a matter of hours. Vehicles drove along Genesee Street and it did seem as though there were more police cars than usual, but Jesse knew it was part of the coming change. He also knew that in other towns and cities the police, National Guard, and the new civilian security force were staging for events coming later that day while an apathetic, unaware, successfully dumbed-down sheeple went merrily along their way. But even the civilian security force was for the most part in the dark, believing only that today was the day that the President was going to begin taking guns from the "right-wingers" and "Christian extremists", and that they were to be a big part of enforcing the so-called "buy-back."

Carousel Mall on the north side of Syracuse was already getting busy with Christmas shoppers at 9:10 in the morning, but as the U.S. economy was being steadily deteriorated by the elites through Omondi's policies, many would do more window-shopping than actual purchasing. The food court was bustling with coffee drinkers and mall walkers, but in a few hours it would be a scene of mayhem and panic.

The President and his family had packed up everything deemed necessary and were waiting for word from the "inner circle" that it would be time to evacuate to the “secret, secure location” where the Vice President and the top members of the Democratically-controlled House and Senate would also be moved with their families, pets, and most-valued assistants.

Jesse was no Isaiah, Ezekiel, Jeremiah, or Daniel. But he was given dreams and as he sat while Chittenango and most of America carried on that morning without a clue, he knew that his prophetic dreams were coming true. He was reconciling in his mind that last Christmas really was the last, and whatever December 25th of this year brought it would not be cheer. Likewise, the image of the empty bulb of the hourglass called “the Church Age” portended to him that while he knew not the day or the hour, that day and hour were potentially hours away.

He knew that he would be on the streets later and panic would be ensuing. He could not stop what was coming, but with the help of the Holy Spirit he would serve as a source of light in the physical and spiritual darkness.

But what about Erica and the boys? What about Steve Sandifer, Galen, and Trey? He tried to contact Galen at his current number, but there was no answer and that was troubling in Jesse’s soul. And even though Erica and the boys were not in the dream that involved the scene of mayhem on the streets that he believed strongly would take place that day, he knew in his spirit that they would be okay.

There would be peace in the valley; and as Steve Sandifer, Eileen Sandifer, Jerome Wooden, and Galen Moss already walked in the most peaceful of valleys where they would be forevermore. Their bodies were lying dead on the floor of the Sandifer’s kitchen at the hand of Trey Emerson - those bodies still warm as was the 9 mm used to shoot them as Trey ran out of the front door to meet Jerry Walters, Kenny Case, George Mackinaw, and Stanley Bobrowski in Matt Carrier’s Dodge pickup.

“(There’ll Be) Peace in the Valley” was a song that Jesse had sung so many times as *Jesse Same - Elvis Impersonator*. And now, as he sat on the bench at the edge of Dr. West Memorial Park, he began to sing with no accompaniment and his voice was a dead-ringer for that of the father he never in this world knew:

*Oh well, I'm tired and so weary*

*But I must go alone*

*Till the lord comes and calls, calls me away, oh yes*

*Well the morning's so bright*

*And the lamp is alight*

*And the night, night is as black as the sea, oh yes*

An elderly couple had been strolling from the opposite direction, and they stopped and marveled at the mellifluous voice that sang *there will be peace in the valley, for me, some day - there will be peace in the valley, for me, oh Lord I pray...*

As he sang on, others gathered as Jesse was again standing and his voice echoed through the park. Dan Furman, who had an hour prior resigned from the Chittenango Police Department because he as an Oath Keeper would not carry out the new Constitution-defying duties expected of him, stood and clapped and sang along as the chorus was repeated many times. While the scene later that day in the park would be one of chaos and calamity, as for now it was one of joy as after Jesse finished singing he and Dan Furman prayed with a group of six people who were moved to accept Jesus as Lord and Savior.

When they finished praying, Jesse felt a hard object get shoved into his lower back as an anxious male voice barked "Dan, you should know better than this and you, singer, get moving or I'll put this nightstick over your head." As Jesse looked over his shoulder while he was being pushed forward, he saw two young Madison County Sheriff's deputies - one male and one female - dressed in full riot gear and sunglasses.

"No religious gatherings in public places. Either you go inside the big church over there or you go home. Now move out or you'll all be arrested" the female deputy commanded loudly; albeit nervously.

As the group of six new followers of Christ, the elderly couple, and the few others that gathered began to disperse, Jesse asked the deputies "are you going to cast out the demons too?" As he asked this, Dan Furman stood defiantly on the sidewalk with his arms folded across the chest of his black leather jacket.

A translucent, five foot tall semi-anthropomorphic being that was missing one eye but had two small, toothy mouths on its left cheek in addition to its primary gob leaned against the female deputy while the male played fretfully with the over the shoulder microphone of his portable radio that didn't seem to be working.

The demon now licked the exposed skin of the female deputy's neck as she became discomfited by something she could not pinpoint.

"Look, we're just trying to do our jobs, okay? Either you leave or we'll call for reinforcements! We're not playing!" The female deputy who was a sergeant spoke with no confidence while her subordinate tried to get his radio to work.

As the demon suddenly vanished while Jesse and Dan stood resolute and the male deputy pointed his shaking Glock in their direction, the sergeant who was becoming more unhinged spoke “look, I have two kids at home and I hope that you won’t kill me. If I take this riot gear off right now you’ll see that I don’t want any trouble. You know, honestly, this job sucks and I quit. They can shove their pension that I won’t get any way!”

“You’re a lousy cop, Mike” the sergeant continued as she pulled off her vest and threw her helmet on the ground. “You’re an immature hothead who is going to wind up getting killed by a perp that has more on the ball than you do!”

“I’m walking home to be with my kids because the terror attacks are coming in a couple of hours. My kids need their mom, so please, don’t kill me…please!”

Jesse and Dan were confused as the woman walked toward Russell Street, having dropped her gun belt on the sidewalk. And as the male cop holstered his Glock and likewise started to walk briskly away, they were both befuddled by her plea of “please don’t kill me…please.”

The two leather jacket bedecked men did not see what hovered behind them. It was a seven foot tall, silver-robed angel with an iridescent pearly-white 15 foot wingspan and flowing golden brown hair; and he had easily frightened the demon as well as the deputies. When the male cop pointed the Glock in abject fear, it was at the angel and not at Jesse and Dan. When the sergeant asked for her life to be spared, it was because the angel held a medicine ball-sized orb similar to a Christmas snow globe, and in it she saw an image of herself in full riot gear and bloodied face lying in the snow and being trampled by a frenzied hoard.

The angel had not come to kill her but to warn her and to likewise “discourage” her and her partner from shooting Jesse and Dan.

Dan Furman patted Jesse on the back and started to walk away. After going several feet, he stopped, turned and spoke, his face revealing equal parts distress and fatigue:

"I'll grab her gun belt before someone else does, and then I'm going home, Jesse. She's right, it should be starting sometime around noon, according to intelligence that the White House has. They believe it will involve a number of cities along the east coast, and they're concerned about tanker trucks being used as weapons around Syracuse. There was some manner of biological release near Syracuse days ago, and it was tied in with the situation at the Motel 6 and the bomb threat on Wednesday. It's amazing how the mainstream media knows about this and yet they're keeping quiet about it until it happens because their beloved Marxist president asked them too."

There was a few moments of silence, save for the sound of vehicles proceeding along Genesee Street and the sound of a four year old girl who was walking through the park with her mom saying "mommy, there's five police cars over at the fire station. I can count 1-2-3-4-5. How come the police men look like the Power Rangers?"

Dan and Jesse both looked toward the beautiful blue sky, and with that the former cop drew in a breath and continued:

"We trained with the National Guard to implement and maintain Martial Law and it will start going into effect later today. What sits in the White House is pure evil and he could have set the wheels in motion weeks ago to stop what is coming, but instead he's using it to put the final nails into America's coffin. He's a tool used by the elites - some call it the Illuminati - but he's a willing tool handpicked by them and groomed. The people in this country have no idea as to what is about to hit them. It's the end of the world as they know it…"

Being that she was a pedestrian, it was easy for Allison to make her way through the checkpoints that chilly yet sunny Saturday morning. Cars were backed up on Route 5 heading in and out of Chittenango as police, National Guard, and the new civilian security force checked I.D. of drivers attempting to enter not only this sleepy little burgh but those all around the northeast and within days all over the country. If you weren't a resident of a particular city or town, you were turned back and this was causing people who chose to be argumentative to get arrested and in a few cases shot.

There were scattered firefights that took place between armed citizens and those who were in the employ of the government, but in most cases the armor of the government prevailed. And on this crisp Saturday morning six days before Christmas, those who visited the homes of "flagged" registered gun owners did not come bearing gifts or offers of buy-backs but instead to take from those who had long believed in the implacability of the Second Amendment. But despite the best efforts of a government gone rogue while thousands suffered in the wake of Friday's attacks, not all of the weapons would ever be bought-back or confiscated…

Allison had walked a long way in an effort to see her son and to try to reconcile with her ex-husband. She had long given up on reaching Jesse by phone as cell service had been down since around noon the day before. Indeed, her mind had cleared since she quit taking the meds, and she knew it would be better to make the four hour walk from her parents' house than to drive and get blocked from Chittenango - if she could even reach the end of the street.

The windows of the Sunrise Market had been smashed as the result of looting. All of the cash, beer, and cigarettes had been taken from the convenience store, as had some of the milk and groceries. The gasoline inventory had been pumped dry and the empty parking lot was littered with broken eggs, squashed donuts, and other unidentifiable food items. The only vehicle parked there was a Chittenango Police cruiser with a napping officer behind the wheel.

The town was eerily quiet and as Allison walked along, all she could hear was the barking of dogs and likewise she smelled what seemed to be burning rubber. She sensed that people were up and around but would not leave their homes. Despite having walked for miles she was moving with a quick gait as adrenaline and desire fueled her. The man that she had fallen back in love with and their son were only blocks away, and in this time of turmoil and tragedy she needed them both more than ever. She was impervious to the scorched wreckage of two Chittenango Police cars in the middle of the street and a Military Police SUV in the same condition that rested on its side in the vacant lot - but she did note that one of the police cars appeared to have exploded and its hood was resting amongst the smashed glass of the Subway restaurant's bay window as pieces of tire, glass, and metal lay scattered about the immediate landscape.

She was jogging now, the physical activity combined with stress and adrenaline pushing her heart to beat at a dangerous and irregular 200 times per minute, but what she saw at the edge of Dr. West Memorial Park caused it to stop beating for two seconds before it assumed its disorganized rhythm. Two German Shepherds were gnawing hungrily on the partially-uniformed body of a police officer who had no head or neck. A smaller black and tan mutt chewed on a piece of scalp with hair, and as her legs became like liquid as she nearly passed-out she saw skull fragments, brain matter, and blood splatters over a wide area of the snow. A Madison County Sheriff's Dodge Durango was parked in the snow on the middle of the park lawn, but the officers inside only sat motionless as though they awaited orders as to what to do next.

She was jogging again, her heart having assumed a normal sinus rhythm as she crossed the street and approached the Ten Pin Restaurant and Tavern, whose windows had also been smashed, and its main door torn off and lying in the parking lot. Lights were on inside of the Ten Pin, unlike many of the blocks behind her that were without any electrical power. In the same parking lot were several cars - all with shattered windshields. Next to where the establishment's front door lay was a black Ford pickup truck with one of the dining room's tables having been used to smash its windshield. Even the oft-humorless Allison found it funny that the white tablecloth was still partially covering the table as it rested at an angle while it protruded from the pickup's cab.

Thirty seconds later, she stopped running and as she heaved and tried to catch her breath she opened the bottom door and ascended the stairway that led to Jesse's kitchen.

As she knocked at the top door, she could hear Dean and Cassandra shouting on the lower floor in what sounded like a heated argument replete with the tinkle of breaking glass. As no one was answering Jesse's door, she found it unlocked and let herself in. As she stepped into the kitchen she realized that while the arguing came from downstairs, the glass she heard breaking came from upstairs and it was Jesse's coffee pot.

Her brain had endured so much over the last month, but despite the trauma it had suffered it took it but two seconds to process the fact that the coffee pot had just been "dropped."

On the kitchen floor tile, in a pool of fresh-brewed coffee and broken glass was Jesse's green hoodie, a pair of his jeans, a white t-shirt, his black underwear and his white socks, now stained with Maxwell House. As her head swirled, she saw several feet away in a pile a grey Memphis Blues NFL sweatshirt, a purple t-shirt, a black bra, a pair of purple panties, blue jeans, and white ankle socks.

Save for the shattered coffee pot, the scene looked as though laundry was being sorted for washing. But instead of detergent and dryer sheets, there was for Allison merely panic in the realization that the soils of maliciousness and arrogance had been unexpectedly bleached out of the fabric of her life.

She walked unsteadily into the living room, where there were three piles of pajamas and undergarments on the floor. There was a set of Teenage Mutant Ninja Turtles pajamas and a pair with red and blue vertical stripes on a white background. But, the pair of little boy's pajamas, underwear, and socks that caused the panic to escalate to a precarious level was those bearing action images of Spider Man. While those did not come from Jeremy's bedroom back in Manlius, she knew that they were nonetheless his.

Jesse was a fan of FOX News, but CNN played on the TV in the living room, as this section of Chittenango hadn't lost electrical power. Before she set out on her journey earlier that morning, Allison had heard her father bemoan "those bastards took FOX off the air and all we get now is the Communist News Network!"

The network had been providing around the clock coverage of the aftermath of the attacks that had been perpetrated on a number of cities near the east coast the previous day. But then, as Allison picked up Jeremy's pajama top and held it to her face as she stood in stunned realization, news was breaking that "flying saucers" and "unusual aircraft" were being spotted streaking and hovering in skies all over the world. And interrupting those reports were others that large numbers of people had just been "abducted."

Dennis and Allison had mocked Jesse behind his back in regards to his belief that Jesus would suddenly and unexpectedly come and take his church of true believers home to Heaven in the "Rapture." They had both warned Jeremy not to believe his father's "childish ravings" and it was Jesse's strong faith in Jesus and that belief in the Rapture that fueled their desire to take away Jesse's unsupervised visits and joint custody.

As Allison came to grips with what really happened, she screamed at the television "the UFO's are a lie, they're a lie" - her voice muffled by Jeremy's pajama top - the realization burned like lava in her heart as she was forced to come to grips with the fact that

Jeremy had been taken away from her and not from Jesse, and that Jesus now had full parental custody of both of them.

# 19

# The Day After

Pastor Dan Duncan looked out over the crowd of one hundred and eighty that had gathered at Four Corners Community Church for the 9:00 a.m. service on Sunday, December 19th. There was no worship team playing music at this service; nor were there to be any announcements of upcoming events. The drum kit was set up on the small, red-carpeted stage behind the pastor, but no drummer sat behind it. There were two guitar amps with wireless receivers behind the pastor, but no guitars were connected. The Korg keyboard was on the floor in front of the stage to his right, but no one sat behind it. It would go without saying that the three metal boom stands behind the pastor supported microphones that would not be sung into on this day. Indeed, the worship team had rehearsed on Wednesday evening for the Sunday service, but it was a rehearsal that was in vain.

"This is the largest congregation this church has ever had" the pastor remarked, and a look of abject disgust was painted onto his goateed face in a dour shade of grey.

Pastor Dan removed his round-lensed wire-rimmed glasses and set them on the wooden podium that he stood behind. As he surveyed the nervous, murmuring crowd, his anger rose as he shouted "there are too many familiar faces in here!" With his proclamation, the murmuring ceased and all eyes were fixated on him.

"We missed it, ladies and gentlemen, and I don't mean a ride in a flying saucer" the angry yet heartbroken preacher announced by using his diaphragm to full effect as he looked out over the congregation, and to the astute observer it would have appeared that Dan Duncan was ready to jump out of his skin.

"Jesus came early yesterday morning. While we were all distracted by the Martial Law that was being declared all over the northeast and down the east coast; while we were terrified by the events that had transpired not only in Syracuse but in Manhattan, Miami, Boston, Albany, and possibly some other cities, he came like a thief and took home those who were watching for Him. Yes, people, those who had oil in their lamps saw Him come and in a twinkling of an eye they are all gone!"

The congregation remained quiet and transfixed on the preacher. Some of them were discomfited by the way he stared, seemingly accusingly. Indeed, some of them were unnerved as they felt as though they were transparent and he could see inside them and right through them. He stared down at the podium for five seconds as if to read something there then returned his gaze to the congregation. He furrowed his brow, unclenched his lips and continued speaking:

"Do you know who went home with Jesus? Our erstwhile pastor Matt Carrier did! You know - the one that our dearly departed former head elder fired! You know who also went home with Him? Well, I'll tell you who also went home; that fellow who interrupted our service some weeks ago, the day that Matt was fired. You remember the guy who looked like Elvis Presley, right?"

Duncan was interrupted by attorney Max Biederman - a fetching, dark haired, suntanned young hotshot who had just set up shop in Chittenango a few months prior:

"So, pastor, if you're a preacher on behalf of Jesus, why are you still here?"

Yeah, pastor, what the hell? It musta been UFO's and not Jesus, or else you'd be gone! I mean, shit, I saw two little green men with big eyes on my back porch yesterday mornin' when all the Jesus freaks disappeared" a sober Ronny Ramsden taunted through a crooked grin.

"I dunno Ronny, I think yer drinkin' again" Earl Skidmore remarked, eliciting a round of laughter from a number of those making up the congregation.

Pastor Dan clenched his lips, gritted his teeth, and waited 14 seconds for the laughter to cease. When the laughter stopped, all eyes were again fixed on him and the congregation and Skidmore, Ramsden, and Biederman all looked like naughty children who had been caught with their hands in the cookie jar.

"You can joke if you want, and you can fall for the deception of the little green men, but the bottom line is that every one of us in this room was left behind. As for me, I graduated from the Dallas Theological Seminary puffed-up with head knowledge, but my heart was empty. I knew how to walk and talk like a Christian and I knew how to teach on the Bible, but my desire to actually follow Jesus was lacking. I did not truly see Jesus as Lord but instead myself as a grandiose teacher and pastor. I did not deal with sin in my life and loved this world a little too much. I can blame John McMurtry for part of that - but the bottom line is that as an adult I did not have the faith of a child. I did not recognize the danger of un-repentance, the danger of not turning away from things like pornography and it got worse…"

Pastor Dan paused and again looked down at the podium while nodding his head in agreement with something unseen. When he raised his head, his face was flushed red with hues of anger, self-pity, and heartbreak while moisture glazed his eyes. As he looked over the gathered crowd of fools and buffoons, he saw interspersed a handful that looked as though they honestly sought truth and comfort. It was mostly for them that he spoke candidly:

"Quite honestly, Jesus was only my job and not my God."

"The preacher is gettin' too preachy. I came here to find out what the hell is goin' on, not to hear a sermon" Earl Skidmore complained as he stood up in his Sunday best white t-shirt, blue jeans, and camo-patterned baseball cap with a spare cigarette resting in the notch between his left ear and the edge of the aforementioned cap. As Earl headed for the double doors to leave, Ronny Ramsden remarked "Earl, sermons are what church is for!"

The members of the congregation murmured discontentedly amongst themselves, before they were quieted by a strikingly sober Ronny asking aloud:

"So pastor, what do we do?"

There was something powerful in Dan Duncan's stare, a sort of humble yet contrarily overwhelming charisma that made the man with medium-build who stood 5' 10" tall appear larger than life. It was a stare that made Earl Skidmore nervous, and as he turned and met eyes with the pastor as he pushed open the double doors to leave, he was compelled to run - tripping on the grey carpet in the foyer before regaining his footing and blasting through the fire doors at the bottom of the steps.

With that stare, the pastor glared at the one hundred and seventy-nine that remained and provided the answer to Ronny's question:

"You must confess with your mouth that Jesus is Lord, and believe in your heart that God raised Him from the dead, and you will be saved. If you still don't believe this after what happened yesterday, than you should get up and leave now."

"I didn't come here for this Jesus bullshit, I came fer information and I guess I ain't gonna get it here so screw this shit" Murf Murphy proclaimed as he got up to leave. And as he stood up and stomped toward the double doors, most of the room began to follow suit.

"I can't believe I walked all this way for this religious crap in a time of crisis! The damn National Guard wouldn't even let me drive here" a broad-shouldered, portly woman in her fifties bellowed at the pastor as she joined the exiting throng.

"Yeah, John McMurtry wouldn't have allowed his church to deteriorate to this level, bless his soul" an elderly woman with a cane carped while glaring at the pastor.

After five minutes passed, there were nine left seated in the congregation. All of them had to walk to the church, and a few of them came a long way.

Dan Duncan walked out from behind the podium and down to the floor where the nine were seated. They were spread out around the room, so he asked "would you please all sit down here together in the front?"

The pastor sat down on the lowest of the three steps to the stage and continued: "I see there are nine of you left. Do you all believe that Jesus is your Lord and Savior? Do you believe that He is the Way, the Truth, and the Life?"

They all answered in the affirmative.

"Alright then, let's all bow our heads, close our eyes, and pray…"

"...Lord Jesus, I acknowledge that I am a sinner and have fallen short of your glory. I know that I, no matter what I do or what works I perform, cannot make it into Heaven on my own. I know that you died on the cross for my sin and have paid its price in full with your blood, and have risen from the dead, victorious over death. I ask you now into my heart to be the Lord of my life and I promise to follow you from this day forward. Thank you for loving me, dying for me, and calling me to yourself. In the name of Jesus I pray, amen."

They all raised their heads and opened their eyes. There were no fireworks and no angels singing in the building, but each of them now knew that they were children of God, as did the three hundred and fifty-six unsettled, nervous demons that hovered amongst them unseen. And it was Tony Zonnerville who wistfully spoke first:

"I remember when Jesse sang "How Great Thou Art" at the Turning Stone. Man, it was glorious, but I was too prideful to believe that I needed Jesus. Still, Jesse made me think and now I know. I miss my friend and I hope I join him soon. Maybe Jesus would have us in a band together."

Mickey Starnes was next: "Jesse got me thinking too. There was always something different about him, I mean, what a genuine, loving guy he was. He wasn't perfect and he had his moments, but I knew he believed and he pointed the way for me. It's too bad that it took the Rapture to bring it all home for me. I hope I see my friend again soon. Thank you, Jesus, that I knew Jesse and starting today I know you."

Andy Dudzinski wasn't on the pickup truck that carried the militia members that was responsible for the destruction of three police vehicles and for the death of two Chittenango police officers and two military policemen. If he had been, he would have been killed by the Hellfire missile fired from the U.S. Army Apache helicopter as Trey drove the truck down Lakeport Road into Lakeport. Andy had no desire to take part in any offensive maneuvers by the North Madison Militia, and was true to the desires of Steve Sandifer and Galen Moss to remain as a line of defense against a government gone rogue. He was now the only surviving member of the NMM, and he offered this:

"I'm like Mickey and Tony. I was too prideful to believe that I needed Jesus. I heard Matt Carrier talk about the Lord and I wanted to believe, but I just wouldn't give in. Well now I believe and I'm sad because I know what we're going to face here in this world. There's an underground bunker behind Steve and Eileen's house but we can't get into it."

"Oh yes we can" was the response from Allison Dalton; the erstwhile Allison Same. "I have a key right here. Yeah, I showed up at Jesse's apartment just as the Rapture happened..."

Needless to say, it was at that point that Allison broke down. Ray Bullock - the man who got under Galen's skin at Donna and Sam's - put a beefy arm around Allison as his wife Annie took her left hand. "Der der honey, it's okay...yer wit friends" big old Ray who was also driven to tears spoke as he consoled the the heartbroken woman.

She gathered herself quickly as a new fire burned inside but it brought a new crown of beauty instead of the ashes of an old life. And flowing through her now was an oil of joy instead of the pharmaceuticals of mourning. Still, her broken heart was self-inflicted, and it would require the hands of the Great Physician to repair it. And with that, she continued:

"I freaked out as I walked into his kitchen and he had literally just dropped the coffee pot as he was called up to meet the Lord. There were his clothes on the floor, and there were the clothes of another woman. And I'm sure she loved him for who he was and not for whom she wanted him to be..."

She began to cry again, but she fought back at the tears and resumed her tale:

"I ran through the apartment and found the empty pajamas of my son Jeremy and two other little boys. I knew what happened…yes, I knew that it wasn't the flying saucers that everyone was seeing. I saw CNN reporting the news and knew it was all bull. But as I was in a state of panic I ran back into the kitchen and I inadvertently kicked the mat that was on the floor by the door to the stairs. And when the mat moved, I saw this note and this key that was underneath. I don't think that anybody knew it was there."

The note that the key was taped to was dated for Friday, December 18th. Allison had already read it herself, but now she read to the other eight and the pastor:

*"Jesse, it's zero dark thirty in the morning and you might still be sleeping and I don't want to wake you. You know what's funny? I had a dream last night, and it involved the key to the bunker. I dreamed that someone you know would need access to the bunker because of a crisis of some sort. It was after the shit hit the fan and the militia was gone. I don't know for sure what happened to us, but I have my suspicions.*

*In the dream, I slipped the key under that brown mat that is at the top of your stairs. You know, the brown mat that I've never seen! Despite Steve's claims that he and Eileen took turns being the key holder, I too had a key and in the dream I slipped it under the brown mat. And now on Friday morning when I snuck up your stairs and opened the door that you should have locked but didn't, there was the mat.*

*Someone will need the key and they will find it, because brother, for some inexplicable reason I know I won't ever need it again. The bunker has everything that Steve and I stocked it with, and I was sure to load in some extra ammo. Somehow, I believe that whoever gets in will know how to use it.*

*God bless you Jesse, and may the Lord be with whoever finds this key if it isn't you first.*

*The G-Man."*

"I know where the bunker is, because I'm the only one left from the militia and I can handle the guns and ammo" Andy Dudzinski offered staidly.

"And I think that four years in the Army before going to seminary may have taught me a little something" Dan Duncan said as he looked toward the double doors, thinking that he'd heard something in the foyer.

"I played paintball and I hunted. I guess that's all I've got" Ronny offered as he stared at the floor.

There was a five gallon can of gasoline in a maintenance shed behind the church. After the ten of them agreed to meet at the bunker at 2:00, the fuel was used by Dan Duncan to saturate the foyer carpet and burn down Four Corners Community Church.

The fire department never came, and as it was a church that burned the enforcers of the new Martial Law had no interest in investigating.

There would be a new North Madison Militia and it would defend itself. But in that defense against a government gone rogue as Tribulation approached, some of the nine remaining in the congregation would die.

Still, that death would have no sting as they were reborn cubs after all; cubs sired by the Lion of Judah who defends and intercedes on behalf of His children - and who promised to build mansions for them that would put even the most well-stocked and fortified underground bunker to shame.

CPSIA information can be obtained at www.ICGtesting.com
Printed in the USA
LVOW011817130613
338487LV00018B/653/P

9 781484 049792